BRIEFLY
VERY
BEAUTIFUL

BRIEFLY VERY BEAUTIFUL

ROZ DINEEN

THE OVERLOOK PRESS, NEW YORK

ABRAMS The Art of Books
195 Broadway, New York, NY 10007
abramsbooks.com

Remember, Rosa, that every day you quicken into motion waves that undulate on to the very confines of existence; you stir up waves that break upon the shores of eternity itself.

—Halldór Laxness, *Independent People* (1934); translated from the Icelandic by J. A. Thompson (1945)

PART ONE

BRIEFLY, VERY

1

She knew that there were other parents in the streets nearby silently planning their terror runs, just like her, just then. This was reassuring, like a superstition, or a community.

Hot magic-blue night. She said, "Whisper."

"What if I'm scared?" whispered Vito, who was eight. "Of the insects, maybe?"

"There is nothing to be scared of, Vi," she told him.

"There is something."

"There is nothing. Just. Close" (and she kissed) "your" (each) "eyes" (of his eyelids).

For a moment he lay very still on top of the old, sweet-smelling sheets, with his eyelids kissed shut.

She took a band from her wrist and held it in her teeth while she pulled back her hair.

Then she took the band from her teeth, and her fingers looped it into her hair, through and up, in a way that was both unthinking and complicated. She came to lie down beside him on the bed, propping herself up on an elbow. She rubbed sandy dirt off one of her feet with the other.

She waited. His profile was immaculate. Ten seconds passed. Fifteen seconds.

His eyes sprang open and he let out a great, worldly sigh.

"I have just checked," he informed her, solemnly, "and I cannot sleep."

"Don't think about sleep," she said, rolling onto her back, disturbing the old photos that he'd taped up along the wall. There were soft toy rabbits bending their heads over notebooks on the floor. The rabbits were held inside a protective circle made from the belt of her dressing gown. Beside them: a flowering branch from the back garden's tree, and her bra, the dust off crackers. "Don't think about sleep. Just close your eyes, and breathe."

"I am. So. Hot," he said.

She inhaled loudly and deeply for him, so that he might copy.

The girls were asleep already in the room. Maggs, who was four, went down first, and then the baby, Daisy. You couldn't say that they always went down like this, went to sleep in this order, for they would have nothing about themselves committed to stone, not yet. But it was something they had been trying out between them for a while: Maggs first to sleep, then Daisy-Baby, leaving time for Vi, who was, she must not forget, only eight.

"What's it like to be nine?" he asked, sounding so grown-up.

"Shhhhhhhh . . ." She smiled.

As each of the children fell asleep, one by one, she liked to picture an anchor, dropping from their soft warm bodies with a whirr, into the night's deep seabed.

Maggs's anchor plumbed down straight, quick and true. Daisy's needed a bit more guidance. Daisy didn't seem to trust yet, didn't know that she wouldn't be carried down with the dark weight of sleep to the bottom, and never rise again. How could Daisy be sure that this awake world was for keeps? That it couldn't be all changed once more, as it had been ten months ago when she'd slipped out of the womb world, slick in a bag, while the sun was a full white circle in the sky. When Daisy's anchor set out for sleep, her panicked eyes would ask, *Is this it? Is this life? Am I here? Will you stay?*

This is it. This is it. You are here. I will stay.

And Vi? It could take Vi an hour to get to sleep. It could take him two. Each time his anchor eased down a little he wanted to check, to see if he could roll it back up again at will. It was his agency, his power in this process that troubled him the most, and kept him all the more awake.

The electricity surged and went out for the night. Fridges for miles around ceased their collective backchat. The fans in the room began to slow down. Outside, in neighboring gardens, the music coming from speakers died, and a group of nearby people moaned about the death, affectionately. The lights in the hallway, the lights on the street, vanished. Then the fans stopped.

"It's dark!" said Vi.

4

"One minute," she replied. She pulled herself from the bed and went downstairs for a new candle.

They'd left the back door propped open with a brick, and so the kitchen, lit by a door's breadth of moonlight, was alive with winged things, with half-forming doubled things, with what Maggs—their coiner of terms—called "creature crawlies."

She tossed stale water from a cup, refilled it, and carried it back upstairs with two pink candles.

"Thanks," said Vi, sitting up in bed at an awkward angle to take a gulp from the cup, thirsty like he'd been at work, toiling, mining, for days. "You're a lightsaber."

When he was finished with it, she took the cup from him and placed it down on the floor. She fished a broken pen from under the bed and used it to scour out the old wax in the candlesticks; she added the new pink fellows with force, and lit them using the lighter kept on top of the wardrobe. Then she sat cross-legged on the end of Vi's bed.

There was a small piece of plastic film stuck to the sole of her foot. The wick of one of the new candles popped in its flame. And in the inner ear, like in the deep, whaling night sea, another pop, which was followed by a silence, this time so all-encompassing. The boy turned on his side and pulled his knees up to his chest. The night grew deeper. The anchors settled in. The children's dreams began to move them slightly further out and away from her.

Apparently alone, with her thoughts, for the first time that day, she tipped back her head, stretched out her neck.

Other parents in the streets nearby silently rehearsing their terror runs. Just like her, just then.

She started rehearsing.

Rehearsing. Rehearsing how she'd get the children out. Rehearsing the paths she'd make silently across the rooms to find the items she needed as quickly as possible. Exactly how, at night, she'd fill the car's trunk with this much water, in the deeper part, on the left, leaving space for that much food, the diapers, the particular clothes, the medicine bag, the green knapsack into which she'd stuff handfuls of precious children's objects and Maggs's crew of pirate dolls. She mentally practiced how she would get the sleeping children into the car one by one; the way each small head would loll against her shoulder, the order she would do this in—oldest first—how she would lock the car after she put each child in, and go back to the house for another. All of this had to exist, prearranged. She explored herself in this projected future, and made contingencies for whatever disturbances to her nature came up there. Taking, finally, the plastic folder of documents that she kept on the high painted shelf, she'd let the cats out to fend. Lock the front door. Pour some water over the windshield. Clear off the sticky creature crawlies. Get in the car, put a boiled sweet in her mouth to mix with the adrenaline. Suck. Pause. Clutch. Brake. Engine.

Vi stirred.

You had to be two, with kids.

She took a deeper breath. Calmed herself.

You had to be two: you had to separate your inelegant thoughts from your body as much as possible, rub out the connection between them. If you did not, you ran the risk of conveying your panicked mind to your young accidentally; it could beat out of you on your heightened pulse, or be carried out in your pheromones, on sweat.

The body could do things for the children that the mind could not, like birth them, or take impact on their behalf; you had to leave it alone to do its work, and not let the mind interfere with it too much.

Her legs moved into a shape of more comfort. She watched the sleeping boy. She watched for the heat that felt visible in the room. She watched the open window, which was covered with a mesh screen. She had lied to her son when she'd said there was nothing to be scared of. He knew.

She watched as, outside, an extremely large moth fluttered itself violently against the mesh. It was drawn, she suspected, not just to the candlelight, but to the particularly heady golden smell of her children's slumber. It was making sounds like it was breaking itself up. The moon was nearing full. The sky was yellowing black now, molding itself subtly to the earth. How was she going to understand everything tonight?

Before everything became awful, it was briefly very beautiful.

She listened to the children breathing. She was always listening out for their breaths, she was always picking their things up off the floor, she was always following them with her eyes, or some other knowing sense inside of her. Her gaze on their skin, their expressions, their scalps, their little teeth, their big, crystal tears. She was always stooping to contain one of them.

There was kids' paint on her legs. Her arms and boobs had bite marks on them. Peanut butter in the crescent beds of her fingernails. She needed a shower. She blew out the candles in the circles of light, slipped from the room and went downstairs, took out the trash cans, which trailed behind them clouds of tiny black flies, and then she sat, suddenly overwhelmingly tired, on the front doorstep, to have conversations in her mind with people she used to know.

She was so tired that: when she had been kneeling beside the bathtub earlier, and the two older children had pulled down their shorts in front of her face, to climb into the bath, she had been uniquely surprised by their genitalia—she had been sitting there oblivious to which child was which, or who they were entirely. Sometimes they were only a series of tasks that she needed to complete. She was so tired: the thought of seeking and lifting her toothbrush—it was impossible. So tired she was wondering if she could leave the soiled diapers where they were.

She missed her husband. He was very good at thumbing out the stain that connected her body to her mind. He was capable of floating her on his fingertips. He rubbed her feet with his. He extracted the salt from her skin with his tongue. She bit his proffered thumb.

She looked up at the dust-hot sky from her perch on the doorstep. She'd known for weeks now that the people in the house opposite had died or gone, but only just this second did she let herself acknowledge it. What else, she wondered, did she know and not know? She was alone, did she realize that? And no one used her name anymore.

She was Vi's mom, Maggs's mom, Daisy's mom, honey, darling, love. When he was home, her husband used her name with derision, like it was a joke. "*Cass?*" he said. "It doesn't do its job."

Or he'd say, "Cass does not represent you."

"You do have a fucking ugly name, though," he'd whisper sometimes, when she was right about something.

"Your feet are fucking filthy, though," he said when he walked in and found her lying in bed, in that way he found both wholesome and disgusting.

"Fucking ridiculous eyes you've got there." She missed the fucking. One of her eyes was brown and one was brown with a missing bit that was pale. "Your pupils," he said, holding her face in his hands and gazing, "are big and black as stars." He always spoke with a disturbing sadness when it came to her eyes. Once, in a cafe, apropos absolutely nothing, he'd said, "Your eyes should have been blue."

His name was Nathaniel. His eyes were solid, green, and milky. His pupils went tiny in the sunshine. He took care.

From the doorstep, Cass heard Daisy let out a cry in her sleep. It was a cry like she'd glimpsed some gaping, horrible truth on the seabed. Cass got up and went back inside. She let herself into the children's room with the faintest click of the door, bending and collecting up things, and listening on the way. But whatever had troubled Daisy had passed; the child's face was at rest, very still, apart from that dewy film that seemed always to be morphing in growth over the baby's cheeks and nostrils. Cass turned to Maggs, who slept with her head against her hands held in prayer, like a parody of a sleeping cherub. Even in her sleep, Maggs got the joke. Vi was wheezing in a way that could almost be mistaken for light snoring. He often complained that his lungs felt "heavy." Cass had spoken on the phone to a doctor about this, who'd told her that there was a shortage of inhalers and to "make do, as best you can, until things get really bad."

Cass liked to imagine the children all grown, and living away from The City, in a cleaner place, where they enjoyed long lives around her. Free from the depression, lung disease, and cancers The City's air promised. Growing their own food. Curing their own minor ailments. Untroubled. She closed her eyes and could summon visions of the three children as three noble adult bodies, whose dignity and certainty made her feel small, spent up, and glad.

She wondered what she would tell them, when they were grown. How they would regard her. How react to her? What would she say?

Before everything became awful it was, briefly, very . . .

When the summers got longer and longer, she'd tell them, there were blooms as big as heads in the front gardens, all along the street. There was that ease between people. That ease that comes in heat. When strangers pass things to each other, exposing their wrists and holding eye contact a beat too long. A wink and a whistle, a lick and a promise, the air was transactional and pleasure-set. Every aspect of society had grown slowly worn and useless over years—the hospitals, the schools, the transport, the food, the bills so heavy, the bureaucracy slow-motioned into a farce, nothing quite as reliable as it once had been—and every citizen had learned how to make their own imaginative way through the fainter provisions, where once they hadn't needed to, where once they had leaned against the steady forces of what they were entitled to. The summers became longer and longer and hotter still and extended into the other seasons. People built their own private economies of barter, borrow and play to your strengths. And, for some weeks, there was a plague of butterflies. Thousands and thousands of butterflies, all at once, so many, crowding the streets. Dead ones, becoming undone, floating on the river. Dancing circles in the trains, then getting underfoot.

At first the children had picked their way down the hot pavements, eyes to the ground, determined. "I will not to step on the flutter-bys" was the promise made daily by Maggs. But it became impossible to avoid them. There'd be butterfly wings stuck to the undersides of the children's plastic clogs, butterfly bodies smashed and sticky, with still-twitching legs. The butterflies landed in the children's hair. The air was all misty and full of smoke sometimes. At Vi's school they fried sloppy eggs on the asphalt and called it a science lesson. They learned how to lie on their backs and surrender all of their playful thoughts, accepting nothingness, and they called it Physical Education. They watched Christmas movies full of snow and called it Creative Reflection Time. Maggs laughed from her belly. The baby went cross-eyed in her stroller as a flutter-by that had landed on her nose slowly flexed its wings.

People were skin-warmed, often barefoot; there was birdsong, and a slowed-down, lingering pace, more laying down—of tools, ambitions, selves. Longer soccer games in the park, between neighbors. A morale-building cricket match down the middle of the street all the way through the early evening, and then, candles, burning in the windows. People had more time. Less work. Fewer things available to procure. Sometimes the internet worked, often it didn't. Sometimes electric fans made gauzy curtains cascade, billowing out from private rooms, like the beckoning dancer in one of the films they projected in the park at night using the generator, or the mains, depending. Singing in the rain, when it sometimes came.

It was too hot for everything. Heat in the cradle of the brain, making thinking fuzzy.

That's what it was like, initially, she'd tell them.

Daisy, in her cot, took in an enormous shuddering breath, shaking the rigging of her finely boned vessel.

Cass realized she had been holding herself, bent uncomfortably, entranced, over the cot for some minutes, and now her whole body felt pained. She went to call Nathaniel, knowing that she wouldn't get through. She stood under a cold shower, and had almost four hours of sleep before Daisy woke her.

2

They rose early, to get some hours in before the heat of the day. But, even at six in the morning, parts of the kitchen floor were too hot for bare feet. Taking Daisy-Baby on her hip, and a coffee in the other hand, Cass went on tiptoe to sit outside, where the back garden was still in shade. Maggs, which was short for Marigold, followed out behind them, shouting, "Ow, ow, ouch" at her burning toes. She ignored Cass, kissed the baby, and took up the paints that had been left in the garden overnight. Blithely, Maggs stirred the brush in a jar of dirty, pink paint water and tiny dead creature crawlies. She began painting a garden pebble, before moving on to paint the skin of Cass's legs once more. Bright colors on golden skin. Cass nursed her coffee and watched, blissing out to the child's rhythmic little breaths and holy concentration. The cool hushing paint strokes on her legs.

Soon Vi appeared and Maggs quietly said his name: "Vi!" They all pronounced it "Vee" like "bee" and "tree" and "key," which was how he liked it. He stretched theatrically on the threshold between kitchen and garden. Attaching his plastic clogs to his agile feet, he stepped outside and, joining his sister without speaking, took up a small-headed paintbrush to attend to Cass's toenails, each a different watercolor, as if she were his unfinished masterpiece from the day before. He paused, dissatisfied with Cass's small toenail, which was neither big nor smooth enough to take the pigment. He made an artistic compromise and painted the entire toe instead. Finally, putting down his brush, he stretched again, and said, in his pure, clear tones, "Good morning, Mommy. I'm hungry."

Inside, there was a washer-dryer, a skillet, a nutmeg grater. There was a record player, and an old radio, and two wireless speakers, and, in a clean jam jar, headphones and hairpins. There were two

11

mobile phones, and two laptops and a tablet. Lamps, and art posters in frames. The front room, the darkest and coolest, was entirely given over to the storage of bottled water. The windows had the cheapest insect screens over them, the hinges of which were spectacularly cruel traps for little fingers.

The plan had always been to leave as soon as Nathaniel got back. But he couldn't tell her when that would be. The children had circled the sun together for ten months. They were eight and four and a baby. They were used to breathing air that tasted burnt and did things to their perfect bodies that they didn't know about yet. They liked the smell of diesel and turned their heads toward it. They were not all hers. They were entirely hers. Their future had become all-consuming for her.

She made some toast for Vi. He ate it while going about the garden with a pair of blunt scissors, cutting off overgrown stems at random. He picked up one of his cuttings to give to Cass. She twirled it between her fingers upside down to slow the gush of clean green sap that was issuing forth, and then, because she knew that Maggs was only about to wonder out loud what the sap would taste like, Cass licked it, and Maggs laughed, like bells, at being known and anticipated so well.

"Can we save this one for Dad?" asked Vi, proffering another stem.

"It might not be very good by the time he gets back," Cass said.

"How long will that be?"

"I don't know, baby."

Vi's shoulders fell but he quickly recalled his braver self and said, "It will be fun when Dad gets back."

"Like when Daddy found you again!" Maggs squealed. "Will be like, Daddy say: Hello! Found you! Again!"

Nathaniel had "found" Cass squatting on the pavement, on the street with all the bars. She'd been tending to her friend, a tall man who was being dramatically sick over the curb. She was rubbing the back of this friend's thick neck. Nathaniel had come over and asked Cass, "Can I help you there?" and she'd replied, "No, we're alright, thanks." And then Nathaniel had lingered too long, and too awkwardly, until he finally came out with, "Sorry. I actually don't want to help. I'm drunk too much. I just want your number?"

He had not *found* her. She had looked up, and liked his face. It was handsome and clean; it was unmessy, even in drunkenness. It seemed open to her. His eyebrows so dark against those sea-glass eyes. His fine white work shirt sweat-damp. She deduced and invented: he hadn't meant to come out, his friends had insisted, he'd agreed in the last instant to go for one drink after work, and he'd got carried away; he wasn't usually like this; it was sweet, his befuddlement at letting go, sweet and out of character. He was good. She was surprised that he'd approach a woman when he was so drunk. Like he didn't know the lay of this nightlife landscape; like he wasn't fully up to speed with how it worked. And she decided to match his naivety—faux or not.

She spoke her phone number to him clearly. She had to do it twice. All the while her friend, from his head-between-his-knees position, hit her on the back of the shins and said, "Stop it" and "Don't give it him."

Don't give it him.

She recalled well the sensation of nipping out from the office in her lunch break to purchase something new for one of their dates. She bought a cheap red dress, and a thing to put in her hair, and earrings that she'd wear once. The thrill of it all gleamed off her. As the dates built up, this became a lunchtime ritual: procuring adornments to bless their burgeoning relationship and bring it success, and it was smiled upon by everyone; her co-workers, the girl in the shop, the man selling lunch who would notice the spring in her step and the promising little carrier bag. "Don't have too much fun all at once," said her friend who worked the reception desk.

For that first date, she'd arrived at the rooftop bar a full half an hour before Nathaniel. But when he appeared, and asked if she'd been there long, she said no.

He stood at quite a distance and she watched as he processed her lie, her face, her posture, and the smallness of the table.

He became visibly resolved on an idea and made steps toward her. But, instead of sitting down, he placed his leather bag slowly onto the chair. He opened his fist to reveal his tie balled loosely in his hand. He took it and wrapped it properly, slowly, around his fist. He put the perfected coil of it gently into the bag. He moved the bag to the floor and sat—all in silence. Then he picked up the menu lying there on the table and said, "What looks good?"

They decided that—before alcohol—they would order the mint tea, because they were both nervous and dehydrated. After ordering, Nathaniel sat back in his chair and regarded Cass with laughing eyes, like he'd found the holy grail and it was kind of trashier than he'd expected it to be. She relaxed. The tea came in a bronzed teapot, on a silver tray, with two old little painted glasses. Nathaniel poured the tea from a great height, and it twinkled down in a long line. Cass remarked that they were recreating the circumstances of their first meeting, but in opposite: the sky was light rather than dark, the line of falling liquid was enriched water, not bile, and they were sober. He took a beat and looked at her as if she was slightly, endearingly insane. And then—when she expected him to recover—they both realized that she had made his thoughts stumble quite substantially and he didn't know what to say next. His face looked panicked. Tongue-soft and tongue-tied. And so—even though she found the question boring, and believed she was fundamentally incurious as to the answer—she asked him what he did for a living. As he said "doctor" she was tipping the glass of tea to her lips and she saw something large roll over the base of the glass and come toward her with the liquid.

"What the hell is . . ." she asked, jerking the glass from her face and holding it up high to the light.

He reached to meet her touch on the glass. His fingers covered her thumb, his thumb lodged between her fingers. He rearranged his hand to grasp the cup from its lip, and as he did so he saw something too, shadowy, in the base. Taking the glass directly from her fingertips, he quickly stuck a teaspoon into it, and withdrew something which he flicked loudly onto the tea tray.

A tooth. A large molar. Four roots. Like a table. An ancient natural table.

"Is it yours?" He could not wait to know.

"No!" But, with her hand covering her mouth, she was running, laughing, her tongue over her teeth, right into the back, to check.

"Let me see," he said, and he leaned over the table, and she, with an obedience that played like defiance, opened her mouth as wide as it would go.

He took her chin in his hand, held it firmly and, having pulled at her bottom lip with his thumb, he looked right down—past her teeth—into her gullet. She heard the air leaving his lungs, and she tasted it filling her mouth. And it tasted like . . . It tasted like . . . She was all apart, all her senses were blown and rejoined wrong, so she was smelling his touch, and feeling his sight, and hearing his aroma. *So be it.*

A dance inside her then. A scramble while the other men who had been occupying her mind left, as if bidden to go by this man, this Nathaniel—with the golden watch catching the hairs on his arm, the barrel chest, the brown leather bag and ironed shirt. Cass opened her mouth wider. Stretched that neck back and up, proffering to Nathaniel the red that remained once the others had gone.

Nathaniel stayed still in front of her. He did not dance away, did not dance from mind, did not strike one as a man who would ever dance. He seemed graceful but stocky, steady on his feet, and his center of gravity was peculiarly low. The way he'd unbuttoned and rolled his shirt sleeves on first sitting down, with precision: exactly like a fancy doctor would. He was very close to what he claimed to be. And he was very proud of this. A bit superior, the way he'd glanced at his watch, the way he'd flicked the menus into the server's stomach. And then he was very, very close, looking into her throat. His gaze moved, from her tonsils to her eyes, and she noticed him noticing the pale flaw in her iris. And—possibly for the first and final time—their thoughts aligned completely: they were grossed out and betrothed. "Shit," one of them said. He pulled himself back, sat down, and beckoned the manager over to their small table with the slightest of gestures, to discuss the tooth. The manager actually ran toward them.

Nathaniel had a house and two children; a mother, a brother, and a job. There were two former wives and a river of grief connecting the pools of them, which kept him up, pacing the banks, late at night.

His first wife, seriously weakened by childbirth, had caught pneumonia in the hospital, and died of septicemia, which had "come on like a train."

The second wife was only presumed dead; it had never been confirmed. She'd gotten sick, thought it was one of the foreign viruses (particularly she feared the rare one, the one that made your eyes bleed; Nathaniel said he frequently found her staring into her own eyes in the bathroom mirror), and, when she'd felt herself strong enough, had gone abroad to recuperate at her mother's, and was never heard from again. "I think she was still unwell when she left. I think she didn't want to die in front of the children," he said.

Nathaniel revealed these parts of his life to Cass slowly and carefully, but still, his timing was off; he really couldn't dance. Each new piece of information felt like the peeling away of dead tissues of skin before they were completely ready. Each freshly revealed layer threw Cass off course in a unique way. But then she'd enjoy how Nathaniel stepped in with his comfort, his adoration, and course corrections. He was very offbeat, but he was also talented, and subtle. The first time she met the children and witnessed their lives—Vi from the first marriage and Maggs from the second—she felt deeply depressed by the stale, restrictive humdrum of it all; by the low-quality cartoons on a device, and congealing cornflakes in plastic bowls, formula bottles cooked to sterility in a pan, and what looked like hundreds of purple syringes in two mugs on the kitchen counter ("No! They're not sinister. You use them to *squirt* infant acetaminophen into their mouths, not their veins!" he had to explain, because she knew nothing). But within months she was seeing the world through Vi's eyes, and finding it extraordinary. The first mother had departed when Vi was weeks old. The second mother had gone when Vi was four and Maggs was six months old. Now they were eight and four. Vi liked to make very direct eye contact with Cass when they spoke. Maggs liked to lie over Cass, as if Cass were a landscape.

In the garden, Cass removed a piece of what was almost certainly Maggs's hair from her own mouth and thought about Maggs's mother. Wasn't it a death wish to return to your motherland, when that motherland was so dangerous? A country that had been written off by remaining global powers. Nathaniel had refused to believe in the death at first. He'd wanted to see official confirmation, not simply an email from his wife's mother, which he'd had to get translated, to be sure, because he couldn't accept what he thought it said. Knew it said. He'd wanted to go and look for her, but his colleagues, whom he trusted, advised him against it. Too dangerous. He'd hired a nanny. None of it made sense. He was angry. He spent six months at war within himself over it. And then he met Cass.

"Found you! Again!" Maggs repeated, pressing Cass's face with her little hands from behind and pushing her chin into Cass's back. "Tell me the story when Daddy found you!"

Cass pulled Maggs around to face her, to plant kisses on, to glory in, as she said: "Daddy found me outside the Duke of York. Then he

16

took me for tea at a fancy place called The Archipelago, and there was a tooth in my tea! When I first met you, I thought you were the best things I had ever seen. On our first anniversary, he took me for tea again . . ."

"At the . . ."

"At the Archipelago, and there was an engagement ring in my tea!"

"This ring?" Maggs asked.

"Yes."

"I like this ring. It does flashes. Can I have it one day? When you die?"

"Sure."

After the ring, Nathaniel had plied Cass with more things, but none of them had landed with her as he seemed to want them to. Then he'd said, "Let's have our own baby." And she'd thought, *Why on earth?*

And now their own baby was laid out on a towel on the earth, moving her little arms and curling her back as if her belly button were connected to the sky via a piece of taut, miraculous string.

Cass liked to hang out with her face right up close to her baby's, so that they completely filled one another's vision, with not a millimeter of anything else in the periphery. It felt so right, this obscuring of sight, in this case. When Cass breastfed the baby, its little tongue would come away all covered in white particles. Particles like a wet, white dust. She was all sunlight and sun, this child. Definitely of this world she had landed in. Her naturally pale skin, already tanned by it. All on a cusp.

3

They ambled, late, to drop Vi off at school. Then they would usually move off to join one of the various long lines for the things they needed: that day's withdrawal from the ATM, street-market toilet paper, and to see what had materialized in the good shop. Maggs excelled at playing up and down the long lines, inquiring into the characters and well-being of all, with such openers as, "I like your shoes. Did you steal them? I stole a thing from Mommy. She does not know. Yet."

But as they walked away from the school that day, one of the other mothers thrust a piece of paper at Cass. "Do you want this?" It was a flyer-ticket to a toddlers' art class. "We can't go," said the mother. "My cat is sick. It eats all the flowers." Which was strange, as cat food was one of the few things in plentiful supply. Cass had seen her quiet neighbor, Steve, return home with boxes of it, and she seriously wondered if that was what he ate. All the beasts were adapting. She had a box of tomatoes from the pizzeria garden, and some rapeseed oil—perhaps she could take those to Steve. She had a box of printed photos from her wedding day, and a box with her certificates and some work, alongside the many boxes of her husband's things. She had cat food, like everyone else. On the way to the art class she saw a cat sitting out, openly chewing a butterfly; the bright wings were still peeking out from the cat's jaws. Each animal qualmless in its own way.

Heavy blossoms everywhere. Jungle city.

In the art class, in the room out the back of the cafe, five little children sat at a round table decorating crowns. Maggs eagerly joined them. Five women stood behind their charges. The bright sunlight came through the frosted glass, softly hazing the lilac walls.

It became clear that three of the women were close. Cass guessed they spoke daily. They had group habits and responsibilities. The other two women were doing impressions of the faces they'd pulled on the first day the internet went down. They aped their own expressions of helplessness, confusion, terror, and then rolled their eyes at their own patheticness.

Daisy was still asleep in the sling on Cass. Cass gently bounced to keep herself, and the baby, tethered to themselves.

"But it's amazing what you get used to," one of the women said. "I simply stopped looking to my phone for the answer."

"It does feel like losing a friend."

"It does."

"My phone was my friend!"

"But you *have* lost a friend, because you lose *connection* to many friends."

"You invest more in your local community."

"You simply have to."

"It was very traumatic, though."

"It really was."

Everything was running together. Cass remained quiet. The other mothers were dressed in thought-through outfits, and they had proper, structured bags. Cass put her face very close to Daisy's. Cass wore her husband's volunteer military T-shirts, and his watch, and all her mother's jewelry, all the gold, all at once. The T-shirts were big enough that she could take the baby under them to breastfeed in a red tent of their own personal smell.

The other mothers were leaving little pausing chances for her to join in their conversation.

Cass had been defensive against other parents. At the start of her relationship with Nathaniel, she'd turned up in the playground, inexperienced and quickly unimpressed by the ways and means of adults with their young. Everyone had thought she was the nanny for the longest time. As soon as he proposed, Nathaniel had encouraged his children to use the word "Mom" when they looked at Cass.

Maggs took to it easily, shouting "Mah!" with chaotic relief, while Vi was naturally more cautious; when he came to call Cass "Mom," it was with a meaning that was pleasantly layered. They ran with it in their mouths: "Mah" became "Mam-ma" and "Mom" became

"Mommy." Cass, in turn, softened. She grew into her own way, became consistent, felt mercy, realized that the reason she fended off other parents was in case they took something she hadn't meant to give. She often made sure to give very little, outside of the home. She remembered when she was a child and nothing was too much for her, no amount of love.

"Yes. It was. That's the word: 'traumatic,'" said one of the women.

It was, the radio had said, an Exceptional Danger Day. New fires. Some of them chemical. There was a chance they'd close the schools again for the rest of the week, if the air quality didn't improve.

"Mam-ma, come here," whispered Maggs. Cass bent down, cradling Daisy's head, and let Maggs put a shiny foil sticker gently on her forehead. Cass thanked Maggs, and stood up too quickly.

Cass looked about and felt that there was something passing between the mouths of these insistent women around her, beneath their words and over the kids' heads, that was protective, that was keeping out the orange sky and the air that smelled of burning. She felt unexpectedly, inappropriately woozy with love.

"Your nose is bleeding."

Cass didn't immediately understand that they were speaking to her.

One of the women said, "It's OK, the bathroom's right here," and started leading Cass to it. Another said, "Oh God." Daisy remained asleep in the sling, with her little bow mouth open. And Cass said to Maggs, in a voice that conveyed there was not a problem in the world, "It's OK, baby." And her tiny green earrings caught the sunlight and flashed a reassuring signal to the child.

Cass wanted to look at the bleed in the bathroom mirror before cleaning it up. The nose blood was thick. It oozed out. Like a slug. The surface tension of the liquid was as tight as the color was dense. The edge of the mirror was beveled and making, she noticed, strata of them all. But the other mother was unclipping the sling, taking Daisy carefully and hurrying Cass along. "You need to pinch your nose," she said, while catching the edge of the sticker with her nail and peeling it off Cass's forehead, as if it had been distracting them all.

Cleaned up, and sitting with her head against the frosted window, Cass was handed a glass of lemonade on ice. The cafe had small ovals of ice. "Ice!" The clink of it in the glass was one of those sounds that reminded you of the Old World. The woman in the group, who was the tallest and most beautiful in that way which is undeniable, and which makes the bearer of it quickly bored by the desires of man, said, "Do you trust me?" as she squirted a pipette of brown liquid into the drink. Cass felt sick. Behind the frosted window, an old man went slowly by with a tank of air on wheels, wheezing. The cafe manager was saying he would throw a tarpaulin over the dead German shepherd outside. A teenage girl in the apartment building across the street was smoking on the balcony; the way she was holding herself made Cass nostalgic. Cass remembered occupying her body like that and a particular moment when she had leaned her forearms just so on the rail of a similar balcony and had realized that the only way she could get the rising, terrifying sensation out of her body was to get a boy to roughly rub it out of her until it left on her voice in yelps, and through her frame in shudders. The children were getting up from the table and wearing their crowns. Cass could see halos around them, auras, like the corona of the moon, each a different color.

That night, if the connection held, she would tell Nathaniel all of this. And she would want him to hear the unspoken moral of her story, which was: "It's time to go." She wanted him to sing it back to her as a clear directive: "You have to get out of there. You're being poisoned. Don't wait for me." But that night the internet was still down, the landline was dead, the power had never come back on after lunch.

4

Throughout her early adulthood, Cass had barely registered the people leaving The City. They had gone innocuously, giddily: they'd miss (they'd pause) all the things, City things. But they were vague about which things. They popped and left like dew.

Now Cass was older, and people left The City differently, in droves going heavily toward their only options. In many cases they went to ill-fitting family members outside of town, to share the costs of life. Cass no longer had family. She considered herself, in this regard, free.

Nathaniel had family but not in the close way. He had a mother, Eden. And he had a brother, Arthur, who was apparently troubled and who troubled, in turn, whatever happened to be in front of him. Arthur "partied." He binged until he reached a brink, he'd be unreachable for months, and then he'd appear unannounced at Eden's to detox, from where he would depart again, on a whim, all without saying hello, without saying goodbye. Phones and keys fell through his fingers like water. He went "from the face of the earth" for months on end, then turned up with scabs on his face to fall on his mother's chiding. Nathaniel claimed to not like either of them. Often he could not tolerate them. Sometimes he shouted: he did not want his children in their vicinity, neither around his brother's aggressive unpredictability, nor around the strange enjoyment his mother seemed to get from suffering it. Nathaniel did not like the silent, blanket fury that came down on him in their company. It muffled him.

And yet. He took Cass and the children to stay with Eden at least twice a year, when Arthur was definitely absent. And yet. He kept up a regular, entertaining conversation with his mother over the phone. And yes, Cass understood: Nathaniel had a family, but he maintained a strange adjacency, which was actually a distance from them.

22

Simply: he was only visible to them because he was guarding the perimeter of his own dominion, watching out for their approaches. While City dwellers were streaming away to find relative Edens, Eden's was a place that Nathaniel found he could go to in theory, but not in practice.

And in many parts of the world, it seemed, the direction of travel was quite the opposite. People were trying to get into the cities, not away from them. In other countries, urban spots had fared better than the rural places. Cass thought the migration of people flowing out and away from her city had something to do with her hometown's urban infrastructure, which was more like an old, abandoned wedding cake than cool and calculated. It still had its columns, its touches, its architectural flourishes, cornices, railings, like decrepit icing. It seemed to have been envisioned once with all this coming decrepitude in mind. Cass's city was sinking, as all the liquid was sucked up from beneath it. It had become an indentation, where all the gases and nightmares pooled. It took forever to get in and get out.

In Cass's fantasy, Nathaniel would surprise her soon on the doorstep, and they'd take off immediately with the children, to live off his savings, somewhere safe and clever, far north, where it was generally cooler, and the air was cleaner, while they tried to sell the house. Although it was no longer common or easy to sell a house in The City.

Cass craved fresh air like she'd craved things in her pregnancy, with a scary gorging hunger: anchovies, baths, apples.

*

She took a bite and realized that the apples she had bought for breakfast were bad. There had been no fresh milk in the shops for three days; it went off in the heat before it could be delivered. Everywhere was out of bread. No eggs. Some peanut butter, some beans in tins.

"Dry cornflakes or beans, my loves?" Cass said to the children, brightly.

Maggs asked for cornflakes, got them, didn't want them. Cass took out an old box of icing sugar, broke it up with a spoon, and dusted some of it over the bowl of golden flakes, and the backs of Maggs's hands. They watched it fall, pretty and light. Maggs ate.

23

Afterward she wouldn't brush her teeth until Cass had chased her with the toothbrush, caught her, covered her in kisses, and still the child wouldn't. Then Cass playacted despair. For this, Maggs would do anything. She liked to feel that she knew exactly where Cass's wits' end was located.

*

A parent at the school gate. A father who managed both a hangdog face and a countenance of constant surprise: "People need to start questioning what they feel entitled to," he said.

He had been watching a child going into the school with a brand-new birthday bike. There were plastic birthday balloons tied with streamers to the handlebars. Cass and the man stayed together as they walked away from the school, and discussed how much such a thing would have cost: twelve times the price of five years ago? More? The man was of the belief that, no matter how much one could somehow afford, those who bought unnecessary new things were—according to any thinking person's rubric—wrong. Every single purchase represented to him an extraction of resources from a depleted planet. "We don't have to buy better, we have to stop buying!" he said loudly. But Cass privately contended that this man had only managed to develop his distaste for wealth by having it. And—anyway—everything about the world had altered so shimmeringly, and by the slightest of increments, not enough all at once to bring your faiths, or capitalist cravings, directly into question. The sun was high. There was just enough. And, once in a blue moon, there was more. The evenings were candlelit. Then the holy pleasure of the sun on your face, reliably, once again. People died and people left.

Another day. Pick-up time. "I've got something for you," said a mom, running from the gate with her twins. "Wait here"—and she jangled off. Cass waited. And while she waited she read through a poster announcing a "Parents for Truth-Speaking Forum" which was plastered on the school wall. Over it someone had written in marker: "Let Kids Be Kids." The parenting dilemma of the day: Do you tell the children what is happening? Or do you preserve their innocence for as long as possible? Giving them at least a memory of something idyllic to fight for. Graffiti had recently been washed away from the same wall, but it still grinned through: "'They are killing me'—Mother Earth." And that word again: "Gaia . . . Gaia . . . Gaia."

"What is Gaia?" Vi would ask several times a week. He always got the same reply from Cass.

"Mother Earth," she'd say, with finality. But Vi knew this was not the answer, in its entirety.

He pushed her on it: "Daddy said they're in cells."

When he was at home, Cass enjoyed Nathaniel's private takes on things. He reserved them for her.

While most dismissed Gaia as unremarkable—another climate activist group, only this time organized exclusively by and for men—in Nathaniel's analysis the Gaias were incels. "Load of losers finally found a woman who won't reject them," he said. It was a love story, in a way, when Nathaniel told it: how a group of violent, misogynistic men had turned to the goddess, Earth, and finally found a partner, a woman who would accept their protection, and who allowed them to relish in her bounty. Her allowance was divine, endless, and indiscriminate. The men felt bliss-love in her presence and would defend her at all costs. "That's why they're always meditating in the woods—they're not meditating, they're spunking up the trees," Nathaniel said. "*Communing* with Nature." He said that word, "communing," in a camp way.

Cass had never seen a man spunking up a tree, but Nathaniel's read on the strange Gaias did fit. The Gaia men set up protective pickets around the downs, forests, and streams with violent love. They attacked sewage plants that dumped waste into fresh water. They admonished people who left their trash behind in untouched places. These men, it seemed, who felt locked out by conventional women, they turned to Mother Earth, felt her embrace, and they heard her speak. And she told them, she made them know, that the people, especially the procreating people, were parasites who were raping and suffocating her.

Nathaniel liked to tell Cass—told her many times—how the political extremes of far left and far right always met, in the end, and the line of polarity became a circle.

"Where are you, on this circle?" Cass asked.

He didn't reply immediately because he was moving himself to do something. "In the center of it, my darling," he said eventually, kissing, delicately, along the line where the edges of her underwear met her skin.

"I think we're at the bottom," she said, like they'd fallen down.

"'They are killing me'—Mother Earth." It was plastered on walls by the Gaias. Especially around schools. Especially wherever procreating people congregated.

But that was all it was: a bit of slightly sinister graffiti, a purposefully misspelled "suffercating." Only graffiti, and a slow increase in the numbers of men walking about town dressed in a way that was both borrowed from the military—the combat gear of many nations mixed together—and adorned with the symbols of woodland Nature. An ammo belt studded with badges of forged leaves and silver acorns. A beret with the insignia of yew, ash, oak. And daisies.

"I don't think that lady's coming back," said Cass.

"But she said she had something for you!" said Vi.

"Let's go home."

*

Another morning at the school gate. A jubilant mood. Three weeks had passed without a school closure: a new record for the academic year. The parents were energetic as they stepped away alone, or with big babies in strollers accustomed to the hot tides of air, some with smaller babies squawking and clammy all over.

Another dad, Ivy and Dale's dad, a friend of sorts whose name Cass didn't know, stopped to talk to her. He told her that he was moving his family to a compound owned by his company, where the air was cleaned and cooled by machine, where there were well-designed spaces for communal working, a school and an artificial glade, fish in the stream, and the internet had a governmental guarantee. ("Is that a thing?" "Very much so.") There was a roof over the whole, he explained, a semipermeable barrier, as well as special staff to take deliveries and clean and quarantine them. They'd managed to sell their house and their car to get themselves in ("Not that they're worth anything anymore"), and he'd have to work much longer hours to afford it, had taken a demonic promotion, but the net benefit . . .

Cass listened to herself saying, "Good for you" and "I'm really pleased for you all. That will be great." She could hear the enthusiasm in her own voice. But she also did not believe him. And she found herself worrying about what this fantasy of the compound could possibly be masking. Where was this man taking his family?

"You should consider it," he said. She watched him as he remembered some opinion he had of her, and his eyes grew sticky. "I'm sure your husband could get a place."

"We can't."

"Why?"

"We just can't."

"What about your work? Would they . . . ?"

"I left."

That was all it was and life was briefly very beautiful. Gaunt faces, bright eyes, and darkening skin. Little transfixing bursts of light in the corners of your vision. Auras and the brazenness of those who threw all their energy behind convincing you that everything was the same as it ever had been.

5

Vi called out to Cass, casually, across the playground, "Mom! Where's my bag?"

"By the bench, there."

"Is he yours?" asked the mother of a very blonde child.

"Yes."

"But not *yours*-yours?"

"Mine-mine," Cass replied.

A different parent changed the subject: "If I had somewhere to go, I'd go now. If I had somewhere."

"Would you?" said the other mother. "Now, see: I wouldn't. I want my friends. And my places, you know? Things aren't—they aren't—that bad."

"Not yet. But when do you call it?"

In the playground, the parents talked. They compared niceties, and summed each other up along the terms of a particular question: Is what you want for your children the same as what I want for mine? And, more frequently than they gave themselves credit for, they verbalized the generally unspoken things: "When do you call it? When it's time to leave, will you? Where will you go and how?"

Most of Cass's friends had left The City. Many of them had never understood why she'd caught herself up in all these children.

She took her children home, pulled Vi onto her lap, and said, "Mine-mine." Inside the house, in the dark hot dusk, the shade of their skin was almost the same. And the night unfolded as ever. Always the same, and never quite.

Cass woke suddenly in her bed that night and wondered why the children sounded alert, speaking in their room. She looked at Nathaniel's watch on her wrist. 7:05 a.m. Not night, then. Usually daylight at this point. But it was dark around the edges of the blinds: no sun.

The children were calling for her. She got up and went to her bedroom window to investigate the darkness. She opened the blinds and stood there as the children called and she muttered, automatically, "I'm coming," too quietly for them to hear. She was trying to work out what it was that she was looking at.

Perhaps it was a very darkening smog. A kind of beautiful black swirl, in gelatinous air. A shoal of night spirits, dancing through the morning. She could not see through it to the buildings on the other side of the street. She could not clearly see the pavement below. All she could see was this dark airy mass, like something CGI, as if her brain was being tricked into believing her bedroom window was a screen. It felt like she could tip her head to the side and the whole world would pitch with her.

She accepted that there must have been a big fire, very close by. And the smoke confronting her was not from regular things burnt, but from something more noxious.

The heat inside the house was drier than ever. She ran about shutting all the windows behind the mesh screens, and closing the curtains and blinds, so the children might not see. She clicked a light switch and electricity came in like grace, but there was no internet. She put the fans on and tried to call someone; everyone was busy, or maybe the lines weren't working.

She put off everything she had to do, brought breakfast up to the children's room, and sat on the floor with them until they became dementedly bored and crazy. They climbed all over her, and rolled their heads across her breasts until she wanted to cry out, but instead she gently, yet forcibly, moved their blessed heads away.

The air outside started to clear by the early afternoon. People came out and were going about their business as if nothing had happened. Still, she didn't want the children to go outside into whatever lingered in the air. No internet that day, no reports, no acknowledgment. No event. Only your personal experience, without corroboration.

*

When the internet had become unreliable, the newspapers started coming free through the door, full of adverts. "Just In Time: Just Not

Possible," the headline had read. The global networks of exchange had, through the span of Cass's childhood, become so refined as to be insubstantial, wispy in the air in the face of such crude threats as wildfires, economic crashes, border policies, overheating. It had only taken a few disasters, simultaneous, interconnected; life had worn down slowly, gradually, and then—pop—the wheels came off.

The First Great Fire had devastated the southwest, around the time Maggs was born. The following year, The Under Floods, further north, but still to the west. Recovery had been scant. The Second Great Fire had been in the true north, but it was relatively well managed; lessons had been learned.

Now there was something new, The Midlands Fire, beyond the outskirts of The City. You heard a lot about the toxic load in the air, especially from the factories burnt, the things released by fire. There was escalating mortality, from the air, from the insufficient medical services, heat deaths, the floods bringing mosquitoes, bringing disease. Death became usual again. It was a convergence of disasters. The agreement between water, soil, and pollination was weakened everywhere. There were disasters at home, and disasters abroad, which brought shortages of imports and destabilized export markets. Fires and lockdowns due to air quality, random and common, poverty. Death by impoverishment. Diminished tax bases. Fuel prices escalating. It was no longer possible to rely on the perfectly timed arrival of anything exactly when it was required: the chemicals that cleaned the water, the fruit that was ripe, certain medicines.

Yet, you could still do things. If you were one of the few who had the right sort of job, which had held, you could still take a plane. You could go to a restaurant, where the menus were limited but the service was Old World. You could pay to be submerged in water so pure that it was purported to remove the toxins and microplastics from your system. You could pay for all kinds of osmosis: mental, sexual, spiritual, where what you held too much of would be offloaded to someone who convincingly pretended to have none of it.

It was confusing. Everything was still just about possible. Just about possible, if you had the money, to take a plane and watch the place where the sea was on fire, from a cliff-edge restaurant. It was possible to descend into a sci-fi underwater glass tunnel and see the last surviving pair of orcas, who swam to the people for company. It was possible to swim above the ruined empire of the bleached-out reefs. It was possible. It was possible to dedicate yourself to extinction, and attend parties for days. It was all possible. You just had to really want to.

Often Cass sank below thought. She was watching, bemused. Waiting for something. Plotting something. She shrank from her friends, attuned herself to the kids, and worked out how they could hum along together best, until their dad got home.

For a short while, Social Health Policy had it that you were not meant to leave your borough without good reason, but this had not been effectively policed. You were not meant to stockpile water, but everyone did. On the days it spluttered to life, you were ill-advised to follow news leads on the internet, but how could you not? There were periods of frenzied action, followed by periods of neglect, followed by reaction. Some people still worked for large corporations on whose behalf they crusaded like beleaguered activists. Some went abroad to see the end-times sights, but such trips were vanishingly rare. The first time Nathaniel told her he was going abroad she was in a cold bath. She thought he was purposely trying to confuse her, perhaps as part of a game that she'd forgotten they were playing, forgotten because of the ice shock of the bath. She got out and sat on the edge of the tub, dripping all over the tiled floor as she put her T-shirt back on and said, "What?"

"Why did you put your T-shirt on?"—clicking and then pointing his finger with concern, from hip level.

"So I could understand what you were saying?"

"It's wet, I can see everything."

"I didn't put it on so you could focus. I put it on so *I* could focus."

"You know, I am very capable of thinking straight in front of your naked body."

"I can't think when you're looking at me naked."

"You're not making sense."

"Where are you going?"

He did not need to go; there was plenty of work for him at home. He wanted to go. "For a month or two, baby. That's all it'll be. I have to do something big. I can't sit this one out. I can't. I'll come back any time, as soon as you want me to, I'll come back."

31

6

By the time those in power had no choice but to act on behalf of life, it was too late. It was no longer possible to secure a "liveable future for all."

It was during Cass's pregnancy that the government became truly a black box, retreating, to serve the interests of those within it, with blinds closed, and assets to preserve. The Black Box Government no longer proclaimed a plan, or what it stood for. It had no spokespeople. The silence spoke. Protests were illegal. People protested.

The police never came. Not for protests. Not for many things. They hadn't come when called for the small things for years. When they did come, for the big things, they were strange, deader, paid off, more frightening. They were no longer protecting the people from the rulers but the rulers from the people. You were grateful not to see them.

Cass thought that society was still kept slightly in check by the idea of a police force. It was only a memory but it influenced behavior. Soon, though, Cass suspected, enough people would realize they could put their hands straight through the protection—there was next to nothing there. There were already screams at night. Deaths were not reported. There were no numbers. Who could tell who was killed by a virus, and who by neglect? Who was left behind? Behind that door? Someone was always dying. The police gathered around the Black Box. The Black Box retreated behind the police and treated them like a small private guard service. The Black Box paid out the minimum to keep services barely going. It gave no directives. There were births and there were deaths and not much in the way of care in between. The schools and hospitals defaulted to an almost constant state of emergency—eking out the funds, closing bits down. Many people took to homeschooling. Cass heard that there was a correlation between days of high heat in The City and incidences of schizophrenia walking into the hospital waiting room.

The internet went off for the first time when Daisy was five months old. For a day, at first. "To protect the population from dangerous information." From stories of conspiracy, and poisoned food, at a guess. From incitement to riot. It came back on. There was a run on the banks. Then it was off again for a day. Jobs evaporated. Roles and money consolidated. Couriers took everything by hand. People took to the landlines. There were wars abroad, and wars within your neighbors' minds over how much of life they could claim back. The electricity was rationed. Decisions were made, somewhere, about which services to retain, and which roles of government to let go, and the criteria for making these decisions could only be understood as cruel. An Old Testament God in the air, coming down like the heat. He who was inscrutable and displeased.

Some said that the Black Box Government was in the process of relocating, or had already relocated, to the far north, with its families and advisors, its own teachers and doctors and police guards. But no one knew.

And there was some commotion, far away on a Southern Continent, over access to irrigated acres of salad crops. At the time, it was mostly hard to fathom. If you crossed out all the theories that you picked up on street corners and forum dives, it came down to this:

The Black Box Government to the Foreign Power on the distant Southern Continent: *We pay for these fields. What grows on them is ours. Stop your people stealing from them. Get off them.*

And the Foreign Power to the Black Box: *These fields are on our land and our people are starving, and also, what assholes you are and always have been.*

As far as could be told, the Black Box had sent troops to the Continent to secure the fields. These troops would have arrived armed, big-booted, with their energy drinks, and in various states of silence. Their mandate was expanded: they were to secure the fields (which had been rented by the ancestors of the Black Box, for a pittance, through antiquated agreement) and also the water systems that supplied the fields and crops. The troops claimed to be protecting these waterways from "national extremists" who would violate the pipes and attempt to siphon them off. The Black Box troops claimed to be doing the local people of the Southern Continent a service: protecting their infrastructure. Yet you did not have to dive deep into a forum to hear that the "extremists" were only trying to tap into the waterways out of basic need.

The boots were on the ground to ensure that the piped-in clean water went directly to wet the crops, which would be airshipped away. They were there to ensure that this water bypassed the local population. It was not that the Black Box troops lied directly. It was that they did not tell the truth. The nature of this dishonesty, displayed with such militaristic nobility, grabbed the people of the Southern Continent in the guts and made them wild.

At this juncture, those who lived around the acres of salad would rather break the pipes up in a way that led to the water being wasted, would rather let their annual fires grow out of control, let the land burn, than let these foreigners have it. The people of the local towns made a point of being straightforward about this. Their sword of truth was all aflame. It became a war of fire. And Nathaniel—an emergency medicine consultant—was a burns specialist.

7

At home, there were fires in The City now, in the museum, half a mile away, fires breaking out at random in the suburbs, fires in the surrounding lands, fires on the Continents. The earth cracked under the sun. Fires on purpose, fires by accident. Watchmen, atop City tower blocks, looking for fire. The hot days led into one another, with no fresh night-air break between, and the fires spread. Up sprang civilian firefighting squads. It was normal. Then the internet came on again. Nathaniel sent Cass articles. An article about a therapist who cured his patients through exorcism. An article about a talking cure that used words as hooks to lift out the offending notions. Nerves. New viruses. Possessions. The mind makes up incredibly complex rules. You must follow the rules if you wish to belong.

He video-called and said, "Look at your face." He said, "Did you read the piece I sent you?"

Cass had scrolled through it, reading one paragraph about how the line below which we swore we'd never go kept moving.

She'd clicked on the journalist's byline and studied her picture. Melanie Thomas was smiling.

"I read it."

"Interesting, right?"

"There was a massive fire at the museum."

"You told me."

"It's terrifying."

"You don't sound scared."

"Maybe I try not to be around the kids."

"I'll come home soon."

"Should we go to your mother's?"

35

"Absolutely no way." They both laughed at the sparkly burst of violence in Nathaniel's voice when he said this, and they each remembered to glance directly into the cameras. "I'll find a place for us, baby. I'm almost done here."

*

She admired his work.

She reached back in her thoughts to her own last season at work. It was the winter that never came. Warm storms took its place. Wet and warm. Mold in astounding patterns along the walls. How she cleared the house of all the cold-weather things. Fleeces, gloves, the parts of the broken heater. Everyone mourned the crispness. There would be no more December parties in the hold of cold nights that required glittering jewelry, and lipstick, and coats like their grandmothers wore. No more of this. Among other things. She left all the wintering stuff outside for the scavenging spirits. What remained there after two days she moved to the driveway of an abandoned place down the road. *Just try me*, she thought. *Just tell me I can't leave this here.* That night, the night before her last day at work, she scrubbed the floors and started to pull up the carpet on the stairs, heavily pregnant.

8

The office had been Cass's backdrop: when she was eager, youthfully illuminated from within; when everyone would leave work to drink together, all night, and back to work together the next day, to fix their hangovers as an ensemble; when she was depressed; when she was in love; and, finally, when she was pregnant and heaving herself out of the marital bed each morning. From when the world had been relatively akin to something she recognized, to when it had gone all strange.

Nathaniel had had a nanny back then for Vi and Maggs. This nanny would let herself in early each weekday morning, and would be cutting little nails and making little breakfasts when pregnant Cass padded down to brew tea before getting ready for work.

As her belly grew, Cass's nose became horribly sensitive, discerning, unable to bear certain foods, particular roads, and the aroma that this nanny brought into the house each morning. It was impossible. Cass would greet the nanny, put the kettle on, and go to vomit, like clockwork. Nathaniel enjoyed very much the conversation he witnessed one morning in which Cass discreetly tried to ascertain from the nanny what the source of the smell was: the name of her perfume, of the incense she used in her morning meditations, which clung to her clothes and hair intently, holding on until it could make its way into the children's hair and skin. And it wasn't the nanny's fault. The nanny was sweet. Not her fault that pregnancy rubbed Cass up the wrong way, and that Cass found the nanny's pointy nose and her terribly thin lips, her tiny, over-plucked eyebrows aggressive, her way of saying "Enough" unbearable—not the nanny's fault that all this made Cass irrational.

In the evenings, Nathaniel would look to Cass and say, "Shall we rub you back the right way?" He would massage her gladly, he would wash her hair. Any time he walked by a place that might sell a fancy shampoo, he'd get it for her. She loved climbing into the bed with him on those nights, when his hands cradled her bump, his nose in her hair. But in the morning the nanny would whine "Enough" from downstairs, in that voice again. And the children were scared of upsetting the nanny's feelings. And this made the nanny extremely powerful.

"The nanny is a Jungian, the nanny has a very long body, she irons Nathaniel's shirts and speaks randomly about community. The nanny is extremely particular about food. The way she puts salt on rice like she's . . . like she's . . ."

"The nanny has to go," said Cass's friend who worked the reception desk.

And while the nanny traced her finger over every single plate in the stack, rather than just touching the one she needed, and while Cass felt this trailing finger movement in her very nerves even from the distance of the upstairs bathroom, while this took place, Cass would assemble herself into some version of pregnancy that the office would find suitable. And then, dressed as primly as she could manage, she'd leave for work by kissing Vi and Maggs's heads and hoping they didn't smell of the other woman yet. The nanny stood at the kitchen sink and stared upon Cass with a look that Cass interpreted as one of pity and menace.

On a whim, one Saturday morning, while they watched Maggs and Vi in the playground, Cass asked Nathaniel if he'd let the nanny go, and to her astonishment he simply agreed. She almost wanted to argue him out of it immediately: the nanny and Nathaniel ran a tight ship, they kept it impossibly clean and tidy, Nathaniel hated mess, he couldn't even make a feasible mess.

But Nathaniel sliced things cleanly and Cass loved this about him. "We can manage without her, if you're sure you want to," he said.

Then, between them, with the nanny gone, Cass and Nathaniel made and remade the children's breakfast, hunted down items of clothing for them. Cass took Vi to school, Nathaniel took Maggs to nursery, and then they'd each go to work. Nathaniel became emotional; to do all of this alongside a partner once more was moving to him. He was grateful, and terrified that Cass would die. She promised him that she wouldn't, and she made the children smile. And when a call came to pick the children up early, because they were running a temperature, or had nits, or the nursery had shut due to lack of staff, Cass took the call, because she wanted to, and because, when Nathaniel went to work, he went to heal people, while all Cass did at work all day was read and write emails, or bullshit her way through meetings. She hated work; he didn't. She worked in exclusive client management, which was ego management. Her own, and others.

At work, clients got angry over nothing, daily. Usually they did this via email. They shouted, in caps, wordily. Everyone was losing, stressed. Cass knew that these angry emails had very little to do with her—personally—and that everyone in her office received them. But she also knew, when she received a client's anger, that within twenty-four hours, or less, the sender would apologize. And that apology would require her absolute forgiveness, which felt like work. She collapsed the two things and felt them simultaneously: the anger directed at her, and the work she'd be required to perform to make the shouter feel better about it when they apologized. She couldn't parse them out. She thought it made her soul weary.

She wished to reserve her soul, and all her care and forgiveness, to spend extravagantly on the actual children in her life. But she was ashamed of caring so little for work. And her shame was so visible, particularly once she was pregnant, her shame for being so helpless to the forces of sex, in an office space created by men who had not carefully cut twenty toenails before their day began, who could not be physically transfigured by the opposite sex. Men who were busy being masters and then begging forgiveness. One man gave her more responsibility, going over the head of another man, so the latter man took her out for coffee to tell her, with concern, "You are becoming ungovernable."

"Cool," she said.

"Well, no."

There was not a single value in her workplace that she felt comfortable about passing on to the children. There was only the humiliation that she had played into it all a hundred thousand times, for the money. She went into the office bathroom, which was an interesting little cave with a mirrored wall behind the row of sinks. It was where she came to understand that expression about not being able to look yourself in the eye. It was in a cubicle here that she suspected, then confirmed, that she was pregnant, and here that the child began to exist in her head, privately. So many children began their existence in that bathroom. So many children began their conversation with their mother in the office bathroom, before they existed anywhere else. Even if that child never made it, the connection began. And so many wished-for children did not materialize in that bathroom. It was here, hidden away, in the untended ladies' room, that real life happened, quickened—according to Cass, all else was only a vision.

She'd tell Nathaniel these things. He'd lie with her. Stare at the ceiling alongside her. Do nothing with her. Their relationship constantly demanded the consumption of something—food, energy, or gasoline, or gifts, or cards. She liked best those brief scenes when they really did nothing together.

That's what she liked best with the children too: doing nothing. Sitting in a room, in lapping silence, with three children. Even if it barely lasted, it was better than everything.

Maggs was the one to break the reverie; she was always the one to break it. She burst open with a new thought: "Who is your mommy?" she asked Cass.

"Not here."

"Where is she?"

"She died."

"You only have your daddy."

"No. He died too."

"Only we are your family?"

"Yes."

"Good." And Maggs went back to her coloring-in.

The office had closed now. The work they'd done there had been subsumed into a larger organization and then curtailed. The nursery had closed too. It had become impossible for the owners to cover the overheads and keep it affordable. The school was carrying on, noble but intermittent.

The children gave Cass constrictions and then little puffs of relief all day long. The children made her laugh. They did ridiculous things when left to their own devices. She'd find four crusts of toast in a tower on the toilet seat, and a pile of pennies under a pillow. They blamed everything on the baby.

40

And then the internet was on and he was there, on the screen again.

"Did you read the thing about theory I sent?" he asked her.

"Yes. Shall we leave without you?"

"Maybe soon."

Vi was eight. Maggs was four, and Daisy was ten months. They'd been nearly once around the sun together.

*

"There you are. Sorry about last time. I've still got something for you," said the other mom. Cass walked with her to her door and sat in the front garden, with the cactuses.

"Are you OK?" asked the mom, coming out with a book.

"I'm missing Nathaniel at the moment." She was embarrassed to start crying.

Before everything became awful, she would tell them one day. The children were golden, and how they hummed and the trees flowered, and everything was slowed sometimes to the breath and pace of an infant.

9

Vi was watching older boys play soccer in the parched park, on the asphalt pitch which was dusky red, tonally in keeping with the tea-brown grass around it.

Cass was with her friend Ally and the girls on one of the four benches that framed the pitch. When Nathaniel had left ("He's leaving." "He's leaving?" "He's going to that war."), Ally had altered her daily rhythm—purposefully but without declaration—so that her constitutional walk always coincided with Cass's four o'clock trip to the park. It was a pledge to their deepening friendship, without making a big deal out of things.

In the mornings, the soccer pitch would be occupied by little children who hurt themselves easily and did not see the point yet in sharing their balls. But by four o'clock, it was always the same group of teenagers, tapping lightly the nightmarish spin of the ball and controlling it, maintaining it. A heroic redirection of flow, sometimes. Chipping it so it skipped over the ground. Booting it into directed soars.

"I do have concerns," Ally said.

"Tell me."

"Does this game not give them the impression that they have agency?"

"When they don't?"

"They do not."

The boys in these afternoon matches were all familiar to Cass now, and even more so to Vi, who studied them with dignity. But there was one that day she did not recognize. Fourteenish, bold, both king and jester in his movements. He had plump lips. He was confident enough to have arrived alone, sure he'd play with whoever was there. The other boys were introducing themselves to him through their tackles.

Hardly any words had been exchanged. They came in particularly close to him when he had the ball. They were pelvis to pelvis, eyes down. Each time, he got it away.

The game paused to reset between goals and Cass heard one of the players, who had been jiving hip against hip and leg between legs with the newcomer, say, "Seen you before. You up the other field?" The curiosity and delicate pride in this was loud to Cass.

"Yeah. You seen me there."

"He's good," Ally said.

All eyes were on this new boy. It was almost unpleasant, really, the surprise when it came, when he turned his attention suddenly to Vi, on the sidelines. "You want to join in?" he asked. He was showing the other players how his skills extended to kindness, and reminding them of how it had felt when they had been included once by older boys, and what a mark it had made. He was shaming them, lightly.

Vi entered the game. Cass was immediately in pain from the tension in her body. Ally noticed Cass's tightness and laughed, "He's fine! He'll be fine."

"I don't want him to be humiliated."

"He has to experience these things."

After some minutes, Vi got the ball. Cass braced for what might happen next. But the other, older players changed; they slowed their pace around him; they did not crowd on Vi, they gave him time to make a good pass. There seemed to be rules at play here that were protecting him. Cass felt estranged by this protection that was not coming from her.

Vi's team scored a goal, aided by his assist. Ally cheered Vi's name. The new boy rested a hand on Vi's head, smiling as they strolled back to the center of the pitch, and Vi was smiling. Cass had her nose in Daisy's ear, and her happy sigh traveled all the way through the globe of Daisy's head.

Ally began talking about her wife's urinary infection but stopped to say, "Uh-oh. Here he comes."

Rising and striding from the opposite bench came a much-adored and locally famous father. There was something he did not like here. He was trying to help the boys improve on something.

Cass watched him carefully. She was finding his intrusion aggressive and believed he was received by the players with more patience than he deserved. She noticed a few of the boys spin on their toes to walk away from him, only to decide better of it. His words, which she couldn't fully hear, must have carried an authority that she didn't understand.

Ally grew quiet and focused. The father directed and pointed. Perhaps he was an actual coach—better a coach than simply impatient. It was becoming obvious, however, that his commands were particularly belittling of the boys who were Black, as if they were less able to understand him, more unpredictable.

"That man's confused by Vi," Ally said. "Not nearly black enough, not quite white enough."

"I've seen that father before," said Cass. "He's not too bright."

"That he isn't." Cass could see that Ally was looking around for a distraction. She alighted on: "Gosh . . . Your eyes are very bright today." It did not sound like a compliment; more like Cass's eyes had affronted her.

"Nathaniel says my eyes are scary."

"Does he, now?" Ally's friendship did not extend to Nathaniel. "Now, tell me, why do you wear all your necklaces back to front like that?"

"Otherwise they get too hot, and irritate my skin here." Cass landed a hand flat between her collarbones.

"Oh."

"Also, if they're round the back, stops the baby grabbing them."

"Why don't you take them off?"

"Don't want to." Cass said this with insolence, and Ally's eyes flashed with a succulent pleasure.

"Shall we pull your boy out of this?"

"Yep."

"Time for apple cake, I think."

"Apple cake!" delighted Maggs.

"Shhhh! Don't broadcast it. I'm only sharing it with you."

*

It was widely (among themselves) believed that Vi had learned to read early in order to impress Cass, when she was still new. First, he'd read the words out loud. Then he'd begun to mime them with his lips, making only wispy sounds. And then, one day, as he was mouthing the words, a puzzled expression crossed over his features. Cass stopped what she was doing and caught the very moment he decided to close his mouth. He read on, internally, poker-faced. And she lost him to himself a little bit. And that was a good thing. It had been her first lesson in letting them grow, and go. Vi taught her everything first.

Daisy looked like Cass and when Cass looked at Daisy she could only describe it—for want of all the better words—as a coming home. A feedback loop. The closest thing to having God inside the room that she had ever felt. Which was intensely narcissistic, she knew, and possibly also the very biological arrangement that had perpetuated her own existence. She didn't get the same feeling with the other two. And, as a result, she actually felt more inclined toward them. Felt that she had to give them more than she gave Daisy. Wanted to. It was all volition with them. With Daisy it was need.

Maggs talked about her "fizzity" feet; she had mousy hair; she gave herself vocal encouragement when she was painting; she kissed her own knees better. She called the car "the driver," her pants were "tunnels," the sky was "the zoo," every color was called blue, and all the meals of the day were breakfast.

*

When Nathaniel left, Ally had started inviting Cass and the children over for Sunday lunch. She lived nearby with her wife, Rose. Cass apparently reminded Rose of her younger self; Cass made Rose feel, in fact, like "a time-traveler." Rose burnt parts of the lunch on more than one occasion when Cass was in her kitchen. Vi loved going to Ally's, "because you're really laughy there, Mom," and also because it was so full of things that had stories attached to them which interested him. Ally noticed his small wonder and took him each time on a tour of the house and its resident storied artifacts very respectfully, speaking to him like an adult. Cass overheard Ally saying to Vi one day, "I am Black first, a lesbian second, a woman third, and a national fourth. Those are the priorities of my identity."

Ally liked to walk. She occasionally invited Cass to take a long walk with her, while Vi was at school. Ally pushed Maggs in the stroller, and Cass carried Daisy in the sling. Ally brought along hats with extravagant brims to protect them all from the rays, and they

45

walked slowly, rather proudly, as though they were walking through the streets of an entirely different era. Ally taught Cass to block things out. Piles of uncollected rot, lines outside every shop, broken windows in abandoned buildings, people selling their things spread out on the pavement, a hair extension stuck in the wheels of the stroller outside a salon—Ally seemed to transform it all in her mind into something lovelier, and she nodded upon it all like a lady regarding her estate. "What are we pretending not to know today, sweetheart?" was Ally's favorite line. She was a full thirty-seven years older than Cass. She had given up on a lot. "The -isms and -obias," she said, "are only problems of the *collective* when there is economic stability."

Ally treated Cass like she was regal, and Cass was flattered; she carefully repaid the compliment, but she also suspected this was all a very good trick. Ally was the cleverest mix of warmth and discernment that Cass had ever known.

"What's your secret?" she asked Ally as they promenaded.

"People do not want you to do what you are told. Men most of all. They are subliminally telling you what to do all of the time. And they also want you to ignore this completely. Put your blinkers on. Get back to your own business. Don't be what other people need you to be."

"OK."

*

Vi showed her a picture of a deep-sea mining machine on the screen. She loved the dance of his eyes illuminated.

10

"When's Daddy coming home?" Maggs wailed.

"I don't know."

"Oh. I really want Daddy."

"We'll try to call him tonight."

"Are we leaving soon?"

"Maybe."

"But Daddy won't be able to find us if we leave."

"Of course he will! Oh, baba! Don't cry. Or do. But don't cry all the way over there. Come here to me."

One night, drinking gin, Nathaniel had spoken about Vi's mother and Maggs's mother. Cass sat in front of him, inviting honesty, inviting truth, ready to mop it up. But the stories: "She had the purest heart I ever knew. The kindest person you could ever meet." And: "She was a visionary. Ahead of her time. The wildness of spirit. But an empath." The stories danced like little sprites through Cass's thoughts and the layers of her defenses. They took up residence with the gin in her center. Agitating her there. He saw. He grabbed her hand and pulled her to him on the sofa. She straddled him comfortably, and he plunged his hands into her curls. He said, "But you are my life, you're my wife, you're the shameless bedazzlement."

She just didn't know how to make him understand how much she loved him. She wanted to make herself insect-small and burrow directly into his chest and proclaim the love within the chambers of him. He looked at her often with an expression that was kind of at sea, helpless, kind of panicked, kind of awed. He bought her more shampoo, and antique gold chains, and gave them to her on Sundays. He kissed the arch of her foot while she laughed at him. When Daisy arrived, and would not sleep, he took the baby in his arms and said to Cass, "Go to bed. We'll come up soon." They were not up soon. He paced Daisy around all night, singing gently. He brought the baby to Cass to feed, and then took the baby away again, to walk. "It was a pleasure," he said the next morning.

When Daisy began to sleep in chunks of hours at night, Cass could tell that Nathaniel was at a loss. From bed, she heard him move from the kitchen to the garden and back again. He took a chair outside and, eventually, the gin; he sat for hours, talking to himself, cawing back at the crows in the morning. When the kids led her downstairs, he was making their breakfast, with eyes like a terrible crying clown. He put a movie on and slept between them all on the sofa, waking in the afternoon to kiss Cass's feet, go out for food and drink, play soccer with Vi, pull Cass in for sex while the baby slept and another movie played. Gold chains on a Sunday. She loved his smell. She loved how he made her feel glorious, even when her baby was small and she herself was oozing still. Whenever he walked in the front door, she was all relief.

It was only once she felt a disturbance. Maggs wrong-footed him one morning. Maggs told her daddy he was stinky. He took real offense. He came up close to Cass, who had Daisy in her arms. "Am I stinky, Daisy-doo?" he said. He opened his mouth and stuck out his tongue, crossed his eyes and went "Ahhhhhhh" at them both. The red-wine-tongue smell was foul. He was drunk, though. He wasn't often like that, Cass reasoned—everyone got fucked up sometimes. He slept it off and woke to fill once more all the lonely, empty rooms in her head with himself. She loved how together he was when he presented himself to the outside world. He was respectful and polite; old-school, charming. And then he came home, unbuttoned his shirt: fuck and you, you, you.

"Don't give it him," her friend had said.

It was tribal between them; like they'd done it all before together. It was all set out ahead of them, for them. It had been so easy: to take his thumb between her teeth, to take his proffered keys and use them to enter his front door. *Just come here, Cass, just step through, close it behind you, be my beloved.* Her father had died two months after her first date with Nathaniel; her sister had gone to the other side of the world a decade before, in anger; any remaining relatives had been so offended by Cass's parents, they did not know how to speak to her.

48

When the news came through about her father's death it was exactly the same as it had been with her mother's: Cass had felt at first very naughty, as if she had caused it. She hadn't. But her parents' passing was a relief to her. And maybe they had known that it would be. She took the keys to Nathaniel's and closed the door on the lot of them.

And there could be more family. Cass told herself this. They didn't have to be alone—a five. She longed to be part of a much bigger web, didn't know how just then, but found that she had not written off the hope. Ally and Rose gave her hope. There was also Eden. Eden who had welcomed Cass with open arms, draping sleeves and an opinion on everything. But Nathaniel kept them—his wife and his mother—apart. Very distinct. He was watchful when they interacted. Sometimes his focus sent not-unpleasant shivers along Cass's nerves.

It was clear that Eden had done something strange to her sons. Or she'd allowed something inverted to bloom between them. Arthur was six years younger than Nathaniel and yet Arthur ruled. Arthur had no respect for Nathaniel's decency. In fact, he found it highly amusing, like it was a pose.

When the brothers were forced to cross paths, Nathaniel's posture grew taller, he filled out, and every inch of him, Cass could see, was ready, live on a trigger as fine as a hair, a whisper away from violence. Cass was surprised to learn the two had never come to blows. The way Nathaniel told it was like this: from a precociously young age, Arthur had undermined Nathaniel's sweetness and embarrassed him for it. When Nathaniel had behaved well—to win the toy, the affection, or the parental good mood—Arthur had waited until Nathaniel had earned the prize, and then seized it for himself. Arthur pretended that Nathaniel didn't exist for weeks on end. Arthur invited Nathaniel to parties that were imaginary. At sixteen, Arthur "stole" Nathaniel's girlfriend. Arthur took the money Nathaniel earned, and blamed the theft on someone else. Arthur could not take Nathaniel seriously. It had all caused Nathaniel a great deal of pain. Each time Nathaniel had shown excitement as a young man, Arthur had deflated it, and Nathaniel had learned to blink away the injury. He had become fascinated by self-control. He was deeply unempathetic when Eden called to report on Arthur's latest drug adventures. He sensed that she exaggerated. He also sensed a detestable hint of pride in her voice when she recounted stories of her younger son's dramatic acts.

"Some people," Nathaniel said as he lay with his wife, "are born wrong." It had nothing to do with your childhood, he said. It was all in your cells. Cass found this idea chaotic, knew it was incorrect, and yet felt the subject to be somehow unbroachable with him.

The few occasions she'd met Arthur, he'd actually been very nice to her, as if she were meeting him in his dressing room, offstage. He'd had that alarming scent coming off the nest of him. He was beautiful, in the same way that Nathaniel was, like Vi. She'd never witnessed anything like the much-retold scenes of his dereliction.

"Are you there? Hello?" said Ally.

"Oh, sorry. I didn't see you there." They were by the pitch again.

"You were really gone. Where did you go?"

"I was thinking about my mother-in-law."

"The batty lady."

"She's not that batty. She's OK."

"She pretty batty."

"I dream a lot that she's going to take them away from me."

"That's nice and weird," said Ally, who looked upon people she didn't know with severity. Ally with her occasional cigarette, and her seventy-four years, and her wife like a blue-eyed rose.

Cass went on to say that she was always surprised by how quick strangers were to criticize her parenting. Ally sat beside her on the bench in the sun and said, "It's because of how you dress. You dress like an adolescent." And then she stretched her legs out in front of her and said, "It's time to go. My body can't take this place anymore. Neither can yours, though."

In the north, which was higher and cooler, fresher and emptier, there was momentum to secede. The north was slowly putting up a wall, a border to keep the climate migrants from the south out. Nathaniel had spent every summer up there as a child in the same pretty valley. He said for all that to break away, to become off-limits to him—it would be impossible. Beyond belief.

What to believe? Cass's hatred for the outside world was growing as the skin on the planes of her shoulders prickled and blistered in the sun. She knew that it was fear, really, this anger. She found a sapphire ring on the pavement and kept it.

It had become commonly accepted that the parents, particularly "the mothers," were at the forefront, and would lead the new generation into a cleaner life. And then everyone had sat back and waited and watched the mothers do apparently nothing to save the world. Many had turned their scorn on them.

Another Exceptional Danger Day. Wildfire smoke, from The Midlands Fire, came in and did not clear. There were the newly named Moorland and Heathland Fires. Cass's head ached. The children were grouchy. She proposed that the air was affecting their brain chemistry, and there was no evidence to the contrary.

11

They did have to go out for food, though.

The selection at the shop was particularly poor that day. The place smelled sulfuric. *I'll take that, wrapped in plastic*, Cass said to herself, tasting bitter. *And I'll take that which sucked water from the ground beneath starving children, and I'll have two of these that required the deforestation of a magical place, the likes of which will never be truly known again. And all I know is this dirty shop, under this flickering light, where every single other asshole is buying all this shit. And I am too tired to do better. I am alone, with three children, and all I have to comfort me is convenience. Worse, all I have to comfort me is a convenience that means death.*

She let the children choose sweets and she paid. On the thin pavement outside the shop she smiled, automatically, as she let another mother who also had a stroller and shopping bags, and children, like Cass, pass by. Maggs was trying to give Cass the bag of sweets, saying, "Will you open this? Will you open it!"

"Soon," Cass said, aiming for the wider pavement around the corner, where they could stand aside, out of other people's way, and open the sweets, and she could check that the children knew she wasn't angry at them.

But there was a commotion at her side. The stroller wheel had jammed.

"It's my shoe!" Vi said.

Cass bent to release Vi's shoelace from the wheel. As she did so, two great big hands came down roughly onto Maggs's shoulders and pushed her forward, so she stumbled and landed on her hands and knees. It took Cass a second to compute that a man was physically clearing her child from his path. He was followed by a much older woman. "Do try to think of the elderly," he barked grandly as he helped the old lady with him to navigate around Maggs. "I did not mean to push her to the ground," he said. "But you must try to think of others."

Cass told herself, out loud, to calm down.

The man assumed she was telling him to calm down. He looked horrified by her lack of repentance. His parting shot before he turned away was an expression of disgust.

Cass felt that if she allowed her throat to open again she would unleash such a fury that her body would follow her words and she'd bring this man's head crashing to the pavement. Perhaps he had no idea how strong she was, or how intuitively she could project the course of her attack. He was not strong. She could tell from his posture that he had no core strength, and his ankles were weak. Whereas Cass was baby-strong from all the begetting and the mental, physical, emotional carrying of children. She could lift her children high off the ground, and run, and hold tantrums still.

Maggs was stunned, quiet, and watching Cass for a reaction.

Cass knelt on a level with Maggs. "I'm really sorry, darling." She spoke very loudly. "That man is pathetic." She hoped he could hear her. "He only had to wait a moment. We wait for people all the time. But he is not as considerate as us. He is not as good as us."

This had been the most surprising thing to Cass about her thrust-upon motherhood. It beggared her belief how difficult passers-by found children.

She didn't know what it was that she was making the children feel.

She was still crouching on the pavement in front of Maggs when Vi said, "Your phone's ringing, Mom." This irritated her. She rooted for it in the bag. It was Nathaniel calling. She thought he must have sensed the terrible day they were having, and was calling right on time to prevent her from attacking a weak-ankled man. But instead he said: "Where are you?"

"Outside the shop?"

"Get home. Run home now. Run."

It took an hour or two for the news to trickle in, before they fully understood what had happened. Then the internet went out.

12

No one was completely surprised by the first Gaia attacks. Something had been building. Like fight night in the suburbs on a Sunday. What was surprising, though, on that first day, was quite how indiscriminately the killings took place. Numbers were clearly all that mattered to Gaia. And their efforts were redoubled by the fact that the Gaia soldiers were happy to die in an orgy of limbs, along with their victims, to rid Mother of themselves and return to her. Which meant that they took their homemade explosive devices and their few guns and their knives like swords right into the center of things.

That afternoon, when Nathaniel called Cass outside the shop, Gaia had taken out a playground three miles from where Cass and the children stood, as well as eleven crowded buses, and they had made a deep welt into a market on the other side of the river. These attacks had been coordinated, simultaneous. Someone had let the soldiers of Gaia slip through and organize undetected. No one was protecting the people anymore.

Cass put the kids to bed and waited until she could tell, from their breathing, that they were deeply asleep. She tried the phone again, but everything had gone down soon after the news of Gaia broke. She slipped on her clogs and went outside.

She knocked at the doors of neighbors, to see if someone would sit with the children, but no one came out. "I'll be twenty minutes," Cass said to herself. And she took off. It felt newly safer to leave the children locked in the house alone than to ever have them out in The City again. The longed-for rain, light and eveningish, was coming in. She imagined that the remaining Gaias would feel it on their upturned faces like a benediction.

Cass kept her face down. She had never left the children like this before. She never walked at speed anymore. She had no memory of the last time she'd walked quickly, alone, at night. Her whole self was urging her to go back to the children immediately. But she overrode herself and strode out. This was her town, where she had grown up, and she recalled a way of moving through it that felt borderline invincible. Late at night, hood up against the rain, quick, but not scared. *I am not delicate*—and her body reached forward. *I am not to be drawn into conversation, or looked at. I have no problem with you, passer-by, so you have no problem with me.* She remembered how, when she had been at school, the special girls, the ones who were well looked after, had signaled their vulnerability. At the time, their fragility, that sense of preciousness, had felt like a touted luxury, the preserve of the loved girls, the lucky ones, the cared-for; it had been attractive. Cass had envied it, but now she wasn't so sure.

There was no answer at Ally and Rose's front door. She went around to the alleyway that ran along the back, where there were tall wooden doors in the wall. Cass went to the right door, and she yelled out their names, to no avail.

She jumped once, to gauge her reach. Landed. Her hood fell back. She jumped again, with a bit more force. This time she touched the blue-glazed pot on top of the garden wall.

A train was coming through, along the tracks, behind her. She waited for the noise to clear away.

One more time, leaping off the earth. With a full palm she got the pot, which was terra-cotta and contained a large aloe plant, as big as a toddler. She pushed it and it fell onto the paving behind the wall, where it smashed beautifully. It smashed with a largesse that made Cass pout in admiration.

The sound had the desired effect. At the other end of the garden, a door swung open on its wheeze-hinge, and a voice shouted, bravely, "Hello?"

"Rose. It's me."

"HelloCassieDarling," one word, one exhalation. "Wait. Wait. I am finding my keys."

Cass turned and leaned against the wall to wait. She was different without children. She tried to blow air out of her mouth and up into her nostrils. *As quiet as cats*, she thought. *As blue as a sealed-up, velvet* . . . Someone was shouting. The sky was inky smoke now, a distant wildfire blowing in. Someone, a man, was declaiming. It was coming from the cemetery, on the other side of the train track. Indisputably, "I hate you!" A man was standing in the graveyard, on that quiet misty blue night, screaming "I hate you," extending the vowels, giving it all he'd got.

"Crikey, baby," Rose said, appearing. "He doesn't sound very happy. Do you think he's having a little word with God?"

"No, I don't." Cass kissed Rose on her cold, soft face and smiled because Rose had clearly moments ago applied the frosted-pink lipstick that was kept in a bread basket by the back door, for greetings. Cass knew all about this, and all about this place, and she was taking her leave.

"You look pretty," Cass said.

"Thank you, baby. Just a bit of lippy. Coming in?"

"I left the kids—can't stay long."

"Awful things today. I was just going to have a smoke, darling. Want a cigarette?"—said like something that never usually occurred to her.

What the hell. "OK."

"Tea?"

"No time, really."

"Alright, baby."

They'd reached the metal chairs and table, which sat in a shape of candlelight coming from the kitchen.

Cass leaned forward for Rose to light her cigarette. She widened her eyes as she did so to soak in every particle of what was before her: her whole view was taken up by Rose's pink-varnished fingernails, Rose's huge arthritic knuckles, all of Rose's chunky silver rings, worn on each finger apart from the pinkie, which had once broken and then healed crooked. The flame from the lighter was switched up too high. Then there were the blue veins on Rose's inner wrist, which matched the blue of her eyes. And the skin under her unsleeved arms.

"You alright, darling?" Rose said, as she always said, repeatedly.

Cass inhaled from the cigarette, and got it out quickly, as a question: "I think it's time to go?"

Rose nodded. She silently nodded again. She waited until any emotion had tempered down before whispering, "I think you're right, baby." Winking, smiling, touching Cass's knee. "I think you're right."

Before everything became impossible, it was briefly, unspeakably beautiful.

Ally's voice came from the kitchen: "Who's with the kids?"

"I left them."

"Why?" She came out in a long robe.

"I wanted to check you were OK. And I need some fuel, if you've still got it. I don't want to queue for it with kids in the car. I want to get them out of here as quick as possible tomorrow."

"You off, then?"

"Yeah. I've got to get them out of here."

Ally smoothly crossed the garden and went to the shed, moved some things around in there while saying, "A half-tank is an empty tank," and came out with the first of two pristine khaki jerrycans. Cass left her cigarette in the ashtray and moved to help Ally shift them.

"You should have brought the stroller to wheel these back."

"I should have."

"There you go . . . I always did hate that plant, you know."

"I did know that, yeah."

"It looked like a young alien popping its head over the wall. Frightening, actually."

"It did."

"Well, there's no point in being scared of aliens now."

"Not anymore. There are too many real things to be scared of."

"That is exactly what I said."

"It is."

"Why you coming round here only to repeat what I say?"

They smiled at each other in that succulent way.

And Rose said, "Where are you going, Cassie-Baby?"

*

The next day, Cass hovered over her phone, agitated, until she caught some bars and called her mother-in-law, who said: "I've been waiting for this call. Darling, I am so happy. Come. Yes. Come. You must come right away. I'm dropping everything. Drop everything, right now, and come. Is there someone who can help you with the packing? Arthur's just this minute left, you know. Your timing couldn't be more perfect for me. You cannot stay in that place. In fact, you mustn't. God knows what's in that air. And that's if you're not stabbed in a playground. It's very bad there now. Think of that! Just come."

Cass hadn't tried to call Nathaniel to square it with him first. She was reaching around him. The pressure had built too much.

Once upon a time, at a party, in an apartment, with a concierge, and an elevator, where the host was projecting silent porn onto two massive white walls, Nathaniel had undone his tie and gone to get them drinks. He'd come back with two brightly colored and humorously decorated cocktails, and he'd commented, sadly, that a group of people in the kitchen were using competitive cocktail-making as a stand-in for personality.

"Lucky for us," Cass said, sipping the drink. And he kissed her on her sugary mouth. She dug her tongue into the kiss, and ran the tip of it where his teeth met his gums, which was a thing he liked.

She didn't see Arthur arriving. All of a sudden there was this man, with one arm around Nathaniel's shoulders and the other hand on Nathaniel's chest, and they wheeled around like that, like an apologetic two-headed beast, to face her.

Nathaniel, tight, grimacing, said, "Cass, let me introduce my brother."

Arthur looked at her from under his brow, like *Oh, there you are.* She took him in, and thought, *Don't look at me like that.* He allowed his features to settle into a puzzled expression, as if to say *Like what?*

Hungry and mean. Displaying his appetite, and her rightness for it. Like he would.

Arthur released Nathaniel—who immediately stepped to make his body a shield between Cass and his brother—and pulled a pretty girl with long hair into his side instead. He began again. He was quite genial and funny with the girl, whom he introduced as Jem, and he listened attentively as she began to speak.

"Well, she was insufferable," said Nathaniel, later, in the elevator down. Then he said, "My brother's a cunt." Then he said, "This is a sexy elevator." Cass yawned and felt glad because they had a parlance: elevators were sexy or unsexy; when one of them was drunk, the other wasn't; rice was "extraneous" or "substantive"; they checked one another's teeth with their tongues; they cared about the same things. They were a fit: in balance, and love, and just enough lies.

58

13

INTERLUDE—NATHANIEL

His life is lonely. He takes the back stairs of the Hotel Gloria, which were once reserved for staff, where his trainers slip on the very worn carpet. There are brown stains on the ceiling. A pile of sweaty Bibles on the hot window ledge, and a cat coming up toward him. Where has he heard that phrase before—"sweaty Bibles"? His brain can't reach back through the etymology of his thoughts like it used to.

It's not his phrase. He must have heard it somewhere and taken it. His cognitive tendency is to steal; he knows this about himself. Cass's father told him at their one meeting: "Artists borrow ideas, but geniuses steal them." Admittedly this was said in relation to Shakespeare.

Nathaniel skips the last step. It is entirely possible that he came up with the phrase "sweaty Bibles" himself, and then considered it too good to take credit for. Too good to have come from his own badly catalogued mind. He diagnoses himself: a man given to bouts of inspiration, followed by a self-deprecating cover-up, he sidesteps the glory, gives it to someone else.

He steps to the side to let a smirking young officer pass. He interprets the smirk as youthful superiority.

It is deserted downstairs. There are chocolate biscuits on a tray on the bar, in packs of three, a bit like the ones they'd had at school.

"Eat those." There's the woman who works in the kitchen, Marie, whom he's befriended. Older women always love him. They spot him and take care of him. This one, appearing, has eyebrows that are permanently high, and she is carrying a plastic basket of tea towels, nodding at the packs of biscuits. "The fridges are off, they'll all melt."

Above the bar, the Christmas decorations are still hanging from the ceiling. It is almost July. The glasses remain gathered and unwashed from the night before.

The power is off in the kitchen, in the bar, and now he understands as he steps, wincing under the sun, onto the terrace, the power is off across the entire town before him. No hum. The sun is putting down more complex layers over them all, and will continue to do so. Washing on a line is strung between buildings. The sun is crisping up the cells on the back of his neck and he moves his head to feel it reach different parts. He imagines that his head is leonine and his neck serpentine, but he knows this is not accurate. "What's your problem, anyway?" he hears, or asks. He looks up and sees a midday eagle, wishes for a meaning.

He sucks the chocolate off his finger and goes inside, toward Marie.

"Don't suppose there's anything else melting back there?" he says.

She stops what she is doing to work out what he means. Confirms it to herself. "No," she says. "Nathaniel, I mean it: no. I have to account for it."

He is returning to the staircase with Marie's plastic basket of tea towels under his arm when he re-meets the smirking young officer, who is on his way back down. This time the smirker has decided to be someone else entirely: he is bashful. Red-cheeked.

Nathaniel admires this young man's willingness to flit so quickly from role to role. Usually the fiction of one continuous self is compulsory. Nathaniel knows that he himself moves between different selves, but not in such an open or speedy way. The smirker seems to want something from Nathaniel.

And then Nathaniel remembers who the smirker is. They met yesterday, at the workshop. The smirker is called . . . "Tom, isn't it?" Nathaniel recalls the taste of yesterday's tea with the unusual addition of long-life milk, mixed with the cigarettes, and the ballroom with the green material. He recalls how Tom gave off the whiff of decency, seemed to be seeking decency in others, and how all the gathered men wanted to pass young Tom's decency test.

He greets Tom warmly, shifts the basket to his other side, and leans against the banister. He tells Tom encouraging things, while discovering that he is bathing in the light coming down the stair shaft, coming

60

adoringly off this young man, from off the playing field behind his old school, a place that Nathaniel can picture easily; they are all of a type.

But then Tom asks, "What did you get up to last night?"

And Nathaniel senses that he cannot trust this young man. Nathaniel grows taller.

On the way back up the stairs, the pores of the sweaty Bibles are more open.

Nathaniel reaches his floor. It is ten past noon, too hot for exertion. His T-shirt is soaked. His vision is going black around the edges. He finds he must lower himself to the floor. As he does this he keens with the swirl of the staircase below him, making awful noises, and thinks he will have to throw up into the plastic basket of tea towels. Then he does. He retches and gut-spills. He wishes to not be seen like this. Primal need to not be seen like this.

The door to his room swings open and there is a woman. He knows her, and he is grateful. She brings him inside his room and guides him to sit under a cold shower, where he vomits some more in a helpless way, so it sort of rolls out of his mouth and down his chin and forms a bib covering him. She is speaking urgently in the background.

He has his eyes shut. Inside, he is stuck in a triangle between the long-life milk and the cigarettes and the green curtains and will wait this bit out and then he'll be fine. And then he can do his thing and everyone will recognize him.

The subject of yesterday's workshop in the ballroom was "Well-Being and Well-Doing." It did not sit well with him. They were all taken through the principles of meditation by a dude too humbled. They were asked to close their eyes and tune in to the energy of their hands. Nathaniel felt the bar of his chair cutting into his back, and his back felt ruined anyway, from what was either a repetitive strain injury from the gym or a deeper pain consistent enough to be an alarming lung complaint, and his bowels felt full, and the sweat from his palms and underarms made the fabric they kissed feel rough and full of hooks. His insect bites roared. His heart palpably hurt—indigestion or actual heartache, he wondered. He knew. He knew enough to know he should not inquire any further. He stood up slowly and left quietly, smiling in a *What can you do?* way at the senior physician, who opened half an eyelid to see him go and then used it to wink him off approvingly.

The Hotel Gloria, sequestered, is unkept: if you run a finger along anything it gives up hairs and a gray powder. The air vents and air cons are visibly clogged with ghostly floating cloaks. Kit has been abandoned in the corner of the second-floor corridor and will be missed soon.

He has moved himself from the shower, has removed his clothes, and is sitting, in his shorts, on the edge of the bed. All is uncertain. The world shifts and freestyles. He leans delicately toward the tea towels in the basket and flips them to the side in a way that will not disturb the vomit too much. Beneath them are two warm bottles of gin. He rinses out a small tooth mug and fills it with gin. He sits by the door to the balcony and will wait now, between sips. Rubs his face, checks his hands, sips again. He notices smoke pouring upward outside the compound. He is sick again, this time into the metal trash can. He brushes his teeth. Begins again, small sips.

Petal, her legs folded beneath her on the bed, says, "You should see a . . . I don't know how to say."

"A doctor?"

"Yes. Docto."

"Doctor."

"Yes. Please."

"I am a doctor." He smiles girlishly. "You should get off. I'll be OK."

"Get off?" Her grasp of his language is not as strong as he likes to believe.

"Time to go."

She pouts and gets her things.

He sleeps. He gets up. He locates his jacket, empties the pockets. He observes himself as he places his key card on the glass-topped table and aligns it with the handle of the gun. The first bottle of gin is unlocatable. Perhaps Petal took it with her. He knows she put the second bottle in the mini-fridge, which is only marginally cooler than the room. He wishes to brush his teeth again. He opens the bathroom door and reaches for a can of DEET, which he sprays into the airless space. The tube of toothpaste is nearly empty, limp and curled in on itself like a natural thing. The mirror, he notices, is spattered with dried spittle. As he brushes his teeth he tries to rub the mirror clean with a piece of toilet paper.

From the bathroom mirror he can see back into his room and it's the gun he notices, mostly. It has a strong personality. Its presence sometimes prevents him from feeling lonely (did he steal that idea too?).

His life is lonely, but there are things he can do about this. He can call his children. He can call his wife. (He misses their warm heads resting on him. He would like to curl up with them.) He can sit in the hotel bar and if that becomes too depressing there is always the jeep to take him back to the camp, and the rinky-dink hive where the journalists drink. But, he muses, those journos are all so wrapped up in their own drama: trying not to fuck each other as if the world depended on it. He thinks of them laying all their lust on a stone drinks table every night, covering it in vodka and setting fire to it, calling it a sacrifice to a god called Professionalism. And then they act in mock-horror every morning when they wake to find that their lust has only bloomed and bloomed in their sleep. It's a charade, boring to watch and impossible to get in on. Which is why there is also the girl named after some flower (he muddled up which flower from the outset, and has resorted to calling her Petal), who acts like she doesn't know that what she is doing is prostitution.

He doesn't mean that. They haven't had sex. He wouldn't do that.

He's bought her dinner, drinks, shoes, medicine for her grandmother.

He brushes his teeth until his gums bleed. He spits out the bloody toothpaste and swears simultaneously. He leaves his toothbrush on the side and sits on the bed and hears the snap of the perforations breaking as someone opens the second bottle. Someone? Who? Oh. Him.

The gun on the side shares quite a lot of its personality with the man who taught Nathaniel how to shoot. Nathaniel observes that yesterday's meditation workshop would have been better coming from Nigel, the gun guide. Both activities seem to require a similar set of skills: deep breaths, pure focus. Nigel is the more . . . Wait, this isn't an original thought either, is it? Someone has said before that meditation and guns require the same skill set.

What time is it at home? They'll be out by now, taking Vi to school. He doesn't like to call when Vi is at school; he doesn't think it's fair. He doesn't like to call in the evenings either, when he's in work mode or drunk mode. He is very proud of his children. Exceptionally so. He cares about them deeply. He talks about them, frequently, any day, to whoever will listen. The special album on his phone containing the best photos of them would be visibly well-thumbed if phones recorded actual physical affection. When he speaks about the children, he falls into justifying why he is not with them. Such deliberate justifications. He is at pains to emphasize that he is not some useless, detached father. He is away from them, doing the only thing he can think of to do at this time, which is to be where he's of most use. He wants them to be proud of him. Cass is wonderfully capable without him.

He misses her like he misses the seasons. He often thinks he glimpses her out a window, and then he is overcome by an urge to run to her, and marry her again, and impregnate her again, with no cool. It is imperative to him, this drive to keep her.

He refills the mug. He is talking to himself. He is explaining himself to the gin.

He is scared of certain things he believes about himself. These beliefs are like a hidden, bleeding internal organ that he carries around; one that would kill him like he was just anybody.

Sometimes he thinks he loves Cass enough to remove himself.

Often his phone is in his hand, and he is trying to call her, but each attempted call drops and then he shouts something like "Stupid piece-of-shit phone," which once, on a hangover, transformed into him screaming "Stupid piece-of-shit me." He never meant anything so sincerely in his life.

Whenever he does get Cass on the phone, she is keen to run through all the things that are wonderful about the children's days, spent without him. When he hears that the children are so happy, he tips into self-pity, and he knows they are happy because he is not there. Ergo: he should not be there with them. He takes a drink. This cycle of thought and action is unrelenting.

To love, he thinks, you have to be relentless. To love them, he has to be relentlessly honest with himself about what he is like, and remove himself from them.

He got so close to Cass, he thought she would see him for what he really was, and help him to untangle it. He lost some respect for her when he realized that she didn't see him truly. She only has eyes for a fantasy version of him. She only has eyes for the children. The first night he met her, she was with a bloke who was throwing up, who said, "Don't look at him." Nathaniel went over this story with her, and found that she remembered it wrong: she remembered the friend saying, "Don't give it him." Either way, the male friend was possibly correct. But this male friend also happened to be too obviously in love with Cass for her to trust his opinion, which helped Nathaniel out in the end. The guy did him a solid.

He lies back on the bed. Nigel, who taught Nathaniel to shoot in basic training, got very close, physically, during the sessions. If he had to call it, Nathaniel would say that it was too close, but there's no reason or opportunity to call it—it's not like anyone ever takes you aside and asks you to call it. He hasn't articulated this closeness, not even to himself, only his body felt it, and then re-felt it. Surely the whole point of being the sort of man who teaches other men how to shoot is that no one will ever accuse you of getting too close to other men unnecessarily. No one will ever accuse you of anything other than being too unyielding.

It has somehow already reached that point in the evening when a decision has to be made about which way is up. What to do? He could seek out Petal again, always hiding in plain sight—is it this bar or that bar? He picks up his phone from the glass table to call Cass, but it rings in his hand. And from this point on, and for several weeks, time speeds up.

It's the night coordinator. She says, "Dr. Maguren? Sir. It's a code green."

"I'm not on," he informs her. *Check the fucking piece of paper in front of you, why don't you*, he tells her, silently.

"I'm to call in all operational medics, sir. It's code green."

"It was a shitshow." He is talking to Melanie, in the journalists' hut, seven hours later. "It was a . . . Jesus Christ . . . a massacre. So much blood. We were slipping around in it, in the blood, on the floor. They were planning it for—Definitely back in . . . back in . . . back in . . . in the talks, they were already planning it."

"Do they know any numbers?"

"I don't know. I don't know. I don't." He pours the dregs of his drink into his mouth and sloshes it around, remembering the sick from earlier in the day and using the alcohol to make sure he's got it all out from between his teeth. "I saw at least a dozen DOA, but I was in one resus room. I mean, I don't know. I don't know how many they even bothered bringing in."

Melanie stands but keeps hold of his arm to indicate she isn't going far, only reaching for the bottle from the bar to top him up. He notices her woven bracelets where her sleeve rises. And then, in a surprise even to him, as she sits back down, he puts his fingers on her wrist in exactly the place you seek a pulse. Tonight he tied tourniquets, assisted amputations. Two bled out on the table. One of them, a lad called George, he knew quite well. He signed him off as "OK to work" after a light shrapnel wound last week. There is an insistence among the men that you do this—none of them want to be taken out or sent home. But there was a barrier between Nathaniel and his personal memory of George as he worked to start the heart.

It's physical work, heart-starting, like digging the earth as fast as you can to find water before it trickles away. Sometimes you hit true, and life comes gushing back; sometimes, at the end of it, you find you've dug a grave.

Toward the end, he held the hand of another boy he recognized in the bay, probably too deep into morphine to know that he was dying, but you never know. You never know. Nathaniel cried.

From the small kitchenette in the medical center he could hear the friends of the dead baying desperately to get back out there, unto the breach. Jaws set, no sleep until tomorrow. And then Nathaniel passed through them, to get some air. They slapped his back and sides tenderly as he went.

The pulse in Melanie's wrist comes through his fingertips, fills his ears, his head, and all the blood rushes to his dick. It isn't an easy decision, because it isn't a decision. He is absent. Grief and booze. They both leave their guns on the glass table in his room while they "shag," as Melanie calls it, taking all their clothes off almost immediately, like it's procedural. The next day they do it twice more having reasoned that, as they skipped the condom, and she was going to take the morning-after pill anyway, they might as well make it worth her while. He isn't going to cheat again after this—might as well make it worth his while too. There is a supply of levonorgestrel in the medical compound and Nathaniel signs out three.

One week later, Melanie is naked, smoking a cigarette in the armchair in his room, and he realizes that she is aping confidence. She has consciously decided to be the sort of woman who sits naked in an armchair, because other women do that and why shouldn't she? But it doesn't work on her. She is fighting against her personality too hard. It makes him see her face differently, like that of an enormous ugly child. The day after that, he can't remember her leaving, and has to step off the running machine in the gym when his heart starts beating out of time, worrying that he asked her to leave. He realizes that he has arranged the drinking into everything so that he has no time, no opportunity at all, to consider.

When he does consider it all, he is taking the back stairs, once (as he always recalls) the preserve of staff. Everything he does at the Hotel Gloria is on a timer. He is setting timers constantly: it is X number of hours before he must stop drinking in order to be OK to work in Y number of hours. He can go home when he likes; he'll only stay for a few more weeks—say, six. Then he can start again.

He walks through the hotel from the back and comes out into the reception area. Petal is there, looking disappointed. She asks why she hasn't seen him. "Where you go?" She seems actually hurt, and not likely to be playing him for money. He thinks about telling her, "Look, I have a wife and I have children. You can't be a child about this." But the forcefulness of his tone might make her cry. And who's to say she isn't totally aware of the seriousness of his marriage and children? Perhaps she is being the adult here, and letting her feelings toward him flow while knowing that their connection can only grow so big and beautiful before falling from the stem. He thinks about telling her the truth, saying to her, "Sorry I didn't look for you, I was shagging a war correspondent." But then Petal might jump to conclusions that the war correspondent is cleverer than her, and therefore more interesting. And then Petal would cry.

Melanie *is* cleverer than Petal, but not more interesting. The way Melanie uses all the stuff she's learned is like the good icing on a really basic cake. Petal has no icing. Petal's mom clearly baked her in love. So he walks with Petal through the market zone, and via the burnt-out factory, to the beach, where they hold hands and sit in a secret spot and he lays his gun and phone and keys to the side and takes her head in his lap, he combs her hair out with his fingers, and tells her stories about his life. He takes sand in his hand and lets it fall out. And she has her period and removes her pants and sits with her legs apart, to let it bleed out into the sand. She says that all the girls do this when they come to the beach together, but never with men, but he is different. He is a doctor, after all. The stray dogs circle them, perhaps, he thinks, drawn to her blood. The sea breathes; she faces her open sex to it. He doesn't know if he dislikes this or not. Even though he is the doctor, she seems to be the one who is more steeped in life and death, truly. He thinks that she is talking to the sea. He hasn't slept. He knows that it is the mythologizing of women that leads to them becoming terrifying and then disrespected. He makes her normal in his mind and places a hand on her belly. An Apache goes overhead containing his colleagues, probably on their way to pick up more dead. From the mountain at night you can watch the fires. Maybe they'll go up there. And this, like everything, is only for a time. These fanning palms, this falling sand. When he is done here, he can go back home, and be the better version of himself. He hopes he can be a benevolent force again, once everything has bled through.

PART TWO

EDEN

14

When it is time to leave, will you?

Cass started to pull the things they might need out of cupboards and drawers and into piles on the floor. She picked her way across the rooms, collecting armfuls, folding clothes, throwing crap away, and then packing the trunk of the car. It took a few days in the end. She wasn't pumping with flight, nor fight. She was humming, in grace, with her message for the children undulating to the confines of their existence: *I know the way, and I will keep you safe.* She knew their favorite toys by heart; she threw away a stack of yogurt pots containing soil and dead sunflower seedlings.

She was constant motion—pulling a grape off its stalk with her teeth, jiggling the baby on her hip, and continuing to clean out the food cupboard. She went about the house adding to her mental list of things she did not care about and could therefore easily leave behind, reaching to change the song, scooping another thing off the floor. Vi asked her how long they'd be away for, and she said, "A little while." She did not say, "No one comes back once they've left, darling."

Daisy opened and closed her mouth against Cass's face. Cass pulled up the neck at the back of the baby vest and blew air down Daisy's spine, to cool her.

"Look, Maggs, I can teach you," said Vi. "Sh-eh. Say it! Sh. Eh. Spells: she." Cass admired him for turning to what he knew for sure when external events were escalating outside of his control.

Maggs did not understand Vi's lessons, but she liked the attention very much. Vi carefully wrote "Tricky Words" at the top of a page, and then a list for her: the, you, he, to, she.

"Geh-Oh."

"Jeh-o."

"Geh-Oh. Go."

To get out of The City, they had to drive through the part of it where Cass had grown up.

They passed the bingo hall, which still operated, and the cinema, which did not. A long, tight line of vehicles, beginning all the way back by the sport club, were waiting to get into the gas station. This forced the traffic out onto the wrong side of the road, but the oncoming drivers were understanding. Then the streets became residential in the sense that Cass recognized most deeply, and soon enough they were driving alongside the grid of places that had once been "hers."

To distract herself from imagining more Gaia (blood: she could picture the pools of blood in the playground; she could picture the approach of the second wave of men, with their brooches of leaves), Cass began to give the children a little tour of her own childhood as they went: once, she told them, there were tiny gray snowballs just here, there was hot chocolate there, breath condensing in the air, everywhere; a memorable fireworks night, a favorite jacket with the patches sewn on, the second-main part in a school play, her sister digging up flower beds in the park, the fry shop where Cass broke her wrist, netball. She told them that her dog's codename had been Opal Fruits the Magnificent, but he was also called Gus.

They passed a row of boarded-up shops. The pharmacy was still marked out with its old medical cross. Cass remembered being Vi's age, and standing precisely there on the pavement, finishing a dough-nut and waiting for her mom. Her mom was always ages, so when the doughnut was gone Cass had taken the change in her pocket to the vending machine to claim a plastic globe that clicked open to reveal a toy. Then her mom had emerged from the pharmacy, unsmiling and triumphant, transferring a white paper bag, crumpled at the top, into her larger handbag, and Cass had quickly sussed out what was inside it: HRT, and the cough medicine that was given to Cass to make her sleep every night, and the energy sweets for mid-morning, which gave Cass the shakes. And Cass's mom noticed the plastic globe. "Let me see that," she said, and held out her hand for it. Cass handed it over immediately. Cass's mom took the globe, glanced at it, didn't give it back. She greeted a passing friend and they became engaged in conversation. They all walked in the direction of home together.

72

Cass's mom kept hold of the globe until she seemed satisfied that it was very disappointing, not in actual fact something she desired. She handed it back to Cass, all greasy.

This memory had never troubled Cass's consciousness before. It was unremarkable. Cass had put up absolutely no resistance to her mother throughout her childhood; she'd accepted everything of her parents. They'd been the air she breathed. They'd constituted her safety. She had not, back then, talked about home, neither inside nor outside it, not even to herself. It would have breached the sanctuary.

Cass remembered the feeling of her mom, more than the visuals. How her mom was always inspecting her: picking up her limbs, looking in her creases, bored. It was safest to unfurl. If Cass withheld herself, or her stuff, her mother grew violent. "You get here now!" she would shout if she sensed even a flicker of hesitation in her daughter. Sometimes Cass missed a cue. Then her mother would be forced to grab whatever it was she wanted, give it a once-over, and release it, while angrily communicating: *What did you make me chase that for? Wasn't even worth it.* Cass was picked up, found wanting, put down. She would have felt like the cause of her parents' depression, but she knew better than to believe she was ever so important.

Cass drove on. The strange tinge of the sky swept into the car, as if it was on its way somewhere, then the sun lit up the golden smears of pollen on the back windows. Her babies' faces in the rear view looked sublime—they were like the glass prisms that break up white light, turning everything into all this color.

When Cass was a child, she had stepped into a shallow hole in the park soil, so her sister could bury her feet in it. Cass had stood, planted, with her arms held out like a Christ, like a human tree, and with crystals of sugar on her lips; there were prisms, prefiguring something, in the plane trees. And her mind had formed, as if grooves were being cut into the wood of it for the water to run through. When she was a child, and by herself, the basic feeling of being her, alive, within her body, had been that of being drenched. Heavenly drenched. All of life running through the grooves. And this had been a secret. Such a secret. In a home where secrets were forbidden—where their mom read their diaries, and sniffed the crotches of their clothes, and insisted on hearing and policing all their thoughts with an accusatory "You're very quiet" several times a day—Cass had learned to conceal not just the secret of her blissful liveness, but the fact that she was withholding anything at all.

She had made the blessed feeling of being her, alive, absolutely tiny, to protect it, so no one could sense it, chase and take it from her, nor give it back to her sullied and say, "What did you make me chase that for? Wasn't even worth it."

"I want to understand," Nathaniel had said.

But Cass had found that cajoling herself, let alone other people, into understanding her childhood was exhausting and point-less. There were only memories of memories. Questions and answers led to nothing that resembled the feeling of the truth. "They made me feel sick," she'd said to Nathaniel once, when he was digging. "My parents made me feel sick. But I didn't notice it, because it was all the time, until I left home and it stopped. Isn't that horrible? That I would say that aloud? That I would even admit to this? My parents made me feel nauseous. They said I was ungrateful. Mom called me a spaz. They always thought I was a cruel child, and I believed them, but I also knew that I wasn't. And that's it. I literally have nothing else to tell you."

The sick smell of growing up. The depression. The depressives' household held a particular smell, a really sweet unflushed-toilet smell; it was the smell of unwashed adults, floating in heavily bleached surroundings. Her mother liked to clean. Or had to clean, because everything was too much. The rags she used to clean the toilet were covered in bleach and used again on the doorframes, and the surfaces, then left to soak in another sink of bleach and water. Cass and her sister were themselves overly cleaned within this fug. Their mother was rough with them, which they submitted to comprehensively, until one day she became disgusted by their bodies and screamed, "Clean yourselves!" No one had ever shown them how; it had been some-thing done to them. Cass thought she was supposed to scrub her skin hot and raw, until her father walked in on her in the bath one day and told her to "Stop it, Cass." He was often walking around naked. Sometimes engorged at the sight of them. His mind gone. When this happened, Cass's mother would be very angry indeed at the girls. But it had been safest, it was cleverest, for Cass and her sister to be loving toward their parents, to think of them, and do sweet silent things for them—leave them notes, tidy up, do everything without being asked, excel at school, where there was order and adults were relatively rational—while keeping themselves, and their sense of being alive, a secret. This was what Cass did. And her parents took whatever they wanted from her, any sweetness, and then she left.

She thought it was both the greatest honor she could pay to her parents and the greatest revenge she could inflict upon them to be kinder than they were to children, to be more skillful at love and life, to have humble, true mastery, and to think of them no more.

Cass put on an audiobook in the car ("From the beginning! The beginning!" the children screamed) and they sang along to the theme song. Vi carefully put Daisy's pacifier back in her mouth every time she dropped it. ("Daisy really likes *me*," he said. "Her eyes laugh when she sees *me*.") The children were asleep by the time they approached the highway.

A barrier was shut across the service road. This surprised Cass but she did not let it unduly disturb her. She was focused, calmly, on her destination. She was powered and blinded by the roaring sun stealing her breath.

One of several men she could see in a little white cabin at the side of the road came out, wearing sunglasses and pink plastic gloves. He walked over slowly, circled once around the car and then came to stand beside Cass's open window. He didn't stoop at all, so she was level with his stomach, his belt, and his crotch.

He didn't say anything.

"Do you need our documents? Which ones do you need?" she asked him.

"Give me everything you've got," he replied.

Cass leaned over to the passenger seat and took out the plastic sleeve from the glove box along with a hard fruit gum, which she popped into her mouth. She passed the plastic sleeve through the window.

The man touched the edges of the papers inside with his pink-gloved thumb. "You're well prepared," he said in an accusatory way. "You got somewhere real to go?"

"Yes."

"OK, I'll be back." And he left, with her plastic folder, without hurry.

Bring it back, please. Now, please, thought Cass. *Please.* She fixed her jaw and moved the fruit gum around her mouth with her tongue, roughly. She turned to look at the kids again. *Still there*, she thought. Their opened sleeping mouths seemed to her a heavenly directive telling her to kiss them. *How are they real?*

She pushed her sunglasses up into her hair, sat back, and made eye contact with herself in the side-view mirror.

She really liked how her face looked. This was another secret.

"Why is that a secret?" Nathaniel had asked her one day, with his head resting on her navel. Cass had sighed. "Maybe . . ." she'd said, gradually. "Maybe, I think people, maybe women, won't like me, if I openly like my face." To this, Nathaniel had made his thoughtful "huh" sound. When Cass heard this "huh," what she heard was the satisfying plop of her thought landing cleanly in the cool central pool of his brain; the part where she assumed he kept his medical knowledge, and past lovers. The real part.

Occasionally, though, Cass worried that the "huh" was only what he said when he didn't really get her meaning. And if that were the case, she'd rather he let her know that she wasn't being clear, instead of allowing her to believe that her thinking chimed in him in some central way.

"Does what I just said make sense?" she'd asked him.

"Yep."

"Also, I like how I look, but I hate how I look to other people. So my liking only works in private."

"But how do you know what you look like to other people?"

"They tell me," she'd replied too quickly. Then he'd been silent in a different way.

Christ. She came round to the view of her face in the side-view mirror again. "Shut up," she mouthed to herself. The man was coming back, without her documents, with a clipboard. The fruit gum was soft enough to bite in half and chew. *Insouciantly*, she said to herself. The man put the clipboard and one proprietorial hand on the roof of the car.

"The purpose of your trip today?"

"Relocating to my mother-in-law's."

"Her name?"

"Eden Maguren."

"Her address?"

"It's in the folder, on the letter from the council."

"No. I want you to tell me her address."

She told him, and he wrote it down on the clipboard on the roof of the car, giving her the crotch once more.

"Reason for relocation?"

"Seeking refuge. I have three minors and no running water," she lied.

"Vaccine status?"

"Here, on my phone."

"Symptoms?"

Internally, a jangling of the nerves. The intermittent sense of not being real. Glee. "Nope."

"Eden Mag-u-ren knows you're coming?"

"Yes."

"I'll need her phone number." Cass provided it. "And your husband knows of this trip?"

"Yes, he wrote the letters you need. They're in there." She'd made him write these letters, just in case, before he left: "I, Mr. Nathaniel Andrew Maguren, do hereby give my full consent for my wife, Mrs. Cassandra May Maguren, to travel with our children, Vito Andrew Maguren . . .". et cetera. The man shifted to look in the back seat. "How did you get them to sleep, drug them or something?"

"Kept them up until midnight, woke them at six."

"Risky strategy. On six hours' sleep, my nephews would be screaming."

Cass discerned a lightness in his tone and took it as a sign from him that she could relax; this was all a formality. She was grateful. He wrote some more.

"I will inevitably return," he said with comically intended melancholia, and he went away again.

The air above the surface of the road ahead shimmered with heat.

While the man was gone, Vi woke up. "Don't wake the others," Cass said. Vi took some water from her and went back to sleep, his eyes brought low by his heavy lashes.

The hair stuck to the back of her neck. Vastness of sun in sky. Light like a plague.

After some minutes, the man ambled out of the cabin once more, with the plastic folder dangling casually at his side. He passed it to her through the car window, and she noticed that he'd put everything back inside neater than he'd found it; the corners of the papers were sharply squared.

She thanked him, and smiled again when he said, "Safe journey. Oh: and there are closed roads up ahead. The closed roads lead to fires, which are very dangerous. Don't try to go down them, OK?" She laughed at the way he said this, with resignation to humanity's basic stupidity and a sing-song lilt. She placed the folder on the seat beside her and looked back at him to say goodbye. Her angle and his were new, and from there she was able to see the silver wide-boughed tree, in the circle, pinned on the shoulder of his shirt, which could almost mean something. Her hand felt for and turned the key, and the barrier—operated by the other men, from within the cabin—opened. Her heart was very quick and felt oversized in her chest: roundabout, exit, service road, uphill, and then a descent to the six-lane highway, which was quiet. At the first turnout she pulled over and checked each document off against the list she'd made on her phone, as quickly as she could.

The children remained asleep for the smooth duration of the highway. Cass drove them under pedestrian bridges that were painted with slogans: Gaia's "They Are Killing Me" as well as "Go Home," "No Migrants," and "Turn Back," even "Parasites." Her awareness of the landscape shifted up and ran with the gears.

They drove the highway for over ninety minutes. She kept her eyes on the road and did not think back, nor look at the families on foot, walking the banks, nor the closed exit points, nor the cloud of smoke in the distance, to the right.

At the first village after the highway, they encountered a rudimentary tollgate that had been driven through. Cass slowed down to go over the broken parts of it. Dozens of brightly colored soccer balls had been released from shop or van and were scattered all over the road.

Vi, fully waking now, struck up urgently: "Can we stop and—"

"No," she interrupted calmly.

"Oh, but can we, please?"

Only: "No."

The next town was covered in slogans from front to back. At the next, Cass swung the car around a corner and was met by a sudden and improbable blockade, trucks and angry drivers. Cass U-turned and went the long way, trusting her sense of direction, enjoying the feeling of it, reaching a site of sufficient abandoned stillness where she could let the children out to pee and run around the bases of the trees a little. She fed Daisy, who kicked and kicked, like a happy little frog. Then they all clambered back into the car in a new mood, and put music on. Now they were traveling down lanes, often single-width, with trees all over and around them. It was altogether lusher here. It was perceptibly cooler already. And the air did not leave an aftertaste. Here was potentially less poison. There had recently been rain.

They arrived at their destination at around five, when the buttery light made crowns and thrones of the canopy. Cass caught sight of Maggs in the mirror. "Don't put the seat belt in your mouth," she said. But—she worried—maybe she shouldn't have said that. Putting things in your mouth was, after all, a comforting act.

Once you'd found Eden's hidden turning, it took at least fifteen minutes to reach the house. There was a long steep driveway, bordered on each side by a low dry-stone wall and broken up by six gates. Each gate had to be opened, driven through and then closed again—so there was a lot of getting out of the car and back in, and a lot of pleading for various things from bored children. After the last gate there was one final hill and then they were in the courtyard.

Cass turned off the car engine and closed her eyes.

"What are you doing now, Mommy?"

"Waiting for those birds we talked about."

"Oh yes. Are they coming?"

"Here they come, baby."

"I want Daddy here."

"It's OK."

Nathaniel was the only person in the whole world who enjoyed the spectacle of the birds. Of all the things it would have been possible, privately, to make fun of at Eden's, Nathaniel would go absolutely no further than the geese at the gate; but on the geese, he did not hold back. He would mimic his mother's voice as he reminded everyone in the car that these were "my Guard Geese, darling." "Here they come," he'd say. "Batten down the hatches." The geese came to spread horror: all wings and sharp barking beaks, and they would swarm around and start jabbing at the car. Their tongues were black. And their noise. Even Eden's bold dogs were frightened of the geese. The dogs would run upstairs and bark down from the windows. "There goes the cavalry," Nathaniel would say. "Cowering in the second-best guest bedroom." Small children were never not scared of all this.

The last time they'd visited Eden's, Maggs had screamed and screamed at the geese until her mouth and eyes had become frozen open in silent, gooey terror. Cass could remember saying to Nathaniel, with uncharacteristic and undisguised impatience, "Is Eden coming?"

"Of course she's coming," he'd replied.

For when the geese were completely gathered and surely making dents in the car, then Eden would appear: first at the upstairs windows, which she would fling open wide so that the dogs did not have to bark through glass but could demonstrate themselves fully, without restriction. Then she'd disappear again and—after slightly longer than a plausible interval—she would open the front door. She came, her pale skin luminous, carrying two long rakes and the air of someone with a great burden ahead of them, a great physical skill, which you were about to witness.

And so she appeared to them now.

Eden put her arms through a series of leather loops that were attached to the handles of each rake. She grasped tightly. Then, with a facial expression of perfected agony, she heaved the rakes out and up over her head, shouted "AWAY!" and brought the rakes falling down to the ground. This she repeated. Up. And down. Up and down, coming slowly toward the car, heaving and pained. She was a small, slight woman. She was the palest woman Cass had ever seen. As the geese began to back off, Eden grew tired and paused. She hung her head, momentarily. Usually Cass would say to Nathaniel at this point something like, "You must help her." To which he'd reply, not taking his eyes off his mother, "She doesn't want me to." She was a gigantic goose. Usually the children would be inconsolable, what with the attack of the big-winged birds and the martyring of their father's mother. But Cass, coming into the present incarnation of the event, realized that there was silence in the car. The children had fallen quiet, even as they were surrounded by the obnoxious geese. Daisy had her pacifier, Maggs was whispering something to Vi, to which he replied, solemnly, "No. Eden can't fly."

Eden was drawing level with the car and saying fiercely, "Come on, now. Move it." Cass realized that this directive was aimed at her, not the geese. She started the engine and pulled right up to the front door to ferry the children inside, while Eden held back the birds.

15

There were two parts to Eden's house: the old part and the new part. They went in, as always, through the old part, which Eden referred to as The Cottage. It had a rough and very small front door, painted cream. The hallway was dark and had a flagstone floor. The dogs were falling over each other in ecstasy trying to get down the stairs and greet the arrivals.

The dogs made Daisy coy. She banged her face onto her mother. Vi put a finger through a belt loop in Cass's shorts. Maggs was trying to climb up Cass's side. The dogs licked their legs. Cass pushed the dogs off.

Eden, relieved of her wings, was standing directly in front of Cass, her fine-spun hair tied back, her angular face beaky. She was placing a palm on either side of Cass's lower back and resting her head on Cass's collarbone, making Cass feel big, and adult, and ridiculous for thinking she'd ever needed help. Eden sighed dramatically against Cass's chest. Her perfume was strong. The ferns and myrtle at the window.

"Let me look at you," Eden said, pulling herself away. "You're nut brown. And look! At least your legs look good, my darling. Do you like my look?" Eden's thin lips were painted. Her eyes rimmed in kohl.

The dogs were padding around them; the gaps in Cass's attention were becoming bigger. In her mind's eye she saw, on the frame above the front door, tiny bright-green baby spiders sitting with their peering mother, all surrounded by wrapped carcasses. She felt or saw the hornbeams in the wood behind the house hush softly. Something rushed up through her, tingling from the ground, and then left. Everything felt achingly detailed.

"I have entered my tomboy era," said Eden, turning full circle with her arms held wide.

"I love it," said Cass.

"One of the old codgers has gone and pegged it, so they leave piles of his stuff out before he's even cold! And I never wash them." Eden held the collar of her shirt up to her painted face and took a theatrical sniff. "Love that smell."

It was, admittedly, a very new look. Maybe Eden was breaking free of something. There was still the made-up face, and little dots of jewelry, but no stockings, or belts, or heeled boots anymore. Her eyes were still powerfully quick, but they were also newly watery. She smiled occasionally and it wrinkled all the way up the sides of her eyes, but never at the children; Maggs had tentatively made her way through the dogs over to a side table, and was dropping its treasures onto the rug.

"Oh no, darling. No, not those," Eden said to Cass.

Cass hoisted Maggs up into her arms with Daisy and followed Eden into the kitchen, where there were towels on the floor under the dogs' bowls, and pretty mugs hung on hooks. The girls arched their backs and pleaded to be set free.

Heavy footfalls crossed the floor above them, heralding the arrival of the woman who helped Eden.

"You remember Bea!" said Eden, delighting as Bea entered the room with a hand on the wall for balance. Bea had been Eden's friend. Now she was Eden's friend, cleaner, housekeeper, hairdresser, and also her driver, since Eden had sold her car to a teenage boy who'd braved the geese to knock at the door of The Cottage. "Mom's amour" is what Nathaniel called Bea. Bea nodded in greeting at Cass and glanced at the children. Then she launched herself more fully into the room and the two women displayed their bond as they weaved around the kitchen like ballroom partners, one big, one small, one slow but committed, one light-footed. Eden said to Bea, "All these things," and indicated with her delicate, aristocratic wrist the few objects on the counter.

Like Eden, Bea had a "new look." Her face was raw and indented in peculiar ways, and she was wearing what appeared to be an old-fashioned matron's uniform in dove gray.

"Isn't it wonderful?" Eden said when she noticed Cass noticing it.

"Saves my own clothes from getting spoiled," Bea explained. She was lisping, like her tongue had grown too big for her mouth, and she did not make direct eye contact. Cass quite wanted to see her eyes, which she remembered, from their few meetings in the past, as particularly sparkly, but these were not offered. Something newly demure in her.

"Saves her clothes," Eden echoed. "Must save things, you see."

Maggs and Daisy were growing very loud in their protests to be let free. Eden, with her attention focused on the boxes of tea in the cupboard, said to them, absently, "Now, what *is* all that noise for? Bea, Bea, where are the biscuits?"

The women became flustered in their attempts to locate the biscuits and grew argumentative. Cass, flushed with the relief of arrival, was comforted by their squabbling. It felt like company. Fuss, like indoor hens and care. And outside, through the open back door, the air swept by in a spell of its freshness. Perhaps it was the hit of oxygen to the lungs from the cleaner atmosphere, to the bloodstream, that was making Cass feel so happy, so high.

Oh, Eden, she thought: *Eden, Eden, Eden*. For there was Eden, leaning her head back to sort through the boxes of tea. It was easy to love that profile, which was iconic in its way, strange, fragile bird bones, the bird queen. Cass could see the orbital bones of Eden's eyes protruding, her poreless skin and her peerless haught. She wasn't easy, Eden. She was dramatic and frequently defensive. She was particular about how things were done, and where things, including emotions, were kept. Eden was inscrutable when it came to her affection for Cass—but hinted that it either extended as resplendently as the universe or was completely non-existent, and nothing in between. Cass was either adored or suffered by Eden, but it did not really matter which. Either way, she could stay. And at Eden's Cass did not have to worry about her children being killed in their playground, nor did she have to think about Exceptional Danger when planning their days; the chemical soup in the air was thinner, they were out of the reach of wildfire smoke, the children could be outside all day. Around Eden's there was so much space. They could go weeks without seeing a stranger, if they wanted to. Cass realized that she'd put up with anything, any amount of Eden, anything to stop her children's lungs from feeling heavy. She had made a good decision. Cass could call Nathaniel and reassure him; she hoped he would journey to meet them at his mother's soon. It would be where he would gather them up to himself again. Then Cass could surrender and relax for a while.

"Terrible business, that Gaia stuff," said Eden.

"Yes," said Cass.

"Do you think they'll keep killing until they've had all the children?"

"I thought we might talk about that when they're older, or later."

"Stop that noise, *now*," Eden snapped at the girls, who were whining at Cass. "Or it will be straight to bed. And"—gently, to Cass—"feet off the table, please, darling." For Cass had stood Maggs on the table so she could keep the child's face close to hers without taking the full weight.

"Don't worry," Cass whispered to Maggs, transporting her like a magic airship and landing her on the floor.

*

Eden's food supply was bountiful. There were apparently local growers who were friends, and shanks of meat in the cool cellar. Eden did not feel like cooking that evening and so, when Bea left to drive home (having shown Cass how to use the washing machine in many small steps, as though Cass were an idiot), Eden instructed: "Open all the cupboards and help yourselves."

An early-evening breeze through the kitchen. Taking the pan off the heat. The house had power every day, reliably, from two in the afternoon until eight at night. The internet barely worked at all, there was no mobile phone signal. But a landline was stationed on the table in the hall, and an unbreakable VCR player, as well as a haul of old films, had been rescued from the outbuilding the year before. Cass set the children up in the den off the kitchen, in front of an animated film, as she made a salad, and pasta with wild garlic she'd picked from the walled kitchen garden, where the sky felt so big and fast.

Eden came in when the food was ready. Cass recalled that Eden hated having too much on her plate, so she asked, "How much would you like?"

"Oh. No. That's massive, darling."

"That's not for you, that's Vi's. How much would you like?"

"Please, don't give me too much. Please!"

"How much of this?"

"Make me a small plate."

"Would you like to make up your own plate?"

"No! Make me a plate. Make me a plate."

Eden went to sit with the children in front of the TV. Cass brought in the food, which was on the old blue-and-white willow-patterned china, with forks that were heavy at the base.

Eden said, "Oh, darling, this portion's too huge. I did tell you."

"Just eat what you can," Cass replied reassuringly, and sat to convince Daisy to feed. But Daisy only opened her mouth wide around Cass's breast, and then caught her mom's eye and laughed.

When the film was over, the children wailed for another, but were led quite easily to the bedroom between Arthur's and Nathaniel's, where Bea had resurrected the old cot. Cass stayed with them there until their sleeping breath had established itself as the dominant air in the unfamiliar room. Then she went back downstairs.

*

Following her husband's death, Eden had used his life insurance money to change her home. From the front it remained goosed and quaint, the rooms laid out in the same old ways, the passages small and uneven; the curtains caught all the dust and the under-sofa was a wild and neglected territory. But if you took the deep-purple corridor that now ran in a too-straight line—plumbed by "an architect with a Jesus complex"—from the front door to the back of the house, you came out, down a few steps, into the expansive New Sitting Room, with its double-heighted wall of glass which looked out over the garden and woodland. The room was all made in clean lines. The sofas were in oyster colors. There was a winding staircase suspended at the center, which led up to a small library on a mezzanine level, from where a door took you, through a cedar-wood closet, to Eden's new bedroom and bathroom. The glass that clad this extension to the property was dark, providing a sepia tint on the inside, while from the outside this dark glass was reflective. Trees and bits of white sky were mirrored on its black surface. Any occupant of the New Sitting Room could see out, but no one could really see in.

Deer would sometimes come up very close to the dark glass, Eden said. Deer and rabbits, and once a badger, not realizing that human-kind was right there.

The whole enterprise had made Nathaniel demented. Why couldn't his mother buy a new place, instead of partitioning off her old life and the new like this, in a weird and expensive way? He hated Eden's lack of self-awareness. How she had never examined herself, nor dismantled the stories that kept her trapped. "She could have started a whole new life when my father died," Nathaniel had said, many times.

Instead, Eden behaved as though her husband were only missing. It was as if she had built the new wing onto the house so as to have somewhere to retreat to upon his dreaded return.

"My father was a very quiet man," Nathaniel had said. "On the surface, he very much stayed out of her way. Excellent lawyer."

Nathaniel never made coming from money seem pleasurable, nor desirable, and yet he'd have it no other way.

*

Cass followed the deep-purple path into the magnificent New Sitting Room, where Eden was reading a battered magazine.

Eden reached a beckoning hand elegantly over the back of the sofa, and as she did so her gold bracelets moved up her wrist. The effect was very elegant. Youthful, even. Eden, who was going to be exactly twice Cass's age for a few more months, seemed to be the younger one just then, and this felt important.

"Let me look at you," she said. "Oh, darling. Have you been through the wars?"

"Oh, it's fine. Isn't it the same for—"

"Look. The thing is. Well. Well done you—for keeping on going."

"Thank you. Thanks for having us to stay." Cass felt ensconced with tiredness; it washed over her all of a sudden, making her feel unfit for thought, or time.

"Don't be silly," Eden said. "I hate to be alone. I loathe it. Nathaniel knows that."

"Does he?" Cass wasn't thinking.

"You haven't spoken to him." It wasn't a question.

"I have."

86

"He doesn't tell you these things."

"He does. I'm sorry. I'm really tired. I do. I do speak to him."

Eden did not reply, but smiled directly into Cass's face. It was a smile that was confoundingly bright and too close. All Cass could see was that smile and those muscle-like eyes flexing at her. Cass felt herself momentarily lose faith, felt painfully, deeply, like she wanted to go home.

"*When* did you speak to him?" Eden insisted.

Cass heard herself then addressing her mother-in-law in her head, using that same tone that she had learned for the children: *It's OK. It's OK. I understand. I'm sorry. I've swum in here, taking over all of your space. And I must seem so possessive of the children, and possessive of my husband, and I must make you feel threatened.* Cass knew she had to downplay her relationship with Nathaniel now, to help Eden feel in balance again. And then they could resettle: two women in the home, beside each other. And this was the safest way forward for everyone.

Cass continued: "We do speak. We haven't been able to the last few days."

"Well, yes. He's away from all that now. Isn't he? God. You know I had Arthur here, and that girl of his? That was a triumph when they left. Arthur's not like Nathaniel. I find it hard to believe they shared a womb."

"Not at the same time," said Cass. *Away from all what now?*

Eden smiled again. A smile that seemed to ask Cass, *What would you know about anything?*

"Anyway, you'll want to go to bed," she said.

Cass did want to go to bed. She kissed her mother-in-law and left for the old wing. She trailed her hand behind her on the wall up the stairs, thinking of the thousands of times her husband had touched the same places. She checked in on the children, turned the bath taps on, and approached the high double bed in her room.

Once: she'd come into this room to find Nathaniel, sitting alone, staring at the patterned wallpaper, wearing a starched shirt. Cass was all freshly cleaned and done up pretty. She was ready to present herself to Eden's friends at the party that was beginning downstairs. Her head tilted once to the side in a mock-submissive gesture of *Will I do?* Nathaniel got up quickly, propelled from his thought, and went to kiss her but landed it on her shoulder, so as not to smudge her makeup. He inhaled her hair, and onward, into her shoulder.

She said, "Let's go down." But he took her by the hand, with his thumbpad pressed hard into the absolute center of her palm. And he guided her to the bed. He guided her to bend over the bed, with one side of her face on the mattress, with her feet firm in the carpet, her knees bent. He folded her dress up carefully over her back, and moved her hair, and tilted her chin, so he could ensure that every part of her remained unrumpled and perfect. Even the lipstick.

She remembered, as he placed his palm down on her firmly, to steady her, as he pushed himself into her, that the edges of the lips of the mouth were called the vermilion borders. And she had colored hers in, up to that border, with Honey Coral 1985, purchased years earlier in a department store that had chandeliers. She felt wrong to still be having thoughts like these: she should join him in sex thoughtlessness. Shut off the dialogue. Consider *thoughtlessness*, she told herself, and he caught at that physical edge inside of her, where he always caught, that made her instantly panic and swoon down stories. She landed on another thought about how, soon, her thoughts would leave her. She would leave her mind. And utterly. And then it would be like floating, just above the surface of a twilit sea; she saw the blue oil rigs full of faceless people. She would float above them, above the air, to where the sky was as wide as your mind, and where you could, finally, breathe—breathe—breathe. Like the shutter going off 360 times a second.

He collapsed on her, pulled himself out of her; he licked the back of her neck wetly, then he got up.

She turned herself on the bed to face him. And when she did she was able to see, from the look on his face, that while he'd been having sex with her he hadn't, as she'd assumed, switched off the dialogue in his head. He'd been completely awake throughout. Very conscious. The whole encounter had taken place in full sentences for him. It had been a scene he was trying out: *And then I'll do this, and then I'll do that.* She hadn't realized. And her not realizing had been part of the turn-on for him. *What a dick*, she thought imperiously.

"You're a dick," she said.

He held out his hand and hauled her up, caught her, and said, "I love you, my queen."

She missed how he chanced his luck with her. She missed being wanted. He was the home she felt too far away from.

While the bath ran, she lay on the bed with her hips loose, her legs wide, knees bent, the soles of her feet together, like an animal on its back, gentling, not kicking. These were physical poses she knew to get into; ones of not resisting your fate.

When she judged that the bath would begin to overflow, she got up. She submerged herself in the cool water, rubbed at the places where sweat had pooled, swilled the bathwater around her mouth and spat it out. Entranced by the sight of white evening light catching on all the peculiar planes of her wrist. She couldn't be bothered to make herself come, nor get her things from the car, like the toothbrushes. She lay her head back on the tub and stayed there until she felt herself dropping off to sleep and got out.

16

Late morning, the next day, and outside all was breathtakingly light; the trees were flapping and waving. The children were baying. Eden thought the girls needed a change of scene. Cass was going to take them for a drive while Vi helped Eden in the garden. But Cass couldn't find the car keys.

"Is it locked?" Eden asked, incredulous.

"Apparently."

"Why did you lock it?"

"Habit?"

"Why on earth would you do that here?"

Cass searched her bag, the bedside table, beneath the kids' beds, then Eden went into all these places for a second look, turning Cass's pockets inside out. "Honestly, Cassandra," she said. And: "Where has silly Mommy put the keys?" she asked the children. And: "Did you at least get everything out of the car before you locked it?"

"Nope. Nothing. I'm losing my mind here," Cass said quietly.

They retraced Cass's steps. She realized that she'd misplaced her sunglasses too. They searched the long golden grass in the field behind the kitchen garden, where they'd played soon after their arrival. The grass would have caught Cass's objects in a friendly, silent way.

"I am sick and tired of this already," said Eden.

"It's fine. I just need to change the plan."

"To what?"

"To one in which we have no clothes, or toys, or laptop, or books, or medicine, or documents, passports . . . Shit, the rest of the diapers. Can we break into it?"

They stood in the shade cast by The Cottage discussing their options, while the geese began collecting together in little groupings as if conferring on whether or not to attack. Above them, between the high winds, high summer coming down, ordering the day, enforcing breaks to attend to thirst and sleepiness.

The day passed. Cass made dinner for Maggs; fed the dogs; took the trash cans out to where Bea had directed; grew privately annoyed that Eden was increasingly asking Vi to fetch and carry things for her. Cass had to explain to Bea why Daisy couldn't have the old bag of marbles to play with. Bea was affronted.

"She puts everything in her mouth," Cass explained. Bea remained visibly confused. "She could choke," Cass said. Bea shook her head and muttered.

That night, Vi stayed up late with the adults for a feast. They used a tablecloth, and lit lots of candles. Cass had made a stew thing and put flowers on the table. Vi was in charge of the music, using his dad's old battery-powered stereo. Eden obviously found the whole thing bemusing and slightly boring, but seemed to feel proud of herself for not having displayed this. Toward the end of the dinner, Vi yawned and Eden got a dreamy look. Cass had forgotten how Eden looked at Vi, like he was something exotic that made Eden more sophisticated.

On their way to bed, Eden led Vi out to the hall and showed him where, every night, she lit two special candles, one for each of her sons, and left them burning on the windowsill by the front door.

"Do you leave them burning all night?" Vi asked.

"It's very safe."

"Daddy says it's dangerous."

"Well, Daddy's not here," said Eden. "Which is why we must burn the candle for him."

Vi turned to give Cass, who was leaning in the doorway, a look, which was beseeching, and ironic, and adult, and a first.

17

Three days went by. "Still no keys, darling?"

Bea was instructed by Eden to search every inch of the property—"Every inch, I tell you!"—in her visibly uncomfortable uniform.

Maggs started up a game in which she would sing-shout from various locations, "Mommy! I've found your keeeeeys!" Then she'd bring Cass the keys to the back door, or a metal bracelet, or some coins, and say, "Are *this* your keys?"

Bea suggested smashing the car window. Eden explained to Bea why this wouldn't solve the problem: "You still can't turn the car on without the keys, darling. Nor can you get into the trunk without the keys, can you, Cassandra?"

"You can't."

"As I said. Why does no one ever listen to me?"

An hour later, Bea made the same suggestion again. "But all the things they need are in the trunk, honey! The trunk!" Eden shouted, was always shouting at Bea. "Please! Don't start smashing windows!"

On the fourth day, Maggs brought Cass a silver compact mirror. It was heavy, engraved with vines and Eden's initials.

"This your keys, Mommy?"

"Where did you get this?"

"Ganmother Eden's room."

It had been made clear that Eden's quarters were off-limits to the children. But Eden was out for a drive with Bea, so Cass said, "Show me where. We'll put it back." Daisy wound her sticky fist further into Cass's hair and held on tightly as Cass rose to follow Maggs down the purple corridor.

Cass could absorb Eden's rooms more fully without Eden present. She noticed for the first time that there was an elegant lip running around the top edge of the room, which held a light source—left, inexplicably, on. The woodland out the back was large and beautiful through the tinted glass wall. There were piles of decorative boxes on side tables: boxes made of wood, and boxes made of stone, inlaid, latticed, dozens of them. A large framed picture of Eden's late husband in ceremonial dress, and another of Nathaniel looking handsome and clean. There were no pictures of Arthur, even though he was possibly the best-looking of them all. There was an old-fashioned phone upon a table with a crenulated edge. There were art books in a stack beside the sofa. Bea's cleaning was in evidence here. Not a smudge on the glass, no dust in the corners of the stairs. Why did Eden let the front of the house stay so dusty, and full, and teeming? For contrast? Eden's preferred chair seemed to glow.

Maggs led Cass and Daisy to the spiral staircase and demonstrated proudly how she had taken the curving steps up so carefully when she'd come to this forbidden place alone. At the top, Maggs pointed and said, "This way, Mam-ma," leading them into a room with a perfectly made bed, puffed like risen dough. The forest felt even closer at the windows here. And, off to the side of the room, a bathroom, where the clutter of the old house was vindicated.

Bottles and bottles of shampoos and soaps stood and fell together in the shower basin. Around the sink, arranged in levels, was a full array of cosmetics and creams, lids off and broken. Mixed in among it all were spray bottles of bathroom cleaner, and a tub of rat poison, and an enormous variety of vitamins, supplements of all sorts, and eye-shadows, and brushes, fake eyelashes and toilet bleach, and a plastic bag full of boxes of hair dye in the corner, and cotton swabs. Perfume. Hair clamps in a variety of sizes. Another jewelry box. A photo of Eden as a young woman, her cheekbones flashes of white. A pile of wet underwear in the shower. Prescription pills. Dry shampoo, teenagers' tanner and glitter body spray, a pencil for filling in eyebrows, allergy tablets. Here were all the things that Cass lived without, because these things were impossible to get, or unethical to purchase, or irrelevant to the life that was required now.

"Where did you find it?" Cass asked quietly.

Then she looked down and saw that Maggs was staring up at her, and the girl's eyes were full of tears, about to spool over. Something about Cass's reaction to this room had changed it all for little Maggs. Cass moved Daisy into her other arm and then picked up her elder daughter. And the three of them caught sight of themselves in the mirror together.

18

Gradually, naturally, over a few days, Eden's food stores were depleted. Cass asked Eden about restocking the cupboards. She was told repeatedly not to worry: "Please don't make a big deal out of this, Cassandra." Cass said she would take Bea's car and drive to the market herself. Eden rolled her eyes at this, explaining that Cass wouldn't find it, and wouldn't know who the scammers were once she got there, and wouldn't be able to get back again, and she'd have to take Daisy, to feed her, without a car seat. "On your lap? Driving? For hours?"

Cass threw herself at a different problem. With the diapers locked in the trunk of the car and blank stares greeting her inquiries about where she could purchase more, she grew resourceful. She negotiated the use of Eden's worst bed linen, cutting it up into square cloth diapers, which she folded and secured to her baby through trial and error, much to that baby's amusement. Eden didn't want these diapers to go in the washing machine once soiled. "She's worried the gunk will block her pipes," Bea explained. Cass cleared out the firepit at the back of the kitchen garden and scoured the black from the large old pot to wash them in.

The first set of diapers were merrily on the boil and Cass was resurrecting an old, larger washing line to dry them on when Eden crept out toward her down the garden path and surprised her with an affectionate squeeze, saying, "Well, you've created an eyesore there, darling." Cass jolted with gratitude at the little splendid squeeze of an adult's hand on her waist. And they laughed, together. They were both laughing at Cass. At her ability. Cass felt a buzz of love. A collapsing. Their fondness like soft fur.

They would never share the common telepathy that comes when you fall truly into step; Bea was the only person fully synchronized with Eden. Bea' always seemed to pull up in her car exactly when Eden happened to need her, with no apparent planning. Sometimes Bea slept over, or arrived at 6 a.m. as if she had slept over, then she'd be gone for days. ("She's a free agent, Cassandra. We're not in each other's pockets.") Bea was more finely attuned to Eden's needs than to her own and she was confused by anything that was not Eden-related. Cass was particularly alarmed that Bea could not seem to follow the simple plot of the children's film they watched together. Bea certainly could not healthily put the children first in any situation, or forgive them for their noise if it rankled Eden. In this setting, Cass's care for the children was sometimes made to seem, in itself, childish and selfish.

Cass ran her eyes over the store of food and planned how she could make it last a few more days.

Then they were down to two more meals, and Cass heard herself ask, plainly, loudly: "Who will bring the food?"

"I've told you. There's a delivery man. Comes once a week," said Eden.

"But we've been here nine days—he hasn't been."

"Something must have come up for him." Eden was flustered. She was arranging red flowers in a green vase. A large pair of seamstress scissors lay open near the edge of the table. Eden was in a dress again and her waist was cinched in tight with a thin red belt. The unwanted leaves were falling from her hands, down to the tiled kitchen floor. "Life's not straightforward anymore, Cassandra," she continued. "Things don't happen at the press of a button. In nine days you haven't managed to get into your car, have you?"

The scissors were perilously close to the edge, right above Maggs's head. Cass moved to close them and push them into the center of the table.

On Cass's wedding day, Eden had arrived early, bringing something old (a Victorian lace collar), something new (a thin golden bracelet), something borrowed (a locket), and something blue (a small bouquet of forget-me-nots). Eden had spoken charmingly with each of the thirty guests, and stayed behind to bargain with the caterers.

But now the red flowers would not do Eden's bidding, and she was pinching them and poking their stems in harder among their cousins.

Cass took a deep breath. "Could you call the man? Because I have to feed the children."

"Yes, yes. Alright, darling."

Cass, the pest.

Eden held a whispered conference over the phone. Bea arrived a few hours later in her car with a box of cereal and cans of beans and some tomatoes. She did not say hello when she entered with the food, nor speak as she unpacked everything. She opened the cupboards and said, as if Cass wasn't in the room, "There's already beans and carrots in here. I don't know what she's complaining about."

Eden held up her hands to Bea. "Don't get me started."

Bea continued, "Middle Fire has spread. It's twice the size they said it would be. I couldn't get anywhere."

"Midlands, darling, not Middle. Makes it sound middling, which it is not."

"How close is it?" Cass asked. Bea and Eden ignored her, and carried on unpacking. Perhaps they each thought the other person would answer. Cass said to the children, "OK. Let's go for a walk."

They didn't go far. Only through the kitchen garden, out the gate at the back, into the woods.

Cass kept breathing deeply through her nose to check for the smell of smoke. The air seemed clear.

She found it easier to see in the woods, because the light was softened, filtered through the leaves. Maggs wanted to pretend they were on a beach. She collected things (casings, leaves, stones, twigs) and said they were shells. The oaks roared in occasional winds, and sounded like waves hitting shingle. The leaves moved in synchrony as if they were underwater, subject to the same current.

They went to what Cass knew to be Nathaniel's favorite tree. It had man-made holes, finger-sized, all the way up the trunk. Vi filled these holes with the littlest stones, smallest twigs, and Maggs's "shells." Daisy started wailing, but Vi would not be hurried.

*

Night. Cass stood at the window, watching for fire. The Midlands Fire. The horizon was still. There were many stars. Beside the window hung a color photo of a valley with a fine white building at its center.

The name "Eigleath" printed on the mount beneath it. Cass had heard the name, could pronounce it, "Eegleeth," but had never seen the word written down before. Hanging alongside it: a piece of tapestry, framed. A nail sticking out of the wall with no reason, nothing on it. Cass had picked up a piece of green thread from the floor earlier; she took it from her pocket and tied a bow around the nail.

The electricity did not go off at the usual time that night. After the children were in bed, Cass returned to the sofa and let a film play. Eden came into the room with a bowl of something in her hand. The bowl was blue and had hearts painted on it. There was steam rising off it. Eden's nails were painted emerald green that day. Cass drew a shape in the air with her flawed eyes between her own green-pierced earlobes, green nails, green baby spiders, green thread on the nail.

Eden remained standing as she took two enormous spoonfuls into her mouth, then she held the bowl out to Cass with a straight arm. "Do you want some? There, take it. I don't want it, darling."

It was apple crumble, with vanilla cream on the side. Cass tried it, winced, and her eyes lit up with the sugar. She decided not to ask "Where the hell did this come from?" because the answer would inevitably be overcomplicated, and more than six words long, and it would, somehow, through exquisite design, make Cass feel guilty or anxious in ways she couldn't anticipate, and she was too tired.

Eden lowered her forehead and was transfixed watching the show on the screen, as if it lent a new line of inquiry to her thesis. And then she said, "Did you try calling Nathaniel again?"

"Yes."

"No joy still?"

"No."

"Oh well. Never mind." She watched a bit more, still standing, and then she said, "Do you know what we *are* running out of, though, darling?"

"Huh?"

"Do you know what we're running out of?" Eden's face was one of the finest things that Cass had ever seen. Noble and yet practical; alarming and yet unthreatening; striking and yet unmemorable in and of itself, which was perhaps why she dressed it up so much.

"No? What are we running out of?" asked Cass.

"Water."

Cass spooned more food into her mouth, and waited. Then she cocked a brow, swallowed the stickiness, and said, "But I thought it was connected?"

"It is. It is. It is temperamental. On a good day. It is temperamental. No, look. I just took my last shower in a while. Let's put it that way."

"I would have put the kids in the bath if I'd known."

"Oh, chuck them in the stream."

"What stream?"

"The stream! North of here. Not far. You've really got to explore more."

"Is it walkable?"

"Not with the children, no. Still not found those car keys?"

Cass detached and looked away. Eden sat down and arranged the colorful cushions around herself nicely. Pleased, she continued.

"I mean, actually you shouldn't venture that far. The fire's getting awfully close. But I know what I was going to ask you. Yes. I remember what I wanted to ask. Do you think he's dead?"

"Who?"

"Your husband."

Cass did not reply. Eden went on, "He is in a war zone, you know."

"No. I don't think he's dead. I don't entertain that."

"Good. Just checking." And then, gesturing toward the bowl, she said ever more brightly, "It's good, isn't it?"

"I don't let that idea in." Cass was about to start crying. It was an unbearable proposition to her, that Nathaniel might die, that he might be so alone, in a box or as ash, all by himself. *All by himself.*

"Oh, don't get upset!" Eden said. "I only wanted to check you weren't catastrophizing again . . ."

"When have I ever—" But if she finished this sentence, she really would cry, which would be a terrible thing to have to sort through with Eden afterward. The energy that would be required to stabilize Eden after such an event forced Cass to control herself. She returned to the previous subject of conversation: "Do you have reserves? Of water." She was thinking of her own front room in The City, packed with bottles.

"No. We don't need those here."

Or Cass could cry from frustration.

She wanted to speak to Nathaniel, not only so that together they could laugh off reports of his demise, but also so that she could describe to him what she was encountering in Eden. She would say, "Eden seems to promise that she'll catch you if you fall toward her, she even entreats you to fall toward her, but then she takes a step to the side at the last possible moment and lets you crash, and then blames you for making her move away." Probably she wouldn't say such a thing. It was too much.

Cass took a deep breath. Both women were looking intently at the screen. Cass finished the food. She licked the bowl clean. She enjoyed the thought that Eden might find her appetite offensive.

The electricity popped off, and everything went dark and silent.

"It's just: he's really never been this long out of touch," Eden said softly.

19

Cass had been dozing and feeding Daisy in bed on and off since dawn. By 6:30, Daisy was wide awake. Cass covered her in kisses, a fresh cloth diaper, her only vest, and they went downstairs. She picked up the phone in the hall and dialed her husband's number, knowing that he wouldn't answer: it was a ritual at this point. She let it ring fifteen times as she read over the now familiar list of names and numbers that was written up in Eden's looping hand and kept beside the phone. There was a complicated coda of ticks and crosses in operation along the edge of the list. Tick, tick, cross. Did a cross mean the number no longer worked, or did it indicate something about the person the number would connect you to? Nathaniel's name and number were happy with ticks. There were many different numbers for Arthur, many crossed out, most accompanied by crosses. Florence had ticks; Tim had ticks; Bea, ticks. A line had been drawn through the middle of the words "Cass and the children" and Cass's number in The City was scratched out. "Eigleath" was ticked. "Marcus and Mary" ticked thrice. Cass hung up the phone and proceeded to the kitchen, wondering if the air might not be a tad smoky. She let the dogs out and turned on the taps to fill the pan. Nothing came out.

The water hadn't run down slowly. It was as though someone had switched it off singularly and completely in the night.

"You OK?" asked Eden, a gauzy kimono floating in on her perfume.

"The water's gone."

"What did I tell you?"

"Eden. Things get very bad for children extremely—very—quickly when there's no water."

"There's no need to panic, Cassandra."

"They can get really sick. We won't be able to clean anything, we can't flush the toilet. We all must be really careful now. I'm going to have to burn the diapers at the end of the day."

"Don't panic." Eden was smiling, her mouth was so capacious.

"Dehydration can set in very quickly." Cass's heart was already racing.

"Look, you have to go to Tim's and get some, darling. It's really not that big a deal. It's three miles! That's all. I'd go myself, but I can't. I can't carry it. I can't. My joints."

"Who is Tim? Wait. Could Bea drive me there?"

"Hmmmmm?" As if she wasn't listening. "Bea's gone off to see her son. Just go. You'll be fine. I'll call Tim now."

"When will Bea be back?"

"Days. I don't know."

"Can we call her to come back?"

"No! She's gone."

"How long would it take me to get there? You'd watch the children?"

"Of course, sweetheart!"

It became clear, as rounds of tea were not made, and the children drank the last of the water from the jug, and the toilet cistern did not refill after it was flushed, that Tim was a neighbor with a water storage system and Cass simply had to leave as soon as possible, go to him, and get back. She gave Daisy one more feed and then handed her over to Eden.

"Please watch her with the little things, like marbles," Cass said.

"I have had children of my own, you know."

Cass dithered in and out of rooms, trying to make sure that she'd done everything in her power to make her departure easeful. She drew Vi onto her lap, and spoke in his ear: "Please help Eden while I'm gone. Watch your sisters. You know what they're allowed to do." Vi wanted to go with her. Not, she felt, because he was needy for her, but because he seemed to think that his protective forces would be put to better use at her side.

"No. I am totally fine," she said. "And I'll be back really soon."

Cass was aware that in collecting the water she'd be introducing herself to someone new, and not just any someone new but a someone new with a water supply. She tripped upstairs and looked at herself in the mirror. She'd found two of Nathaniel's old T-shirts in a drawer to add to the one she'd arrived in, but she hadn't washed them in days, and all were stained in the same ways: breast milk, food, the strong smell of menstrual blood on her only shorts. She brushed her hair through, cleaned her teeth with a finger, and went to ask Eden how much money she'd need for the water guy.

"No money. It's a favor. Speaking of which, you can't go dressed like that."

"It's all I've got. It's fine."

Eden poured the baby back into Cass's arms and went away. Maggs was yelling that she didn't want Cass to go. This protracted leave-taking was nightmarish. Cass felt it would be much better for everyone if she left quickly. Eden reappeared with clothing in plastic dry-cleaner bags flung over her arm.

"I don't think any of this will fit you," she said.

"Eden, I really should get going."

"They'll all be far too small for you."

"Daisy will need to be fed again soon."

"Try this one on. Please." *Why*, Eden seemed to ask, *can you not do this one thing for me?*

Eden thrust a dress at Cass. It was dark tweed, thick, with lining, the label stitched in with gold thread. It was an old-fashioned pinafore meant to be worn over the top of a blouse.

The nape of Cass's neck itched continuously.

She used to pluck her eyebrows into perfect lunar crescents. She used to pop her eyelids up and run a black pencil along the waterline, for definition. She used to spray perfume behind her ears, and meet friends by flower stalls outside train stations, and they would go to bars together after work. They'd see where the evening led them. She went along with Eden's plan: she stepped into the dress, and held it up over her chest as she wriggled her T-shirt off beneath it. Then she put her arms through the sleeve holes and removed her shorts. Eden was behind her, zipping her in. The dress was too big. It hung loosely at Cass's ribcage. The straps gaped around her shoulders; it tapered at the ankle. The lining was silky: her skin rushed against it. Cass went into the hallway to the long mirror. She held her hair up and took in a side profile. *What on earth am I doing?* But her own clothes were pretty disgusting.

"OK. This is fine. I'm going to leave now."

Three kisses for three soft heads. And—*Don't think, just go*—she was out and shouting fierce vowels at the geese. Showing them her teeth in snarls.

She'd got as far as the first gate when Eden came sprinting lightly after her.

Cass turned. "Eden, you can't leave the baby alone."

"Let me put this on you, please."

Eden was holding out a bright-red open lipstick. The gold lid in one hand. The red, unscrewed and pushed out to its full extension, in the other.

"I don't need that. Please go back to Daisy. She's too small."

"Daisy's fine. Daisy's fine."

Eden stopped close, was leaning in toward Cass, aiming the end of her lipstick at Cass's face. Cass's instinct was to push Eden away as hard as she could and run back inside to pick up her baby. But then what? No water. She felt huge. Momentarily felt like she was persecuting little Eden with her horrible strong will, and that, in retaliation, Eden might punish her babies.

Eden said, "Let me put this on you and then I will go to Daisy."

"Give it to me. I'll do it. I'll do it," said Cass, letting out the most fury she had ever displayed in front of her mother-in-law.

Cass took the lipstick and, remembering how it was done, drew a little in at the center of her mouth. She spread it out with her ring finger in a tapping motion.

"Do your arch. Do the arch," said Eden, fixing her gaze on Cass's mouth like it was the only point of focus in the world.

"That's enough," Cass said, passing the lipstick back.

"The arch! There. Please. Let me."

Eden took Cass's chin strongly in her bony hand, and drew on a full-bodied red mouth. The geese were getting closer.

"There," she said. "That's perfect. Thank you. Mind that you don't smudge it on the way."

"OK. OK. I'm going. Bye. Go to the children."

Cass began to walk away. She reached the fifth gate before she felt compelled to run back. The children had embedded alarms in her and some of these went off in accordance with Cass's real, true instincts, which were to be taken seriously, but some of them were triggered too easily by false exaggerations of fear; and she was finding it impossible lately to know which was which. Cass hitched up the weird garment to climb back over the gates, she went dancing and hissing with the geese, to check through the kitchen window that the children were OK.

She had to believe what she saw: Daisy was in Eden's arms and Eden was gently bouncing her up and down, while talking to Vi and Maggs, who were drawing on large pieces of paper. They looked absolutely peaceful. And totally fine. If Eden noticed Cass peering in, she pretended that she hadn't.

"Everything's fine," Cass said to herself. She kissed the back of her hand to remove some of the lipstick as she got away.

20

Surely, if children needed water, and the water man had water to give, then the equation was solved. But—Cass shifted to the other side of the proposition as she reached the last gate—why should this water man feel an automatic compulsion to share with her children? Cass remembered not to assume anything.

Eden seemed to find it pleasurable, necessary even, to send Cass to this water man in lipstick. Perhaps a deep-seated, old-fashioned need in Eden, to please men who hadn't even asked to be pleased, was at play. Or maybe Eden wanted Cass to realize that she was not above debasing herself for her children, and that no woman was.

Cass was struggling against the urge to rip the dress off.

It was highly possible that Eden had been imparting no lesson, and simply wanted to help Cass leave the house looking a bit less feral. The problem was that even Eden's most harmless acts were beginning to create a catastrophe of reaction within Cass.

She looked at her husband's heavy watch. He'd removed some of the links in the strap before he left, so that it would stay comfortably in place on her wrist. She had marveled at how he'd done this at the kitchen table one Sunday afternoon, his surgical confidence being greater than the expense of the watch. As Cass walked the main road, under the climbing sun, she turned to the pearly dial again and again to identify precisely how far off Eden's calculations had been. She moved her necklaces around so they hung down her back.

Eden had said that it would take "forty-five minutes, maximum, darling" to reach the turning. But Cass was fifty-five minutes in, sixty-five minutes in, eighty-five minutes into her walk and she hadn't missed the turning yet. She wasn't slow. She was in her stride once more, in urgency. The lining of the dress was sweaty and clinging. It was so quiet all around. The sound of the material sticking and releasing from her legs was the loudest thing for miles. Not a single vehicle drove by. She thought about Daisy's chubby wrists and Vi's dream. She told herself her thirst was not hers but her children's, and walked faster.

There was no cover. Not even once she turned off the main road. Just bright light all the way along the path, between fields toasted brown and gold and black. The hedges on either side started closing in, teeming with small berries that Cass assumed were poisonous, and still the sun was direct on top of her head.

When the path ended, it did so abruptly, and Cass found herself suddenly at the edge of a wide-open space. Tim's bungalow was an eyesore at the center of it. Cass understood this arrangement of building and space to be an excellent security strategy: whoever was in the house would be able to see her coming long before she arrived; there was no way of sneaking up undetected. Cass trained her gaze on the details of the scene and collected together an array of assumptions which she began shuffling like cards: Tim must be discerning, careful, charming, idiosyncratic. *The second he sees me approaching, he will emerge to wave me in.* The next thing she noticed, the next thing to impress her, was the line of massive blue containers with taps at their bases, down the side of the building. And then she saw the plants—an exuberant jungle of palms in pots and an aloe, like Ally's alien, crowding up the windows of the bungalow and congregating on the deck that ran right around the property. Weird garden gnomes gathered in groups in the fields, among masses of sacking and spades abandoned. A man-sized heap of rubbish. A lot of sky here. More sky than anything else, and the sky seemed deeper and higher, as some parts of the ocean are deeper than others. She felt she had swum very far out.

She stepped up onto the deck and knocked on the door. The wind chimes were hanging in silence. There was no answer. Wait four breaths. Wait seven. Checking the pearly face of her husband's watch once more: she'd left the children 127 minutes ago. No answer. So knock louder.

She circled the place twice. Called out who she was. She backed off and looked into the distance all around to see if he'd gone to the shade to work on something. Eden had telephoned ahead, Tim knew Cass was coming, and Eden said he didn't have a car, so he couldn't be far away. Maybe he was asleep.

She only had to turn the handle a quarter way and the front door swung open. If her quest weren't for water she would never have been so invasive—perhaps. She called out again: "Tim. It's Cass. I'm here from Eden's." Her voice sounded reedy to her.

Inside was all darkness and stale cigarettes.

Framed art hung all over the walls, and Cass could see her reflection in the covering glass. She chose one picture to look at while she waited for Tim to appear. It slowly became clearer as her eyes grew accustomed to the dim room. It was a painting of two gray shapes on an orange table, against a blue background. Each shape had a geometric bite taken out of it. The removed parts of the shapes were not included in the picture. And the insides of the shapes, which were now revealed, were perspectively perfect, and colored in undulating aspects of gold. The insides looked real, while everything else was abstract, without declaring why. These sorts of puzzles bored her. She felt infuriated: was he hiding from her?

She entered a bit further into the room. Black mold spread out across the ceiling. *Imagine if Nathaniel were here. What would he do?* Nathaniel would move decisively; he would find canisters for the water, help himself to it, take it, get away quickly, and pay Tim not a second's more mind. Nathaniel's focus would be inspiring. Cass's breasts were rigid, full and desperate for her baby to drain them. She looked into the kitchen. And instead of seeing the kitchen, something else happened. Something to do with sight and time, and her place within it, slipped. Instead of a kitchen, she saw herself, from behind, framed by the door, hair stuck to the sweat on her neck, in a ridiculous dress, frightened by something. She had to get back to the children immediately. She went outside again.

On the decking this time she noticed her own name written in capital letters on a piece of paper which was secured on a table by a rock the size of a head. She lifted the cloth covering the table and found beneath it two massive carriers of water—plastic, with black screw-top lids. A gasping groan escaped her as she picked them up by their handles.

It took her ten minutes to reach a sheltered spot, and during this time she had to put the water down twice. When she was out of sight of Tim's, she unscrewed one of the lids. The bottle was so full that she was able to sip from its neck without tipping it. She felt watched.

She set off and reached the main road again. The sun had not yet gone over its peak. The plastic handles cut into her hands. And the smell of breast milk leaking into the tweed dress was strong. She stopped to pee by the side of the road. Dehydration made the urine smell thicker than milk. She was too heady and slow to rearrange her feet in time, and the pee soaked into the edges of her plastic clogs. She really could not bring herself to care. Her brain was slurring. And it felt as though the bones in her hips and her arms were splintering under the weight of the water; it felt like irreversible damage. She started to sing to herself as she went up the hill and through the several gates. She had to keep stopping and placing the water down to let her hands re-form where the plastic handles were disfiguring them.

The geese were at the final gate. She called for Eden, but it was pointless over the noise streaming across the birds' black tongues.

She could leave the water in the lane, climb the gate and frighten the animals away. Or she could open the gate and simply let them escape. She heard herself say "Fuck it" and let the gate swing wide. All the geese were excited to leave and filed out officiously.

And then, on that last slog from the final gate to the front door, Cass softened. She caught herself smiling. In a moment or so she'd be granted the sight of the children's faces. And those little faces would tell her things without words. And this was love. This was the love that her soul had been sent to seek in this life. It was possible to comprehend now, quite clearly, that her younger self had been mis-sold. The world had conspired to teach her that romantic love would be her savior and her keep, but the world had been wrong. It was not romance, with its conditions, but her love for her children that was the most almighty thing life could ever have put in her path. She loved them, and she asked for completely nothing in return except that they be alive and free. She loved them, and they would love—not always her, but life itself, and this was the deal.

She had reached the front door. She put the water down and stooped deeper, to pick up a flower's petal that had landed on the paving stone there, which she would put between Daisy's thumb and finger. Imagine how that would feel, for fingertips so soft and new and petal-like themselves. Like kin touching kin. Cass leaned on the front door and turned the handle. But it did not give.

21

The front door was locked. How strange. The front door was locked and the dogs were not barking as Cass knocked.

The dogs were not barking as she called. The dogs always barked when someone was at the front door.

And the front door was never locked. Just as there was no point in locking the car, there was no point in locking the front door.

Cass stayed there, disbelieving. Postponing, for another second . . .

She knocked very hard on the door, and called out Eden's name. Called out Vi's name. Knocked again, too hard this time, so it sounded panicked.

She left the water where it was and looped the property, calling at the windows, looking out over the grounds, calling their names, her heart beating a bit too hard.

She tried the kitchen door. It was locked. For the first time.

It's alright, in a minute I'll see them. She spoke to herself nicely: *It's alright. They're just around the corner.*

But they weren't. They weren't just around the corner. Where were they?

Returning to the front door. Knocking again. Thinking, *Even if . . . even if they'd all gone out, they'd leave the door unlocked for me.* The questions: *Where are my . . . ? Why can't I . . . ?*

Even if . . . even if Eden had taken the children for a walk, somehow, to the river. *But how would they manage it, in their thirst and the heat?* Eden couldn't carry Daisy far.

Or perhaps someone—someone like Bea—had arrived and taken the children to a place in her car. But that didn't explain where the dogs were. There'd be no room for the dogs in the car, they'd certainly leave the dogs behind. The dogs would be at home, here, now, barking at Cass. Even if—even if Bea had come in her car, she would

109

have driven along the road Cass had just traveled, *wouldn't she?* Would have picked Cass up on the way. *Wouldn't she?* And, in all eventualities, they'd have left the front door unlocked for her.

Cass bashed on the front door with her closed fist, shouting for Vi.

They must have gone . . . They must have gone to get help. There was some kind of emergency. Three kids, one old lady, no water. An emergency was the most rational explanation.

She was running now, around again, in the opposite direction, past the roses and the shedding bougainvillea.

"Eden doesn't want me inside the house." Cass said this out loud, as if she was alone on a stage. Then every single thing that had happened, for the last several years, was relit to perfectly corroborate this new truth: *Eden doesn't want me inside the house.* The fresh light bounced from remembered scenes of Eden and converged on Cass, bringing her thrilling clarity. From this place, Cass's mind took a balletic leap and landed impressively on a new conclusion: *Eden has locked me out and taken my children away from me. And this was Eden's plan all along.*

Was this true? How was it possible to know what to believe? She only had Eden's logic for balance, which was so mercurial.

Cass was circling the house, calling; putting her face right up against the dark glass of Eden's rooms and using her hands as a shielding viewfinder. There was no one.

She was looking for a clue. She had to get inside, and see if there was a clue as to where they had gone. She had to get away, in her car, and catch the old women as they fled with her children. Get in, or get away? She thought of getting on her hands and knees in the long-golden-grassed field, and sweeping for her car keys. Immediately even the time spent having this thought, let alone acting on it, felt like a waste. *Break the car window*, she thought. *Are they hiding in the car?* That didn't make sense. Why was her thinking failing her at a time like this? Break the car window? *But you can't drive away without the keys.* Look for the keys? *In that field forever.* Why would they take the children and the dogs away? It didn't make sense. There had to be a reason visible inside the house. There had to be something she could see that would make this make sense. This was the way of the world. *Use your eyes.*

The kitchen door would be the easiest way in.

She picked up a flowerpot from the little grouping to the side, and took one of the small bricks it rested on. Then, having checked through the window that there was no one crouching behind the door in some hideous game of Hide-and-Seek to terrify her, she took a step back and threw the brick hard, at the thin pane of glass in the kitchen door. It smashed, first time.

"Mommy?" She heard Maggs's tearful voice coming like a puff of warm familiar air through the broken pane. Cass's eyes adapted to the dark inside, and there was the sad figure of crying Maggs, very still, on the other side of the room. "Why did you break the window, Mommy?"

Cass had her arm through the hole in the glass, and she was grappling for the key that was always left in the back of the door. She felt the skin on her wrist split, and took a sharp breath in, but didn't stop patting for the keyhole. The key, which was usually kept in the door, which was always kept in the door, wasn't there. But look, there—her mind sharpening in focus now that she could see one of her children— Cass saw the key on its ribbon, on the kitchen table, and was able to guide Maggs to bring it to her, and she was in.

"Where are the others?" She picked up this child in front of her and held it to her fully.

"They're asleep."

"Where's Eden?"

"She left away."

Why isn't the baby crying?

"Where's Daisy?"

In the den, Vi was curled up, asleep, fetal, on the sofa. Daisy was face down on a cushion on the floor, which must have been placed there to break her inevitable roll and fall off the sofa. *Face down?* Oh God. Cass picked the limp baby up. She couldn't undo the zip on the back of her own sweat- and leaky-milk-sodden dress. She went to the kitchen, took up the seamstress scissors from the center of the table and, holding her limp baby in one arm, saying, "It's alright, it's alright," she cut the dress right down the middle. She let it fall, pushed down her bra, and brought the baby's mouth to her nipple. How was Daisy so far gone? The milk started spurting. "Wake her up," Cass commanded the milk. "Wake her up. Please." The milk squirted in the baby's eye. Daisy's mouth opened feebly, and her tongue tried to latch on, but it tired, and fell back. Cass

111

held the baby's head semi-forcefully onto the nipple. Daisy, alarmed by this insistence, awoke a little more. Something occurred to her. She was getting it; she got it. She latched on. The baby's chin started moving determinedly and rhythmically. The relief poured all the way through Cass and out with the milk into this baby. Who would be OK.

Cass walked with the baby pressed against her, and tried to wake Vi. "Come," she said. But he roused, noticed her curiously, and then turned away and went back to sleep. In only her underwear, bra hanging down from her ribcage, her baby still latched to her, Cass went back outside to pull the water in with one hand and start administering it.

Five hours—she checked the watch, she grabbed a cup, she counted—five hours and twenty minutes, she'd been gone for the best part of six hours. Is this what six hours with no water did to a child? She brought the first fill of the cup to Maggs, the next to Vi. She had to put Daisy down so she could haul Vi up, his eyes still closed, his head lolling, and put the cup to his lips. The baby cried as she did this, which was music to her ears. Vi's reflexes were strong: he grabbed the cup instantly and drank. She filled it a third time, for herself. Then, for the fourth, she put it between Maggs and Vi and told them to take small sips and drink it slowly between them. She sat on the floor, mostly naked, her back rounded, trying not to cry, while Daisy fed and Vi and Maggs sat beside her quietly.

She didn't ask them anything, she simply tried to re-establish some normality for the evening. She got them comfortable in their bedroom, and the older two picked at dry cereal and drank the water slowly. They remembered and pieced together, imperfectly, their favorite storybook, which was locked in the trunk of the car. They each chose a song for her to sing. She counted their toes, their fingers, and their eyelashes, which made them giggle and made her feel safe. Vi and Daisy were very sleepy throughout. Daisy fell into a full-bodied sleep in Cass's arms, while Maggs stayed wide awake, unable to settle, hiding the pebbles she'd collected from the forest around the room. Two completely opposite responses to stress, Cass thought: *One sleeps, the other imposes order.*

The sun had set in a blaze on one face of the building. Vi was struggling to keep his eyes open, but he was certainly waiting for Cass to ask, "Where did Eden go?"

"I don't know," he said.

"Was it soon after I'd gone?"

"Yes. Quite soon."

"She didn't say anything? Where she was going?"

"I heard her get in a car. She gave us our medicine. And then she got in the car."

Cass thought the green baby spiders above the front door were growing bigger and darkening beside their mother.

"What medicine?" she asked, casually.

"I don't know." In the next instant he was completely asleep.

Cass regarded him as he went under. She let an empty mug hang by the handle, let it swing from her finger, while she watched him. She took a deep breath. And then she said, out loud, "I don't think I should let you go back to sleep." But Vi wouldn't wake.

"Maggs, did you have medicine?"

"It was disgusting. Horrible. Yuck. Spat it. I spat it out. Then Grandma Eden was very bossy to me. It was horrible." She said this matter-of-factly. She was busy: her pebbles were feeling exposed and would require the most tricksy of hiding places for the night ahead.

"Did you swallow any of it?" asked Cass, calm.

"No. I wouldn't. I got in trouble."

"Did the others? Did they eat the medicine?"

"Yes."

"Did Daisy?"

"Yes. Daisy had it. She liked it. She kept the spoon. Eden was mean to Daisy. I do not like Eden, thank you."

Cass's initial wish kept her calm for one sweet moment longer: she wished and almost believed that she could make herself throw up, and this would purge the children's stomachs.

Maggs was trying to carry too many of her pebbles at once. A couple of them slipped and some fell against each other; they ricocheted.

What was possible?

"Excuse me," she wanted to ask someone, "what is possible here?"

It was possible that she needed help. It was possible that her children had been given something. Drugged. Drugged to sleep. It was possible that they'd been given too much. It was possible that she had to assume they had.

It was possible to scan ahead in her mind and see which routes of action were blocked. These she closed down and the remaining

113

paths connected quickly: she must walk to Tim's for help. She could carry Vi on her back, and Daisy in her arms, and Maggs would have to walk beside her. All the way. But Tim didn't have a car. And all he could give them was water. And she'd already collected water. What she needed was a doctor. Like her husband. A man who used to talk to her, every single day, about whatever she was thinking.

She dialed his number and let the phone ring fourteen times, hung up and dialed again. She did this ten times in a row. Then she hung up the phone, stepped away, and he called her back.

"Honestly? You sound insane and you're really frightening me, Cass. And there's not a lot I can do from here," Nathaniel said. Cass was holding the phone extended to the furthest reach of its cord, in the nook of her shoulder, and she was rifling through the trash can in the kitchen, looking for the brown bottle that Maggs had described, to find out what was in it. She felt insane. She felt wild. Wildly flailing.

"Anything," she enunciated, "anything could be in our children's systems now. It could be damaging their organs right now. What if they never wake up the same again?"

"Cassandra. Cassandra. Listen to yourself."

"Why aren't you here? You could have gone to collect the water. What if she's given them something that's damaged them? Their cognitive functions?"

"Listen to yourself."

"I am. I am. I am. Please come now. I can't do this." Said in a desperate way, when it felt too late.

"Cass, I can't. Look, it's a positive thing that you've gone to Mom's. I'm glad you're there. I know how she is. Hard work. But she would never harm those children."

"She left them on their own." It was coming out in a wail. "She gave them something to make them sleep and she left them on their own."

"There will be a really good reason for this."

"Yes. There will be. Because nothing is ever her fault. Even if she killed them, it wouldn't be her fault."

She felt him wince, far away.

She pressed the tip of her nose into the palm of her hand and scrunched her eyes tight. Then she said, "I'm sorry. I'm scared. She drugged them and there's a bad noise."

114

"What? Noise? Coming from the children?"

"No. It's outside. I only just ... But it's been going on the whole ... Stay on the phone, don't go anywhere."

He started to speak urgently, but the receiver was on its side on the hall table.

It was too dark out to see. The noise was coming from the long-grassed back field. It was a pining song. There was movement over there. She approached it cautiously. She had a sense of what she was walking toward as she got closer: she thought it was the dogs. But they had something with them. Something that they were tugging at. It was a large, knotted, limp mass.

Removing herself as she walked forward, she pictured the phone on its side back in the hall. One of the darkening green baby spiders above Eden's front door puffed itself up and died. There was a clock that ticked loudly. The unlit candles on the window ledge. Spots of their colorful wax on the floor. When this was over, she told herself, she'd pick that wax from the floor because someone had to, at some point, they couldn't let it pool like that on the flagstones forever. It would look mad. The children.

And in the long grass, with the owl's hoot, and the burnt-wood smell, evocative, carried on the air from fires coming closer, and the insects at her ankles, and walking toward the dogs, desperate, was Cass. Her foot landed over a baby frog, but her high arch sheltered it with a grand sweep of roof, and she did not crush it.

"It's their leads," she said with relief, to the baby frogs, the owl, the trees, her husband, who was never there, and yet constantly.

The dogs were all tied together, to a tree at the back of the field. Their pained whimpering turned to hopeful barks when they saw her. They had tangled their leads up with playful complexity, and had pulled the knots too tight with their exertions; this had created a body-like mass of rope. Cass released each animal at its collar, and began walking back to the house with the grateful dogs running ahead and then beside her. They were licking her bare legs and toes and snuffling for baby frogs.

She was about to break into a run, but instead she was surprised to feel her body crouching down onto the ground, into a ball. What if the worst was happening? Who could answer her that question? Now. Please. Fuck. Please. She did not know if she was suffering from premonitions, or the extravagant machinations of fear. What was instinct? She looked up at the building ahead of her. She was searching its windows for movement. For something real to represent her dread. Something that Nathaniel would believe in, could be convinced of. From where she crouched, the dark glass of Eden's rooms reflected the stars. What's the mirror image of a wish? A curse?

*

She picked up the phone again in the hallway and explained quickly what she'd found. "The dogs could have died of thirst," she said. "I've given them some water. I don't think they were in shade all day."

Nathaniel was very quiet at his end.

Eventually he spoke. He was sullen. "Do you really have enough water for the dogs? Maybe they were tied up to spare the water."

Cass grew phenomenally still.

"I feel like someone's put a curse on me," she said at last. "Someone's doing voodoo."

When he spoke next it was as if he'd come to stand beside her: she felt the brush on her arm, the shimmer, the opening up in the fabric of the night, the vortex that was him.

"No one is doing anything to you, Cass."

This was the loneliest she had ever felt.

She said, in her most normal voice, "Can you come now? I can't do this on my own any more. Please come home. Meet us here, and we'll find somewhere to go."

He didn't say a thing.

"The fires are spreading. I think we need to go north," she said.

There was a long pause.

"I'm not sure you get it," she said.

"Cass, you've had a very hard day." He was speaking to her like she was a patient. "Go to bed."

"I'm not going to bed," she said. "I'm too worried about the children. I've got to go."

She hung up.

22

For the rest of the night, she kept waking Daisy to check it was possible. She paced the room with Daisy's little breath in her ear, and promised the child things, both big and small.

Cass did not sleep. She wanted the children to drink as much water as they could. To flush out their systems. Even Maggs.

Even Maggs, who'd taken none of Eden's medicine; whose refusal to respect authority would get her in trouble and save her, always. Cass marveled at Maggs's face, which looked defiant, even in sleep. Her spirit of refusal was settled into the taut plane of her upper lip. It was a beautiful defiance: a defiance that Cass hoped would lead her daughter to forsake conditional protection. Cass promised that she would loathe and seethe at anyone who tried to take an ounce of Maggs's defiance away. And how they would try: *You have to go along with what I need you to do, sweetheart*, they would say, *or else I will tell everyone you are unkind. And then you will not belong.* She hoped that every manager, every weak man, every strict lady, rule-obsessed, easily horrified, every judgmental fool, she hoped that all these people would hate her daughter for her continued, happy defiance. *If the world will not change, then please may it always disapprove of Maggs*, Cass prayed.

Time and again, throughout the night, Cass held her children up in a sitting position and put the glass to their lips. Once more, Vi clasped it in two hands and gulped. But after that Cass only succeeded in dripping the liquid onto and around his chin. The baby would put her mouth on Cass's breast and automatically begin to latch, but then she'd realize she was full and asleep, and release and stop.

Cass left them for short spells and went looking for evidence of the medicine they'd had. In Eden's bathroom there were so many things.

She stood at the kitchen door, and watched the forest for a sign of morning. She breathed with the forest until the sky started turning white and the birdsong struck up again a chorus. And the body of night drained out.

"Mom?" It was Vi, behind her, the early light cast in the shape of windows across the floor. Glass still shattered from the broken pane. "Are you OK?" asked Vi. "Your foot is bleeding. And your arm."

Other mothers would not have let any of this happen, she thought.

She held him and realized he was OK. And realized, too, that it was necessary to find somewhere safer than here. And perhaps it was also necessary to find someone safer than her.

23

Trying to flush the children's systems of whatever Eden had given them had used up a lot of water. They would have to make another trip to Tim's. They would go all together. It would take all day. Tim would have to give the children some food and help her walk them back. He'd have to show himself this time. She called ahead, using the number on the list by the phone. No answer. Nonetheless.

They were setting off in the early afternoon, when the sun was past its peak and the day was certain. They had reached the third gate, and were slowly beginning to have fun spotting the recently rewilded geese, when they heard music. It was loud and moving, coming toward them. The children looked to Cass with their eyes all huge and impressed.

Bea's white car swung around the bend, blaring. Bea looked grim behind the wheel. Eden in the passenger seat, however, was dancing. She made an exaggerated O with her face in delight at seeing them, and reached out for them through the window.

"There you are! There you are!" she sang.

Bea lunged forward to turn down the music, apparently grateful for the excuse.

"We've done a food run!" Eden shouted. "Where are you going?"

"More water," said Vi after a while, because Cass was silent.

"No! We've got tons in the trunk. Hop in."

Cass said quietly, definitively, "No." It went unheard in the car so Vi spoke up again: "We'll walk back. We'll meet you there."

"Well, run ahead and get the next gate for us, Vi, there's a good boy. I'm not doing another of those damn . . ." Bea drove on so Eden's voice and the music trailed away.

They all gathered by the broken kitchen door, where Bea made the children sit in a row and handed the older two buns with bright white icing. Eden said she was boiling water to soften carrot sticks for Daisy to try. She didn't mention the shattered pane. She stepped over the glass carefully, moving closer to her daughter-in-law—who stood, adrenaline searing through her, ready to attack, or run, or bite, or scream. Eden handed Cass a box, raspberry red, swirled with gold.

"Open it!" she urged.

But Cass stood there, apparently struck dumb, so Eden whipped the lid off for her, with a flourish.

A bar of chocolate stuck out the top, at least three soaps, an expensive-looking shampoo, more things, buried.

"Treats!" said Eden.

"What medicine did you give them?"

"Pardon?"

"What medicine?"

"What? What medicine? I don't know about any medicine. I didn't give them any medicine," she stage-whispered hurriedly. Eden was all of a sudden like a confused child in the face of injustice, as if she might fumble her words and be prone to tears.

"They said"—Cass also kept her voice low—"that you did."

"Cod liver! Cod liver oil. Because it's hydrating. It's not bad for them. I thought, for my peace of mind, just one top-up of liquid before I left. I couldn't bear to leave them so thirsty. I could not bring myself to do that." Eden's emphasis was on the "I." "I didn't want to leave them," she continued, conspiratorially. "But I didn't know what else to do. Bea doesn't offer to take me often. She was going to the good place. It's very far away."

"How could it be so far it took all night? You and Bea should have waited for me to come back!"

"The fires!" It sounded very much as though Eden was making it up as she went along. "The fires! They're closer." Her dramatic emphasis, her trembling pool-like eyes. "My darling, they're very close. We dashed so we could get back before they got to the main road. To be completely honest, I wasn't sure we'd make it back." Then she said, "But it was exciting!" and Cass, speaking simultaneously, said, "You shouldn't have left them . . . You could have waited."

Eden was visibly upset by Cass's directness. "We looked for you, anyway." She was barely coating her switch to irritation. "We drove all that road looking for you. It was a waste of time. You must have gone the wrong way! You weren't even on the right road! And I wasn't worried about the children because I knew you'd be back very soon. And I couldn't take them with me. Not Daisy, especially. I can't feed her, can I?" She slapped her own bosom. "Imagine that! No, don't imagine that. You need to sit down. You don't look well." Aggressive. "Sit here. Now. Smell. These. Soaps."

Eden held the raspberry box under Cass's nose. The soaps were wrapped in paper marked "The Three Kings" and they smelled of treasure.

"The dogs were dying," Cass said.

"But I had to choose, Cassandra." Eden's tone was resolute now, she'd had enough of the conciliatory stuff. "I couldn't leave the dogs in here, thirsty. You hear awful stories. They are wild animals, you know, they can turn on the young, especially if they're not genetically related."

"I couldn't get in." Cass's teeth were jammed together as soon as she said this.

"I left the key in the front door for you!" Now angry. "Oh God, you haven't gone and lost another key, have you? Wow! That's beyond"— she turned to Maggs and changed her tone—"beyond belief, I say!"

Bea had unpacked apples, carrots, bags of dried pulses, sugar, sultanas, fresh herbs, salad, bread, flour, salt, milk. "I think it's better if I do the cooking now," said Eden, beaming at Bea. "Yes. I'm taking my kitchen back!" She bent her knees and punched the air in triumph. Bea did a peculiar little bob in response, and smiled toothily.

"See," he said later. Returning her call. His voice bleaching her of all else. "You're safe. The children were fine. They were tired and a bit thirsty."

She didn't say anything back. She was lying on Eden's sofa, Eden's old-fashioned telephone in her hand. The children were in bed. Daisy had taken her first meal, mashed-up carrots and boiled apples, which meant that she'd rely on Cass less. Eden had taught Maggs how to write "M." Eden had led Cass here, to the blankets on the sofa, made her lie down, placed cushions under her feet, tea on the floor within reach, a newspaper on her stomach, a kiss on her forehead. Eden smelled bad.

"I'm so worried about you," Nathaniel said. "Who is this Tim guy anyway?"

"I assumed you knew him."

"I've never heard of him."

He told her that he missed her, he told her that they'd talk about the future when she'd rested, and that he had to go. She said goodbye, hung up, and gazed about the room.

She felt like a starlet on the embroidered cushion, and a monster, and a freak when she thought of herself walking the road in that dress, and the loneliness was a pressure from the outside forcing itself so strongly on one particular region of her mind, forcing so hard that it physically hurt.

Later, from the phone in the hallway, she called Ally, who listened while Cass went careening through her troubles (in whispers, in case Eden heard her). Then Ally said, "Listen. Listen to me." Cass loved how Ally said that "lissst" sound. "You can't come back here."

"But . . ."

"The sky has been pure orange for three days, baby girl. Do you hear me when I tell you that? Huh? Do you understand? You cannot come back, Cassie love. It's awful. There is no protection. There has been more Gaia. There will be more. The air's so bad. It smells of burning hair even from our beds. We've gone out thirty minutes a day this week. That's it. It's over. This place is over. It's not safe."

"Anywhere would feel safer than here."

"That's not true. You're suffering. We're all suffering. But you are safe."

"I would feel safer if Nathaniel was here." The two candles were alight by the front door. Cass let her eyes rest on the shape of heat around one of the flames. It distorted everything. Nathaniel was shimmering to her, he was shape-shifting things. "Is he not coming back because he doesn't want to?" she asked Ally.

"Is this the first time you ever thought that?"

"I guess. When he left . . . I'm sure he was so in love with me . . . and the children. That can't change."

"OK."

"I think he needed something really frightening in his life. You know? Baptism by fire."

"What do you mean?"

She meant exactly what she'd said: that she believed he'd gone because he needed a shock and a purging, a period alone and in service. It was a new theory of hers, fast developing. He carried in him—didn't he?—guilt over the deaths of his first two wives. He had thought he could protect them—his first two beloveds—with his mere presence, the fact of his existence, but, of course, he could not. (Eden had led him to believe too much, perhaps, that his mere existence carried miracles. It didn't.)

He needed to be purged of the guilt he carried around; and Cass needed for him to be purged of it, and the children did. And the only place he could think of to go and release the unpleasantness he felt for himself was in some hellhole of fiery war, among men. He would release his shadowy feelings far away from his family.

There was not enough energy within her to explain all this to Ally over the phone. Unless she could speak to Ally in person, their shared understanding would inevitably dilute.

Cass said, "I think he minimizes any problems that come up because he doesn't want to admit to himself that he can't help from there."

"OK."

Yes, OK, Cass thought. "I think he'll be making plans to get back now."

As they finished their conversation, Cass stretched the phone cord to the two candles by the door. Her toes touched the blobs of wax that had hardened on the floor. She licked her thumb and finger and brought them down on one of the wicks to extinguish it. Her fingertips came away inked a little black in cindered wick. She tried to trace a C with the cinder on the window ledge. It didn't really work.

24

August. Fires were closer, the horizon was mist, the days sizzled out. The water came back on again. Cass found a drawer of things that she and Nathaniel had left behind on previous visits. She pulled out his old T-shirt and the smell of him was almost detectable on it. She inhaled it, seeking a trace, a trance. She found an old mascara, the brand she used to like. And a bikini top. A travel itinerary they'd printed out. The key card to the hotel room they'd stayed in, beside the tropical sea. A white denim dress. Everything was big on her. Meanwhile, the children's bellies got rounder. Maggs poured make-believe tea and ate real pie. There was good food again. Daisy turned one. She'd been once around the sun. Cass imagined the colorful scenes she wished to create to mark the occasion. Eden organized a tea party for them. There was an enormous to-do over the acquiring of cake ingredients. The colors were muted. Eden did all the cooking, complained about it endlessly, and refused all offers of help. Structures were slowly being put in place so that Cass did not have to think. She could also elect not to eat. There was nowhere to go from here. She was suspended, waiting for Nathaniel, who hadn't said he wasn't coming. Her mind could be clouded all day. No logistics required. The kids painted her skin in the garden. "You'll need a lot of paint to do Mommy," Eden said.

One day, Cass put on her bikini. One day, she was holding Daisy, and she dropped a platter of roasted vegetables on the floor. Eden didn't react. But there was an air change. By the end of that day, everyone had cried for reasons unrelated to the spilt tray of food but also, seemingly, not.

Eden became more herself. Eden and Maggs grew close. Cass melted into the walls and found memories of her own mother in there. Her days were taken up with reliving a time when her hand was small and fitted within a woman's hand. It was horrible and equally riveting. Cass felt disgusted. Everyone needed her less. Eden and Bea took the children for certain portions of the day. Bea spoke to the children in exactly the same way that she spoke to the dogs, which was not necessarily nasty, but was detached, as if protecting herself from something they might do or say to her. Cass's telephone conversations with Nathaniel picked up, and fell into a rhythm, coming from an autopilot heart.

August, still. The water ran dry again. This time, to no fanfare.

Eden got off the phone. "Bea's not answering. But he's in. Go now. As you are."

Cass was wearing her bikini top, her tiny shorts, with her legs brightly painted in green and red by Maggs. The children seemed to be happy. They only fought when they were with her. She walked to Tim's with little demons swirling her head. She was having nasty conversations with her mother, taking both roles.

Wildfire smoke was tracing in the air again. It added to the creeps she got as she approached Tim's. This time, she did not suppose he was watching her: she knew it. She could feel his gaze. It forced itself upon her pattern, it was insidious. It was not unpleasant. It lit up all her tender parts in bright shame.

She went straight to the spot where the water had been the last time, and found a piece of paper again—this time carrying her full name— under the big rock. "CASSANDRA MAY MAGUREN," it said. Eden must have shared this information with him over the phone. It felt as if he was showing Cass's name to her to make her see the ridiculousness of it. No less than seven overblown syllables. She felt his joke: *Look at all those pretty letters hoisted together, to signify something so unimportant and meaningless.*

She had carried the water quite far from Tim's bungalow when she heard his door slam shut. He must have come outside to watch her away. And then he went back in, noisily. She hadn't so much as attempted to say hello to him this time. It occurred to her that this might have upset him. It was easy for her to forget how rude she could be when her default was anger.

She found herself thinking about him for the rest of the day. What did he do next—after he saw her? Did he pour himself a glass of water? Did he take it in large gulps? He took up residence in her head.

Two days later, because Daisy had required an emergency bath, Cass returned to Tim's again. "And wear proper clothes this time, please, Cassandra," Eden sang. "The upper rail on the right is all for you. You should be able to reach it, I imagine."

Cass was relieved to see pants folded over the hangers in Eden's cedar closet. Why couldn't these have been made available to her before? Practical, comfortable. But then her hand brushed a green dress and she took this down from the rail because it felt soft to her sun-peeled skin. It was fancy and full. A bodice, with a cocktail skirt. Eden was thrown off course when Cass walked down the stairs wearing it.

"You look so pretty," one of the children said.

The dress aided Cass in concocting a fantasy that lasted the whole journey to Tim's, in which she was going to a party where Nathaniel would meet her. It occurred to her that she was having an imaginary relationship with someone who was only her husband in name.

She was sweating through the top of the dress. She would ruin it. She pulled her arms out of it and let the bodice hang down, walking bare-breasted for a while. At Tim's, covered up again, she knocked, she went inside, she looked for him; he wasn't there.

There was a dream. There was a dream Cass had once. And it was not this.

*

"Tim really likes you," said Eden one evening.

"We haven't met."

"Yes," said Eden, like she was talking to a mad person, "you have."

"No. We have not met. We have not exchanged any words."

"There's more to meeting people than small talk, Cassandra."

"Eden, I don't know what he looks like."

"I told you, he is very attractive. He's working very hard at the moment. He's an artist, Cassandra. Or, you know, artist adjacent. Something."

Cass got a fever and went to bed for four days. That's when she really had to release the children. She couldn't do a single thing for them. She had read somewhere that, when a mother is ill, someone needs to demonstrate to her that the children will be cared for, or else she will be ill forever. And they were cared for. Daisy was brought to her for feeds. But fewer than usual. Somehow water was acquired without her participation. One morning she came to, and found Eden sitting on the end of her bed expertly making Daisy giggle. Then Eden said, "Bea thinks that illness is a sign your soul and personality are not in alignment."

"I think I'm dehydrated."

"No. That's not it."

Maggs had an allergic reaction to something in the forest and her hand swelled up. They plunged it in off milk. Telephone calls were made for antihistamine. She sat in the crook of Cass's legs and wailed. Cass couldn't do anything but hold the child and pray that this would be over soon. The room swung about.

In her fever dreams, Cass entered Tim's once more. Its hum of bad wiring was exaggerated. The clearing it sat in was a crop circle. It all buzzed. Tim was there, visible to her, although he was blurred. He was in the dark, sitting at the table, painting with his eyes: wherever his eyes traveled, lines appeared there and stayed. He looked from the wine glass to the laptop, and an orange line was drawn between the two things, suspended in the air. And when his gaze swept from the center of Cass's forehead down her sternum to her pelvis, and then, swoosh, down the inner line of her leg, she felt the paint of his gaze land on her wet. She stepped back and the orange paint line hung in the air before her and she considered it. It was shaped like half a wishbone. Each line Tim made with his gaze had a different color. The colors did not mix but stacked on top of each other, layers and layers over every single place. Paint collected and drooled where he stared. The colors were ruling her. Then "Tim" became, actually, Nathaniel, and while he spoke and Cass replied in lines that had very little to do with what he had just said, she leaned on the kitchen counter and smoked a cigarette. She felt closer to youth than in forever. They were on the porch; Nathaniel put his arms around her and encompassed her completely so there was no light between them. She allowed her whole self to collapse into him, thinking, *I could stay here forever.* He put his lips on the crown of her head, and kissed it as though it were the relic and he the pilgrim. And they stayed there for too long, swaying in the breeze they were jointly imagining. Seeing if, and how much further, and deeper, she could relax. But, when she looked up, she perceived the real Nathaniel approaching from across the bright circular plain toward them. She had been caught in an embrace with a fake. She felt guilt for having been so close to the fake Nathaniel, who might actually have been Tim all along. When the real Nathaniel reached her, he vomited canary-yellow paint at her feet, like an offering. He was very unwell. She threw a duvet over his back and led him inside. Daisy woke her.

Cass did not enjoy dreams anymore, but in this one she had felt important. This feeling kept her high for a little while. She stayed with it, and it moved her away from the children.

25

"I'll take Daisy with me," she said one day, ready to go to Tim's. She was wearing the ironed blouse and pencil skirt that Eden had left hanging for her on the upper-right rail—because it seemed to make sense that day to please Eden as much as humanly possible. When Cass wasn't pleasing, she felt the children were fully subjected to Eden's moods.

Cass's confidence with the children was thinning out. She had started to wonder, late at night, whether she hadn't stepped into their lives with too much certainty. Had it been a grandiose act on her part? But she was excited to make the trip, because she'd resolutely promised Daisy an adventure. Just the two of them. She was holding her exhilaration outward, ready to take her baby.

"I'll take Daisy with me," she said again to Eden, who hadn't seemed to hear her the first time.

Eden did not reply with an easy phrase like "Are you sure?" or "Don't be silly, honey." Instead she firmly and quite horribly yelped, "No." And she held Cass's baby tightly to her own perfume-misted chest.

Cass shifted her weight backward. "I promised her."

"She's barely turned one. She doesn't understand promises. She doesn't understand you." Eden was speaking aggressively. Cass must have been winding her up all morning, unaware.

Cass would have liked to cry. Instead she helped herself out in a better way, by placating Eden.

"You're right," said Cass. "Sorry. It will be far too hot for her. We'll do something else, later."

"How were you going to carry her all that way?"

Cass had not been sleeping. Eden was right. It was a mad idea. "I'll say goodbye to Vi and Maggs," she said.

"What is all this? What is wrong with you?" Eden's face had that bewildered look. Daisy's was a blank.

"Nothing."

"Bea's taken them out to the woods."

"Who? Bea's here? In her car?"

"No." Eden was extremely irritated. "Her car's broken. I told you that. That's why you have to go. You should have left by now."

Cass watched her own feet on each step down the spiraling staircase from Eden's bedroom, wondering if she'd fall. Burning into her mind: the sensation of how the wooden stair felt against the palms of her feet. Palms of her feet? Soles. Down the purple corridor she went, back through to the kitchen, slipping on her plastic clogs, stepping outside. *I want my baby*, she felt all the way. But she couldn't actualize anything. She elected to go first to the edge of the woods, to find Vi and Maggs and check they were OK before she left for Tim's. But when she reached the place where the trees formed an edge, she couldn't hear them. They must have gone quite far in, she reckoned, and it was late, and she wanted to be back before their bedtime, so she had better go.

As she walked away from the forest, a deep, angelic cloud passed overhead; stormy and lavender. It caused a fault in the usual relationship between the sky and the dark glass of Eden's quarters. And under the cloud's shade, from the particular place where she stood, Cass was able to see, ghostly, through the reflective sheen.

There was Bea, inside, on Eden's mezzanine, standing in full uniform, part of a tableau, holding Daisy dispassionately. On either side of her were Vi and Maggs. They looked like a strong group together. They were all looking directly at Cass. Staring at her.

What did they see? Whom did they see?

Someone retching with fear. In elegant clothing.

Cass left. She came back with water.

That night, Eden swung open Cass's bedroom door and stood on the threshold. "He knows what you're up to."

"What?"

"He knows what you're doing, and it's got to stop."

"I really don't know. What are you talking about?"

*

130

"Are you still there?"

"Yes," Nathaniel said.

"How long will this go on for?"

He didn't reply.

"When can I see you?"

"I don't know, Cass. Sometimes I think that this is it now."

"What do you mean? We can't stay like this forever."

He did not reply.

Daisy was practicing walking up and down the hall.

"I can't live here forever," said Cass. He stayed silent. She went on, "Vi has to go back to school. The girls have to grow up somewhere. We need to be together again. Decide where we're going to live. But I can't live here."

"You might want to do something about that bit."

"About which bit?"

"Their education. Maybe you teach them yourself? That will give you something to do."

*

There was a bang. Followed by a pause. Then the sound of crying. Cass ran to where she'd left the children in the bathroom for "two seconds" while she grabbed another towel from her room.

Maggs had slipped over in the shampoo that Daisy had poured all over the floor. Maggs was lying stunned on her back, letting out long moans. Daisy had the shampoo bottle in her hand, and shampoo in her mouth. The horrible taste of it was beginning to reach her and she was on the verge of screaming. Vi was ignoring them. He was standing on the rim of the bathtub in order to lean out of an open window as far as he could. As he leaned, a little pot holding a nondescript plant fell from the windowsill and Cass heard it explode onto the paving stones below. She shouted his name three times in quick succession to bring him away from the window. It startled him. She wished to be back in Ally's garden having just smashed the aloe pot.

"Get inside! What the hell are you doing?"

All she did was disaster limitation.

*

September.

"Come on," he said. "You have to talk to me." Then Nathaniel took a pause. These silences were frigid now. "Is this how it feels to be alone?" he asked. "Because this feels awful."

"This is how I feel every single day." Her tears were leaking on everything, and the watermarks she left were revealing the grain of the paper behind his designs.

"Tell me about the children," he said.

She said nothing. Let the line go dead. He didn't call back. She thought he would. Because they always saved things between them. All the little drawings and designs. They always collected them up when one of them had thrown them down. She'd pass him her favorite pen, so he could redraw over the lines. Always.

*

As she was passing Eden the baby, Eden said: "There's a stain! There, look. Your top is stained. Wait here."

Cass waited, completely still.

Eden came back with Daisy and yet another white shirt. This one had small, delicate buttons and something complex at the wrist. Daisy watched her mother take it.

Cass turned her back to remove the stained shirt and put on the new one. Did it up. Said bye.

The body is heavy when the spirit has left it. But Eden, in contrast, seemed so happy at last. So light and moving. So full and central. *Maybe*, thought Cass, *my soul feels more comfortable in Eden's body. Maybe that's where it's gone.*

"It feels like, above all things, we must give ourselves to Eden."

"Cass," Nathaniel said on the phone, "I am so sorry." But he wouldn't do anything about the things he was sorry for. At night she worried that he wanted to come back, take the children from her and start again with someone else. Probably, the most decent thing she could ever do in her life would be to let him.

*

Downstairs, Eden was saying to Maggs, "Cass's wedding dress was cream."

132

"It was white," Cass said, entering.

"No, it was a deep cream."

"It was white."

"It was not, Cassandra." Eden said this furiously, as if all Cass had ever done was lie, and for once, having borne enough, Eden was correcting her. The children looked up from their coloring, and looked wearily at Cass.

Above all things, when Eden walked into the room, Eden became the center.

Cass was wearing the mascara she'd found.

"What have you got on your eyelids?" Eden said, unhappily.

"Nothing."

"Yes, you have! What makeup have you got on your eyelids?"

"No makeup."

"What color, I mean."

"Just mascara."

"Yes, I can see the mascara. I'm not an idiot. I'm not talking about there"—she poked her finger toward Cass's eyes—"I'm talking about *there*." She jabbed her fingernail right into Cass's eyelid. And for the rest of her life Cass would be able to call up the feel of that digging line of nail on her lid.

"I've got no makeup there," she said.

With nothing left to resort to, Eden stuck her thumb in her mouth for wetness, pulled it out with a small pop and dragged it hard over Cass's eyelid. Then she inspected her thumb for traces of color.

"It's just my eyes," said Cass.

*

Tim's door looked different. It didn't usually sit like that in its frame. Cass touched it, and realized it was locked. That was the first time. An entire pack of cigarettes lay open on the porch table. One had been turned upside down in the pack, one was missing, the foil still in. She understood these to be a gift and took them as such, but there was no lighter. She went around to the back, where there was often a lighter left on the flaking sill.

All this in the hot mistiness of nearing forest flame.

"Was Tim in?" asked Eden when Cass got back.

"I don't think so."

"No. He had to go and see his lady friend in town. I'm sorry."

That night was the first in Cass's three years as a mother when, for a full six hours, no child stirred. And yet, and of course, Cass didn't sleep at all. She stayed outside, smoking cigarette after cigarette from the pack Tim had left for her. There was nowhere to go. Even if the piece-of-shit car could be accessed. There was nowhere she could think of to take it.

She was wretched and burning with frustration. And she was confused. For hadn't the day begun well? Eden had been in a pleasant mood. She had called up to Cass, first thing that morning, "The internet's on, darling. Come." Cass had been invited to sit in Eden's chair, with Eden's laptop; Eden had brought her a cup of coffee and smoothed down her hair.

The news online that morning had been thinner than it used to be. The titles were very limited. Cass imagined that the Black Box was propping up the few remaining outlets and influencing their agenda. One slightly more reputable news source carried warning banners over nearly every story, and there were child locks on the browser, which prevented Cass from clicking away the shielding boxes and the pixelation. She had to read the vanilla version of things, but that was bad enough: August had emboldened the fires. The Midlands Fire in particular was making unpredicted gains. There was now a possibility, where there hadn't been before, that it might merge with The Moorland and Heathland Fires.

Cass clicked on a map to enlarge it. The current breaches of The Midlands Fire were marked in red, and the forecast spread was in orange. The orange reached very close to Eden's, but didn't encompass it. How close was too close? Cass queried the map's accuracy. Clicked off and looked for stories about The City. She learned that fires were being doused in the parks there every day, and the air quality demanded an undignified lifestyle. The skies in The City were mustard seed. The summer had turned vast tracts of surrounding land into a tinderbox. The City had its own new color code: on orange days you were to avoid strenuous outdoor activity; on red days you were advised to limit any time spent outside to an hour; on Exceptional Danger Days you should stay inside. On the homepage there was a new running tally of estimated deaths by pollution (100,367), deaths by fire (1,058), and, now, Gaia deaths (3,972) for the nation, for that year, so far. But if this count was sanctioned by the Black Box to appear on one of its approved outlets, then she suspected it vastly underestimated the true numbers.

There had apparently been five more Gaia attacks since Cass had left The City. She read of a forming practice, one of "gardening": once the bodies had been cleared after a Gaia attack, groups of Gaias would come along in the night to plant gardens at the scene. In the dark, saplings were dug in between the rubble, and swings, and blood. Financial donations to the movement were beginning, quietly, to accrue, allowing the night-time plantings to become increasingly sophisticated. Grass had been laid. After the most recent attack, in a concrete playground, trees in giant containers had been lifted off trucks, and placed into the scene. The public seemed more agitated to stop this planting than the deaths themselves, because these beautiful manifesting gardens were not tributes to the victims. This lush overgrowth was a reclamation; to show that Mother Earth had won, against the people. Cass read an opinion piece about how bringing flowers to a funeral was no longer acceptable, in light of Gaia. The symbolism surrounding death was changing.

A different news source reported the war dead. An opinion piece in the sidebar, headlined "Death By Laziness," ranted at the jobless:

... who have taken an unfortunate spate of national crises as an excuse to give up. "Life is too hard!" they cry. "What about the social contract?" they demand, while contributing precisely nothing to society. These young men and women cry out for the benefits afforded to previous generations, without understanding that work, any work, is the only solution. It is the sad truth that their grandparents would be ashamed of them. Not long ago people were too embarrassed to live on handouts and live in such unkept conditions as our feeble youth today.

The thinker behind the piece was lazy, but Cass had grown in laziness too. She knew in her bones that there had to be a baseline of nurture within society for it to function. She knew that when there was no safety net, ideation became violent and suicidal. But she did not know where to go with this train of thought anymore. She had lost any ability for robustness of argument. Her temples ached and pulsed from

135

the exertion of simply being in the heat, in the house. Even if there were a way to leave and a place to go, Cass was not sure her brain would spot it. She felt drugged. Scrolling on, there were several stories about the illegal border wall which had risen in the north to keep the southern climate migrants out—but these stories, too, were thin. There was one "exclusive" about how the wall had been constructed, which did not investigate its funding nor cite a single source. Another story "revealed" how the border was run day to day, and gave thumbnail profiles of the people who'd been turned away. It did not voice any condemnation of the wall. Which was strange. There was no word anywhere, nor action promised, from the Black Box on this unauthorized intrusion of a wall across the nation. Cass clicked on a healthy-looking face, which led her, via an article, to a video of a makeup tutorial that was as old as Vi. She watched it, transfixed by the products because they looked so edible; they were made to look like that on purpose, perhaps. Feeling sick, she closed the laptop and went to change. Then she'd put on the mascara, which had got Eden all worked up and led to the nail on the eyelid.

Cass, outside that night—after the internet, the fingernail on the eyelid, Tim's locked door—as the children slept through for the first time. She sent smoke from Tim's cigarettes out of her nostrils. After a while, a troupe of small, late moths was there to mirror the dance of the cigarette smoke against the night sky, which was vivid and had a density to it given by the nearing wildfire. The proximity. She remembered: being in a foreign city, her friend walking ahead of her, leading her somewhere, smoking like her, on a beautiful morning; she remembered, in a different foreign city, seeing other friends across the street—they hadn't spotted her yet, they looked so beautiful. It wasn't much, when you put each memory into words. But she had witnessed such beauty, such beauty that it made her feel sometimes she had seen enough. Cass felt, herself, like leaving. She felt herself in between.

There was a sound from the kitchen and she reflexively hid the cigarette, in case it was one of her children wandering about.

Instead, Bea's face appeared around the door, her small white nose noticeable first, followed by the rest of her.

They'd never really been left alone together before. It was an unpleasant proposition, just then.

136

"Can smell that a mile off," Bea said, nodding at the cigarette. Then she added, "Yes, I'll join you," as if she'd been invited.

Bea launched forward and came to rest against the rough exterior wall, beside Cass. She was copying, checking with her eyes to see if she was doing it right. Cass left the wall and moved away, using the cigarette smoke as a plausible excuse to purposefully stand beyond Bea's reach.

"There was poachers in these woods once, you know," Bea said. "It's an art form, actually, poaching. It was all artists around these parts. Used to be like that." Her features settled for a moment in fondness. A prettiness. "Not artists in the modern way that they have now. I mean artists in the proper way. Real. Every moment of their lives, they're an artist. Makes a cup of tea, here, look, that's beautiful. Sweeps the floor, say. If they were sweeping the floor of their studio, or the floor of their kitchen. The same. Art. That's what it was around here."

It was a surprise, how the words were flying from Bea's mouth, as if she'd been saving them up to be released together. Bea was speaking not with speed, necessarily, but with force. The unexpectedness of it was quite frightening.

"Is that what Tim's like? An artist?"

Bea expelled air in an exaggerated puff through the side of her mouth.

"Oh no. No! Not at all is that like Tim . . . So, tell me." Bea nodded her nose up and down in a gesture to invite Cass closer. "Tell me. Did you get on the computer, on-the-computer, on the thingy, this morning? Seen the news?"

"Yes."

"You seen those fires are all heading up this way? There's a little mappy online. It's interactive. Don't know if you saw—if you saw that?"

"I did."

"Good." Bea sucked the night air in and was satisfied. "Still, it's been nice having you here. Not like when Arthur was here. With that girl of his. That girl! That was all hell. Eden was very unhappy." She shook her head in the knowledge that Eden's unhappiness was the very worst thing that could befall them. "That girl of Arthur's had no . . . What's her name? Jem."

"Jem," Cass echoed closely.

"That's it," Bea said. "Jem. She couldn't . . . keep herself. Still, it's nice where they are now. I'm happy about that. It's safest there."

"Where are they now?"

"You've really helped Eden out, you know that? You've done Eden a real . . . a real service, here. I am grateful. We're on a more even kneel now—keel now than we were before."

Cass let the cigarette butt fall to the ground and fiddled with the packet for another.

"Yes. It's been nice having you," Bea reiterated. "Sad to see you go."

Cass lit the next cigarette, felt the slow sparkle along her nerves. She understood the smoking as the small introduction of alarming compounds into her system, followed by a recovery: roughly ten reminders per cigarette that recovery was still possible.

"You know," Bea continued, "Eden was devastated when he stopped calling on her. I tell you, she was devastated. They were quite a thing. Quite the conversationalists! Tim got really . . . under her skin. But then Jem! Arthur!"

"I don't understand."

"Oh, I stay clear of it all. Very clear. You know me." Bea stopped to touch and then to scratch the back of her head. "They're not bad people," she continued. She was sincere, a sudden genuine loveliness at the thought of them softening off her speech.

Something about that sincerity made Cass feel a crack within her; she could not tell why.

"Who? Who are not bad people?"

"Why, Jem and Arthur." Bea's eyes were pleading to be met in a meaningful way. "Now, I know Arthur's not like your Nathaniel. Not golden, like Nathaniel. Obviously."

Oh God, Cass realized; the crack was a fissure upon a much bigger broken piece.

"But I always love Arthur. I do. He upsets Eden so much. But that's because they're the same, those two, aren't they."

"I don't know."

"You're a clever girl," said Bea, "you'll work it out. It's difficult— we think we shouldn't take children into the dark. But sometimes you have to, for what's on the other side of it." She looked back out to the

138

dark horizon, as though she'd only recently acquired the wondrous ability to see it. "Oh, I feel odd," she said; her face fell. "Help me?"

"What do you need?"

"Nothing."

Cass stepped toward her, with a hand offered out.

"It's nothing," Bea said. "I feel strange sometimes. Must be the smell of Tim's horrible cigarettes."

"How do you know they're Tim's?"

"Where else you going to get those from?" Bea snapped. "Oh." She bent at the knees and slid down the wall. She sat. Her dove-gray uniform in the soil. She turned her head to the side and spat.

"Let's get you inside," Cass said quietly, understanding, fleetingly, that Bea was only having a truthful, physical reaction to the conditions of her life.

"There is a place called Eigleath." Bea spoke with a child's voice. All of Cass's nerves sparkled up alive, alarmed by a specter of terror, and went down again.

"No, Bea," Cass said gently. "No, Bea," Cass said sadly. "Not Eigleath. They sold Eigleath. Years ago." Cass spoke kindly, like a good mother.

"That's a rhyme of Eden's," said Bea. "*There is a place called Eigleath, / Can be taken by no thief.* I've been there, you know? Once, when they were youngsters. Heaven, is what I said. I told Arthur, 'That's your heaven, right there.' That's the one good thing that father did for those boys. Couldn't show his affection in normal ways. Tale as old as, isn't it? You'll need your freedom, though. I mean freedom from yourself. From all this."

She gestured vaguely at Cass's entirety, with the modicum of disgust that Cass was more familiar with.

"So." Bea took Cass's offered arm and heaved herself up. "You'll clean those nasty butts up before morning. Well, then"—and, wishing Cass "a restful night," she scowled, following her nose back inside.

26

Cass did not sleep. She lay in bed in confusion and unease. Nothing Bea had said had meaning. But the exchange had left a troubled impression on her. She could taste Eden's rule on the air. It was not clear. It was not clean air. No wonder Nathaniel wouldn't come to her here.

When the children woke the next morning, Cass carried them into her room, climbed back into bed and ignored their sleepy squabbling. She wondered if Eden or Bea would watch the children now, when Cass required it, rather than later, when Eden found it convenient.

Then she heard Eden right outside the bedroom door, saying, "I really am sick and tired of this." Cass pulled herself from the bed and went to swing her door open, to find Eden bending on the other side of it.

"What are you sick and tired of now?" asked Cass. She asked her question blandly, which brought out the violent expression in Eden's eyes. It was an expression that Cass found boring now, her boredom expressed on her face. This only escalated matters.

"Well, if you must know, I am sick and tired of picking up after you all, all the time," Eden said.

"Leave it. I'll do it."

"You won't."

"What have you picked up of ours?"

"This sock!" Eden held it up.

"And?"

"Oh, it doesn't matter."

"It does."

"No. Forget it."

"Forget what, exactly? Forget that you just said you're sick and tired of picking up after us, when all you've picked up is a single sock?"

"I am sick and tired of having to watch what I say all the time."

"I don't believe you're capable of that."

Eden pointed her outheld index finger at Cass like a sword. "Watch it, sunshine," she spat. "Mark me now, my girl, you had better watch it."

Cass slammed the door.

The children looked up at her like sad little wolves.

Vi asked if Grandma Eden liked them. Cass told him that of course Eden did. Vi asked if Cass loved Eden, to which Cass replied, "I hate her." Vi started to cry. Cass held him tightly.

"How can we make Eden like us?" he asked.

"I think we've got to stop worrying about that."

Through the open window they heard Eden's voice down in the courtyard, almost yelping in emotional pain as she was escorted into the car by Bea.

"Oh, Bea," Eden said, breaking down. "It hurts so much. I miss him so much. I cannot take this anymore. The pain. The pain is too much." Car doors were opened and then closed; the engine started quickly. Cass believed that Eden was talking about Nathaniel.

"Poor Eden," sighed Maggs.

Cass began to pick their clothes up from the floor. She resolved to tidy up, so that Eden would have less reason to be angry when she returned. But then she worried that the children would remember this sad, shouty morning, and she wanted to make it nicer. She might as well work with the sun streaming through the windows, rather than against it. She started faking cheeriness. She treated herself to some of Eden's precious coffee, then she let the children lead. She followed them wherever they wanted to go, and did whatever they wanted to do.

They built a castle with sofa cushions before leading Cass into Eden's sitting room. Cass let them. She followed them. Each step felt endless. Her thoughts were turning to her part in all of this. How she had helped create this situation with Eden. How she was un-good. She felt like she was being tried in an internal court presided over by Tim, by Nathaniel, by Eden. And she was found wanting. Each step was painful, sickening, but she smiled, and she was patient.

The children were tentative in Eden's room. Cass picked up an art book and drew Vi and Maggs onto her lap and said, "I'm sorry, I'm

141

sorry" into their ears. She gave them the task of picking their top five pictures in the book. They leafed through it together; meanwhile, Daisy pulled little things off low tables. This was making Vi anxious, but Cass smiled at him and said, "We'll tidy it up before Eden gets back. Don't worry. She won't know." Daisy picked up a crystal ball; an amethyst half-encased, still, in hard volcanic rock; an old address book full of bits of loose paper. Her new skill was dropping things on the floor without them landing on her toes. She made her way over to a collection of trinket boxes. Three silver ones formed a thin tower. Five others were stacked in a pyramid. Some were smooth metal. Some were beaten with a pattern.

Nathaniel had gone away to deal with his grief. He had found Cass and then asked her only to hold the fort a little, while he took his grief for his dead wives somewhere far away. This made sense. He was protecting her and the children from his mourning. He would come back. She had to calm down. She could not continue in this way. The facts of the story, not the wild emotion but the facts: Eden had taken her in and life was hard for Eden. Eden felt abandoned by her favorite son. Irrelevant. Unlovable. Times were unprecedented and everyone was doing the best they could. Cass's imagination had always been elaborate. She was not imprisoned in a nightmare dreamt from an old woman's gnarled glands. "No one is doing anything to you," her husband had said. He was right.

As Cass thought this, the lid to the uppermost trinket box slid off with ease under Daisy's baby fingers, revealing marbles and pills. Ah! Cass felt scolded. So there was an excellent reason for keeping the children out of Eden's rooms after all. It was not due to Eden's preciousness, but because this area was not child-proofed. This was where Eden had taken all the dangerous stuff—like pills and marbles—to keep out of the children's reach. Maybe Eden had been thinking only about the children's safety when she'd made these rooms out of bounds. And perhaps there was a just and right reason for every single thing that Eden did and said. Only Cass had not taken the care to open up the channels of communication properly and see. She shook herself gently free of Vi and Maggs and jumped up to take the pills and marbles away from Daisy.

Then there was Maggs's sweet voice saying, "Mommy, Mommy. A deer!"

Cass looked over her shoulder.

There was a deer. The deer had come right up to the dark glass. Not knowing that people were right there. It had something like bracken caught in its antlers. Its nostrils, trembling. The wonder.

The deer's eyes were globes. It was too close. It was too beautiful. Its heart was very visibly beating under its ribcage. Its softly furred antlers removed the human breath from them through the room and through the glass.

Cass was looking over her shoulder, her mouth wide open, her teeth visible, looking through the window in breathless delight at this perfect apparition of a deer. So she did not see. She did not see Daisy opening the next box. Did not see what Daisy took out of the box and put directly in her mouth.

But Vi was paying attention. For Vi, the deer did not intrude upon his vigilance. Vi saw. And Vi declared it, out loud.

"Mom," he said, "Daisy's got the car keys."

27

INTERLUDE—NATHANIEL

Petal, beneath his sheet, fails to understand him, yet again.

It is morning and it strikes him—as he gets up to open the oily curtain, and then the gauzy net curtains beneath it—that his inability to talk to and be understood by Petal, and her inability to talk to and be understood by him, means that nothing about them can be explained away, in trite phrasing.

Strangely, thanks to their linguistic limits, they cannot be limited. Not by "I am this," "You are that," "We are a particular thing."

Not only this. The language barrier has another advantage, one of inspiring him to be resourceful. He has to find other ways to tell her who he is without words.

She is padding across the room now, indicating that she is going to take a shower. He picks up her strappy top from the floor and hangs it neatly over the back of a chair.

He likes that they do not seem to get swept up in each other's feelings. Petal appears to be a genuinely even person and he is able to retain his sense of self around her. It is perfectly clear to him where his domain ends, and hers begins.

Last night, he recited to Petal the only poem he knows off by heart, which he enjoyed doing very much. She seemed to understand the meaning of the poem through the sound of it, rather than its literal sense. She sang the rhythm of one of the lines back to him. Da-da-da-dada-da-da-da-dada. She has a freckle on her left ear rim.

He thought of reciting this same poem to Cass once, but on the brink of it he was overcome by how basic, inferior, how obvious, his only poem was. He anticipated Cass's opinion and felt it as his own.

In his room, the wardrobe door will not close fully unless it is lifted off its hinges. It drives him mad.

He is unfair. Cass is not a snob. She is never sniffy nor elitist. Quite the opposite. Often she is not nearly discerning enough for his liking. Too welcoming of anything, and of anyone. Low standards.

He knows he has been villainizing her recently. It is not a great way to deal with everything. But if he starts thinking about Cass as she truly is, then everything becomes unbearable.

He has lifted and popped the wardrobe door shut. There is a song he's been wanting to play.

He could not always differentiate between Cass and himself. For example: when she felt anxious, about the nanny or something, he thought it was him who was anxious; when he was in a low mood, he assumed it was Cass who was down, and he waited (he knows he waited impatiently) for her to snap out of it.

Sometimes, when there's an unexpected knock at the door to his room, sometimes he thinks it is Cass come to save him and he is not above welling up instantly with his love and gratitude just at the thought of this.

"No one's coming to get you." He talks to himself out loud.

There is a song that Petal particularly likes. When he hears the shower jet turn off, he puts the song on for her so it's playing when she comes out of the bathroom wrapped in what is, essentially, a hand towel. He has recently acquired speakers.

Petal can sing the first line of the song alright, but after that her wording is wrong.

He laughs. "The word is 'down,' not 'brown.'"

"S'only aiiiiii," she sings.

"Look at you," Nathaniel says, "over there, murdering a perfectly good song."

She interrupts herself singing to say, "My hair feels bad." He does not like how she looks so critically at herself in the large oval mirror on the bedroom wall. "Is the hair . . . bad?" she asks. "Is the water?"

"What's this song ever done to you?" he replies. "Wait, that's the good bit"—and he goes over to the laptop to skip back ten seconds, twice. He picks the line up in his low voice.

He puts his shorts on and steps out—brushing against the curtain— onto the balcony. The new compound wall obscures his view. He used to be able to see the winding road, and the growing fields. It was a friendly scene, with the curved backs of workers over the crops, their backpack spray machines, and the little haphazard vehicles, and the people walking up and down, taking a stroll after eating their evening meal. Before the wall arose, he could watch the satisfying display of the water sprinklers darkening the earth of the fields slowly, in patterns. But the conflict moved closer, and firmer divisions had to be made. All he has for a view now are the concrete blocks of the wall, which have thick black wires taped—literally taped—against them, connected to loudspeakers and aerials up top. There's the patrol of local guards in the inner yard, who like to lean against the wall until they are whistled at by the man in the cap to move on, and there's a parallelogram—yes, a parallelogram—of sky still visible. He used to get more daylight in the room, and full sunrises. Now he gets indications of them through washes of color in the shape of sky.

"In the illness?" she asks. She is trying so hard to get these lyrics right.

"Stillness," he says clearly. "Come here."

"No. I must to go."

He could watch her all day. That's all he does, really, especially since he lost his view. When she's with him, he watches her walk about the room like she's a small goddess, he watches her on top of him, underneath him, and when she's not there, he replays her. And that is all. That is quite all. He was in surgery the other day, thinking about the proportion of her waist compared to her hips. He was trying to get some rough numbers together for the circumference of her parts, to calculate an abstract ratio, in an attempt to confirm to himself that she does indeed have the golden ratio about her. He can't quite believe the delicate work he was able to complete while his mind was entirely on Petal.

Ever since that wall went up, his focus has been trained on Petal. He feels like a schoolboy having his thoughts bent, by a walled institution, onto the lesson of the day. Biology: petals, and how to pick them; how to label diagrams of them.

Diagrams? Maybe he should draw her.

He does seem to have a knack for picking the good ones. It is possible that he has been drinking less, quite naturally, thanks to Petal. She has brought this out of him as if by mother magic.

Petal is leaving now with a little timid kiss and a hand on her hair. He is unashamedly sad about her departure and has decided he will treat himself to a relatively rare drink when she is gone. He's not due in the hospital until four, and—he's checked—the junior currently on shift is quite the most competent one, making it unlikely that Nathaniel will be harassed. Often the juniors phone in questions from theater indicating an alarming lack of basic medical instinct. "Do they not teach these kids coming up anything anymore?" his senior colleagues say, frequently, as their lanyards tap and click together around their necks.

He likes that sound. He appreciates that he and his senior colleagues are really—and they know it; you couldn't not know it; it would be stupid to act like you didn't know it—they are really quite exceptionally good at what they do.

Petal is gone. He can put that song on repeat and have his fill of it, and a beer, or something stronger.

All except one of his senior colleagues are fathers like him. He wonders if they feel it too, the parental guilt. (Something stronger.) It garrotes him sometimes out of nowhere: a father should not be this free. At least (he consoles himself, all the while believing he deserves no such consolation) at least he (he hears the crack of perforated teeth around the new bottle neck) at least he is an improvement on his own father, who worked many long postings abroad without a palpable touch of guilt.

As he sits on the red plastic chair on the balcony with his tooth mug of gin, a mosquito the size and texture of one of Petal's eyelashes gets in his face. He catches it and smudges it out in one quick move against the arm of the chair. There was something about language he toyed with earlier, when Petal was padding all over the room. Her presence helps him to think in a way he prefers. Why does she always leave?

The gin tastes peculiar. He takes some more in and sloshes it about his mouth to get to the bottom of the peculiarity. Then he swallows and releases a gasp of inquiring breath. What is it? Is it that . . . ?

Oh.

He drinks some more to be sure that it is, yes: he is absolutely correct.

The odd taste he is experiencing is that of fresh gin meeting dried. The gin tastes strange because his mouth is full already with

147

the taste of gin from last night, and he's actually, so far this morning, managed to misplace the fact that they were out drinking until 3 a.m. It is possible he is still drunk from yesterday. Possible.

Did Petal realize this before he did? Is that why she left?

The smudged-out mosquito has left its store of blood on Nathaniel's hand. Nathaniel leaves his drink and goes to the bathroom to wash it off with soap. While he's in the bathroom, he realigns the wet towel on the rail; he sings along again to the song, very quietly. See? He's fine.

Very quietly, thoughts of Cass, who likes this song too.

There's his face in the bathroom mirror again. He leans his forehead (he believes casually) against the mirror and checks his eyes for bloodshot. He uses his tongue to check that all his teeth are in place. Checks the pulse in his wrist.

In a moment he will be back on the balcony. He already knows how everything is going to go. Everything. The inevitability is so boring.

Cass couldn't see.

His phone beeps. He receives a text to inform him that the boy he worked on so tirelessly yesterday has passed.

"Fuck."

As predicted, he is back on the balcony refilling his tooth mug. He drinks. He closes his eyes.

"Why die?" he asks the boy.

Nathaniel knows he is a man who takes these things particularly personally. He thinks he is possibly too sensitive.

The people who've died on Nathaniel's watch were all unusually intelligent people—his father, his two wives, those young men on the table with clear smooth skin beneath their eyes—intelligent and decisive individuals. Because of this, each of their passings has felt to Nathaniel like a very deliberately done thing on their part. He simply cannot escape the belief that they *died on purpose*. He experiences regular bouts of hatred for each one of them for it and, at the same time, he gets it.

He has entertained the possibility that dying is what the truly intelligent people do to avoid the squalor of living too long: they realize the rationality of it, and they choose to die, by giving permission to the brain to begin closing in on itself and shut up shop. He wonders, *Is death what the ballsy people do? Am I not ballsy enough?*

He is on the red plastic chair, with the gin, as he knew he would be.

He is never much charmed by those families who remove their loved ones from hospital, when the time comes, to die peacefully at home. When it's his time, he would like to go out on the theater table, surrounded by a handful of top medical minds, all fighting for him until the last. Giving it all they've got. To go out fighting. Now that's ballsy. Even if he had no chance of survival, he'd rather die at the center of a ring of experts, and the accumulated findings of hundreds of years of medical science, medical technologies, battling death, than at home, on a sofa.

The red plastic chair beneath him is simply too uncomfortable. It always is. He knows one day he'll toss it over the edge of the balcony. The inevitability again. He goes inside. He notices Petal's cotton underwear under the bed. Most women left their undies around deliberately so that, he assumes, you'd stumble upon them and recall the sex you'd had, leaving you unable to deny the existence of the woman who'd been in your bed. It was as if these women didn't believe you had object permanence. Petal doesn't play tricks. Her underwear is there innocently.

He can speak to Petal about anything. Sometimes it's as if she understands better than anyone ever has before. Even though it is hardly possible she understands at all. He has told her awful things. Awful things about the deaths of his wives. His awful theory.

His awful theory: that the children's first two mothers left life because they could not bear reality. They saw how the world was turning. They could see that the world was on a quick trajectory to its end. They could see the inevitability of it. And they found that they could not witness the death of the world with their own children in it. So they left. It was the obvious development of a maternal instinct within them: it was not possible for these mothers to keep breathing in a world that would not sustain the lives of their children. This is his theory.

His children do not know yet that the earth will not sustain them. Neither does Cass. She is living in a dream. Her insistence on leaving The City was maddening. There is nowhere to go! He wanted to yell this at her. There is nowhere that will be left untouched by the death of the world: there are only places living in willful ignorance of the coming ending.

149

He had to leave and be somewhere the real conditions of life were actualized. Fire, death, desperation, up close.

He must find out if he has a clean shirt. Petal has a habit of hanging his dirty shirts in the wardrobe, which misleads him into believing he has lots of clean shirts ready to go when he doesn't. Also, Petal is incapable of closing the wardrobe door properly. There is a pleasant burning sensation in his gut, and a consistent balled pain in the middle of his left foot.

A mortar explodes off at the yard line, which is about a mile from the compound. He takes pride in how these surprises do not instigate a physical reflex in him.

His mother says he never cried when he was a baby. He can absent his instincts. He can be somewhere else. Like when he was operating the other day, and the bleed-out got too great, and he said, "Alright, alright," and he set the tone for the team, and ran through the procedures, but still he remained internally with Petal. Very calm. Events did not reach him.

That poor kid on the table didn't make it either. They were on a dying streak with him. The outcome would have been the same whether or not Nathaniel had stayed internally with the comfort of Petal.

At the point of death, he is sure that he would like to be surrounded by top medical minds, working tirelessly to save him, minds that are also privately occupied with the sheer unbelievability of the girl they had in their beds last night. With a song like this on in the background. He'd like that.

It is unconscionable, what he is doing.

The softness of her skin is unconscionable. The smell of death around the morgue tents is unconscionable. The fidelity of his senior colleagues: unconscionable. The softness, the smell, the fidelity, each has its own range and operates on a different part of him, but there is an area of overlap between them, somewhere near where his sense of his children resides. None of it is manipulative. These things affect him because they are real, not performed, not artifice.

The first two mothers left because they saw what was to come. Their prophecies killed them.

150

After giving birth, Cass looked up at him from the hospital bed with her flawed eyes mesmerized and lost, as newborn Daisy emitted little screams. Unconscionable, to keep Cass trapped in a dream.

Wake up, he wants to tell her. *Where are your prophecies?*

He refills his mug and wonders for a moment if he could repaint the railings on the balcony himself. The thing about living in a hotel is you see how shitty hotels are without constant maintenance.

If he had never stemmed down his nerves. If he had never pleased his mother. If he had not bent his head to learn all the rules of courtship and marriage and decency. What might he have been? As free as Arthur? An exploding bomb, experiencing the world.

He considers the balcony railings again. The drop.

Where else could he be at such a time as this, in all good conscience?

PART THREE

THE BORDER

28

Cass was sitting on the ground by the side of a wide, empty road. She was resting back against a huge, rigid knapsack.

Her skin was so dry and sunburnt that her lips looked like they were blistering out from her face. She had a full mouth, and freckles, and dark lashes not sun-bleached to fawn yet. Her youthfulness continued, like the give around very ripe fruit. And her lips were moving slightly, she was speaking, but you'd have to be up very close to hear her. As the children were. Three of them. Their eyelids were burning. They swatted at flies. The tarmac was melty. Everything around them woozed and spun, it woozed and spun. The air burnt gentle lungs.

Cass was trying to stay alert. She kept resetting her eyes on the horizon to her right. She was waiting for a vehicle to appear there. This vehicle—if it appeared—would be coming either to drag them backward or to propel them forward, she didn't know which: either way, she was extremely motivated to stay watchful. They could not go a step further on foot.

She was making a series of small movements with the musculature of her jaw when the face of a truck came through the heat screen on the road's horizon. It got closer, it was enormous, in a cloud of fumes. An eight-wheeler. It slowed gradually to a stop in front of Cass and the three children, casting them up in shade. Cass had been stroking one child's perfect nose from brow to tip. She stopped. Reached back and squeezed another child's knee. She put a hand down on the road, and pushed to rise.

It turns out that when it is time to leave you will find that you have the children out of the house before a thought has formed. You will find that you have ready in mind an inventory of valuable and useful things, which you will collect with an efficiency and a calculated foresight that, later on, terrifies you. (*Were you sizing up the haul all along? Unconsciously? Did it show?*)

Even if the engine of your car doesn't turn over, even if you and the children have to go it on foot, you will not falter, you will put off despair.

You will unlock the places that have been locked. You will feel immediately, gratefully, for all the things within your reach, like official papers, passports, bottled water and money, clothes, a baby sling and proper shoes. Chargers. Jewelry. You will shake out the big bag and repack it, exacting. The children will not question you. The older will help the younger to put on their shoes as you try the engine again, accept that the battery is flat and decide that you must leave anyway. You may leave behind signs of your inconvenient existence: a half-eaten biscuit balanced on the arm of a sofa, long strands of hair in the plughole, your car keys hanging in the ignition. You will choose the path that will lead you away as quickly and as far as possible. Even if that way is dark. Through the woods. You will not wait. You will not wait until morning, and you will not wait to be talked out of it. When the time comes, and not a moment before, you will know exactly what you must do. It may be the first time you encounter that experience of knowing so completely. And all the mistakes you have allowed to coagulate into a personality that you take everywhere with you, like a heavy preamble, all of that will be irrelevant. You will move. When you have to. With a message for your children undulating to the confines of their existence.

The driver of the eight-wheeler offered to help lift the children up into the cab.

Cass nodded her assent.

When the moment comes, you will hear the sound of your own voice drop to a natural, deeper tone. You will realize that you have been speaking on a falsely high note all this time. You have been constricting your throat. You have been lying. There has been a thick, heavy stage curtain between yourself and the quick of things, and when this is released it will fall with an elegant heavy sigh to the floor. And this is one of a series of noises that will haunt you: the sound of car keys jingling, voice drop, curtain sigh. Then the sound of children's feet running urgently, not in play but after you. They will train their eyes on you, as if you've been absent for so long and they can't believe you came back.

The driver of the eight-wheeler wore a worn pink sweatshirt and was neither he nor she. The sweatshirt was pushed up at the sleeves, and it covered soft rolls of body flesh and large breasts. The driver's head and arms were shaved, inexpertly, without assistance. The driver got in and rocked from side to side, spreading in their seat. They spoke in a voice that was neither way. They did not seem to blame Cass for withholding herself. Quite automatically they deployed a reticent, irrefutably masculine patter. But then they succumbed to a shiver that rippled through their upper back, and they stopped. The children sat with Cass on the long front seat of the cab, and each found a part of her to bury their head into.

When it is time to go, you will leave suddenly, as if commanded.

On the open road, in that hinterland between the place that everyone has left and the place that everyone is heading, before you reach the border, you will bend to brush the end of your nose against the children's cheeks.

The driver of the eight-wheeler was heading far north anyway. They worked for an independent weather monitoring agency. They asked Cass, "Have you been to the border before?"

"Not since I was a kid," said Cass. And there had been no border then. Only a welcome sign coming soon after a huge wooden winged beast on a hill near the road.

"What happened to you?" asked the driver of the eight-wheeler.

All the wild possibilities happened. "Can I charge my phone?"

"Of course. You walked far today?"

"Yes."

"Couldn't get a ride?"

"Car wouldn't start, in the end."

Cass plugged her phone into the cable dangling from the dash-board. When the phone turned on, it beeped and beeped with messages that kept arriving for several minutes. She read them as they came in: they were love notes, and sex notes, and admin notes, all sent by her husband before he'd realized that her phone was dead and locked in her car. "Baby . . . ," "Hi baby . . . ," "Baby, I need to tell you . . ." She was waiting for him to hear from Eden that they had fled, and for messages of his alarm to start floating through, which she would need to read before she could work out what to tell him.

157

Cass knew that when people were close to dying they slept a lot. They might also experience death throes—violent convulsions of the body.

She thought that the close death of a civilization might be similar. There were increasing sleeps. These sleeps were times of peacefulness, as general productivity faltered and halted, when the roads were emptier, the skies clear of planes, there was birdsong, detail. There was an incredible awareness, at times, of the microscopic layer of cells where you ended and the rest of the world began. That layer, that boundary, could take all of your focus in a waking dream. And you visited this state more frequently. As did all of life all around you.

And then there were sudden bouts of the throes. Unexpected violent movements. A border closed. A truck turned over. A storm. The yelling of the dispossessed. A flood and then the water system is infected. A disease, and nowhere to bury the cattle. More burning; of flesh, of land. More bad air. More depression. Lung weakness. More flies, drawn to blood. A weaker constitution and a reluctance to work. Less money. More reaching for the cheaper hit, which is more brightly packaged. The more packaging, the more waste. The more the factory spews its guts. The more rivers die. The pump must work. The more the seas burn.

There was a green shell on the dashboard. They came around to talking about the Plagues of Egypt. The driver introduced the subject—how the plagues could all be explained away, rationally. Cass had learned about this at school, the driver had seen a climate scientist give a talk—and they started piecing the plagues together: in the first plague, the Nile runs to blood.

The driver began: "The Nile *could* turn red, just not with literal blood."

"There was an algae, right?"

"That's right, a particular algae that grows in extreme heat. It is toxic . . . in quantities. It multiplies, turns the water as red as blood. And that's your first plague. Caused by overheating. A climate change."

"And that algae kills the shellfish, the fish, and drives out the amphibians—so plague of frogs, plague number two."

"It wasn't a plague of frogs, it was a rain of frogs."

"Oh, yep."

"When it's very hot, frogspawn can evaporate into the clouds, I think; then baby frogs rain down. It's unbelievable, but . . . That's plague two."

"So meanwhile the dead fish who were killed by the algae wash up on shore. They attract the flies."

"They attract the flies, exactly. Or the lice, which are the third plague."

"Then it's bigger flies?"

"Bugs are plague four, which get at the livestock and kill them off, the fifth plague."

"Then—what comes next? The pox?"

"It's boils. The stress, from the bad water, from not being able to drink and clean . . . There is an outbreak of—I suppose you could say pox, but boils is the sixth plague. Followed by a further extreme weather event, climate again: hail, plague seven. And then the first-borns die."

"No, we've missed some. There's the hail but—this is the bit I remember—they think it might have been a massive volcano erupting. And the ash from this volcano could have been mistaken for hail. It really rains down. But—but the ash creates the . . . the perfect conditions for locusts, which is plague eight."

"I did not know that."

"And the ash also makes the darkness, which is nine." Cass could feel the blood returning.

"Then the firstborn? Did they die from the algae at the start? Or maybe they all got the boils, the pox."

Maybe, unconsciously, they did not wish to inherit all this and they wriggled free.

"It didn't happen quickly, like it seems in the Bible, back to back."

"No. But there is some domino effect."

"Some. That's right. Dominoes."

They drove through the day. In the late afternoon, the driver and Cass noticed that the fields they were passing looked uncultivated and were therefore likely to be free of irritating pesticides. They got out; they put Daisy down on a woven blanket the driver had. The driver tentatively suggested a game of It ("Is that something children still play?"). Vi picked up on the driver's apprehension, and he threw himself into the game to please the driver, and Maggs followed suit for different reasons. It was here, with the feel of crickets brushing her ankles, that Cass took herself off, a few steps away, turned her back on the children and took a piece of paper out of her pocket, which

159

she had grabbed from Eden's hall table without fully understanding why. She dialed a number from the paper. Her limbs jolted in surprise when someone picked up. The conversation was a long one. Cass had hoped for, but not expected it. The driver kept the children entertained so that she could concentrate.

The evening before with Bea; the handwritten numbers by the phone: it had been enough, just enough of an opening.

Back in the cab of the truck, Cass was much more at ease. "It was in front of my eyes. And I could not see it."

"Yes," the driver said. "At least you can see now." After a while, they added, "All the damage in this world is done by the people who cannot see the truth in front of them."

But Cass was looking at her children.

"They'll be OK," said the driver. "Will you?"

"Who knows?"

The world turned on its back, stretched onto the parts of itself that hurt, and it settled, inflamed. More and more people were manifest at the sides of the road. In groups. Carrying boxes and bags and water, water, water. Dirty water spilling from something burst beside the road. The eight-wheeler slowed and joined the line of traffic into the border camp.

Getting dark again. Ahead of them, the tent-and-car city at the makeshift border came into view. It was lit up by huge floodlights. It rose like a great landmark, a tor, on the horizon. Cass was surprised by how terrifying a prospect it was. She was surprised at herself, for coming here. Surprised most of all by her surety. There were seemingly thousands of cars parked up. Beyond them, thousands of tents, spreading, spreading, to the camp's edge. There were so many people.

"Is this where all the people went?" asked Maggs.

All the people united in an aim: to get through the border. "When you feel like something is being taken away from you, you want it all the more," the driver said. They explained to Maggs that, when she was born—when Daisy was born, even—the land beyond the camp had been seamlessly connected.

Cass looked out over it all; she could see a portion of the hastily constructed, armed-guarded fence made of concrete, shipping containers, and razor wire.

On the other side of the border, people knew the land was higher, and the climate slightly wetter, the crops supposedly better, and the air cleaner. It was where, so it was rumored, care and order had been taken into the striving hands of a few socially minded individuals, not given up on. There had been only one Great Fire behind the border, the second, and it had been dealt with. Magically, there had been no Gaia beyond the border. It was not irrational of the people gathered at the camp to believe in this North Way; to believe that it was their only hope, and their birthright. And they were demonstrating their insistence on access to it by amassing here. The music coming from the camp was aggressively unpredictable. Heavy bass.

At the top of the rise, the driver helped Cass and the children down from the cab. The driver had explained, several times, that if they were caught trying to sneak the woman and children through, they would lose their license, the whole body they worked for could be closed down. "I'd take you, I'd smuggle you through, but they check everything, the stakes are too high," they'd said. Cass hugged the driver, and they hugged back, and then tighter. The driver left Cass, and Daisy, and Vi, and Maggs, standing on the edge of the border city at night. Having pangs.

When you have to leave, you will be able to. You will get the children out of there. You will carry them away. You will reassess: you will hear the sanity in what you'd thought was madness, and the madness in what you'd thought was sane. You will be subjected to horrors of obsessive thinking, remembering how every advertisement, how every item bought, how every drink, every sugary high, and every aspiration you held only contributed to this destruction, to this chain of interconnected events. Filthy liquid will trickle past your toes, staining the hot earth blood-colored. You will think everything you see is overly symbolic. Kind of crass. Obvious.

A preacher on a box was shouting, "Forgive us. We were only seeking transcendence, Lord. To make the moment bearable."

Cheap transcendence through beers, and through marriage, and through belonging.

She thought for a moment of her husband.

And now nothing can be born. And we are on the run. And the preacher said: "This is the way it ends, baby, I always told you. This is it for you and me."

161

29

It was extremely loud everywhere. There was nothing Cass could do to stop the noise reverberating seismically through her children. In the past, she'd acted as a shock absorber for them, but they were going to have to feel the full drop of this bit.

First, they had to weave through hundreds of densely parked cars and the people who were living in and out of them. Each stereo seemed to be turned up full. Every single person here was trying to control their own environment—still. Cass kept noticing piles of fresh feces kicked underneath vehicles, with bits of tissue attached.

The vehicles gave way to many more people, to dogs barking, children crying, to tents that seemed to have grown across the land, games and arguments. One like this:

"You cunt!"

"You can't call me a cunt, I'm your daughter."

"You're a cunt, cunt, cunt, cunt, cunt."

"No. You're a cunt."

"You can bet your life on it. And my mother was a cunt, her mother was a cunt, you come from a long history of cunts. YOU ARE NOTHING SPECIAL. YOU. CUNT."

"Bitch."

Both smirked.

Leaflets, bursts of laughter, strings of red lights, acquiescence. People keen to display who they'd been all this time, when they were back in their homes. Cooking meat and texting.

The pathway through the tents and the mud was made from sheets of corrugated iron and honeycombed plastic. Twice, the pathway split and Cass had to ask the way.

Where the mud became unnavigable, Cass was so determined that she and her children would not slip in the fetid mess, where everything was mixed, that she felt unearthly powers of steadiness. Daisy was strapped to her front in the sling, leaving her one hand free for Maggs and one for Vi, with the enormous bag heavy on her back. Thus was the entire universe constituted and in the balance.

They finally found and joined the correct line, ready to be processed when the center opened in the morning. Cass heard herself inform the children that, after a short interview in the building at the head of the line, they would be free to continue on their way. They would not be stopping here, she explained. They had every right to pass through the border, unlike most people, and they would be met on the other side. She spoke with great certainty, as if her firm utterance were all that was required to make anything be so. The man and woman standing ahead of them in the line turned around as one and gave Cass the eye, as if to say, *Why the hell would you tell your children that? You have no guarantees.*

Cass's phone had been ringing on and off. And now that they were in the line, she could release the children's hands and answer it. She squeezed the little fingers before letting them go, but they clung on to her, so she had to shake them off. Then Vi stepped up and onto Cass's toes. Maggs bunched up the hem of Cass's T-shirt and put it in her mouth to suck on.

"So look, I'm here." It was Arthur. "I'm in the van. It's blue. I mean, you'll see me. I'll see you. I'll be seeing you soon. So everything OK, yeah? We know what we're doing?"

Cass's gaze flicked and landed on a long flag. It was shaped like a serpent's tongue, and was lying, unable to catch any wind, over a yurt that stood out, ridiculous among the normal tents. And here is what she thought fully, so it absorbed her entirely. She thought: *I am porting these children to their inheritance, to their fated futures. They are fated to live, and live well, on land that is beautiful, in air that is clean. I have commanded it. And it will be so. We will be let through.*

It's not always enough, though, is it? Motherly insistence. Cass deflated her lungs, and levered the bag from her back and sat on it. She replied to Arthur that she knew what she was doing, sort of. She caught the moment that Vi decided, with a triple blink, to keep his questions—about his dad, about Arthur, now apparently on the scene, about all these people, and the rights they had or did not have to cross the border—to keep his questions to himself for now. Cass got off the phone, released Daisy from the sling to stand, and hung her head between her knees for a second. Daisy tugged at Cass's cascading hair. Cass looked up. Her bright smile caught the children unprepared.

The aid people brought them leaflets, water, and, later on, plastic cups filled with rice or curry. They offered to take the children to the bathroom when they needed to go. They gave the children tags to wear around their necks and gave Cass a pen to write her name and number on the tags. They gave the children plastic bags to sit on. Eventually a softly spoken lady came up close and asked if the children would like to go with her and sleep in the charity's tent. Cass said no, thank you, firmly. Cass had to remain in the line; naturally the children would stay with her. How could she protect them if she could not see them? The lady left, but she came back again, and asked again, went over it all, again. Cass did not care for this.

The lady's reasoning began to take on a patronizing tune. She was slowly revealing herself to be well-versed in insinuation—"I would never judge a parent," she said, "but I am always invested in the best outcome for the children." She went on and on: "It's best for Mom to have a rest. Moms are no good when they're tired." It went on until Cass felt poked and red hot. It went on until Cass barked, "Don't shame me. It's not kind."

The lady received Cass's words like a physical injury, recoiling. She backed away and turned her attentions to another mother, who looked so clean and ready to work with others. Looked so trusting.

There were lots of cats and dogs walking about, hunting for scraps. The children wanted these animals to draw closer. There were so many bodies pressed together. They were all suspended here. The people had come to the camp with each other, and their pet carriers, along with all their worldly goods, on a chance. If enough bodies built up, maybe the undeniability of the mass of them would smash the border through. Not long ago—the pet-owning people remembered, they repeated, incredulous—there'd been no border here at all, and the north had been part of the southern people's land too. The border was ridiculous to them. Surely it would go. And when these pet-owning people realized they'd be here for a while, and that you cannot keep a pet boxed up indefinitely, they released the animals and hoped their ties of loyalty would remain. But the cats left, at liberty to curl up with someone better. The dogs went to the man with all the wasting steak. This hurt the pet owners' feelings, and caused arguments, some of which, so it was said down the line, had turned deadly.

As the night continued, Cass heard how the army came to the camp fortnightly, to clear it. Everyone was sent home. Or, if home was no longer viable, they were bussed to hotels and to schools that had been refitted, which was surely the work of the Black Box, though they had made no public declaration of their actions. Cass could imagine the sort of statement a spokesperson of a functioning government might make in such a situation: "Any border across our parts is illegal. But we have to accept now that an illegal border has been erected," they might say. "And we have a duty, therefore, to protect our nationals from gathering unsafely around it, until such time as any border can be peacefully dismantled. To avoid the northern regions from being overwhelmed, the border will come down gradually and professionally. The regular clearing of the camp, meanwhile, is an act of safekeeping, to prevent the border camp from taking root." But the Black Box had said nothing. No statement. No spokesperson. Instead the silent clearings prevented the camp from taking safe root, in terms of reliable infrastructure. The army came fortnightly and only pushed bodies back, and then the bodies resurged. A push was due in a day or two. Hence the particularly het-up atmosphere.

It was said that the Black Box Government had moved itself north of the border, for safety, when they'd first received intelligence about Gaia, when the internet first went down, when the records for the highest temperature recorded were broken and remade several days in a row at the airport in The City, when the runways melted.

It was said that the Black Box had been complicit in the construction of the border wall.

"Is it an illegal wall if the government wanted it built?" wondered the talking couple ahead in the line. This couple were saying that their neighbor back home had been nearly killed by Gaia. He had suffered abdominal injuries, had only been treated at the scene, an explosion, and sent home, when he should have been taken to the hospital. The hospital had been too full—this was the gist of the story that Cass was able to overhear. The voices ahead were then lowered to say, "He lost his—" and Cass raised her own voice to speak to her children and exclude herself from hearing what or whom (she suspected whom) this neighbor had lost to Gaia.

The camp was exposed. It was entirely unprotected from a Gaia attack—and wasn't it ripe for one? Wasn't it perfect? So full of bodies intent on consuming some more heavenly patches of earth. And wouldn't a Black Box Government even welcome, privately, such a clearing—a mass clearing of inconvenient citizens, by Gaia? "Wouldn't it solve their problems? Deter more migrants?" said the group of people ahead, later, speaking more loudly, emboldened by whisky.

The same people turned to Cass and told her to mind the children's feet, that there were rats in the camp as big as dogs. Nits as big as mosquitoes. An experimental vaccination program. Thieves like you wouldn't believe. Squads of good-lookers selling "nightly relief, if you know what I mean."

Later, a man walked up and down the line, apparently looking for something he'd dropped in the mud. Cass was very aware of him; he passed by half a dozen times and each time she rearranged herself to stand between him and her young. There was nothing particularly alarming about his appearance. An unremarkable face, glasses, head covered with a sports cap, clothes that lent bulk. It did seem as if his wish was to preoccupy her, though—particularly her.

And then, perhaps sensing her unease, this man came to a standstill right beside her. He looked up suddenly from the ground to the sky; in unexpected wonder he said to the stars, "Golly."

Cass's whole body was prickling. He turned to her and inquired, "Hmmm?" as if she'd just spoken and he hadn't quite caught it. She raised her eyebrows and shook her head at him—*No. Don't even think about it.* Yet he got down on one knee to address the children at their level, around their mother's legs, and he said to them, "It's a beautiful night, don't you think? What are your names?"

Maggs told him all of their names. Then the man took several chocolate coins, which were wrapped in bright, gold foil, from his military waistcoat pocket, and he handed them to Maggs, brushing Cass's leg as he did so.

"Share these," he said. "Are you scared here?"

"No." Proud Maggs.

"Good." He stood again and looked back up at the stars, saying, with something of a poetic timbre, "There is no reason to be scared." A performative thought broke his reverie: "I am forgetting my manners." He turned, businesslike, to Cass, grabbed her hand quite violently to shake it, placing his other hand further up her arm, and said, congratulating her, shaking her hand, "You have beautiful children."

Cass pulled her hand away. He was made smug by her unfriendliness.

"My name," he said, "is Fred." Then he pulled down at the neck of his T-shirt, so Cass could see on a leather thong around his neck he wore a large wooden pendant in the shape of an oak tree leaf. His smile stung her. She tried to take her eyes away from him, but he was trying, she'd swear, to burn the image of his face and the pendant more deeply into her brain. He was not looking at her in an invasive way, not so that he could see Cass more closely, but so that he could be sure she got a good long view of his face.

And she did not forget it.

He made his salutation: "Gaia with you," he said, and moved off.

"What's Gaia again?" asked Maggs, still confused, having not managed to build a picture from the limited facts she'd been given.

"I think he was Gaia," said Vi. Finally getting it.

30

A little while after 9 a.m., the doors opened. As the line moved forward, Cass and the children saw that the checkpoint occupied a building that had recently been a large school. This caused mild excitement in Vi and Maggs. Through the double doors, they passed a school office, which still contained trophies in a glass display cabinet, and a chest marked "Lost Property," which was padlocked. Collection times were on laminated signs on the walls; "Medication must be signed in to Becky in the school office."

Inside the assembly hall, Cass and the children were directed to stand in a square marked out on the floor in tape. At the other end of the hall were five cubicles made from plastic scaffolding and sealed in with plastic sheets. After each claimant had been interviewed, there was a fierce whirr and spray as the cubicle was blasted with atomized disinfectant from above, smelling strongly of fake lemons. Vi said it smelled "bright yellow." There were twenty-nine groups ahead of them. Cass tried to sit on the floor to feed Daisy, but was told she had to stand.

When it was their turn, extra chairs were brought to the table. One of the gashes in the tabletop had been colored in deep blue with a sparkly pen. Cass knew that Maggs would try to touch this. Daisy started bleating and writhing.

"Tell me your story," said the woman on the other side of the table. Cass told a story that Vi had not heard before. He didn't question it.

"We came from The City." Cass faltered. Her mouth felt cavernous, her voice foreign in it. "We were there for the first Gaia attack, in The City. It was close. Really scary, so I left. I took the children to my mother-in-law's." She wished to stop there.

"And then what happened?" asked the woman.

"It is hard to explain."

The woman put her pen down and pinched the shoulders of her top up to rearrange it. "You have to try," she said.

"She hid my car keys, so I was stuck. The water was . . . It stopped. I had to walk to get it. But that wasn't it. I can't explain really how bad it was. I was losing my mind. And she was OK with that, my mother-in-law. She didn't mind. She wanted me to lose it, I think, secretly. And she lied to me about things. Confused me. With my husband. They both lied. They lied by omission, but still."

"About what? What did they lie about?"

"Eigleath. There is a safe place we can go. Apparently it's wonderful. I didn't . . . It's called Ei—" Cass came to an abrupt stop because the woman sitting in front of her bashed her elbow on the edge of the table.

"What's your claim on Eigleath?" the woman said, holding her elbow.

"It's my husband's."

"You're married to . . ."

"To Nathaniel Maguren. I've got documents here to back all this up." Cass passed her folder over. "I just don't have . . ."

The woman released her elbow, readjusting the angle of her head upon her neck. "The most important one?"

"How did you know?"

"This isn't my first day."

"My brother-in-law is coming now with the title deeds and inheritance papers. He's called . . ." A strange thing happened then as Cass was sure the woman got to the name "Arthur" before she did.

But this was only Cass's exhaustion playing tricks with her.

"Arthur."

"Arthur."

Later they were taken into a sports hall and given out-of-date protein bars. The children were reassuringly talkative despite their lack of sleep. After some more waiting, they were led far, far down several quiet corridors and into an empty classroom, which looked directly out onto four ball courts fenced with chicken wire.

31

The man who eventually came in to them was harried and thin. He looked at his watch twice in quick succession, performing his disbelief at how the day had got away from him. He said, "Take a seat up here." He drew Cass's folder of documents out from under his arm, set it on the table between them, and spun it to face him. He began leafing through the pages. Cass furiously shushed Maggs twice as he read.

"I'm sorry this is taking so long," he said. Cass thought he was referring to his slow consideration of her papers, but he added, "One of my officers was caught partaking in cocaine in the toilet with a vulnerable person. I had to deal with that. And there's the hunger strikes."

"Hunger strikes?"

"Families on hunger strike. Starving children. Won't eat until they're let through."

Cass didn't want him to talk about this in front of her children, but she also felt compelled to help. "What do you do there usually?" she asked. "Are the children OK?"

He shrugged. "You'd think there'd be a case for removing them from their parents. But when the children are doing it apparently of their own volition . . . it's complicated. Anyway, we don't like to be emotionally blackmailed here. Particularly by members of a southern population who have been, traditionally, through these eyes anyway, entitled oppressors. And now you want us to welcome you? Well, no."

She took his point. He brought his chin right down, and he regarded her.

"Where else can you go?" he said.

"Nowhere," she replied.

"Where else can you go?" he repeated.

"We've got nowhere to go," she said clearly.

"And your husband?"

"I don't think he's coming back."

On hearing this, Vi gathered up a shaky breath, like he might begin to cry. But Cass and this man were locked into something, and they paid Vi no attention. There would have to be other times, in the future, for Vi to be reassured. There'd have to be. No matter what. She had to get them all somewhere safe. And then she could retrain them to trust.

She heard herself speaking again. "We have a fair claim," she said. "I have recently learned that my husband is the joint owner of the property, Eigleath, with his brother, Arthur, who lives there. This is my marriage certificate. These are the birth certificates. These are his children. We have a legal right to go to our land."

She had been firmly touching and pressing down on the relevant documents with a pointed finger as she spoke. The man did not like this at all. In fact, he watched her finger with an exaggerated expression of alarm, while holding his pen between his teeth.

"My brother-in-law is on the other side of the border. He is in the car park. Right now." She was pointing at the wall behind the man.

"It's not that way," he interrupted. He took his pen from his mouth and used it, wet with his saliva, to steer Cass's pointing finger so that it was aimed away from him, out the window. "He'd be over there."

"Fine. My brother-in-law is over there, with the title deeds."

"Yes, but it doesn't work like that."

"Like what?"

He leaned right back in his chair and turned his attention to the window, thinking.

Cass believed she knew what he wanted.

This man wanted her to tune in to him, to suss him out, to sense him out, to supply him with some version of emotion that was nice and comforting and tailored to him. And for what? For safety: in exchange he would allow her to reach safety.

On any other day of her existence previous to this, Cass would have bent. But on this day, at this time, she decided that she should be let through the border, as was her right, without having to give an ounce more of herself than was legally required. No prettiness, no eye-gazing, no hero worship, no subterfuge. The papers she had provided were exactly enough. Why should she give more? Give

171

essence? Beg and flirt and wonder with blatant eyes what would soothe him? Apologize to him for taking up his time and plead prettily? For safety.

This man sat back expectantly, like he was waiting for her to break and play. Like he was capable of becoming very disappointed in her.

"If we can't go through tonight," she asked, "what happens?"

"Yeah, we have some rooms, but they're not very nice. You're better off back outside, to be honest. So, this is your husband's brother you want to live with?"

Had he not been listening at all? "Yes."

"Biblical."

"No." She was emphatic. "He has space for us. And it belongs to us. There is space there. And other children."

"How will you get there?"

"He's picking us up. He is outside now. I just said. I already said this. I told your colleague this. Arthur's here, now. Wherever it is that you wait. That's where he is."

What was this man doing when he looked at her, if not listening?

"Yes . . ." He sighed and turned his gaze to the ceiling, as if for strength. "OK." He smiled weakly and then he got up and he left.

Cass raised her T-shirt, lowered her bra, and latched Daisy on. She took Vi under her free arm. Maggs was expressing how thoroughly unimpressed she was by the situation, sighing loudly, shaking her head, and getting up to look in the low schoolroom cupboards. But Vi didn't know how to act. He told Cass that he needed the toilet. She didn't want him to go alone; she also didn't want to move her whole troop from the room. She told him to open the door and look for any signs of a nearby bathroom.

Vi was halfway to the door when the man swung it open again and came back in. "I've spoken to the supervisor," he said, "and I'm going to need some more information." Cass didn't like how the violent swinging open of the door had made Vi jump, scared.

"I have given you everything I have," she said. "My husband's name is on the title deeds to the house. There is a man behind this building, in the car park, with those deeds in his hand, waiting to show you."

"OK, well, we can't find him. OK?"

"He has told me he is there. We can phone him now. Did you go yourself and look? We'll come with you to look."

"Excuse me? I do not work for you. Yeah? Do you get that? I do not work for you."

"I know."

"There are people in the world right now who have lost access to their primary residences, yeah? Not their second homes. Not their in-laws' third or fourth houses. I don't work for you." He pointed with the files at the children and said, "What are you doing bringing them to a place like this? A place like this place you intend to take them? What are you doing with them in your care? Are you fit? Are you sure? Because we can get that assessed."

It didn't matter what documents she had. They'd only let her through if they liked her. And they'd only like her if she anticipated their needs and became what they required her to be. Maybe this man needed her to acknowledge that in another life, in a bar, say, she wouldn't have noticed him. She would have dismissed him. Maybe he needed her to make amends for that.

He was turning away from them to leave, but Vi, desperate for the toilet, asked bravely where he could find a bathroom.

"You don't look much like your mom, do you?" said the man to the boy as he left, and closed the door behind him.

And then he locked the door.

Cass was still breastfeeding, but she put her pinkie by the corner of Daisy's mouth and pressed her breast down there to break the seal. She sat the baby quickly on the floor so that she could go to Vi and hold him. He was frozen to the spot and crying. It was particularly important to him that the men he met liked him—she'd forgotten about this. Daisy was crying now also. But Maggs, electing for a moment to act with the grain rather than against it, picked out Daisy's pacifier from Cass's pocket and put it in the baby's mouth with great care.

They found that the classroom windows were pivoted: they could be pushed outward and opened a chink. Vi stood on a chair and directed his pee through the gap. Cass complimented him on his aim. She suggested that he seriously consider entering the Olympic Pee Championship one day. He'd probably win gold, she said. "Will you be there?" he asked her. She replied that, embarrassingly, she'd probably insist on joining him up on the podium when he received his medal, and so would his sisters, all weeping with pride. He started to giggle, first with his eyes, then the rest of his perfect form followed.

As this went on, Cass was also trying, unsuccessfully, to make her phone work. It had no reception. There was little charge left. She plugged it into a socket beneath a whiteboard, and found that the electricity was off, or the charger broken. *You had better be there*, she pleaded silently to Arthur, while vocally she elaborated on the Olympic Games. Maggs would be entering the Tearing-Up Pieces of Paper event. *Is Arthur for real?* But they really expected Maggs to excel in the Forward Roll on a Bed event. *Was he only telling you on the phone what you wanted to hear? Maybe he was lying. Arthur lies. Not being where he says he is—that's exactly the kind of stunt he pulls, isn't it?* Yes, the Institute for Silly Walks would be involved in the Olympics. *Making promises he can't keep. Haven't you been told all about him? Didn't Nathaniel tell you?* Daisy would, obviously, be representing her country at the Wobbly Walk Mixed Relay. *Was I stupid? Maybe he could never have pulled this off?* And Daisy might also, at a stretch, receive bronze in the Pacifier-Losing events.

Cass had let herself believe, for a day, that Arthur was the sane one. She had decided, over the course of an instant, that Eden and Nathaniel were so far from sanity, their disapproval of Arthur must indicate his rightness.

And now she was locked in a classroom on a makeshift border with no way out. And there was nothing she could do about it. Except try to change the color of her children's experience.

The man must have heard their laughter as he came back down the corridor several hours later. It possibly angered him. He opened the door and leaned in. Cass supposed he wouldn't step into the room due to the smell from Daisy's diapers, which Maggs had also had to use.

"The children can wait here"—he directed this at Vi, who had poked his head out in alarm from the low cupboards he was exploring.

Cass said, "No. They come with me. We stay together."

The man held the door open for her. "Come on, now. Just you. Come."

"Why can't they come with me?"

"We're going to sign some paperwork."

Cass's mother would have gone with him. This thought reached her next. Cass's mom would have gone obediently with the man and left the children. Not because she thought it was the best thing to do, but because, when a man indicated that he wanted you, you filed away after him.

"I'll sign the paperwork here, or with a chaperone." Cass had met people who were very different from her mother.

The man looked infuriated by the insinuation; he was flustered, leaving. "I am trying to help you now," he said, locking the door on them once more.

Cass had noticed that Vi had spent the last few days studying her intently, balancing his sense of self on hers. If her heartbeat was steady, so was his. As Cass played through in her mind the sight of her own mother walking meekly away with this man, full of awareness of the uses her body could be put to by others, she felt that Vi saw it, too, in his mind's eye.

32

Later, when they were quieter, when the whole northern sky was enacting a spell again through the classroom windows, when Daisy was finally sleeping on Cass's chest, and the other two were beginning to doze, curled up in the empty cupboards, which they had been pretending were the secret belly of a pirate ship—Cass got a whiff of her husband, unfocused her eyes and drew comfort from addressing him as if he were there. *I miss you. I think about you. But you're not here. You're so far gone. One day I will have to let you go. I think that you might have left us on purpose, but I can't think, right now, what the purpose could be.*

She could feel him all around her. She sank into him, played her own game: that he was present, in the room. He was. She could feel him precisely. The effect of his form on hers.

Maggs interrupted Cass's reverie with a forcefully awake sound: "Do you want to play I Spy again, Mommy?"

Cass felt an unusual and compulsive spasm of revulsion at the child's intrusion.

Then came a terrible, hurtling idea: *What if the children die in this room?*

Cass saw, unbidden, a picture of her children's lifeless bodies in a row, in this room, in these clothes that they were wearing. Their limp limbs. It was too real. *I shouldn't be conjuring images like this.* She burst into helpless tears, and, looking at the girl, she thought, *Shit. We need to find your real mother. Where is your mother? Maybe she didn't die. Maybe she needs to come back and rescue you. Maybe I am your caretaker, until your real mother comes.*

Late dusk into night. *Where is your fucking mother?*

Cass stayed up all night. The children were up and down. They talked about things like bubblegum.

What's bubblegum? *You've never seen it? You chew it and then blow bubbles.* Bubbles come out of your mouth? *One bubble at a time. It's bright pink and smells of sweets.* Can I try bubblegum? *Sure. We'll find some.* Can you teach us now how to do it? *Not really.* What's going to happen now, Mommy? *I don't know.*

Just more whispering, in the night, my love, like we always do and always will.

Have we messed up, Mommy? *No. You haven't.* You haven't either, Mom. *Maybe I should have gone with him.* You're tired, Mommy. Is Uncle Arthur waiting? *I really damn well hope so.* Don't swear, Mommy. *Sometimes it's OK.* I know all the swear words. *All of them?* All. Of. Them. *Like?* Damn it. *Jam it? Oh, you mustn't say that one.* Why? *It offends the bees.* Do they get upset? *Terribly.* What do they do? *Protest dances.*

Cass was forming a nascent plan. When the sun came up, and the center opened again, and the corridors were full of people, she would start making as much terrible noise as possible to draw wider attention to her case. Yes, this was her plan. She was delaying it. There were few ways of making the required level of noise that wouldn't frighten her little witnesses.

She also knew, after that long night, that Arthur was not coming to get them. It had been a fantastical plan concocted between a single-mother in exile and a junkie, over the phone. She'd have to start again. Think of somewhere else to go. Perhaps she'd trace her steps back to the charity tent. She could apologize. They'd forgive, wouldn't they? They'd be kind to her children, and let her charge her phone and try.

Birdsong. Big skies. White-light morning. Someone would bring them food soon, hopefully.

A snake traveling across the ball court outside looked like it was levitating. It had such sure direction; it held its head very high. It did not seem sentient to Cass; not in the same way the deer through the window had just two days before. Its sentience was less commingled with her human understanding, more piercing, more acidic. It was astonishing. That was a word Nathaniel liked to use. "Astonishing," he would say. And, beyond the court, the hedges were shaking. Maybe some foxes. Or maybe the birds could make the hedges shake like that. It was all astonishing. How the natural things were shaking, so unnaturally. The hedges were shaking with shrill. Cass was enjoying watching them. They shook, and they shook.

And they expelled a foot. A side. A man. An entire man was coming through them.

He was always taller than you expected him to be, and he dressed in a variety of faded colors. He looked bouncy-jointed as he hopped out of the bushes and continued to shake parts of himself free. He scratched under his chin. He yawned. Then, with an unconscious hand, he reached down and undid his flies, took out his penis, threaded the fingers of his other hand through the chicken-wire fencing, and started to piss over the edge of the court, chatting to himself.

Cass was right: the children had never heard her make great frightening noises before. Apart from Daisy, perhaps, when Cass was birthing her, but how could Daisy remember that, except at her very base, the very unreachable part of her knowing? Certainly the children had never, in their general, daily lives, heard their mother scream like she did just then in the classroom. With all her frighteningly endless might: "ARTHUR! ARTHUR! ARTHUR!"

It took him some moments to work out where the screaming was coming from, and in those moments he looked vulnerable, befuddled. When he realized that there was a woman jumping and waving at him from a window, he automatically spun away to hide his member from her, marking nearly a full circle on the ground with his piss.

33

Arthur's way was not to try to get them out of the classroom by going back through the system. Arthur's way was to get them out of the classroom through the window. He fetched a screwdriver from his van. From inside the classroom, Cass was able to unscrew the metal restrictors and the window levered open fully. Arthur lifted the children through, and then held his hand out for Cass.

His hug was strong. His smell was rich and royal. And Cass with her face in his armpit.

He pulled away to take her in, to release his strings of mischief, to smile and to say, "I reckon we could run now." He understood the dynamic immediately without needing anything explained. "Vi, my main man," he said. "Show me how fast you can go."

Arthur, running with Maggs in his arms, and Cass's big bag on his back, was all eyes, fingers, and gaily leaping legs. There was something wondrously comic about his run—his knees came up high, his toes almost pointed, you could call it a gallop—and he seemed aware of this, and he didn't care at all about how funny he was, not in the slightest. Cass could not hold all the joy she felt, running, with her baby's head tightly against her.

The van was on the other side of the bushes, at the very center of a large open car park, where they would likely be seen by the border workers arriving for the day. Arthur hurried to it, helping Cass strap the children quickly into the back. He had a baby carrier installed in there, ready for them, and two booster seats, with a cuddly toy propped up in each, with bags of chips, chocolate, and water. When he took Daisy from Cass's arms he said to the baby, quietly, "Hello there," in a voice that signaled to Cass a bounty of tenderness. Cass's joy was strangely displaced by this. It made her panic: tenderness? How

179

could she ever repay such a thing? Tenderness was ruthless. She had no weapons or consignments against tenderness. Maggs proclaimed loudly that her new bear was called Shark and they said, "Shhhhh!"

The two adults got in the front; her door slammed shut, then his. He started the engine and they pulled on their belts all in one swift movement, like they'd been rehearsing this.

But the panicking sensation was rising in Cass. She was newly able to see the peculiar violet-and-green geometry of her own unique bind. An idea of action came over her.

"I need to go back in and get the kids' passports," she said. "I don't have the passports. My marriage certificate." She had released the seat belt again and was letting it run back through her guiding hand. She was about to open the car door and rush toward the school buildings.

"Why?" Arthur asked her. And his unwieldy eyes, which usually roamed, stayed on her. He said it again: "Why?" He did not look away. She couldn't breathe. "You don't need passports. Look . . . There's nowhere to go after this." And he left a good pause to let that land.

"But they'll need their passports one day . . ." she tried.

He raised one side of his mouth, closed one eye. "Maybe I . . . maybe I come back for them another time," he said, convincingly, that tenderness again, and even in his hurry, he waited for her to put her belt back on before he released the clutch and maneuvered them smoothly out of the car park.

They were still within the gated perimeter of the border. There was one further manned gate to get through. When Cass saw it up ahead she started swearing under her breath, but Arthur was steady.

"They're going to stop us!" she said, high-pitched, but not moving her mouth too much, as if the guards at the gate might read her lips. The children were alert to her fear and it completely silenced them.

"These boys don't know anything what's going on," said Arthur, quietly. "This place don't know tit from elbow."

Arthur grew jovial as the checkpoint drew near. He touched the upper rim of the open window, his nose with his thumb, the car again. He swung his genial greetings out to the young men—they looked like boys—who were gathered there, and he called to them: "I got my cargo!"

"You have their papers signed out OK, Arthur?" said one keen young boy with cheek fuzz.

"Oh, what? Christ, yeah. Do you wanna see the bits of paper? It's in the back with all the shit." Arthur didn't turn the engine off, but he made as if to undo his seat belt and get out.

"You're alright there, Arthur," said another of the boys, with a deeper voice.

"Don't worry, Arthur, you're OK." They all liked to say his name.

"I've got something extra for you lots next time," Arthur said.

"Good lad, Arthur!" And they waved him on.

When Arthur started accelerating onto the main road, the wet air blowing through the van windows felt clean, right to the bottom of the lungs. He put the radio on and drove, both of them checking the mirrors.

After about thirty minutes of driving, rows of housing having made way for countryside, Arthur asked Cass, "Are you OK there?"

She started crying as the road went down behind them.

He let her cry for a while, before offering, "You want to talk about it?" But she was unable to verbalize. She pulled her knees up and bent her head down, so that her kneecaps pushed into her eye sockets.

Arthur put his enormous hand on the back of her head, where she knew her hair was greasy and her pale scalp grinned through. She was embarrassed. She felt him turn to look at the silent children in the back and check on them. She had become so alert that she could feel looks, see noises in sharp shapes, her taste buds were prophesying unbreachable pain. And yet, and yet, as she felt the heat of his palm on her head, she imagined that it radiated down through her, and she softened in a way that she had not quite forgotten was possible.

A song she liked came on the radio. Perhaps her anguish might soon change over into relief. She took a breath, released her legs down, and sat back in the seat. The car was clean. A Mickey Mouse on a keyring, and a Jesus on a cross, dangled in a bunch from the mirror. Cass had a *Mona Lisa* keyring hanging from the mirror in her own car: this thought comforted her. She noticed the red stitching up the side of the long handbrake. And the passing land, which was sage-colored, heather-colored, moor-like.

"What did she do to you?" he asked, and it was immediately clear to whom he was referring. He seemed to be looking beyond this sad Cass, beyond the immediate environs, to her broader experience. He was trying to help her place herself within it. Giving context. He was long-distance. This much attentiveness felt very alien to her.

"Everything and nothing at all," said Cass.

"Yeah. I'm sorry about her."

"It's as if she thinks I'm the dangerous one . . ." she started.

"Yeah."

"She's not safe."

"No." There was a sticker of Ganesh on the dashboard, picked off around the edges. There was a Virgin Mary on a plastic rosary wrapped around and hiding behind the Mickey Mouse.

"She is worse with women, though," Arthur continued. "So maybe you do have to tell me."

She told him: Eden, Bea, dogs, Tim, water, keys. Calling it up electrified her with anger. It enlivened her. She was passingly aware, as a bridge flashed darkly over the car, that this anger could fuel her for the rest of her life, if she let it. She was caught up in it. She was saying "Eden would bring me so low" and repeated it:

"She would bring me so low, and she would stand on anybody, anybody, to save face. And I think she's made Nathaniel think I'm crazy. So crazy that he won't even come home. Why won't he come home? Am I so terrible? And I hate him, and I wish I'd never crossed paths with this awful family. You know, if you spoke to Nathaniel, I'm not sure he'd say I had anything going for me. But I do. People do like me." She felt suddenly ridiculous, ashamed, as well as so bored of her shame and herself.

She had been addressing all this to the road ahead, but she turned now to the driver. Arthur's profile was—distinctively—exactly like Nathaniel's. And she saw, in that instant, not Arthur but her husband beside her in the driver's seat—and she felt her whole self dilate with fear. Nathaniel would not be able to withstand her tirade. Nathaniel would do something about it. He'd surely stop the car and tell her to get out—no matter that his mother had entrapped her, no matter that Cass had seen his children through an ordeal. He'd get out too (wouldn't he?) to spit at her feet and then drive off without her. She would never speak like this to Nathaniel. Would she?

Would she? The confusion. All her leads and cords were connecting into the wrong places. What would really happen if it were Nathaniel in the car with her now? What would he say?

Surely—he would tell her that he loved her. He would say that he'd *never* spit at her feet. He would entreat her to, *please*, bear in mind that Arthur was a *cunt* who stole money and girlfriends. Remind her that Arthur would *never* think of you unless he needed something. Arthur was shifty, and always had his eyes on the door. That was right, wasn't it? Arthur was always high, and if you tried to help him he would only break your heart.

Yet here, in real life, not in the subtle tricks of her memory, was Arthur. Arthur with his bracelets and rings, and his verses tattooed up the arm, and his ear rimmed all around with more rings, and the slash where one piercing had split through his lobe. The dirt under his fingernails. The lines of red scratches down his neck, which were perfectly spaced to be clearly the marks left by the nails of someone writhing beneath him—this was Arthur. His rattails had beads in them. His shirt had a single fine red thread stitched down one sleeve, with a tail loose at the end, like the stitching in the car seats, which was red, unusually, on cream. Arthur wasn't taking any of what Cass said personally. Not at all. He was accepting. And the ends of his mouth were touched lightly up. He said, like it was a fact that she was going to have to accept at some point, "You're going to be OK now. Our place is really nice. And you can make it your home. She did that to Jem too, sent her to that bloke's place."

Cass was searching everywhere rapidly for evidence that would match this Arthur she was witnessing with the profile she'd always carried of him. As she looked at him, the previous image yielded, until there was nothing to match with and only this fact: he'd actually come. He was physically propelling them forward and out of the situation, unlike Nathaniel who was present only in her mind, like some sort of psychosis.

Here was Arthur driving so carefully, mirror-checking metronomically even though the road was basically empty. There was no crap and litter in his car. He was letting the irate presenters chat on the radio without allowing them to disturb him. She felt that she could close her eyes and go to sleep without having to check with him first that this was alright.

How insane this sounded to her. She had been in a contemporary marriage to a modern man, so why did she find herself wired in this way? Why did she think she needed to check that the man beside her would not punish her for sleeping?

The children's heads in the back had lolled forward ten miles in, their little mouths had fallen open once more with sleep; they were fifty miles in, a hundred miles in.

She kept her eyes open.

"So how is my brother, then?" he asked with intentional airiness.

"I don't know."

"You think he's alive?"

"Yes. He is."

Arthur had Nathaniel's eyebrows. The hairs down the back of his neck were the same. His nostrils. The same pulse in the arm. But a stranger.

"Would you be relieved if he died?" The question was not posed as if her answer, either way, would be judged. "I mean, he's pretty much checked out at this point, right?"

Cass put her feet up against the dash. She said, "He told me Eden had sold Eigleath."

"Yeah, well, he'd be lying. Wasn't hers to sell. Dad left it to us. To me and him. Equal."

"Why do you think he lied to me about that?"

A number of expressions indicating various levels of discomfort chased over Arthur's face. Then he said, "Maybe, Cass, maybe, he knew that he would be leaving you—leaving you and the kids soon."

"Even more reason to tell me about Eigleath."

"No. No. Not at all. If he's getting out of here, the last thing he wants is to imagine you shacked up with me—with us, I mean. Last thing. I swear. I'm his worst, you know that. He doesn't want to leave and for you to be totally-fine-thanks-darling without him, does he? They don't think like that."

"Who's 'they'?"

"Not us."

Two more songs played. She rested her elbow on the windowsill and closed her eyes. Could it be possible that Arthur believed she was an essentially decent person? Not wrong in her bones. A decent person who had been in a difficult situation.

184

It felt now like she was being taken onward by someone who thought her truth was reasonable. Arthur had collected his brother's wife and was transporting her to safety.

She dropped into deep blasts of sleep, broken up each time her elbow slid off the car door.

34

She was dreaming. She was standing on the edge of an empty swimming pool. She needed to jump down into it and begin gluing her darker tiles into the gaps where the old pale-blue tiles had come away.

A male voice said: "I need a piss." She woke quickly and did not know, instantly, where she was. She pivoted in her seat and looked out through each window, searching for visible dangers.

The children in their seats behind her; the colors of the land pronounced around them; the fields almost jewel-like in hue. There was a dense thicket by the side of the road ahead where Arthur was standing wide-legged, broad back, urinating.

Which bit of life is real and what is safe?

What was she waiting for? What did she fear? A police car, in all seriousness. Officials from the border coming to take them back. A vigilante's car, sensibly. Ragnarök. Eden. Her own husband, with loving dread. Vi's mother. Maggs's mother. Her own mother. All the mothers. Her father's decayed body. Her mother screaming, "Come here. What do you think you're doing? Stop crying before I give you something to cry about!"

She forced herself to breathe slower. Arthur was opening her car door. "Come see this," he said. "The kids will be fine," he said. *The kids will be fine. What a notion.* "You relax now," he told her. *Why am I here? Why am I here?* She felt she was slipping through safety's fingers. "Come on," he said again. And then he thought about it: "We'll keep in view of the car."

She got out and followed him toward the thicket of trees up ahead, because she could see and hear what he was leading her to and she thought it would help. They came out on the other side, to where the sea was changing gray and white beneath them. The sea always behaved with her as though it knew she'd be coming back. It was rolling, fresh in sound. Its spray was in the air, lightly touching her face. Arthur lit himself a thinly rolled cigarette, careful to watch it, not her. She could hear a bat squeak in the rustle of the trees.

He started speaking: "Me and Nathaniel used to come out here," he said. "I was ten, he was sixteen. We had these canoes. You can get out good, over there, and past these rocks, see?" And he proceeded to tell her a story that she had heard before, about when the storm came right into the bay and Nathaniel was knocked out cold in his canoe, and . . . Arthur must have known she wasn't listening and, she contended, he probably knew why: first the sea air, then the sight of the water. The air, the sight, the flow had all been restricted. And here she was, her whole self, rising and falling, and she was grateful that he knew not to look at her.

Back in the car, she tucked her feet beneath her and regarded herself in the side-view mirror again. She noticed the directness of her gaze, the violence in it. She recalled, unexpectedly, the ease with which Nathaniel used to get his fingers into her soft spots, under her shell. She had thrilled—a bodily thrill—in happy fear of his easy access. But today, if he were present in the car with her, what would it be like? She did not think she could enjoy fear again.

This onslaught of changing thought and feeling was exhausting.

Arthur said, "Sleep more, if you want to. There's quite a way to go yet."

35

Interlude—Nathaniel

He is packing. They are being evacuated.

"It's really OK," he is telling Petal, who is lying on the floor in a pose that seems altogether too dramatic. She is not rubbing away her tears. He crouches down in front of her and helps to raise her, saying, "This place was a dump anyway, sweetheart." There is fire all around them on the outside of the building. Petal looks hideous. "The embassy will be much nicer," he is telling her. All at once she is scrambling to her feet in a burst of tearful anger, running past him and locking herself in the bathroom.

While the corridors and staircases of the Hotel Gloria rush with spilling activity, he stops in front of the balcony glass in his room to feel the frightening heat. He basks in it. There is a veritable wall of flames that goes up behind the wall of the compound, into the parallelogram of sky. This is the sort of adrenaline situation he's been seeking.

He has three sets of cuff links in his hand. His mother taught him, fiercely, to be the sort of man who always travels with cuff links, and so he is, even here. How ridiculous.

His mother is calling him, as it happens. The phone has been ringing for days. He hasn't been able to answer. It is not a good time. He intuits it is Eden calling him from the phone in her hall or sitting room, rather than Cass using Eden's phone. Cass has stopped calling. She knows that something is wrong within him and until he presents that thing to her she can't fix it.

He has always tried to answer his mother's calls. Wherever she called his name, in the past, he responded. He might be different now.

He can change. It is allowed. Perhaps he does not have to answer her anymore.

His mind is wandering. It has become strange to him recently that so much store is set on creating idyllic childhoods for one's offspring. Can't life improve? Shouldn't we start off life with all the worst conditions, and fight our way past them to reach the heights? Isn't childhood for feeling everything, so that we might practice all the emotions while we still have a guide beside us? Not that he'd had a guide. He'd been the guide.

This—today—is the first experience he has had of Petal's fear. He does not like it. He finds it distasteful. Cass would be much braver in the given situation.

He is resolved entirely to make his life with Cass. Only perhaps theirs won't be an easy resolution and he will have to live with that. He cannot lie to her. They cannot be in innocence anymore. They have been expelled from it. She must know what has happened. What he has done. He will tell her about his sticky unfaithfulness. And he hopes that she will forgive him. He can imagine her forgiving him. He really can. This is the miracle. Cass's miraculous forgiveness is the only thing he can imagine significant enough to compete with the effects of adrenaline on him for his attention.

It is a big love he will hurtle home to. Cass Love.

In his recent days' conceptions of it, their love has gone through a process of maturation. It feels real and everywhere, even though they're not speaking at the moment. His mother won't like their new, deep love, forged through difficulty. She will certainly try to undermine it. But she may not even recognize it. It could happen in front of her nose, and she might not know what she was witnessing.

He has to focus on his wife now.

He has confused them in the past. The women have occasionally presented as all the same to him. The heavy need that he feels coming off his mother—he thinks it emanates from Cass too. Is this his fundamental mistake? Could he lose his confusion here? His mother be damned.

He convinces Petal out of the bathroom through a process that is dull, stupid, and drawn out. He steers her from the room and down the chaotic stairs to the transport that is waiting. She is shaking. He tells her that she should go on ahead, but she doesn't want to leave without him. He kisses her. It's fine. He is not entirely repulsed.

The new female consultant on his team calls them over from her transport. She is in the back seat and she persuades Petal to climb in beside her. She makes the photographers in the darkness of the vehicle scoot up to create room. She has a superb bedside manner, this consultant, and she uses it on Petal to great effect, but she shoots daggers at Nathaniel. He knows—he knows—how it looks. "Colonial," he supposes, is the word. "Toxic." "Exploitative." He wishes he could tell this new consultant, "It wasn't like that. It's not what you think." The whole thing between him and Petal came from their equal childishness. But he can hardly defend himself now; there isn't an audience interested in hearing his defense, nor is there time for it.

He has to hurry back to his wife: she is the only person he is willing to explain himself to.

He would like more for Cass than a normal marriage can offer. He wishes to have her all to himself and he wants her to exercise her power over him. He wants her to be led exclusively by her desires and fulfill them completely, while remaining exclusively his. He doesn't see why there has to be a contradiction inherent here.

He refuses to be embarrassed.

He is back in his room, alone. He tries, he tests, touching the balcony glass that stands between him and the fire, he feels the flames on his eyeballs, feels the heat swell the back of his retinas. Astonishing. She is calling again. Why must she always call? Everything he has is so neatly stowed that he can lift piles of folded clothes straight from the shelves in the wardrobe into the bag in an orderly fashion, just like his mother taught him. She taught him everything. She taught him not to test her. To protect her preciousness. But—Arthur. Arthur invaded Eden's solitude. Arthur invaded Eden's body, when she was pregnant with him. Nathaniel could remember how much she hated it. Arthur stretched Eden's stomach. Once born, Arthur needed to be held constantly. But Nathaniel could see that it was not what Eden wanted. Nothing is ever enough for Arthur. Arthur always requires more. Arthur is so angry at not having enough.

And Arthur acts on that anger in ways that Nathaniel never could. Arthur is the most manipulative of them all.

Will he leave the wardrobe door open, or shut it—to burn either way? He will open the glass balcony door before he leaves, just to feel what it is like to stand before the flames. He might use that moment to ask for Cass's forgiveness, for mistaking her for someone else. Cass is not Eden. He does not have to simultaneously adore her and protect himself from her.

Cass welcomed pregnancy, unlike Eden. Cass was only happy when she was holding her baby, unlike Eden. Cass worked out, privately, the puzzle of how to be loved. There is something simple in that. A simplicity so stunning that it rivals complexity, surely? He wants to meet her there, in that simplicity. She is his mother's opposite in every regard. It is time for him to honor her. The confusion he suffered, where one woman standing in front of him stood in for every woman that had ever stood in front of him—this is a form of suffering that can end.

She is still calling. Nathaniel used to love her call. It felt like food. Like shelter. Even when it wasn't. Engaging with her ways has made him clever and complex. He could never stand her, and he could never live without her. He could not let her too close; but he had to have her in his sights so he could anticipate what she'd do next. This has made him sick.

He will wrap his hand in a pillowcase before he takes the hot balcony door handle to slide it across. He will be purged by the intense heat of fire. He would like to be rid of Eden and Arthur forever. Cass is the alternative to them, not their continuation. He is going to get Cass from his mother's and find somewhere safe for them to stay, and let her teach him how to be, now that he is new. They will be man and wife, post-innocence, in adult understanding, and all the world will be new. They will be a team that can take on anything; anything at all. They can absorb anything. Even the heat, which is coming in against the glass, against the compound wall, in the parallelogram of sky, and beyond.

PART FOUR

EIGLEATH

36

They drove down a lane into the valley. From a passing place on the lane, it was possible to glimpse the whole of Eigleath in one glorious view. A white house nestled in deep greens and long growth. This was where Cass's husband had spent his summers growing up. He'd talked about it so dreamily. In what world did he live, where he could deny his children this?

From the passing place, it took another fifteen minutes in the van, downhill. It was quickly clear to Cass that the more accustomed a driver was to this stretch, the more frightening the experience would be.

Eventually the lane smoothed out and leveled in front of the white house, which was covered that early evening in a screen of sunshine. There were potted plants climbing trellises, no spills, all swept.

A woman came to the doorway wrapped in a large emerald-green cardigan.

Cass got out of the car, the pale gravel underfoot.

The house was wide and seemed, in its proportions, in its makeup of windows and sills, to be smiling. Again, there were dogs. These ones did not bark. They were grandly shaggy and wolfish.

The children, awake now, did not plead to be let out of the car. They were heavy with compliance. Arthur, surprised by the children's inaction, flung open their door. "Come on!" he said. "Gambol!"

This is a gamble, Cass silently acknowledged.

From their seats, the children looked out at her, waiting for her. Sometimes children are only their eyes; the rest of them shimmers away. She respected their proud fear, leaned in to undo their belts one by one.

She walked them toward the door, where the lady in emerald green said to the children, "You won't remember me. I'm Jem," and knew to look each of them, in turn, in the eye. And to Cass she said, "Welcome, you." And to Daisy she said, "Well, we haven't met."

The last time Cass had seen Jem, both of their heads of hair had been full of products that gave off synthetic scents.

From the hallway they took stone steps down, emerging into a big room, which was shabby, bright, and clean. The brick floor was old and uneven. Before Cass noticed that the room was a kitchen, she saw that the soles of Jem's bare feet were red from ingrained brick dust. There were worn indentations in the bricks which Jem found with her big toes: it was all molded to her and her to it. There was the longest table. And another. There were brightly colored jugs, and cut herbs in water. Everything was colorful and chipped. Everything was smooth, with a nick. The beams in the rafters were unfeasibly high above them and wrapped with old garlands of dried flowers and hanging ribbons. Cass looked to where the sun came in through a high-up paneless window.

"It's like a meeting hall," she observed.

"Yes!" said Jem, delighted.

"It feels like I've been here before."

Jem made tea and offered bread and biscuits. A man with a lot of dark hair and a bushy well-kept mustache walked in, topless, and he welcomed them. The soles of his feet were red too. He stood at the sink with one foot more forward than the other, so that his toes would fit into their own set of comfortable grooves in the brick.

Other adults came in and went out. Red feet all. Children's drawings were scattered on the very long tables, which were joined together. "We can all fit around," said Jem, looking at the tables. "All of us. It's a happy place here."

It had started to rain slightly over the sunshine. Jem—expecting little from the weary travelers—filled the space around them with her own lightly tripping voice. "We get more exciting weather up here than I think you're used to. We get loads more than just sun at Eigleath."

"More than just sun," Cass repeated, so the children caught it.

Cass was all at once sickened by the thought of the unrelenting, metallic sun which in The City had left them unfit for much more than lazy crawls and caws. The air in The City which had tasted hot

196

black. Which made children's lungs grow small. Cass could hardly believe she'd kept the children in that city for so long. And that thought insistent, angry, again: how had Nathaniel denied the children this place? Jem said there might be rainbows out of the window to the right.

The rain, Jem explained, was collected in vats and used for the garden, where the soil had never been cultivated to grow food until a few years ago, so it was, admittedly, peaty, but nutrient-rich. It held carrots; there were pigs, cows, sheep; a river too poisoned to swim in regularly. But on the highest day of summer, which also happened to be Arthur's birthday, swimming was allowed.

Jem ran water bubbling from the tap into glasses and was telling Cass why it was safe to drink: from their own narrow well, filtered through quartz. Electricity was rarely a problem, Jem explained. They had generators and the solar panels had been replaced recently. Money was got in the local town, which was reached in the truck. They had loads of trucks. The money was put into collective jars arranged in a line on a shelf, in full view, above the kitchen sink. "But you mustn't worry about those," she said.

"Do you have a rotation for who does what?" Cass asked.

"Don't worry about that," said Jem, who had no cheekbones, and a crooked smile, and her chin up a little higher than looked comfortable. This was Jem: her face like a golden plate tipped toward the sky; flat and catching the light.

A marmalade cat rubbed its head and then its side against a table leg. Jem said that in the greenhouses there were salad leaves and fruits tended daily without pesticides and sold in the town on weekly trips taken in the trucks, along with meat, occasionally, but they kept most of the eggs. The money was all put back in the jars.

While Jem was speaking, another man had come in and stepped up in his huge boots onto a chair, and from there onto the kitchen table, to hold his phone aloft like an antenna.

"It won't work," Jem interrupted herself to say.

"Vinnie said he got signal last week."

"He didn't," Jem replied, then, looking at Cass, she repeated, "He didn't."

A group of children were trying to come in at the back door and say hello, confidently. They were ushered away by Jem and another woman with short dark hair, who appeared from a larder-like room and frowned at Cass.

"Come—come with me." Arthur led Cass and her children upstairs. Every door along the landing was painted a different color. One door had sprigs of yarrow across the top of the frame, another had a line of green shells like the one in the cab of the truck, where they'd been only forty-eight hours ago. Some of the shells had fallen to the floor. Maggs picked one up.

Arthur led them further down the hall, passing by two opened doors through which they saw into two rooms lined on either side with triple-height very wide bunk beds, decorated with flags and littered with toys and pencils.

"That's the gang, the young; I call them the Children of the House." Arthur nodded into these rooms as he passed them; his gait carried a reassurance, a confidence of being. "Here's you," he said, and he opened a pink-painted door at the very end of the hallway. Behind it was a bedroom where the windows looked out and over and into the valley, impossibly green, and the bed was made up in a blur of blues; there were flowers in two little glass receptacles of water on a side table.

"Think these are for you, Vi. You read?" Arthur gently kicked a cardboard box of old children's books with the side of his foot. There were towels folded on the bed. The towels were rigid and orange-gray from lack of bleaching soap and softening products. The valley was painful to look at. So lush it was overstimulating. Cass went, internally, somewhere else. Somewhere more mono-chrome. To a hotel room where, pre-Daisy, Nathaniel had drunk so much that, when he'd wheeled around from the toilet, he'd slipped on the wet floor and split his lip open. Cass had soaked the blood up using hotel towels that were bright white. He'd grown a lesion like a pupa on his lip. She'd worked out how to kiss him without disturbing it.

"The kids can bed in next door with . . . the gang . . . I call them," Arthur was saying.

"With me," Cass said firmly.

He shrugged, turning to leave, taking a fresh cigarette from behind his ear into his mouth. "Whatever you want, honey," he said. "Whatever . . . want."

There was a twang in Arthur's voice, an accent he'd picked up without affectation. He missed words out. He didn't speak clearly, like his big brother did. He did not have that same monied drawl. More than that, it was as though a blunt trauma had fallen on the connective tissue of Arthur's speech. But at least Arthur seemed to think in straight lines. Nathaniel and Eden might speak confidently, but they were so circuitous in their reasoning.

"And look," Arthur said, suddenly remembering. He bounded to the window and said, "All that land is ours. To the end of the valley—you can't see."

The valley was verdant. It was gleaming vast. It was the same valley that had been looked down upon, unchanging, for generations; it was remarkably untouched by the world's breakdown. It was a rare place. It was glorious. It was too much. Cass looked away from it. She saw the comfort of the bed again—all in blues. She felt the youth and stretch, the strength, in all the limbs in all the bodies she had seen at Eigleath so far, and in Jem's voice. It was too much. Even the tiny flowers by the side of the bed—drooping, small, splendid—were too much. And scaling the petaled beauty of the bedside flowers up, and gazing out again to the reaches of the valley, which was sparkling after the slightest sprinkle of rain, it felt like a joyous insanity to Cass, who thought she might bubble over and laugh, like the water flowing freely from the taps.

And with all this, she wanted to collapse on the bed and sleep for days, but she firmed up one last time to ask Arthur where they could wash. Arthur mumbled something sounding like "Yeah, wash out your wounds" and called for Jem, who took them down and out and around the side to an outdoor shower. Its concrete floor ran away to a drain and its four wooden walls marked out a space big enough for many to fit in at once. It was open at the top to the sky. The shower-head was big. Cass thanked Jem and leaned in to turn the water on.

Jem waited. When Cass had peeled off Daisy's diaper, and folded up its contents, Jem insisted on taking it away herself. Then she came back and stayed. Cass was at first put out by this.

The two women together knelt just out of reach of the shower spray and began pulling off the children's gross garments and throwing them into a corner. The water grew hot. Jem passed Cass a squeezy bottle of liquid soap. Cass cut her fingernails with a pair of rusty scissors found on the side, and then used her finger pads to scrub at the children's scalps. She soaped and soaped and rubbed into their muscles. Jem had Daisy in her lap and with a washcloth went between the baby's toes, making her gurn with helpless laughter. Jem scrubbed the dried poo off Daisy's rear without disgust. Cass watched and felt discomfited. She was territorial over her children's skin. It was a landscape she could not share. Her grip on them had got them here. But, with her own clothes beginning to grow wet under the spray, she realized that her tight hold on these children would need to be released a little soon.

Maggs and Daisy bashed their bare feet on the ground to make splashes. Vi stood directly under the jet and let the water run and run over him. Eyes shut. Black eyelashes sending the water into wider rivulets which ran down his cheeks. So alone and separate, within his mind. Cass couldn't carry these children alone. She could not; she was not physically capable of simultaneously cutting Maggs's reluctant toenails and cleaning the baby's bottom and finding mental space to divine what Vi needed next, wondering whether a man shouldn't talk to him about how to clean under his foreskin. Perhaps she'd come to a place of communality for this reason—to share the tasks.

Jem expertly shielded Daisy's eyes with one hand while she poured water from a jug over her hair with the other. And Daisy let her. Cass rested her own head back against the wet wall, with the spray falling over her, feeling the closeness of all the times the children had wriggled and pushed their bones uncomfortably into her body—in The City, at Eden's, on the floor in the locked room at the border—seeking comfort. All those times she'd closed her eyes and tried to imagine this, the next first taste of life.

After the shower, Maggs lay wrapped in a towel on the thick meadow grass. She began to roll from side to side until she had the idea to roll herself out of the towel completely, and dry her whole body in all directions against the perfect tickling of unspoilt grass. Jem had gone away and come back again with arms full. She let the children choose from the T-shirts, home-dyed in turmeric and beetroot, jumpers and socks darned, all smelling fresh and ready. She had a jar of homemade minty paste and Cass rubbed this over their teeth. Vi put on his borrowed clothes and looked unsmilingly pleased and beautiful.

200

They went upstairs, talking. Jem followed them, this time with a board game tucked under her arm. She pulled Daisy onto her on the bed and started setting up the game. She tossed her head at Cass and said, "Go." Then she said, "Take a minute."

Someone capable and kind was taking the weight of the children. *Good God.* Cass slipped out.

Immediately outside her room, in her way: another pile of clothes.

"Whose are these?" she asked Jem.

"Probably for you."

All the fallen green shells had been replaced carefully on the door-frame further down. This place, Eigleath, worked like it was run by spirits.

A large careworn shirt, a small cardigan, socks, boxer shorts, men's drawstring pants.

Cass went back to the shower alone, but feeling the thread tangible, like a line through the house between her and her children. Accompanied by the sense that no one would try to break that thread at Eigleath, she washed herself, and cried, and washed and cried.

37

That night, all four of them, clean in the big blue bed. Sleeping. Almost. Vehicles had been coming down the lane, one after the other, and their headlights filled the bedroom and then left, filled the room with moving light and shadows, and then gone. Greetings were being performed on the gravel. This woke Vi.

"I don't like it here, Mommy," he said. Cass understood. There had been so much change.

"What don't you like?" she asked him.

"Don't know." He brushed long hair out of his eyes.

She loved the ripening silences that frequently came between Vi's first line of speech and his gathered thoughts.

"Funny place," he said eventually. "I think I really miss Dad"—and by the time he'd said that small three-lettered word his eyes were creased and pushing out tears. "He won't be able to find us here," and then the real problem: "You told that man at the border that Dad was never coming back."

Shit, shit. "Oh my love. Oh my love, I'm so sorry. I said lots of crazy things back there, didn't I?"

"We ran away from there."

"We did."

"Through a window!"

"Yeah."

"Are they going to catch us and take us back to that place?"

"No."

"Dad doesn't even know where we are!" said in an abject way.

"No. But I'm going to phone him in the morning and he will be really pleased to know that we're here."

"But you said he's never coming back."

202

"He'll come. He will meet us here. I had to say things that were not true at the border." She delivered this with resolve.

The boy wiped his nose on Cass's shirt.

Then he undid the button on her cuff; did it up again; undid, redid, undo, redone, calmer.

She stroked down the hair that grew in front of the boy's ear and noticed how each line in her internal poetic verses about his father was changing.

The lines were beginning as always, in the same old ways, but a great many of them had new emphasis and were ending on syllables of anger. Where once there had been poetic harmony, now there was a jagged verse of disrespect, unrhyming.

Increasingly, she could not respect Nathaniel, and this was loosening his attractiveness. Here lay his son, who was scared. The fact was that this lovely boy's father could have done so many things to alleviate this fear, but had chosen not to. Nathaniel could have moved them to this apparently gorgeous place, Eigleath, months, no, years ago. He could have spared them Eden. He could be stroking Vi's perfect ear. He could be around, changing diapers, a watchman over the children's changing. He could have stayed. It would have been so simple, to stay.

Everything Eden had done felt authorized, allowed, by Nathaniel.

And yet, the verses shifted, from hour to hour.

Here was a boy who wanted his dad. And here was a mother who could make everything rhyme.

Another set of headlights lit up the room.

She had to separate Nathaniel and Eden. Holding them in her mind as one wound-inflicting entity would only spell endings.

Amid the peace of the blue room she was still able to detect and keep pace with a pure little promise, a beat, a meter, running through the center of the marriage. She hoped that by stripping away the untameable, ungovernable feelings of her anger, and of Nathaniel's grief, what would remain was a basic bond of care: *I help you, you help me, let's have a competition now, to see how good we can be to one another.* She could not remain angry at her husband for Eden's behavior forever: it would not be reasonable. She could learn all the reasons he had for the things he did. She could become one of them. And how beautiful their marriage could be, if it could hold the necessary things he had to go and do, and hold, and hold, ready for his return.

He had lied to her about Eigleath because he must have believed—truly believed—that it was not safe for them to go there. Not safe to be with Arthur. But he was wrong. He didn't know who his brother had become. Nathaniel had made a young man's ruling about Arthur, and never returned to question it. Whereas Cass had taken on the question, taken a risk, had traveled to Eigleath, and could now demonstrate to Nathaniel that Arthur was safe. Vi was sleeping, safe, beside her.

She suspected that Eden had control over Nathaniel's opinion of Arthur. Eden had portrayed Arthur as her aggressor so that Nathaniel could be her savior.

As Cass was dropping off, she heard all the people who had been congregating downstairs filing out of the house together. She got up to watch them go from the window, as they headed across the meadow and down out of sight. They looked like a midnight wedding party. In relief at their flooding away she had a thought to creep downstairs and make herself something more to eat. "Help yourself to everything," they had said to her.

A teenager with clear eyes was sitting cross-legged on the kitchen table like a little knowledgeable creature. The girl introduced herself as "the babysitter" and held her head curiously as she watched Cass move around. Then something occurred to the girl: "You don't know where anything is, do you?"

"We've been waiting for you!" It was Arthur. He was leaning in through the window, beaming at Cass. "Full moon. Let's go." He'd threaded the end of a feather through one of the holes in his earlobe so it stuck out at an alien angle along the back of his head.

"Where?" Cass asked.

"Party time."

"I'm tired."

"Come on. It's all for you! We'll be ten minutes back if they need you."

Cass said she was too worried to leave the children and Arthur told her that the girl, the babysitter, was a nurse, and the young man who had appeared from the larder was a sage. The girl said she'd check on the children every hour.

"It's all for you!" Arthur said again.

She'd go for an hour. She'd go with Arthur. She could spare an hour. She could last an hour, and join in. All the adrenaline was not yet gone from her journey. On every in-breath it felt appropriate to step out into one more thing she feared. On every out-breath she felt guilty for being undeserving of this reception.

Cass and Arthur strode out together and the night seemed to warp to enwrap them. And then the stars, smatterings, galaxies.

"I'm really worried," Cass said.

"About kids?"

"No. I'm worried about taking up space. Using up your stuff. Is it alright that we're here? Really?"

He spoke down at his feet, something she didn't quite catch, and she asked him what he'd said.

"I want you to make this your home," he replied, quietly, a prayer mumbled. Then he repeated it again: "I want you to make this your home." With resolve. He kept going, repeating it. He sung it, louder, until he was shouting it to the gods, and then, as a god, he dropped down onto his knees dramatically and shouted, "I want you to make this your home!" Cass was laughing.

There were drums starting in the distance.

"I want you to make this your home." Looking up at her now, like he was desperate, pleading.

"OK, OK," she said. "Get up!"

They continued down the track, which curved off around a mound, across the corner of a field, and then down again into a natural circular dip. A large fire smoked gaily in the middle.

"This is . . . The Circle Place," Arthur said, as if the striking unoriginality of the name had only just occurred to him. "It's where we hold our rituals." People greeted him, and he ignored them, looking at her. She had to look away.

The moon's aura was an indecent thing; indecently huge. Around the fire, people were sitting in congenial groups. Drummers up the back.

"Sit here," he said. All she had to do was take the seat that was offered. All she had to do was sit between Arthur and the smiley-eyed man with the mustache who shook her hand and said, "I'm David." All she had to do was take the drink that was offered to her by one of a number of pretty, sprite-like men. All she had to do was answer the mustached man's questions playfully. "How was your journey up here?" he asked, sardonic, having heard things. "Uneventful," she said. Everyone here made it so easy for her. All she had to do was accept her privilege and trust them. Put her weapons down.

It was a happier collection of people than she'd been around for some time. Cass kept guessing at who among them actually lived at Eigleath and she felt the parameters of the place expand, and shrink again, under her guesses.

David—his mustache protruding like a proposition—talked to her about community, his "diagnosis for society," with an emphasis on the "no." The "special small new world" they had created at Eigleath had become, for him, a haven, not only from a violent climate, not only from the violent herd mentality of "the common world," but from the overly abstracted thought of "The Man." David talked of the non-logical, primal thinking that was necessary, in his opinion, to connect humankind back to the religion of the Great Mothers. The earliest matriarchies, he told her, "concentrated on maintaining, not exploiting, life." He said, "No one dominates, or humiliates, for power here. That's the dream, anyway." He spoke of the "absolutely necessary absence" of ownership. He was damning of their parents' society. He told her how the world they'd all grown up in had engendered in them too much individualism. "But community rewires that. We can heal. And when we heal ourselves, we will heal the Great Mother." Cass had heard it all before, albeit in different intonations, but she enjoyed very much the sensation of having him lead her somewhere, on purpose, in thought. She tuned in and out with what David was saying: ". . . because your mother was stuck in a capitalist dreamworld. Love should not be about ownership."

What was he saying? About mothers? About the romantic relationship and capitalism: the symbiotic connection between the two? Monogamy and hell?

The problem was that Cass wanted to be the private owner of her husband's love. Maybe Eigleath would gentle this belief in her, or perhaps she'd keep her belief to herself. She wanted her husband back, as he was before. This simple wish. "This capitalist dream of ownership."

"There are . . ." David was saying, linking up his musings on her behalf, "there are zero ways in which capitalism and the planet are sustainable. You have to choose. One or the other. And capitalism is held together by the monogamous relationship. Marriage is an economic maneuver, to sustain capitalism. There is no way that these sorts of relationships can continue now."

"Can't a partnership be at the center of a community?" she asked. "And be a helpful thing, for many."

"I'm just saying that society should not be so hierarchical, with the married people at the top. It's a system that stabilizes greed."

"For someone who doesn't believe in hierarchy, you lecture quite a lot." She was remembering how to be, the little jest in her expression, followed by the mirroring of it in his.

"Look," he said, "you adjusted your life to enjoy your own exploitation. That's all. That's it! It's quite normal."

Jem, perched on Arthur's lap, spoke up as if to rescue Cass from David: "David lives along your hall," she said.

Arthur heard this and took over. "David," he said slowly, "lives on your floor, other end. He was an engineer in his past life, he keeps us running. Wife died, she was my mate. You see Vinnie there?" Pixie body, tattoos on his face. "Ignore him. He's a proper sweetheart. You ignore him. He doesn't mean half what he says. He works with me. Rooms down in basement. Look—above you." He pointed very straight up, and looked very deep down into Cass, to make sure she understood that he meant above her bedroom, and not above her now, in the sky, among the stars. "Above you, that's me and Jem. And also Ella's room." David proffered a freshly rolled cigarette for Cass, right in front of her mouth so that his fingertips were an inch from her lips. She took it. He cupped and lit it. "For an engineer, you are some shit at rolling," Arthur said to David. "That's gonna explode or disintegrate, give it a second. And there's Ella," he continued as he identified a short woman with cropped black hair and good posture. "Ella's in charge. She doesn't shout about it. But there it is. There's six kids. Nine now, with you guys. That's it. That's Eigleath. Me, Jem, David, Ella, Vinnie, the kids, you. All you need to know. Everyone else is hangers-on, from town or Black Box. We don't mind." He said this last like an order. It became instantly apparent to Cass who among the gathered party was from the Black Box. The Black Boxers were dressed down, in neat plain clothes, as if they were trying to fit in by disappearing. While the others—with more matted hair, and easier gestures, jewelry which never came off—were dressed in full regalia. "Now drink this," said Arthur, "and have a dance." He winked at Cass as he got up.

An hour passed in ease as Cass moved, listened, and laughed along. There were little pinch bags and slushy lines on polished wooden trays being handed around. She noticed how frequently these circled back to Arthur and how coolly he declined them. *See,* she reassured herself. *He's not using. He is here.*

At around one, she walked back by herself. The babysitter and the sage were sitting out, with their toes pushed into the clover and the closed daisies. They offered her tea. She sat with them, feeling a tender ecstasy, saying aloud, "Well, this is ridiculous." She held up her cup in a sort of salute to the world.

38

Her cup stayed in the air. Beneath it, she saw a thin figure coming toward them across the meadow in long skirts.

Jem, drawing closer, was intoxicated. Her face hung all loose, and her shoulders fell forward as she swayed. Two of the wolfhounds followed in her wake. When she was near enough, she addressed the girl and the sage: "I'm going to steal her away now." She was holding out her hand to Cass; it was bejeweled, and it opened and closed all its fingers, once, twice, to insist on being taken.

Cass let Jem pull her up; she smelled of lavender and of smoke. Jem wanted to lead Cass to another field where she said the constellations were mapped out in the stones on the ground, but they got no further than an old oak tree, which stood alone and majestic at the end of the clover meadow. Clover, dew, bare feet. Jem circled the oak's trunk and ran her palm, fingers stretched back, over the gnarled, face-like wood. She hung her head in reverence as she made her circles, and lifted her free hand to the sky in a way that seemed otherworldly.

"You're so lovely," she sighed, eventually coming to rest in front of Cass.

"You're so high." Cass bent her face to Jem's and smiled.

"Are the children OK?" Jem wanted to know. "Are they OK? Will they be alright?" Her teeth were catching on her inner cheeks. "Oh, but they're so lovely and you're brave. Lonely. Brave."

"Do you want some water?" asked Cass. Jem said something unintelligible, and then tried to sit but fell to the ground, her mood altered.

"Everyone," she said, "everyone else here is too fucked, too *fucked*. Too fucked to really see what's going on anymore. They're going to get a problem, if they carry on like this. But I want to know. I want to know what you think about . . . what you think about . . . Eden?"

Cass hesitated. She wanted to detach from feelings of Eden here, by the oak. She didn't want to bring it all up, especially not with someone who was fucked; too much could be misconstrued. Too much relived. Cass was not confident yet that she could be convincing about how much Eden had made her suffer. Eden always had plausible deniability. Cass replied to Jem with an easy question: "You were at Eden's just before us?" But Jem had lost focus and was searching on the ground beneath her skirts. "What are you looking for?" Cass asked.

"My drink."

"It's not here. You didn't bring it."

Jem sighed with Maggs-like extravagance.

"I'll get you some water?" Cass offered.

"No. No. You're fine. You're lovely, by the way. Did we tell you that enough? You see. Oh God. We were only meant to stay one night. Break the journey up. It's far." She stopped and gave Cass a suspicious look. "You sure you didn't take my drink? I swear I saw you."

"No," Cass laughed. "I didn't take anything."

"You didn't? Fine. It's fine, actually. You didn't. So. Yes. God. We'd been in The City. Doing pick-up for Black Box. They don't trust many people. They trust us. It's a long way, though. We stopped at Eden's for a night and Arthur lost the van keys." She rolled her eyes, as if he might have done this on purpose. "We were stuck there for ages."

"He lost the keys?"

"Yeah. Idiot."

Cass was very still.

"I found them eventually," Jem went on. "They were hanging from that tree. You know the tree? The holes and the bits, hanging."

"Yeah, I know it. How did they end up there?"

"Maybe they fell out his pocket, someone found them, put them there. Maybe. I don't know. I wouldn't put much past that lot."

Cass tried something: "I think Eden's kind of dangerous," she said. Jem discovered a steadiness in her torso and managed to hold it, unwavering. Cass continued, "Eden took my car keys."

"It doesn't surprise me." Jem almost grinned with recognition.

Cass wanted to go no further. Not like this. She directed Jem's attention elsewhere. "The Black Box are up here, then?" she said. "Back home that was a rumor, that they were here."

"Black Box?" Jem was overtly shocked that Cass didn't know. "They're based a few miles that way, having a lovely time. Their minions come to us to party. They're twats mostly." She yawned. "Very entitled. Very green. By 'green' I don't mean . . . I mean . . . Oh, it doesn't matter. They're wealthy, obviously. Anyway, we were breaking the journey up at Eden's, meant to be a night." Jem curled her lip. "When Arthur's around Eden, you know, he uses up all the stash. He can't keep it together around her. So it was even harder to get out, once he got stuck in. But he's clean enough now, you know? He's gone back to normal."

"He seems very well."

Jem nodded for too long so that she started rocking. "Did you meet Tim?"

"No . . . I went there, to his place. I never saw him."

"She sent you there?"

Cass heard herself replying to this quickly, with a half-formed thought. "You know, it was like Eden wanted me to sleep with him or something." She let a weird laugh escape, like she didn't truly believe what she had just said. "I felt like a sacrifice."

"But you didn't?"

"Sleep with him? I never even met him."

"Oh, you're much cleverer than me," Jem said. Then she spat out: "Eden would never make Nathaniel's wife fuck for water."

It froze Cass in her tracks, this pronouncement, this combination of words and their implication. "Wait," she said, and then couldn't get her breath behind another word, only repeating, "Wait."

Jem shook her head in refusal; there was someone approaching them.

"Hi, lovely!" Jem called out. "I was just thinking about you." A girl was coming, staggering to sit with them. "Bluebell, this is Cass: she is lovely, like you." Bluebell's skin was glassy.

"Lovely," Bluebell repeated, bearing pointy teeth and eyes so blue they looked like fake gemstones. Cass wanted Bluebell to go away.

Bluebell had come holding a long branch which Cass recognized as yew. There must have been a fight to get it off the tree because the ends of it were still wet, white, and brutally torn. A fight, or a great deal of forceful bending. In the other hand Bluebell carried a bottle of what she called "shine," which Jem took.

"How is it down there?" Jem asked.

"Vinnie's throwing snakes on the fire." Bluebell had a curiously deep voice.

Cass imagined a snake popping as it hit the tips of the flames, transformed, like a phoenix.

"I hate that smell, when he does that," said Jem.

"Yeeeah. I'm just going to lay down here, if that's alright? Just lay down for a bit."

"You go for it. Put your head on my lap here if you like." Bluebell did, and Jem played with her thin hair prettily. It caught on her fingers.

For Cass, something was clearing. There was confirmation—wasn't there?—in what Jem had said, of the extent to which Eden could violently bend the will until it broke.

Cass was unexpectedly relieved of her anger for a moment. She was realizing that her anger was only necessary to fend against the threat of her own compassion, which could, at any moment, if Cass relaxed, softly touch upon Eden's humanity and say, *Poor Eden. Wild Cass.* Cass's anger had served the role of protecting her against the idea of Eden's benignity. Cass's anger would be less necessary if she believed fully in the extent of Eden's manipulation. If she truly believed in her own experience.

But how had Jem gone quite so far with it all? How had the equation been drawn so that it was real sex in exchange for water? Eden must have seen off Jem's defenses completely, in a flooding way, so nothing of Jem remained. Branches broken off by rivers.

Cass watched Jem, long-haired, flushed, cradling Bluebell's head in her lap. And Cass was held by a horrifying fear for Jem's well-being then.

She welcomed it. This horror. It would pull Jem into her care. Cass's rushing fear, channeled into fierce protection.

Jem raised her head to meet Cass's gaze. They stayed facing each other, drawing up, between them, in silence, what they were going to examine, and what they were going to pretend they hadn't seen, heard, known, admiring one another's abilities in this regard. Bluebell seemed to be feeling the exchange of energies between the two women; each breath of hers was audible.

Jem changed tack: "I've got to get out of here," she said, passing Cass the shine.

"Do you want to go back with me?" Cass swigged and did not react to the burn against her throat.

"No. There's no getting away from him."

"Who?"

"Thur," Bluebell moaned.

"You mean Arthur?" Cass said. "You want to get away?"

Jem responded with a smile that woke all her honeyed features. "Eighteen years together," she said. "Since I was seventeen. But I knew him from the start. I always knew what it was with him. That it was necessary. You know? Blue, are you going?"

"I'm going." She was rising with difficulty. Jem waited until Bluebell was out of hearing. "He's nasty," she continued, hissing it. "But his nastiness helped us. He could see. Where things were heading. He knew exactly how bad people can be."

"Nathaniel hates Arthur," said Cass. "I don't really understand why."

Jem gave her a dubious look from out one eye. "You don't know why Nathaniel hates Arthur? You really don't?"

"Well, I've heard all the stories, but Arthur has been really kind to me here."

Jem started to mirthfully chuckle. "Of course he has." She shook her head. "He's not stupid. Of course he's been kind to you. He has the sight. He's a gorgeous, gorgeous . . . shitbag. He's magical. Magic. And I was very, very stupid. Very young. He made us all frightened to follow the . . . the"—her voice became breathy—"consensus. And he was right. That would have been awful for me. But he's horrible, truly."

Cass drew her head back. She did not want everything to be unsettled again. She needed Arthur to be good. "But now he's brought you here and you've created all this. It's amazing."

Jem scoffed and then said, bitterly, "I met him. I woke up eighteen years later, and the whole world had burnt to the ground. And here I am."

Cass let her exhaustion and the shine take over within her. She let Jem go on and on, barely following the meaning, waiting for a hand to turn the page.

39

The night passed. The morning came. Cass stayed up with Jem. There was a morning star. Cass guided Jem back up to the white, early-sun-dappled house and they drank coffee and sat with the children in the meadow and Jem continued to speak, clearer now, as she let Daisy play with her bracelets. "I was always too addicted to Arthur. There was a knot inside me"—she held a fist at her sternum—"and it got tighter and tighter when we were apart, and then we were together and it released."

"I know that feeling," Cass said.

Arthur in the space between the floorboards, and the space between the stars. And in every buttonhole, all along. Nathaniel in every undulating breath. Brothers. Perhaps not quite unalike.

"He used to speak in my ear," said Jem, "right up against it. He was making his deposits, you know, his little *weeviling* secrets. I remember being sat on his stomach, I'm naked at this stage obviously, and he says"—she stopped to laugh at herself—"he says that the opening to my womb was like the entrance to a cave and it was cold. He is so full of shit. I used to wear his clothes. That was all I wore, for years. We all wore only his clothes. I brought nothing with me. He laughed out our pretenses, you know? All the posing we did—we do. He chases it away. He pointed out how we spoke, like the sayings we had, and the way we held ourselves—all the stuff we had copied, unconsciously, from our parents, and their parents, and their parents. He called out our opinions until we abandoned them. And we brought nothing. The boys with him—the other men, I mean—eventually they give up all their ego to him. All their ideas that they might win against him, they run at him, and break themselves against him, and when they're broken, they get his loyalty. They come only as themselves. It's nice,

214

actually. And the girls—the girls get bold for his attention. He promises other women too much. And it makes them bold. And then they blatantly request exactly what they want from him. And he gives it. For a—you know—a season. It is much, much better to be a man in love with him than a woman."

"Was he . . . Is he faithful?" Cass hoped Jem wouldn't find this question insulting, but if Arthur slept around, perhaps Jem did too, point-scoring—perhaps sex with Tim hadn't been such a big deal, not quite so seismic, in that context.

"Not when he's using. He's OK at the moment. I have visions. I mean, sometimes I could literally hear him screwing someone else. In the past he did that. Downstairs. But also, visions are my gift"—as she picked tobacco from her tongue.

"I thought he looked after you?"

"He tells me I'm his world, then he taps out. I keep remembering watching him walk in front of me wearing Mom's dressing gown, walking like a king, and then he turns and spits at Dad's feet, just to show him how important I was." All her smiles were reminiscent. "First time I saw him, he was drinking from the milk carton, then he was escorting me places. I felt fallen without him. I do. And I always thought . . ." she said, slowing right down, "that all your kids were his."

"Why on earth would you think that?"

The light changed, became clinical, and Jem's skin took on a dry ugliness.

"Paranoia," she said. "But the right sort. I swear that most of the kids here are his."

Cass looked up at the other children—the "Children of the House"—who were all standing around Maggs as she explained to them a great heist she had planned. They looked different, these new children whom Cass had barely taken in yet. They looked unchildlike. They all wore an assortment of adult things, and rings, over which they bent their fingers to keep them in place.

"You're so calm," Jem said then.

"I'm not. Tell me another thing?" Cass lay back on the grass and closed her eyes and wished that Jem's stories could pass through her without leaving a trace.

"About Arthur?" Jem said. "Nothing. Nothing. I don't complain. There's no one else for me." Her voice lightened. "He may have fathered all these brats. But he sleeps in my bed every night. He doesn't really sleep around anymore. That was in the past. And, you know, these kids, actually, they're David's, Ella's nephews, our friends left them here with us. It's just my paranoia. Anyway, I knew, from the first moment he touched me. I was done. It's me he needs . . . It's just, I wonder now if it's been too much for me. Sometimes I think I would have had a longer life if I'd gone with someone else."

"What's going on?" It was the man himself calling out to them from across the land. He was with five other men heading with purpose.

"We're fine." Cass did not sit up.

"Where you going?" Jem yelled to Arthur.

"Vinnie's got to go town today, and he's a wreck."

"Shit," said Jem, getting up so fluidly that the air and the grass around her barely registered the movement. She walked at once toward the men.

"I wanted one day off from this shit." Arthur was furious. Then to someone, it was unclear to whom, he said, "I heard you the first time."

Cass found herself left with the Children of the House.

The tiniest of them, who was trying to prevent a draping garment from coming off, approached Cass. "You're new! Were you knowing that? Can we go to Lance now?"

She could not fathom them. They had unfamiliar characteristics. The landscape looked, once more, quite bleak; the night had washed her out and left her not only empty but still emptying.

Cass asked the oldest-looking child, the one with a scar running from cheekbone to chin, where the computer with internet was, and he led them all there.

40

The computer was in David's room. David opened his door to them; he was wet, freshly showered and bare-chested, wearing proper pajama pants. One of the little girls dashed into his arms and Cass realized that this was David's daughter. He welcomed them all into his room—which was three rooms, knocked together, whitewashed, a different space entirely, heavily scented. It was like a studio, sparse, with lots of plants. Piles and piles of books, but otherwise pristine. The children started jumping on the bed. David set Cass up at the computer on his wide desk. While he leaned over her and tried to connect her to the internet, she registered her absolute nervousness.

Vi came up quietly to her shoulder. "Are you calling Dad now?"

"Yes."

"Will I be able to speak to him?"

"Hopefully."

She dialed through to Nathaniel a couple of times, but he didn't pick up. Then she opened her emails, expecting a deluge of messages from him demanding to know where the hell she'd taken his children, and why had she left Eden's so abruptly? But there was nothing. Was it possible that Eden hadn't told him they had left? Eden would perhaps plead ignorance and no responsibility.

Cass opened other messages, including an appeal for food from a parent whom she'd been friendly with at the school gate. There was nothing from Ally. But then a new email popped in—it was from Nathaniel—like a little jolt. It said: "Sorry I missed your call just then. I'll call you this time tomorrow. I hope you're OK. I love you. N x"

She replied straightforwardly, telling him they were at Eigleath, and she moved away from the desk. David had given Daisy a basket of his daughter's toys from a cupboard. His daughter objected to sharing her things with a baby, but he overruled her. Then he suggested that he go downstairs and make everyone a round of boiled eggs. Cass asked if she could lie down on his bed. It smelled very foreign, but the smell was lost to her in sleep.

She dreamt that she stepped over dead lizards on the way back into her old house, where there was a party that she didn't want. Before that was a dream sent from the yew, about a dark place, reflecting. She dreamt that Eden was standing very still at the foot of the bed. These were all in the special category of dream that changed the way her body felt for days after.

41

Nathaniel did not call the next day when he said he would. Cass tried him again: no answer.

She went looking for Arthur, perhaps for reassurance, a bit of counter-narrative to Jem's nightmare, some tempering. She went looking for her conviction. But: "He's not about at present"—a couple of people used exactly this phrase with her.

Her children were absorbing the new surroundings. Their eyes stared, calmly, imprinting. Their hearts were rushing when she held her hand on their chests; but rushing—she identified—with glee, not anxiety. (She believed she could tell the difference. Something in the pattern of the beat.) They breathed fully, without restriction. Jem, who was inclined not to hear what the adults around her were saying ("Where are you going?" "Were you not listening at all?"—"What time's the thing?" "I've told you this three times, Jem."—"Who are you talking about?" "You, pet!"), Jem blinked brightly when the children spoke, she listened to them properly. Cass noticed how the other adults were sensitive to Jem, rather delicate with her; they teased her for being "in your own world" but were nervous of upsetting her, like she might spill. She was only barely the safe side of fragile—so it seemed to Cass.

Dinner was laid out on the table for the children at six. There were often various people in the kitchen cleaning the windows, washing the skirting boards, and prepping food. None of these people were among the five adults whom Arthur had identified as the real residents of Eigleath. None of these people lived in the house. Cass liked it. So this was communality, she thought: even the young men and women who did not live at Eigleath contributed to its upkeep. Eigleath held their community, and so they helped look after it. Seen like this, the estate became like a sacred object to which all attended. Cass wanted to tell her husband about it. About the living, loving home of youthful energy that was waiting for him.

Days passed and Nathaniel did not call and he did not answer.

Arthur reappeared, but Cass couldn't get him on his own. She wanted to hear from him explicitly how Nathaniel would fit into the picture of the household. How the brothers' torn bond could begin to heal. They needed to coexist as joint owners of Eigleath.

Every time she looked for Arthur, she saw him engaged in a series of longing dances with Jem. This in itself reassured Cass. Arthur so clearly did not fit with the nightmare Jem had described. He appeared to be very much a man who felt gratitude for his partner; if anything he displayed a surfeit of concern for her. Jem was surely unbalanced. This is why she had been manipulated so far by Eden. And Arthur had not protected Jem. He had doped himself out to evade his mother and in so doing had left Jem to defend herself, and she couldn't. He was sorry. Cass could see this reflected in his efforts, as he put things right. Cass had only witnessed an Arthur who played excitedly with the children whenever they approached him, an Arthur who definitively refused drugs at The Circle Place. Arthur was steady now. Exactly what he claimed to be. Just like Nathaniel.

*

Ella, with the short dark hair, was in the kitchen, washing up from all the bacon she'd fried. She had thick wrists and smooth skin. She was strong: she lifted the huge heavy frying pan from the sink with one hand and shook off the excess water violently, once, twice.

No one would let Cass do anything to help. They told her to take it easy. "You're still recovering from your journey," Ella said.

Cass took the children out to explore, venturing further each time: the expanse of fields; some cold, stone outbuildings; the animals; rows of polytunnel greenhouses. After dinner one night, Eigleath's ensemble of children dug clay out of the earth and made little pots. They used the clay to mark their faces with patterns that dried to green.

She was visiting David's room at regular intervals throughout the days that passed to call Nathaniel, sitting expectantly at the screen. No reply.

She felt that David had started looking romantically upon her pilgrimages to use the computer in his room, as if this were the beginning of a new chapter for him. The prologue. But Cass's dislike of him was growing. She didn't like his hands, or his barely concealed intent. She was annoyed that she was unable to convey to him that her husband was furiously possessive.

She got caught on the memory of her own stocky man, with his thick arms cradling their infant daughter in a soft-play center, as he ate Maggs's unwanted cheese sandwich.

*

Three of the older children were doing somersaults out of the old oak tree onto a large trampoline which had been carried there by several young men. The trampoline was blue and its springs creaked loudly when each spine landed. Cass's children had gone, sweetly hand in hand, halfway toward the tree to watch. She loved their backs. They seemed to be growing in those very seconds.

Jem sighed and Cass felt the movement of it against her thigh, so close did Jem sit. They talked through long hours, sharing experiences and tearing up grass.

But Jem refused in these talks to touch on the subject of Arthur or Eden, instead making insightful observations about the children and the growing herbs, and what they promised. Jem was the queen of evasion. Her looks were mocking and wicked if Cass tried to steer her to speak about something she didn't want to. Jem made Cass feel like a healing force. At least Cass could give her that.

Every day there was someone new in the kitchen. Sometimes the place felt too open.

Every day Ella sat down at the kitchen table with them, wiping her hands on a tea towel. She was beginning to fold Vi and Maggs into the basic lessons she devised for the children. She put down a jar of colored pencils, all sharpened, and an instruction.

While the children bent their heads one morning, Ella was infuriatingly curious about Nathaniel.

"I love him," Cass said, matter-of-factly.

"But he abandoned you, basically."

"No, he went to do his job. He will come back. He's a good man. He's a wonderful father." Cass had nearly said "was."

"Is he? He left them. He left you alone with them."

"No. It wasn't like that."

"In that city."

"He had stuff to sort out."

Everyone at Eigleath conferred with Ella over seemingly everything. Her pronouncements directed the flow of activities. She was constantly sought and drawn into urgent conversations. But not by Cass.

Nathaniel emailed eventually. Apologized. Said he'd call the next day. He didn't.

His emails continued for days like this, making excuses and keeping to the surface of things with "I love you's." He didn't seem to be upset that Cass had taken his children to Eigleath. He did not mention Eden. He did not pick up on Cass's comments that Eigleath had not—as he'd always said—been sold, but was in fact very well kept. He claimed to be distraught that they hadn't been able to speak. The connection was shitty, his end. They'd speak on Maggs's birthday, "come hell or . . . ," he wrote.

*

Cass was plating up rice and lamb for eight children, with Daisy on her hip. She dipped her finger in the gravy and Daisy sucked it. David was beside her, washing out the rice pan. Two people Cass had never seen before were cleaning out the corners of the larder. Daisy was screwing up her face fiercely, trying hard to form sounds.

"What do you want to tell me, huh?" Cass asked. Then she cradled Daisy's head and tipped her back and Daisy laughed, the toothy, firefly laugh.

Yet another new person entered the room. Cass only noticed him particularly because he had scar tissue all up one arm, which she recognized, from images she'd seen on Nathaniel's phone, as burn tissue; it was the way the markings eddied, like a silted estuary. His strides were long, his course pre-set and certain. His T-shirt was nice. She leaned back against the counter, stroking Daisy's thigh with her thumb, dipping a finger from the other hand into the gravy and holding it up to Daisy's mouth. Daisy was watching the burnt man too, but she'd steal her eyes away from him just long enough to wrap her small fist around the base of Cass's finger, open her mouth, and land it over Cass's offering.

In stopping to speak to Ella, the burnt man blocked out some of the light coming through from the window. His voice was very soothing; it resonated. Cass's eyes stayed on his scarred arm and she spaced out there. It was easy to exist partly in a fantasy world. Wherever she went, she was leaving a space beside her constantly for her husband, who would fill it very soon. She had mentally rehearsed the tour of Eigleath she would give Nathaniel when he arrived. She had plans to help revitalize the home school. There was buoyancy ahead.

Her leg was itching. A bite, or a scratch. She put her hand toward it and remembered, as she brushed past, the roll of notes in her pocket that she'd been meaning to add to the jars of money lined up above the sink. She took the money from her pocket and let Daisy grab it, stopped the child from putting it in her mouth, and instead brought her to the jars, picking up the emptiest one.

"Put it in," she told her lamby breathed baby.

The man with the red burns came quite alarmingly toward them from the other side of the room. He covered the jar with his burnt hand.

"Don't," he said.

*

When Cass emailed Nathaniel, she also emailed Ally, not to tell her much, but for a little sprout of joy. Ally wrote back to say that she and Rose were mostly holed up inside, but resilient, and learning an instrument each, a violin and a saxophone, gifted to them. "Yours screechingly" was how Ally signed off several missives. Cass worried about how Rose's swollen knuckles and broken pinkie coped under Ally's musical regime.

42

Maggs's birthday. Cass and her children had been sent outside while surprises were prepared.

"When I grow up, Mommy, I going to paint pictures as big as a house," said Maggs, five now.

"A house!"

"This house! As big as the sky! As big as blue!"

"That's cool."

"Sky painter," Maggs confirmed.

"When I grow up I'm going to be a witch," said Cass.

"But you are grown-up!"

"Yes, but when I'm really grown-up."

"A good witch?"

"There's no other sort."

"What will you be, Vi?" the little girl asked, turning to him.

"A nothing," he said. "I can't imagine doing anything."

Once, Cass might have objected to this statement and countered it with all the different things that he might do. But the world of possibilities had shrunk.

She bent down to Vi's eye level and remembered that a mother's words could become your blueprint, even if you consciously rejected them, and this was why, she thought, some women were known as witches.

"You will be happy. And you will be happy. And you will be a happy man," she said.

Not an assertion, not intrusive, not a statement of fact, but another layer of reality. A spell.

Cass wondered if she knew any happy men.

*

Back inside, the kitchen was filled with scented steam. Arthur was home and he was cooking. He'd flung a tea towel over his shoulder. He was attending to the stove devotedly, chopping, stirring, and Jem was moving around him. There were bottles of wine on the table, and new foodstuffs, all brought by Arthur from a three-day expedition.

"Birthday girl!" he cried when he saw Maggs. "Out to the meadow with you."

The party was sweet. The presents were extraordinary. Not the homemade articles that Cass had expected. The children ate the cake and then played. Cass relaxed. She was aware that this was the first time she'd sat down solely with the residents of Eigleath. She told everyone a bit about what life had been like in The City.

"Did you know," David asked as he finished chewing, "did you know, when you left, that you were leaving for good?"

"More or less."

"So you packed all your treasures," said Ella.

"I left a lot behind."

Vinnie said, "It's like that game: what do you save if your home is burning down?"

"The kids and their precious things, mainly," said Cass.

"My mother's photos," added David.

"Pharmaceuticals," said Vinnie.

Then Arthur said, "What about you, Jem?" and he caught Jem's eye, and she focused.

"What would I save if the house was burning down?" She was wiping food delicately from her hands. "The fire."

David looked alarmed by this apparent insightfulness.

"Where did you hear that?" he asked.

"Read it somewhere."

"Yes, but where?"

"It's Jem's now," came Arthur's ruling.

"There's a curfew down in The City," said Vinnie, whose face was old beneath the tattoos (sunbeams radiating from below his eye, a cruciform thing on the other temple). "An hour you're allowed outside. One hour. They track you on your phone, and you can't be outside without your phone, because the phone has the pass on it. It's a horror movie, seriously. But it was always going that way. People were mega-dumb not to see it coming."

"You couldn't see Gaia coming," David said.

"Could."

"What is it now?"

"Once a week they do a 'clearing,' as they call it."

"Jesus."

Vinnie spoke up loudly: "It was obvious the rich would sail through everything. So why wasn't there a revolution? Anyone could see that, as soon as they wanted to, whatever disaster came, the rich were going to go to their land and make their own little Edens. Take the good stuff with them. Close the gate. To hell with everyone else."

"Watch out, Vinnie," said Arthur. "You've used the trigger word there."

"What, 'rich'?"

"No. 'Eden.'"

"And also, why not?" Vinnie continued, unabashed. "I'm not going to stop being rich out of morals, if I've got a way to feed my kid."

Arthur said, "Well, luckily for us"—he took a sip and then placed his glass down—"you don't have any."

Then, as Jem said, "That we know of," Vinnie simultaneously asked, "What? Morals or children?"

They all laughed a little.

Vinnie said, "I probably do, somewhere, poor little sods." He looked off into the middle distance in a way that was so ridiculously oversentimental that everyone laughed again.

It grew darker out, steadily, from the ground up. Arthur mock-wrestled Vi to the grass and lay down beside him. Ella was leading the clear-up, and as she started making her way inside, laden, she called back, like an afterthought, that it was bedtime. The children all groaned, but they also all, miraculously, made moves to pack up their cards, new sticks, flowers, and start to follow her. A single word spoken by Ella carried so much weight with the children. She said the word "bedtime" with no hint of there being any other version of reality than the one that saw these children quietly in their rooms. She created events with the purity of her language.

Downstairs, the talk from the meadow had moved inside. Cass was due to call Nathaniel in ten minutes. She filled a glass with wine. There were clear plastic bags of bloody meat on the table. Abundance. And eggs. The red dust from the brick floor had worked its way under the edges of her toenails.

She was happy and ready, as she climbed to David's room, with all the things she would tell Nathaniel about the new life that was waiting for him. She would remind him how she still carried his love close and felt it every day and used it, in an admixture with her own, to warm their children. Most of all she'd show him how clear she felt, and how free of hardship for the first time in a great long time.

Daisy had refused her feed, exhausted from the birthday and her first bite of sugary cake. Cass's breasts ached with the last of her milk, but there was excitement in this ending. The end of babyhood.

She entered David's room. It was lit by moonlight. She woke the computer, entered the call screen, and waited.

43

Nathaniel dialed in.

The first thing that there was, was a girl. There was a girl there. A girl's face, on the screen. So symmetrical. Eyes darting around the four corners of the device, setting things up. Cass's initial thought was that one of them had accidentally connected to the wrong call. She was about to apologize, but instead she said, "Hello. Who is that?" sounding momentarily, and horrifically to herself, like Eden.

The girl stepped aside and Nathaniel's face moved into view. He sat.

"Cassandra. Hi, beautiful," he said.

"Who was that?"

"It's wonderful to see your face there, baby."

The girl, having moved away, was standing in the background now. Cass did not know if the girl thought she was out of shot. The girl turned and was, in profile, strikingly pregnant. The roundness protruded from her tiny frame. Cass could see her husband's bed, all neat.

"Who is that?"

He stared at the camera, taking a pause that was too long, so it seemed as though the call had frozen, but it hadn't, because the girl was moving smoothly behind him.

Cass said, "Can you hear me? Who is that with you?"

There was a flash of anger over his face. Then, so coldly, he said, "Yes, I can hear you."

"Who is that in your room?"

Not long ago, Cass would have waited calmly for her husband to introduce the pregnant girl in his bedroom, and given him time to explain who she was in a way that made her disappear (a patient, a colleague, a person in need).

"That's Petal," he said.

"Who is Petal?"

"Can't we just talk. Just us. First?"

"I don't know, can we? There appears to be a pregnant teenager in your bedroom." She'd waited so long for this call.

"Cass . . ." He said it as if they were in the middle of an argument that had been going on for hours, days, weeks. "Why does it have to be like this?"

Then they both started yelling at once. "Like what? Like I, your wife, ask you, what's up with the pregnant teenager in your room. After I've been through hell." And he was saying, "I just wish you would listen to me for a minute and let me explain, but you're always jumping to the worst, last conclusion about me. You look down on me with such *disdain*."

"If you had answered my first question, 'Who is that?' I would have accepted—I would have accepted that the girl was a patient, maybe, or helping with your clinic. But you're angry, and that means you're hiding something. And I am joining the dots, and it's not looking very good." Joining the dots, like drawing the lines between the stars and making constellations, which unlocked something.

"I knew I should have written first to explain." He was exasperated already.

"So. Go on. I'm listening. Explain to me."

"I'm changed. Cass. I don't want to chain you. You don't understand what it's been like here. War. War, Cassandra. War. You don't understand. What it does to a man."

"What it does to a man!"

He said, "You don't understand how heavy your need is on me."

Something was pulling at Cass. Something strong pulling her down by the arm, to the bottom of the deepest tunnel, a tunnel dug so deep that it disturbed all the foundations of the earth above it, which would collapse, not only burying her but making the ground above, where their children resided, where their children were, fall in.

Her hand darted out and she turned the computer off at the screen. She picked up the nearest book and threw it across the room as hard as she could with a cry that came from her center. And then she wailed.

David, apparently alarmed by the noise, had run up the stairs and swung open the door.

"GO AWAY!" Cass screamed as she threw the next book in his direction. He caught it easily. He placed it on the floor with his other hand held up in truce, and he backed out of the room.

Cass threw everything that was unbreakable. Curled up in a ball on the floor. It was as if all her breath had been captured by the world and no one would give it back.

After a while, Ella crept in.

"Go away, please," said Cass.

Ella walked around the room picking up the thrown books and objects.

"I'll tidy it up," said Cass. "Don't tidy up after me."

"I'm not, I'm just giving you back these missiles here in case you need to throw them again."

"What's going on?" It was Arthur at the door now, Vinnie, Jem, David behind him.

"He showed me a teenager who he's having a baby with."

"He told you what?" said Arthur.

"He showed me!"

"But he told you?"

"He didn't deny it. He could have denied it."

"Is this real?" Then Arthur knew it was; he hit his open palm against the doorframe and said, "I hate him," and then, louder and upward, "I hate you!"

Ella hushed him: "Don't wake up the children."

He turned to Cass angrily, shaking a finger at her, possessed to the eyeballs. "He's not coming here. OK? He is not coming to my house."

Jem said, "Arthur, this isn't about you." But Cass felt momentarily protected by his rage, like it was the very kindest thing he could do for her in that moment.

Arthur wouldn't step back. He shouted wildly, "This *is* about me and that asshole. I will kill them all."

This sight shocked Cass out of her own emotion. It seemed overplayed. Jem followed him hurtling from the room.

*

"I'm going to say it."

"Don't say it."

"I'm going to say it."

"Why?"

"I'm going to say it, and I'm going to sound like my grandmother."

"Go on, then."

"You're going to wear a hole in that rug if you keep pacing like that."

Cass had been circling David's room, talking, talking freely as Vinnie sat cross-legged on the floor rolling her cigarette after cigarette, and Ella sat on the chair with her chin in her hands, listening.

"I can see it all now. This whole time. This whole time he's been with her. Making a new family. Without us. Without us!"

David had made himself scarce. Cass could sense that this was calculated—so that he didn't witness her at her worst; so that he could greet her like a new proposition when the time felt right. "Fuck him too," she said, and it probably sounded to the others like she was talking about Nathaniel still. She kept being overcome by waves of despair and curling up on the floor under the force of them. Did they lie in bed together and talk about her? Did they laugh about her? Did he like Petal more than anyone else he'd ever liked before?

"Come on," Ella said eventually, when she could see that Cass was replaying the moment of impact over and over and not getting anywhere. "Come with me." Ella, who had never touched Cass before, put her short thick arm around Cass's back.

Ella led Cass through the house, which seemed endless, strange. They went outside and got in Ella's strange truck, and Cass watched the strange trees brush right up against the windows as they drove up the lane. Cass could not think of better words for anything.

"Where do you want to go?" Ella asked. "The cliff above the sea?"

Cass weighed in herself the force that would be required to propel herself into the water from a cliff above the sea.

"No," she said.

"We'll just drive around for a bit, then . . . You can really feel the change of season at this time of night. It is colder."

"I really love him, though," Cass said.

"Sweetheart," said Ella, in which Cass heard "You fool" and also "You'll live."

44

In the kitchen, a few mornings later, Cass was thick with headache from crying all night, and she was tired of stealing away from her children constantly to smoke. There had been no further word from him. Not after her first email, expressing full-throated, nasty pain. Nor her second, reminding him of their love. Her ships had sailed. Whenever the children spoke to her, she could hardly hear them. Her body was irritable, and she wanted Daisy off her. There was a highchair now. It had appeared overnight. She hadn't asked where it had come from. Put Daisy in it.

She had snapped at Vi and Maggs, when they had asked about their dad. And now they were outside and tying themselves irrevocably into the Children of the House bind from which she feared she would never retrieve them.

Yes, she was being cruel to the children, and this was their father's fault. But Vinnie, as he stirred milk into teas, said, "You're very gentle with them." Maybe he meant: given the circumstances. "Want to help me carry these out?" One of the wolfhounds brushed against Cass's bare leg and she hated the feel of it.

"Has anybody seen Jem?" Arthur's call.

Cass's mind had turned ungenerous and churned with daily new regrets.

She should never have let Nathaniel leave for war. Other women would have resisted their husbands leaving. She had let go too willingly. She had lied about her willingness. She should have stayed in The City, made him stay there with her. The brick floor retained no heat now, spilt liquid hung on its surface and did not soak in, and the leaves outside had changed.

She complained to herself: the population of Eigleath was so homogeneous, entirely white, entirely brattish; they were unaware of how lucky they were within their natural bounty and environs; they were spoiled, all dissatisfied despite everything being stacked in their favor. In The City, surely, there remained a vast army of global women who would be making the most of life. The strictures of existence in The City had surely, by now, inspired great creativity and collective action. She missed Ally. She wished she had stayed down there, at the gritty edge of life, where people were still making things new, grafting, grieving. Eigleath felt ossified to Cass; it would go on as it was, unripe. Eigleath had been codified. Life here had been outsourced to a plan that they all had to follow. Nothing was from the body.

"Help me carry these out?" Vinnie said again. She went over and picked up three mugs of tea by the handles. The mugs knocked together in her hands and the hot liquid splashed on her skin and she was grateful for how much it hurt.

Outside, the hood of the truck was up and David was stooped over the engine, polishing his reading glasses on his T-shirt. His daughter came up behind him and spoke into his ear. He assented, and turned a nearby bucket over so she could stand on it and peer into the engine too. She had scabby knees, long pin legs, and she smiled squintingly as though she were always in direct sunlight.

"Arthur, we need more paints," Jem was calling from near the greenhouses.

"There you are! It's on my list." And then, to Vinnie, he said, "Let's be moving the garbage on now. We'll bring the pigs last-minute."

"Aye, aye."

Ella had appeared and was giving Arthur aggressive counsel. The great big sky rushed. The man with the burns was here—unlike he'd been the time before. This time he was huge, carrying full wooden crates.

Cass did not tend to ask about any individual who floated in and out of view at Eigleath—there was a generalized edict in the air to simply accept—but something about this man upset her personally. "Who is that?" she asked Vinnie, who had made himself particularly available to her the last few days, supplying her with cigarettes and with tea.

"That? That is Lance. Used to live here. Like, live-live. Doesn't play well with Arthur."

How short-sighted, Cass thought, to go against the grain of Arthur instead of with it.

Lance loaded three more crates into the back of the van. David called out, "Try it now!" and the two older kids, whom Cass had only just spotted in the driver's seat, leapt into action and tried the ignition together.

"Again!" called David. "Again! . . . One more time. Huzzah!"

The engine turned over, and David flipped the towel that he had been using to hold some greasy part so that it caught Jem on the backside as she passed. She squealed.

"Pigs," said Arthur. Vinnie put down his tea and followed at a march.

David kissed his daughter on the top of the head and said, "Thank you," sincerely. And then he shouted out to all: "That was Ivy's doing! Ivy fixed the engine." And several people called back, "Thanks, Ivy," and, "Well done, Ives."

David, happy, ambled to the rear of the truck and peered into Lance's crates, picking a leaf from the green produce there to smell it, then chew it. He was lifting a crate to look into the one beneath and leaning to ask Lance something.

Ella was telling the children in the front seats, "You cannot go with, so stop asking. No. I said: No." And Jem said to them, "I need you now."

Arthur, carrying with Vinnie a cage containing two piglets, overheard the older children's pleas to be taken to town and he said, "You are not coming—stop whining." The pigs were loaded on, to great catastrophizing. Arthur was in a mood.

He had been avoiding Cass. She supposed that she had brought the weight of his unkind family down on him again. Cass had been cooking and cleaning more in the evenings, even though everyone told her not to. It did not—as the lie had it—take her mind off things; it gave her undisturbed time to focus on her husband having sex with someone else.

Ella bribed the older children to get out of the truck and they ran off together with huge grins on their faces and something secret in their hands. Arthur and Vinnie were in the front seats now, bickering, and then they were off. Ella, smiling, touched Cass lightly with her fingertips as she went back inside, indicating that she should follow.

"Shit, where's Daisy?" asked Cass, entering the kitchen.

"She'll only be with the others," said Ella. "She'll be fine."

Cass ran out the other side of the house to see Daisy holding hands with Jem, walking, tottering, with the other children toward the willows. Cass could not help but call out, "Jem, is Daisy OK with you?"

"I will not take my eyes off her," came the sing-song reply, and the wolfhounds flowed after her.

Cass returned to the kitchen. An unhealthily thin teenager, whom Cass had never seen before, was on her hands and knees disinfecting the shelves in a cupboard she'd emptied. Cass said hello to her, but the girl did not appear to hear it.

"Cass, help me with these?" said Ella from the sink.

David, passing at the window, saw them watching him, shifted his tall frame into a camp hip-swing, and said, "Hello, ladies."

"You'll be careful there," said Ella near Cass's ear.

"Yeah, I know." Cass didn't give a shit about David: she wanted to talk to Ella about her husband's pregnant girlfriend. She wanted to use the words "fucking skank" out loud.

"If you go with David and later change your mind about him, all the men will hate you."

"I know. I'm not interested."

"But he will chase you if you're truly not interested."

"But aren't those the old ways? The Old World."

"I suppose."

"Isn't Eigleath the New World?" She spoke sarcastically. "What are these men even doing here?"

Ella blinked, took a beat, continued carefully: "No one ever said this was the New World, Cass. It's just different window dressing."

On the next full moon, Nathaniel replied to one of Cass's emails. He wrote: "We're coming to you, my beloved. We're going to make this right." Cass sobbed into Jem's skirt over whom the "we" entailed. Jem said, "He's an asshole, he's an asshole," but she was also resigned, utterly unsurprised by Nathaniel's actions, and this made Cass's tears intensify.

Night. The children were asleep once more. David said he'd watch them.

Cass only wanted solitude in which to replay thoughts of her husband licking another woman, knowing another's anatomy, making another hum; to get to the bottom of "Why?" She'd go somewhere private for this. Up the lane, into the great expanse, back on herself, through the stiff gate, her boots, brought to her from town by Vinnie, crunching forward on the pebbles that made the path. She carried with her a large black flashlight, another thing pressed on her by Vinnie. Heavy as a weapon. Enough moonlight to keep it switched off.

Finally, she caught sight of the sea. A beautiful, strong, female sea. She caught it, knew it, greeted it, released it. Then she lay down.

There had been a time when her husband knew her thoughts before she did, as though they were his own. When did that stop? Perhaps it never had. Perhaps he knew even now.

The land was wet and cold against the back of her head.

Before her husband: her parents. She had surely been a vessel for their thinking. They'd battled down her infant walls, and left their own thoughts in her to lie and grow, uncontested. Left her to take each set of their thoughts to its logical conclusion, to that place that they didn't dare go themselves, and left her to deal with the sadness, the inept, desperate poverty of love that she encountered there. They knew her thoughts; they had seeded them.

What could she do with this rooting torment that was shaped like that young girl's pregnant belly and lodged within her? Someone had to rip it out for her. She couldn't do it herself.

She turned onto her front and dug a nail into the earth. Then she closed her eyes and struggled for a while against herself. Something had to give. Something had to break. This state was unsustainable. She would die of this jealousy and of this pain. It would riddle her. Her children would be better off without her if she carried on like this.

She took in a shaking breath. It disturbed a picture that was forming in her mind of her husband and his girlfriend standing together, well-dressed, and being condescending to her.

What did it mean about her, this thing her husband had done? Might it mean nothing? Or was she nothing? Those seemed the only options. And it definitely meant something.

She had once felt bliss with him.

She had once felt bliss. And yet, her impulse had always been to give away the greater part of it. That's what she was for: to feel the bliss of life, to break it in two, to share the bigger piece and become renewed in the process. She had once felt that she could transform the whole night sky into love within her perfect body, and yet her impulse was to give away the greater share. She thought that the world might have forgotten to honor this natural tendency among its creatures. Man had progressed and ruined life by taking advantage of this. The institutions of her society, of education, work, and marriage, had expected, with entitlement, the bigger piece.

If he was coming to Eigleath, where would she go, exactly? He could claim Eigleath as half his. And the children as at least half his. And then what? Did he expect that they would all live together? With his new woman and his new child? Cass could not. She would have to leave. She would not leave the children. There was no promise left. Only necessity.

45

On her late walk back from the cliff, the pebbles underfoot crushed to a beat that felt sympathetic. The lightest rain. Invisible clouds concealing the moon. The beam from Vinnie's flashlight, like a hectic toddler leading her.

When she reached the back field, she spotted a figure walking out. A man. She was agitated. Not Arthur. *No, not Nathaniel.* She moved the beam of her flashlight. It was Lance. His burns were covered up by a red-hooded coat. He was far from her, far away enough that it would have been possible to pass on without them having to properly acknowledge one another, and this was what she wanted.

But she stopped. "Where you going?" she called out, shining the flashlight on him steadily. She was sick of unknowns. Her curiosity was urgent, as if it would save her; she needed to know everything now.

He stopped, then surprisingly altered his path and approached her. And when she thought he was close enough to hear her clearly, as close as she'd like him to get and no closer, she called again, "Where are you going?" He smiled as he raised an arm to shade his eyes from her excessive beam; she directed the light to his feet.

"I'm avoiding the women," he replied. He spoke slowly, irritatingly making almost three syllables out of the word "women." "You're with them?" he asked.

"No," she said. *I come all alone.*

"They're doing a naked thing," he said. "Up by the cliff. Don't think I'm invited." His smile was drawn out, a pleasure—for him.

She saw several flashes of an idea about who this man might be. None of them were complimentary. She let them all go through lack of caring.

"They're not at the cliff, I think they're that way"—and she pointed with the hand that was still in her jacket pocket, along the path that he'd been intending to take.

"Oh." Then he said, "You're Cass?"

"Uh-huh."

"I'm Lance."

"Yes. You used to live in the house," she said.

"I'm not in the house these days. I'm with the stalker. Next valley." He nodded his head to indicate where, but did not take his eyes off her. It was not the same as when David looked at her. David's sticky eyes were full of intent and trained on his future. This Lance was only wondering. At least he was open about it.

"The stalker?"

"Deerstalker. Is it weird if I ask, but—do you need a coat? I just got this." He shrugged in the big red coat. "There were loads down there."

The rain was increasing. Her jacket was borrowed and thin. She'd love a proper coat, preferably with a hood like his under which to hide.

"Sure," she said.

"Down here, then."

She followed him down the hill, across another field, through a gate to yet another yard—she was so bored of this landscape—and to the group of stone outbuildings. They did not speak as they went. He did not walk too quickly. The fingers on his burnt hand looked sore, and the skin there was too new. He moved that hand to rest in his pocket. Cass saw how gently he cradled it in there. She felt a tightening across the back of her own, pocketed, left hand; resented her own curiosity, resented her own feeling, ability.

Inside the cold stone building there were puddles of blood all over the floor and hooks hanging from the ceiling. Lance sniffed. He went into a dark corner, out of the range of Cass's light, and brought forward three waterproof coats for her to choose from. She took them, and it seemed he only then realized where he had led her.

"Sorry, we shouldn't be in here," he said, so slow. "It's where we hang the deer. It's not nice. Is it?"

"I don't care."

Outside, she placed the flashlight on the ground and looked at the coats. There were two feminine, tapered, waterproof jackets, and one huge waxed one, with a large hood. She chose the latter. It smelled, at a guess, of dead deer.

Then he said, "Next place I'm going is nicer. Got to check Vinnie's done my greenhouse. I've been away."

"Stalking deer?"

"Exactly." He looked at her with no guard.

"Never been in the greenhouses."

"Vinnie's vigilant about that."

Lance led her, not to Vinnie's greenhouses, which were tunnels spread over with taut plastic sheeting, but to the muggy orderliness of the original glasshouse, which was kept beautifully, smelling of peas and heat.

Lance stooped to enter through the small door. "This one I kept," he said as he took a match to a paraffin lamp. A little burst of oil smell, and then warm light.

"Were the others yours?" She turned her flashlight off. The plants seemed to sigh in the darkened corners.

He replied, like a secret, "I was here first."

"Since when?"

"Eigleath was empty for a long time before Arthur and Jem came. I looked after it. It was my partner's job, actually. She was the . . . estate manager? Then she left and I took over. Back then Arthur and his family were—you know—absentee landlords. They'd stopped coming. We never heard from them. I had the place to myself for a while . . . It was quite different when Arthur arrived, obviously."

"What happened to your partner?"

"She left. I don't know."

"What are these?" Cass asked. A little row of tiny cardboard boxes in trays of earth.

"I was doing beans with the kids."

"They came in here?"

"We were growing beans under those."

"Under the lids?"

"To show that seeds can grow without light. For a little while, anyway."

"Oh, I see."

"They get quite far without light, to start with."

"The kids?"

"Oh, maybe. I don't know. Aren't the kids all . . ." He flicked a few of the little boxes away with the fingers of his good hand, revealing yellow tendril-like stalks. "The kids are blowing all the roofs off. Letting all the light in. How old are yours?"

They laid their coats down together on the ground and sat on two little three-legged stools. The rain began to land in sheets, thunderous on the glass. Lance seemed, when he spoke to her, to believe she was someone else: his familiar. At one point he ran through the rain to the kitchen and brought them both back a mug of steaming tea; there was a raindrop dangling from the end of his nose, and he couldn't brush it away while he held the mugs in his hands. One mug in the good hand and one in the burnt hand. He passed Cass the mug that had been in his good hand, like he had no expectation of her, or anyone, accepting an offering from his grotesque part. His hair was light, and there were little gray wisps growing comfortably in around his face. His expression had a force to it that she couldn't quite process. There was an energy to it, but not that type of aggravated energy that was rattling, that twisted the face, or panicked the eyes, or jimmied the foot at the ankle; instead, she thought it was the sort of energy like that in the air before a big storm. Strong; felt, and not at all visible. Very peaceful, because very untroubled, because very sure. Not questioning of itself.

She told him about her children without hiding—as she usually did with new people—her general passion for them. He did not ask her— as new people often had—whether Vi and whether Maggs felt like her own in the way that her biological child did. She appreciated that this wasn't due to a lack of attention on his part, but the opposite.

Once or twice as they spoke, the thought struck up in her mind that Nathaniel could in theory appear at any moment, and, if he did, Cass's children would run to him and Cass would not. So she would lose them to him. She blew this out, the flame of this imagined scene. Or perhaps it was the company that blew it out, or the rainy breeze, through the peas and heat air, that extinguished it.

Lance told her about his old life in The City, how he'd traveled and translated operation manuals and, on becoming a volunteer when the second of the Great Fires began, how he'd been trained to burn off ground cover, to stop the spread of fire, how his mother was from one country and his father from a second, but they'd raised him in a third, in the same city as Cass. And his parents were alive, and small, and old, in a fourth, faraway place. She imagined his parents in a mountainous village, on three-legged stools, thinking of their enormous son out in the world. Then she told him about the call with her husband. And he made the link between her husband and Arthur.

"Arthur and I—we don't get on," he said simply.

"Do your personalities clash, or is it a . . . ?"

"No. He's . . . you know." He leaned back and his shoulders expanded away from one another. "He's the big guy in town."

She didn't understand. There followed a silence, which she didn't feel a need to disturb. She waited for him to make things clearer. Eventually he said, "You know, he's dangerous."

"How?"

"With the kids."

"What?"

"In town."

She shook her head to indicate that she did not follow. Or maybe to suggest that she did not want him to continue.

He continued: "Ah, you know. It's because Arthur's the dealer, everybody knows him, he knows everybody. He's some kind of celebrity. But. But he doesn't just sell these days. That's my problem." He leaned forward, quite unblinking. "He is pushing on the people he shouldn't. He's trying to get them hooked through . . . I don't know . . . the force of his personality or something." Cass remained quizzical, so he enunciated: "They're too young."

When he spoke about Arthur it was as if a shadow moved in to cover his whole face, darkening it, pushing the natural energy there, making it stronger. She liked how he had no control over this.

"I didn't know about that . . ." she said, and wondered at once whether she was speaking truthfully. "Where would Arthur get it from?"

"The border." He spoke like this was an obvious fact. "He has it all run up to the border. Takes it from there. It's his border, essentially."

She took a second to fully hear this. She was placing her tea on the floor, and bracing herself.

Lance went on, staring out at the rain now, not at her. "He funds that border. I don't know, I . . . Without Arthur, I doubt they'd be able to keep it going for a week, seriously, the quantities he's shifting. There's so much now. It goes to the town, then down the lines. He pays the border off, they get a good percentage on everything that passes through. So that's why they wouldn't let you go."

"What?"

"At the border. They kept you, right?" He didn't seem to understand her confusion. "Arthur owed them a ton then. He had the money. But he wanted it for something else. So that's why you were . . . hostage there . . . I thought you would have known this."

"Oh," she said.

In the corner, behind Lance, only just illuminated by the lamp, an alien scrum of crickets had been clambering on each other, antennae wild.

Lance spoke again: "You knew this, though," he insisted.

She did not. "So when I was locked away in that room with my children, that was because Arthur owed money?"

Lance just looked at her.

The new form created by his information was settling over her, and it would not dissolve.

"I thought my children were going to die in that room. I was in despair. I've not been OK, really, ever since. Arthur could have told me . . ."

He could have explained the situation when he picked her up. That would have been better, if he'd been honest. So: he didn't want to pay what he owed the border officials, so he had to sneak Cass and the children out? Fine. She would have felt less indebted to him if he'd told her the truth. Everything would have been more realistic. Instead he'd kept his own priorities a secret, and accepted her gratitude. Just as Nathaniel had kept his new priorities a secret, and waited for her to uncover them and adjust herself accordingly. She'd always thought that her husband was what he claimed to be. But the thin, pale, and enchanting barrier she'd perceived between his presentation and his self was—in reality—an enormous, and now misty, grainy deep distance. So, too, the distance between her and him. She'd never even gotten close, he'd only let her believe she had.

Was this true? She was keenly aware that she was sitting in an esoteric greenhouse, hundreds of miles from home, hearing stories. Deeply compelling ones. To round things out, mightn't she also wonder whether Lance had delivered to her this painful detail about

Arthur on purpose, knowing it would turn her against the man he so disliked.

She stayed quiet and Lance let her. He sat very calmly; he was satisfied, or maybe unobtrusive. He was the powerful field of energy in the air, or was he smilingly violent? She could not tell threat from fiction.

"And that pays for everything?" she said suddenly. She was seeing in a different light the clean brightness of Eigleath, the well-painted rooms, the sealed window frames, the generous parties, the wine, the meat, the noble wolfhounds with their wide leather collars, Jem's jewelry, Ella's supplies of tinctures and activities, each resident's personal well-kept truck, the spare tires, her boots, and the whipped handmade body cream gifted her by Vinnie.

"Yes." He held the S sound, like Ally did.

Everything was so well kept and idyllic-looking because Arthur was some sort of drug lord. It was money that made this place, not community, not the New World.

"The people that come to clean . . ." she started wondering, befuddled, aloud, "clean and babysit, and cook, and garden and do everything, tend pigs . . ." The benign adults everywhere. "Are they part of this? Or part of the commune? Or what?"

"They're paid." He covered his mouth, coughed to clear his throat. "Everyone is paid here. This is no commune. Even the drummers are paid off in speed, or whatever's the dirtiest thing going around. Everyone is. They're paid to be here. Or sometimes they owe Arthur money for drugs, so they're here working off a debt. Lots of them work here and go home with a bag of gear instead of notes. The town's suicidal. It's all because of him."

"He always has fuel," she said.

"He always has fuel," he assented.

"The food is incredible."

"It is."

"And Black Box . . . Are they . . . ?"

"Are they what? Are they for real? Yes. They're near. They know. They love the border. They want it to stay. They want to be on this side of it. They want Arthur, they like him, they need him more than he needs them at this point. That balance has just, recently"—he made a clocking noise—"shifted. It used to be he worked for them, but not anymore. He's powerful now. He's not the only one. There are several like him. But I reckon he's kingpin now. Seems that way."

The rain was easing to clear and Lance wasn't exaggerating. These two things felt certain.

"So Jem, Ella; David, Vinnie—they're all in on it?" He nodded. "Why didn't they tell me? Am I too? Too—what? What am I?"

He just looked at her.

She needed to change the subject. Her ignorance of her own surroundings was leaving her feeling too exposed. "Why don't you leave?" she asked him. She wasn't interested; it just bought her time to think.

He repeated the question to himself before answering. "Don't know. It was a beautiful place to be. Once." He leaned back and regarded her, hands in his pockets.

She could not think. "Do you have cigarettes?" she asked.

"Don't smoke." He'd missed out the implied "I," possibly on purpose. Then he released his hands to pick up his tea from the floor and drain it.

Lance had that thing about him that was personal to her.

She noticed how the burns on the back of his hand continued around to his palm, where there was a perfectly circular burn in the center.

A long trestle table ran down the middle of the glasshouse. It seemed to have been recently cleared and brushed. A pair of pink-handled shears on it, and a stack of small yellow flowerpots, but apart from that it was empty. It looked sturdy. And she wondered whether she could simply ask for sex now. She'd ask nicely. She'd be rid of it afterward: wouldn't be weird. The floor was fine, if not the table. With the crickets. It might just help her clear something from her body. Would that be allowed? And the heat rose clammy from her skin, under her clothes. She imagined asking him, and then started to be scared that she already had.

They heard a shriek from outside: a whoop of joy. They both pointed their faces toward it. It was the heralding sound of the women making their way to The Circle Place. They were led by one with a firelit torch which looked newly ridiculous to Cass (*they could have taken electric flashlights, there are loads of them, and batteries*) and they were not coming from the direction Cass had expected.

245

She'd been picked up by Arthur only because he didn't like to be blackmailed. Was that it? She was a pebble in his shoe. And she had been picked up by Nathaniel only because she was right in front of him, and didn't say no. And only because there was something he needed of her—to take care of his children, so he could leave. That's why he'd wanted her to have Daisy so much, to tie her forever to the role of mother in his home. So that he could leave. Was that it?

What did they think would happen when she found them out and decided that she felt used, and hated them? They would call her anger toward them unreasonable and retreat into their curated sanities, having left all their distortion with her. There was nothing about her, specifically, that drove them. Yes, she was pretty sure that was it.

Smoke was beginning to loop up from a fire at The Circle Place. Cass pictured all the people gathering there, racking up lines after a day slogging for Eigleath, that girl, Bluebell, with the pointy teeth and the fake-gemstone eyes, sitting on the knee of one of Arthur's loyal soldiers. Jem and Ella, quizzing Arthur on every aspect of his trip to town. Maybe snakes on the fire again and the smell that no one liked.

She got up to leave. "Thank you for the coat," she said, collecting it from the floor.

"Are you heading down?" He indicated The Circle Place.

"No, I'll go up, stay with the kids." She put the coat on in silence, picked up the heavy flashlight and the thin jacket.

As she turned to go, he said, "I'm seeing someone." He blurted this out so quickly that it caught in his throat and he had to cough again.

And she thought, *When will men stop shocking me with this complete and avowed peculiarity?*

"OK." She was furious. "Do what you want. I don't know you."

"Sorry. I felt"—he laughed, guffawing and coughing at himself—"an impulse to tell you that."

"You shouldn't act on your impulses." And then she went back at him, harder, "I don't know you. Don't assume things."

He remained on his stool, nodding. She was standing on the lip of the greenhouse door, looking down on him, as the rains cleared from the air outside. They were breathing in time with the sea, which they could feel but not glimpse, both of them.

She turned again to go, but he kept—as if compelled, against his wishes—speaking. "I was going to see her tonight, the one I'm seeing,

246

but I won't now." He stood up abruptly, catching his head on the metal beam beneath the pinnacle of the roof. The entire glasshouse reverberated musically from the blow.

"Why won't you see her?" said Cass, almost aggressive.

He rubbed at his head. "I didn't want you to think I'd leave here and sleep with someone else." He ran his fingers through his hair to push it back. "It's not . . . Shit. You don't have to think about me ever again." He was emphatic about that. "I simply . . . I didn't want you thinking that I'd take this . . . use this . . . I didn't want you to think I'd do that particular thing, tonight, after this." He smiled, slow once more, in the pleasure of having regained his footing somewhat.

After what, exactly? "OK." She said it like she was angry at a child, and started to leave, again, but he stopped her, again.

"I don't make her happy," he implored. "We're sad. Something. It's not right. She runs the pub."

"I don't need to know."

"I saw you at The Circle Place, when David and Jem were all over you, like." He took a deep breath in. "And you looked . . ." He trailed off.

She felt guided to walk away—but she needed to know, she needed to know very much, how she might look to a man like this. How he might hate her and dress it up in loving words.

"How did I look?" she asked.

"When I saw you at The Circle. You looked . . ." He was losing his train of thought. ". . . something regal. Like you came to be."

"I don't know what that means," she said.

"Me neither, gorgeous." His was the smile of someone who found himself sharing in a generous world. It faded and he stayed looking at her, his look becoming serious, his seriousness becoming intimate. "You're standing on my coat," he said.

She looked down. She was. It was red. She liked it.

46

If you could stretch back and out of your situation, you would see that The Moorland and Heathland Fires, which had burnt for more than seven months apiece, were under control; but The Midlands Fire, and the southerly blazes—which most affected the large urban areas—were terrifying and all-consuming. Meanwhile trade routes had dried away, without fuel, without coolants. Unemployment was unmeasurable, percentage-wise. Even if you took figures back to the Industrial Revolution, fewer people were gainfully employed now than when records began. The tax base had evaporated. No humidity in anything. No slick. No anoint. Choking smog from fires was the given reason for the curfew in the major cities, which was not, as Vinnie had it, policed via mobile phone, but by how much your lungs could take. There were no good seeds, the earth would not replenish, the crops did not thrive, the flame retardant sprayed from helicopters over the hills, woods, and dwellings suckered out the last natural protective barrier from the skin. The bronchioles were dry, the mucous membrane was diminished in mankind. The quiet streets teemed with masses of rot and rank. The power went out. And went on again. And out. Put all your cables and devices in a basket and tidy them away. And then you wouldn't have to know about the numbers, the rise of Gaia, who had taken over the Heaths and the Royal Parks, their happy death toll, their band of brothers, which had expanded to include many, from more walks of life, men and women. "The blood of the covenant is thicker than the water of the womb," they said.

All this but for a few, in little enclaves, in gentler condition. There were sweet spots where the sea air held dominion. Places that were cut off, in northern realms. Protected by money. And if you were lucky and you got to one of these places, you either blanked out the rest of the world, or shuddered with survivor's guilt. Or neither, if you were particularly entitled.

Before Cass knew him, Lance had been paid to wear a heavy suit and helmet and breathing equipment, and carry around a can of oil, lit at the nozzle, to pour over the bracken and cinder it down, destroying anything that might allow The Moorland and Heathland Fires to spread. Planes had been diverted from the sky above him. Cass imagined the same planes flying low over Nathaniel's digs, where he pushed himself deeper and deeper into a woman who was not his wife.

The air could still be wet around Eigleath. It was winter. They could walk for miles. But the children were straining to be released further into the wider world. Particularly the older ones, Vasaly and Shilo, fourteen and thirteen. No one had told them yet. This is what Cass came late to understand: the Children of the House did not know what was happening. They had been sheltered. They were living a peaceful version of their parents' childhoods, where death was unusual and things were plentiful. It was a fantasy.

In the local town, just fifteen miles away, there was death: from overdose, from lack of healthcare, from botched abortions; the surgery had run out of antibiotics; there was another riot at the border. Unmitigated decline—which had once been up ahead and avoidable—was now undeniable and irreversible. In its poor health, the soil had been giving up archaeological treasures all over the place with alarming regularity. All the playgrounds in The City had been formally closed. Cass closed down the browser on David's computer. It was spring and another wildfire had roared to life fifty miles away.

Cass wanted to go into the local town and see for herself. She wondered what would happen if she borrowed Ella's truck and drove the oldest children and showed them. If she demonstrated to them that the only place to go from Eigleath was down. Would they become less boisterous? Would they recoil in fear, break down, or go into themselves? Or would they grow up into people who wanted to change things? Arthur would be furious if she showed the older children the truth, and his part in it.

Arthur swung, in Cass's presence, from charming cordiality, sharing moments of exquisite play and practiced bonhomie, to the coldest distance, or not even distance: it was more, it was simply a refusal of her existence.

Cass saw Arthur differently now. Through new eyes (sadder, denser, richer, mirrored in Lance's) she saw him heading out on his trips to town every few days, with Vinnie in tow. She saw him get angry at a girl who was cleaning the hall. The girl had oozing sores clustered around her mouth. Arthur said something offhand to the girl, in passing, like he was throwing trash on the ground, and the girl snapped back at him. Arthur's entire being altered then, he ran at the girl with his arms out, like wings, but in total violence, and the girl cowered completely. She shielded her face. Cass heard what Arthur shouted at her: "Nothing for you. Noth-ing. For You." And then he muttered "Fucking junkie" and closed himself in his "study," which was also called The Good Room and which, Cass had noticed (too late, again), was always locked.

One evening, Arthur threw them all out of David's room while they were watching a movie on the computer. He did it irritably, with no grace, simply bursting in and yelling, "Out. Out. I've got a call. A call arranged. I need the computer." David fell to Arthur's wishes simply. He immediately jumped to pause the film and started waving at the children to get up, with not a single drop of resistance in him. Cass was more rebellious. She lingered in the room, pointedly; Arthur noticed and snarled at her as he brought the call up on the screen.

Then he changed his manner for the little man's face that appeared in the new window. He became sickeningly ingratiating. "Mr. McCormack, how are you?" Arthur oozed. "Great to talk."

"Gaia with you," said the man.

Cold shivers flew up from Cass's red soles, and she wanted to get out of that room as quickly as possible. The man on the screen made her think of chocolate coins wrapped in golden foil, which she hadn't let her children eat. She would swear it was the same man she'd seen at the camp. But what were the chances of that? Accidents of fate, coincidences; she usually took these as signs that she was in the right place at the right time, counterintuitively.

Most of all, Cass saw now how the people all around her were frightened of causing Arthur's displeasure. Cass began to see how David and Vinnie performed their entertaining characters just out of Arthur's reach, and never got in his face. Jem attended to him. Cass freshly believed everything Jem had said about Arthur on that first night, and she also understood why Jem stayed devoted. What Cass had shrunk inside of herself to keep safe, Jem had planted in others to keep safe. Jem had not chosen well.

*

Arthur watched Cass from across the kitchen table and rubbed his bottom lip back and forth against his knuckle, so that his head was making the figure of a forceful "No," as if he were changing his mind about her there and then. He had clearly noticed her withdrawal of sweetness from him. She had noticed what tendencies he carried forward from his mother. Cass tarred them all three with the same brush now: Eden, Nathaniel, Arthur. Why had she not seen it before—the family line? The Magurens were incapable of distinguishing people from tools. Old World.

Every day that Cass woke could be the day that Nathaniel arrived at Eigleath. And it wasn't. He'd gone quiet. Sometimes his silence indicated to her that he wasn't coming, sometimes it meant to her that he was en route. She was hypervigilant to the horizon once again.

The only thing to do in the midst of Arthur's activity, and the threat of Nathaniel's arrival, was to leave, but there was precisely nowhere secure enough to go. There was nothing strong enough to break the fact that Cass's children belonged to the Maguren family line. The only silver lining was that Eigleath would one day belong to her three. The only silver lining. She practiced holding herself, sometimes, like the mother of the inheritors of a fine estate. But it didn't work. Didn't work because there was another woman with Nathaniel now, whose child had just as much biological right to inherit. Didn't work because it felt wrong. Cass put it all down.

Ally died. This Cass learned in a bizarre, euphemistic email from Rose. It took Cass several minutes to work out what it was that Rose was trying to tell her. The text came through very large, there were lots of capitals, and a variety of fonts; the meaning was hidden. "ALLY LEFT THE GARDEN on Tuesday. ALLY IS BRAVE DARLING." Cass did not have recourse to grieve. It was easier to go on believing that Ally was still in her garden, in The City, clearing up a smashed terracotta pot. An extroverted cousin, whom Cass hadn't spoken to since a distant Old World wedding, got in touch by email. "Still nannying your boyfriend's kids?" the cousin wrote, before going on to ask if they could stay at Nathaniel and Cass's place in The City. The cousin used the words "stay" and "have" interchangeably. Cass replied to let the cousin know the easiest way to break in, adding: "I've told my friend, Rose, to knock at the door. When she does, let her take whatever she wants from the house. If you have food, please invite her to eat with you. Hug her for me."

Arthur offered Cass, one morning, an opening. He came to her bashfully, boyishly, and asked if he could get her a van, "a nice one."

"Maybe," she said, but it was clear she did not want his gifts. His face froze.

There was nowhere to go from here.

"Thank you for thinking of me," Cass said soothingly. "But where would I go in it?"

He relaxed. They were all in his thrall. They had made their peace with the safest evil.

47

Late spring. The birth of Bluebell's child, followed closely by her wish for a wedding, came to occupy all the available attention.

Bluebell was something of a pet of Arthur's, and the baby's father Stu was Arthur's faithful. Since their accommodation in the town had become "unfeasible," and because the hospital was broken as well as "too medicalized," Arthur invited Bluebell to give birth at Eigleath—attended by Ella and a doctor he brought up from the border.

It was awful. The doctor was too distractingly beautiful. Everyone was ill at ease. Everyone thought that Bluebell was going to die. There were sheets holding soups of blood left outside the room she labored in. It went on for three days. Cass helped through two nights of it with Bluebell's wet face in her lap, or Bluebell's arm in her hands, or Bluebell's foot pushing into her thigh. You had to tie your hair right back or Bluebell would pull it out in fistfuls. You had to make sure you did not screech when Bluebell scratched you, or shat on your foot. Bluebell begged Cass to end it. Cass repeated what had been said to her, "The only way out is through," and Bluebell looked at her so betrayed. Her eyes changed over from their fake blue to a creamy, filmed pale-moonish. She started passing out between contractions, going over to the other place; spending whole minutes there in a silence that terrified everyone left behind in the room.

Whatever met Bluebell on the other side sent her back with new life. The baby was purple and whole. And, on the next full moon, Bluebell wanted her marriage.

*

Daisy's words were coming in and she had taken to sleeping through the night but rising early so as to secure Cass, and Cass's conversation, all to herself. "Wake, Mommy?" she would whisper.

"It's the wedding today," Cass whispered back.

"Booobee"—which meant Bluebell, who was all breasts now, dripping milk.

Then Cass whispered, "It's a bit early to get up."

"Mommy!" replied Daisy. The way she said that word—as if to convey "You are so silly and so great"—blazed through Cass. Daisy spoke the way she had been spoken to, awed and smilingly.

There was no going back to sleep. Cass slipped out of the bed and held the child against her, and they stood like that to watch the dawn over the valley. Daisy, lying against her mother, and sucking her thumb, blinked slowly with inconsolable wonder. Cass believed she was witnessing the pathways of Daisy's brain connect up when she went quiet like that. Cass wrapped herself and Daisy both together in one of Jem's blankets and crept to the kitchen, where they found Ella sitting at the kitchen table, positioned with her knees wide and her feet bent at the toes, and an inward curve at the base of her back, positioned so that each time she looked up from her work she was met immediately by the sky through that paneless upper window—it had been her companion throughout the night. She was busy twisting stalks and twine between her fingertips. Cass made the coffee.

When the rest of the children came downstairs together—like a committee—before 6 a.m., they saw all the circular crowns of flowers that Ella had made, spread out over the table. One of the children whistled in appreciation. The children counted: there were twenty-one crowns so far. They collected the fallen petals from the red brick floor.

Ella told them she needed more flowers—not the common ones, but "the ones like this. See? This sweetpea one? More of that would be good. Orange sits well with it. They complement each other. But then I think you need more green to balance it out, no? Do you see what I mean?" The children ran off, each claiming to know the best spot for what Ella wanted. The oldest boy, Vasaly, carried Daisy carefully down the steps to the meadow. Cass knew that, while the others would run off to the four corners of the wind, Vasaly could be trusted to take Daisy no further than the meadow.

254

Each day she released her children a little bit further. Each day that passed she entertained for longer the possibility that their father was not going to reappear. Perhaps he had decided it would be too much for him to face. He was a coward, she supposed. She was increasingly relieved. She felt the fugues and fumes of him release from her body. Every day her children stepped further, and then ran back to her to check she was still there. They'd stopped asking about their father. Cass didn't know if they had done this to please her, or if she had become enough for them, or if they were forgetting.

The eggs were starting to pop in the deep pan, and Cass was crumbling dried sage over them, as Ella had instructed, when they heard a truck pull in outside. There was Arthur's voice and some accompanying noise as he unloaded the back. Cass and Ella did not look out of the window to see and greet him, for if he was cheerful he would come to them. They realized at the same moment that the milk they'd let Vi pour in their coffee was off.

"We're back," Arthur called loudly on the threshold, to indicate his mood: which was present, forceful.

"You're back! You got everything?" Ella replied.

"I've got news." He had a box of bright-pink candles under one arm, and a half-cut Jem under the other. She couldn't stand. Her hair had fallen over her face and there were chunks of vomit in it.

"What's your news?" Ella asked, while she moved to take Jem away from him.

"We'll talk later," he said, ferrying Jem away.

The guests began arriving early. They were the usual assortment who came for the parties—friends, workers, Black Boxers, and some people from the town who had known Bluebell since infancy—but they came in their finery. The Black Box sent their generously laden private butcher out of deference to Arthur. The butcher was late, and couldn't get his van past a couple of haphazardly parked vehicles in the lane, so the meat was carried down by a group of people who were simultaneously trying to be helpful but also not spoil their clothes. Teenagers in their mothers' dresses and their fathers' hats. Dreadlocks adorned with flowers. Lace sleeves hanging over old wrists. Shy ribbons against puffy skin. A mountain range of acne spots on the back of a shoulder. The remembered things: deliberate handshakes, smiles for days, concern about who should be where and when, and

more flowers. The sound of swearing from the kitchen. Vinnie stomp-
ing out in a huff. Bacon sandwiches and champagne that had been
courted, borrowed, and stolen, saved for months, some of it dusty,
some of it bad, but then someone got hold of a bottle that was good
and kept it by the neck. Mostly there was gin and shine. Arthur had,
over the course of several weeks, built three large pyres out the back,
in place of fireworks for a finale, he said, to make sure things didn't
just peter out. He had a plan that, before dawn, he'd light them, and
all would come together to hold hands around them.

At 1 p.m., the guests started off: through the field of constellations, toward a specially constructed pathway of shells, which led
into a spiral. All paraded. At the head of the line was the celebrant
from town, in green robes and golden ribbons, then came Bluebell
and Stu, both in white, followed by Ella, dressed in black and holding
Bluebell's new baby, and everyone else followed. When the celebrant
reached the center of the spiral, all stopped and turned toward him.
There was throaty singing. A song repeated and repeated until everyone had it. Then the celebrant spoke in an ancient tongue that he'd
learned from his clacky-mouthed grandmother, and as he did so he
bound Bluebell and Stu at the wrist, he took blood saved from the
birth and crossed their foreheads with it. Then he moved aside for
the women. "The women do the marrying," he said. "The women
do the everything. They do the knowing and the holding." One man
had antlers attached to his head, and he started to move them slowly,
slowly, from side to side. One woman swayed, as if she had an imaginary or absent child on her hip. *Missing, or gone, or never arrived*,
thought Cass. She felt tears force a wall against her eyes.

Jem—who had rested, and been topped up with shine—stepped
forward and instructed the congregation to move from their spiral
formation into concentric circles. As they rearranged themselves, the
people crushed and disarrayed the shells into the earth with their feet.
In the center of the circles, Ella laid the unnamed baby on a soft
pillow. The couple stood over it. They directed each of their vows to
the infant, who solemnized their marriage.

"I will raise your father up," said Bluebell in her low voice.

"Will you?" shouted Ella.

"I will raise your father up," Bluebell repeated, louder.

More voices from the congregation joined in this time: "Will you?"

"I will raise your father up."

Now everyone: "Will you?"

"I will!" Gleaming, shining face.

"I will honor your mother's body." Stu's turn.

"Will you?"

"I will honor your mother's body."

"Will you?"

"I will honor your mother's body."

"Will you?"

There was a threatening element to it.

"We will protect you," said the couple, over the baby.

"Will you?"

Can you? Cass asked it within the gentle, silent forests of her mind, and her tears came in more and drenched all her trees.

Lance caught her attention deliberately. He was opposite her, a few rows back. She was beside Jem, who was beside Arthur, who held hands with David, and then there was Vinnie. Daisy was weaving between their legs. They all stank of sweat, having turned their bodies to the task of creating this event, this day, because they understood that their relatively small efforts would make Bluebell feel disproportionately splendid. And they longed, some of them, to represent more than the sum of their compromised selves.

The couple's promises exhausted, everyone stood at ease for a moment and murmured. They let go of each other and clasped their own hands in front of themselves, or folded their arms, and Ella held up her palm for silence once more, and then she spoke.

"Before man, when life bloomed through the seas, all was female. When man is born of woman, he worships her, or he loses himself. And when a man loses himself, we all are lost." She went on like this. Cass listened to it from the points of view of those around her and grew curiouser at all the differences of reception she encountered. Next, Ella sang a bastardized version of a hymn.

Jem joined Cass in crying when the hymn began and Cass tried to squeeze Jem's wet hand. But Jem slipped her hand away and picked up Daisy.

Jem, increasingly, would turn up in Cass's thoughts, not as a knowable person, with a set of characteristics, but as a type of journey. Each time you got your footing with Jem, she led you down a stair, on to somewhere else; her dissembling was endless. Jem wanted to be so close to Cass, but not seen by her.

It was clear to Cass that Arthur would never be bored of Jem. The way she spirited you onward, no one could ever grow bored of her company. Except, Cass suspected, Jem herself.

The singing ended. They all stood in silence, feeling the slightest caress of air on their lips. Then, at the appointed moment, the children's voices started calling from far away. They shouted, "This way!" "Follow us!" "Come over here!" They had the band of drummers with them. The lead drummer gave a yell. A swinging beat ensued.

And the people moved off toward the children, who were all dressed-up in haphazard splendor, in the velvets and stained shirts the adults had lent them. The children led the dancing people through the trees, back to the meadow, where tables had been set up for a feast. Dogs licked ankles. The best stories were recalled and retold. There was fiddle music, airy music. And the newly married couple twirled. He with glad eyes, in a bright-red jacket now over his white tunic, and a bright-red face; she overwhelmed and tearful.

"What the fuck is she thinking?" said Jem, who was drinking shine from a jar.

The men who were together kissed. And the women who were together kissed, and the men and the women kissed, and they looked at each other tenderly, or with aggression, and wondered if they'd ever had any choices, really.

Later, down by the poisoned river which was only swum in on this date, once a year, Arthur removed all of his clothing, climbed up a tree, hung from the branch and bombed into the water. The children screamed in delight. People ambled to the banks barefoot, and disrobed carefully, leaving their fine things hanging on branches. They sank into the water in only their necklaces.

The children couldn't swim, so David, who was sober, stood like a knight with his legs akimbo in the water, watching over them, ready to fish them out if they struggled. Cass kept her dress on and waded in. It floated out around her. She caught the children when they let themselves fall off the hanging branch—just in time—so they didn't go under. Then she floated them on their backs, back to a place where they could stand. They trusted her. Even the older ones looked blissed out with their ears under the stream and her hands beneath them, their eyes adjusting to the bright sky.

When the children were tired, had bicycled their legs, believed they were swimming, David brought them away.

Cass, dress dripping, walked behind them, by Lance who was talking with some of the more elder-like people. Cass craned her neck to see if he was still the same as she had him in her head. He confirmed to her that he was with a slight nod and then a grin.

She found Jem alone, sitting at a table abandoned with the detritus of the feast. Cass pulled up a chair and tried to start a conversation, but Jem blinked and shook her head when it was her turn to speak. Too drunk to return the words. They sat in a companionable silence and watched the speaking crowds. A toddler knocked over a jug of water and started to wail. A woman in a low-cut dress checked her cleavage. A man tripped over his own ankle as he was trying to describe a situation.

Suddenly Jem's eyes went dead, and her body rigid. She grabbed blindly for Cass's arm, which she held on to too tightly. "Did you see that?" she asked.

"What?" Cass tried to follow Jem's gaze into the crowd.

"Please tell me you saw that."

"*What?*"

Cass proving useless to her, Jem released her grip and left her hands startled in the air. Left them there longer; then she got up and followed her vision, disappearing quickly into the crowd, the same crowd that Maggs and Daisy burst out of just then, running to Cass, and she kissed them, *oh*, she kissed them.

And there was Arthur, acting like he was attending the last party on earth. Charmingly deflecting anyone who remembered that it was his birthday ("Not about me, today"). He led the dancing around the fire. He started the girls and the pregnant-bodied and the elders whirling. He drained his wine and looked on, satisfied. When he noticed groups breaking away to talk in bent-headed urgency, he went over and disbanded them. "Not yet, not yet," he said, with that snake-dark stare he sometimes had. He teased the celebrant. He engaged the old men in tales of anarchism. The way he put his fingers into the carcasses on the table and responded to the morsels he found there inspired everyone around him to dig back in to the meat and find it more exquisite.

As the night came in, there was one couple left down by the river having sex against the tree, his feet in the water, her body against the trunk with thick mud all up her thigh. There was a gray-haired woman sitting very upright with her eyes closed on the steps and the butcher passed out at her feet. At midnight, the children were bribed inside with sweets. The Good Room, which Arthur had cleared for the occasion, was opened. And Daisy fell asleep on the sofa in front of the old stone fireplace there, surrounded by her young kin who were river-damp still, and yawning, but refusing absolutely to go upstairs to bed. Ella would stay with them—she sent Cass away in kindness.

Ella had been unprepared when Cass confronted her about the money underpinning Eigleath; how it was less a commune and more a feudal state run by Arthur. Ella had at first responded angrily to the facts as presented by Cass, half-shouting, "What did you think we were doing here, sweetheart? We're not pig farmers. You think people do that shit for us for free?" But then she had turned sorrowful because Cass had not managed, this time, to be ashamed of her own disquiet. Ella had returned to her and told her, "This is the best place for us. I promise. This is it. We are very lucky. Everything can become nothing—overnight. You have to do a deal eventually. Everyone does, eventually."

She sent Cass away from The Good Room, where the river-damp children were huddled in, with the particular shade of kindness that develops through regret.

Lance was waiting for Cass outside. They walked from the wedding party, seeking the quietest place, where the grass was long and soft, and the bats were rustling, and probably there were deer nearby too. They reached the middle of this place and he moved as if he were about to scoop her up. But he experienced a helplessness in his limbs, and he hesitated, giving her pause to step away and regard him. His resting face could be so fully attuned to pity, and then he wavered. His face was both a warning sign and a welcoming beacon.

Cass lifted her hair at the back, took the pendant—a present from Ella—from around her neck, and let it fall on the ground. She undid the belt of Jem's green dress, and let it hang. She reached her wrists up behind her neck, and undid each button down the back of the dress. She let the dress drop. She had nothing on beneath. Only her body, which she did not particularly recognize anymore. It was adorned—scar on her right shoulder, bite mark above her breast, lowered hood of belly button from pregnancy, indelible forever-scar on her shin—over the asymmetry of her ribcage. It had become a body that her mother would not recognize in a line-up. It was a body that her husband no longer knew. She realized that she had been embarrassed by this: to cease to be recognized, naked, by your mother, your husband, what a breakdown of things was this? But there appeared to be a man looking on her and—what was it? Unlike the mother, and the husband, this man seemed not to want to make her body represent anything. He seemed to want to let her keep it. *How about this*, he seemed to say, in his trembling suggestions, *you keep you, and I'll keep me? And I will help you keep yourself, and you will help me do the same?*

Or maybe this was only in her imagination. Perhaps she could make anyone represent anything at all. Maybe it was all her.

He was on the ground, looking up at her, and she had to entertain the possibility that she could not read him. Or there was nothing to read. He had silence in there, perhaps. He opened his lips against her inner, upper leg and her entire body smiled. Smiled in satisfaction. Smiled gluttonously. Smiled and decided, *I will take this*.

When Cass would speak to herself about Lance, as she followed her children around Eigleath on their morning adventures, she would propose that he gave the lie to many subtle gendered conceptions. For example: he did not seem to go about life, as nearly every man she knew did, accompanied everywhere by a female-shaped void that he looked to fill. There was no void with him. He did not need to peacock to the other men how well he could outsource that which he should find in himself. All sides were existent within him. He was terribly strong, and terribly sure, and terribly huge, and his jaw was enormous, and he was tender. He was action, and he was space. He gave the lie to the certainties, to the assumptions, about female fate and the male endeavor. He wanted all things to be alive in Cass too.

She pulled at him, so that he rose all the way up to meet her, and they kissed. She had no clothes on. He wore all his. She started undressing him. His burns. She wondered if he was like a mythical thing to her then. Merman, selkie man, with his shiny, waterproof-looking skin, which had been made in fire. Not real.

They played at being the fold that held the other in place. They played at teasing the seams that kept consciousness in—with palms, and toes, and nails pushing right into the webs of musculature beneath the skin.

But then—"Stop," she said suddenly.

"What? I . . ."

"There's someone there."

There was indeed someone there, watching them. Cass could see an unmistakably human form stepping backward, where the trees met the clearing.

"I think it was a deer," Lance said plainly.

"No. They stepped back. They were watching."

He believed her.

This was the most extraordinary thing: not that his head of hair smelled like it did, not that he was heavier than her husband, not that he didn't slip into that conscious way of being where he thought, *We are having sex now,* and performed the required moves—the most extraordinary thing was that he believed her.

He stood up, straight up, naked, and rose into the form of an alert and violent man. His eyes, focused and angry, stared where she had told them to. He cocked his head to the side, inquisitive, challenged, ready.

"One of the kids?" he said, apparently to himself.

It had been a small person, yes, but not young. "No, not a kid," said Cass.

He pulled his shorts on and walked to where Cass had pointed. Then he saw something and began to run. He disappeared into the trees, where the blue shadow from the elms encased him.

Cass put her dress on. Picked the pendant up off the ground and held it. Far off, she heard Lance yell as if he was scaring something away. Then, after a pause, she could see him walking back, feet planting at a curious angle.

"I did see someone," he said.

"Who?"

"I don't know. They're hiding."

"Let's go," she said.

He bent down to where she was kneeling and kissed the center of her mouth and then moved up to kiss the crown of her head and he lingered there. Then, leveling his face directly to hers, he said, "Whatever you want." It was a promise leavened by the fact that it had already been kept.

They walked back to the house very slowly. Cautiously. Linking hands, then parting. Looking back over their shoulders, edgily.

48

A reddish dark sky as they approached the back of the house.

Arthur spotted them. He was holding some sort of conference on the back step.

"Have you seen Jem?" he shouted out.

"No," Cass yelled, hoping that could be the end of the exchange.

"Where the hell . . . ?"

"Come over," Ella called. "We need you."

Cass whispered, "I don't want to." Vinnie and David were up there too, pacing.

"We should. They look stressed," Lance said.

"Who's with the kids?" Cass asked the group as she drew closer. She liked being seen by these people in the same frame as Lance.

No one replied. Arthur sat rakishly on the step, his head bowed. "I've got news," he said, peering up at them from under his charms.

"I'll go in to the kids," said Cass, not caring for Arthur's melodrama.

"The kids are fucking fine! You're obsessed," Arthur spat. "We've got girls sitting with them. OK? Fucking paid help. I pay the help for you."

As Lance rocked back on his heels, he caught a pinch of Cass's dress and pulled her to him imperceptibly, right when she was realizing how perfectly positioned she was to kick Arthur in the face with her boot. Then Arthur said: "Gaia's blown the border."

"Gaia?"

"When?" Lance asked.

"Last night."

"When did you hear?"

"Yesterday."

"You knew all day?"

"Some of us did, yeah," Arthur said, with a look of *And what? And what are you even doing here?* "Didn't want it to ruin things, did I?"

"Jesus," said Lance.

"It's carnage," Arthur continued. "But it's open now. Everyone's coming over."

They were all quiet for a moment. Six of them, on the steps.

"I guess that's good, in a way," Cass tried. "Letting people in."

"No. It's no good," said Arthur. "It was done by subgroup, splinter-something, they weren't fully knowing the plan."

"What plan?"

Arthur ran his palm down his face, catching his lip and pulling it distorted, while contemplating Cass and Lance.

"Black Box have a plan for Gaia . . ." he started.

Lance sighed with his entire body. Arthur stared at Lance's visibly worn patience with hatred.

"Go on," Lance said.

"Black Box need Gaia to stop, yeah? Stop the killings. It's too much. You can't let that carry on, even if you don't care. There'll be nothing left, there'll be no children left, it is so out of hand. So out of hand. There's been way more mortalities than they say. We're talking tens of thousands. If you leave it, do nothing, there'll be civil uprising to stop Gaia. A civil war. Or they could send in army to stop Gaia. But you don't want to start a war with that lot, 'cos they got nothing to lose."

"So?"

"So . . . it takes giving them their own places, Edens, like here. Give Gaia land. That's the marvelous plan. Makes sense. You give them land, where there's no one to bother them, no people, and the Gaias have the Nature all to themselves. It's like mind-bending for them"—Arthur put two fingers to his ear and twisted them to indicate a bent mind—"but it might work. It might. And in return, Gaia—Gaia's part is that they enforce the border. People are scared of them anyway. Won't want to come up here so much if it's all Gaia. It will stay beautiful here. So it would've worked. It would've. But that's all to shit now."

"Like here?" Cass said.

Ella shot her a look that said, *Be careful.*

"You said, 'Edens like here,'" Cass continued.

"Yeah, like here," Arthur said as slowly as he possibly could.

265

"What do you mean?"

He licked his lips. The cheekiness. "I sold it."

Cass held her breath for a long while and then she said, "Fuck" into the silence.

"I sold it," he repeated happily, his excitement expressed only to rile her. Cass felt like she was falling and wrapped her arms around herself, then released them so that her hands would be free to catch her if it transpired she was in fact falling. "Yeah. I sold my own place, which belongs to me and is mine to sell. I sold it with your husband, actually. We sold it to Black Box, and now we're rich. We're tenants of Eigleath at this point." He looked around, taking them in as if taking each of their places in the landscape into his memory, relishing this. "Black Box gave us a good deal. Made sure of it. I've bought somewhere else, right at the top—s'got an island and everything. It's not as holy. Not where Gaia wants so much. Pretty barren. Lots of concrete. But it's real big. Certainly has potential." He yawned and stretched his arms out to indicate his pretend boredom.

"We're leaving?" Cass said.

"Coming with, are you?"

They stood around Arthur, chastened into quietness, examining the laces and the stitching on their boots, which Arthur's work had supplied.

"Anyway. Now we got problems, where there were none before," Arthur continued. "Now it's all to fuck. Now we got the people coming from the south, who are breaking through the border. Hundreds of thousands of them, I'd say. That border was not meant to blow up."

"That's not really the problem, though, is it?" said Lance.

"No. Problem we got really is the people in towns like ours who want to stop the migrants coming on so quick. They don't want to be overwhelmed. And they're emotional about it, you know? About their homes."

"What are they going to do?" Everyone seemed to know the answer to this, except for Cass.

"Well, darling, the local people, the ones who have always been here, some of them are starting fires further down, to stop the newcomers getting up. On top of that, we got Gaia rushing here, all of them, to secure the border and secure all the land that's been purchased for them by Black Box, before it's overrun . . . And it'll all be at our door soon."

"What will?" said Cass.

Arthur looked at her with disdainful irritation. His velvet coat was very fine. A giant bloom in the buttonhole. "People are starting very big fires, to scare the incomers. But they don't know what they're doing. The way the wind is. Fire's looking to come all the way to our door. There'll be nothing here for Gaia to take, the way it's looking. But there's not a lot we can do tonight," he continued. "Start tomorrow."

"Start what?" said Cass. "You're leaving tomorrow? For this new place?" Arthur could call it an obsession all he wanted, but her life depended on being able to picture the children's next day.

He mocked her: "*You're leaving me!*" he said in a pleading, moronic way. "Not leaving you here, no. You're coming with us." He said this as though it were the most regrettable part of his tale. "Look. I'm not flying us blind here. We'll do what we have to. Look, Cass"—and he began changing the sound of his voice—"of course there's a place for you. I won't leave no man behind. You're coming with. Nathaniel's got his half of the money. Made me send it through Mom, though, so you couldn't get your hands on it." He stopped to chortle at this. "You don't have to worry about him. He's staying where he is. Over there, with her. I'll look after you now. Put him out of mind. You're with us now." He seemed to recall that he was needing something from her. "Darling, OK? You're with us. Your hanger-on there too." He smiled apologetically at Lance. "We're gonna leave together. But you have to help me first: find Jem. We can't leave without her. You know how she thinks. She loves you. Do you know that? She *loves* you. Where is she?" This was Arthur's obsession.

Cass, her lungs bloating with watery shock, felt exhausted by the sight of Arthur's face. "Jem's around here," she said dismissively. "She's around . . ."

"I'm actually worried, though," said Arthur. "Some of the things she said."

"I haven't seen her since the swimming," Vinnie put in.

"I was with her after that," Cass said. "On the meadow. She was fine, really really drunk. She's sleeping it off somewhere." Cass was holding out her hand to take the next puff on Vinnie's cigarette, something dry to cut through the drowning fluids, and he passed it to her.

Several people started speaking at once, but Cass managed to get in over them as she exhaled smoke, which entranced Lance. "Did Jem know? Does Jem know what's happening?"

"Yes," said Arthur. "Last night in town she heard—she got wasted."

Then Ella asked Cass, "What did she say when you saw her last?"

"Not much. She saw something."

"What was it?"

"I didn't see. She was . . . disturbed by it. It was nothing, probably. She was drunk. Seeing ghosts." She looked to Lance, whose clothed form encouraged her to deal in the facts: he was not a myth, and it was probably not a ghost that Jem had seen.

Someone real had been watching them.

49

They went through the house and back out the other side into the party, to search for Jem. Cass was centered in the hunt by Arthur, who followed her closely as if she might lead him directly to Jem on instinct. It felt like a performance as they moved through the crowds together—especially when the people they passed looked at them with reverence, the six keepers of Eigleath: Arthur, Ella, David, Vinnie, Lance, Cass—and where was Jem? Cass did not enjoy the specialness with which Arthur tainted everything he was a part of. She did not want to be part of his court. She did not like his proximity. Jem had surely found somewhere to curl up and sleep. Her brief absence did not warrant this reaction—there was more going on. There was more. But there was also Arthur's expectant face.

"You've checked the whole house?" she shouted into Arthur's ear. "All the beds? Even mine?"

"Everywhere," he said.

"She's scared?"

"She doesn't do scared. It doesn't occur to her to worry about her safety much." Arthur scanned ahead as he spoke and his words brought Cass into his problem, which was Jem's lack of self-regard.

News of the border falling had been trickling out through the wedding. A flow of uninvited guests had begun turning up from the town, and they—having had those extra hours to gather information—confirmed the rumors: "All over the place, starting fires, to prevent an influx," "Gaia's coming to impose order," "Gaia has Eigleath." "That can't be true?" and "Say that again." "Gaia has Eigleath." Terrible incidents were related with a pinch of salty relief. People were coming in on foot, in their regular clothes, to claim one last experience of the valley.

One last party, in the dip of the land.

The six from Eigleath were approaching The Circle Place. The scene in front of them was firelit, hot and messy. The six weaved smoothly through it. As they got further in, they started to lose each other. Arthur waved to call them back to him; they had to lean in and he had to shout to be heard.

"We've lost this. Find her and then we lock ourselves in the house until it's cleared. No one gets inside unless it's one of ours. Let's open up the next field—keep them away from the back. David, Vinnie, you patrol that. Away from the pyres, yeah?" Arthur's three pyres, each twenty feet high, on the other side of Eigleath, would stay unlit. Enough fire already.

They split up. Arthur tried to follow Cass, but she ducked away. Alone, she might inhabit Jem's mind for a moment. She caught sight of Ella and lost her again. She saw Vinnie taking a seat with someone he knew, for interrogation.

Her husband had sold this place out from under her feet. Was it true?

It was impossible. And finding one person amid this chaos was impossible. There were too many faces. Refined faces, and ghoulish ones, the back of a figure with a passing feel of Eden about her. There was a couple cooking up in a ditch. Cass went toward the center of The Circle Place, pushing strongly between close-knit limbs. Elbowing people in the ribs to get through. Treading on feet. Shoving against bare backs. She was collecting anguish for Jem, or from her. Perhaps Jem had kept herself so unknowable to Cass, and others, because she wanted you to believe that you might be able to rescue her, she didn't want to rob you of that hope. But she was hopeless beneath—was that it? Cass climbed up to stand on a box drum at The Circle Place and looked around. Narrowing her eyes. Feeling the central fire too big and too close. And then the balance tipped and she was no longer looking for Jem: she was looking for what Jem might have seen. What had spooked her?

It could not be true that Cass's husband had sold their children's inheritance to a terrorist group that killed children. When she translated his actions into coherent thoughts within her mind, he became truly ridiculous to her.

Standing tall, she shouted, "Has anyone seen Jem?" People noticed her but were not comprehending. Her shouts alerted Lance to where she was. He was there, lifting his hand to her. They wouldn't find Jem here. Cass led Lance inside. He helped her carry her three children from The Good Room up to her bed, and he went to find a sofa to sleep on.

50

"Do you want to go into town with Lance?"

"Why?" Cass was not fully awake. Ella was in her room, in the same outfit as the night before, swigging—so unlike her—from a can of energy drink.

"He's going to town—go with him? Quicker if there's two of you."

"Has anybody seen Jem?" Called from the meadow outside.

It was eight in the morning. The wedding party was still going strong. There were people asleep in cars and holding court in ravaged ways.

Cass asked, "What's happening?"

"There's some stuff we need sorted in town. And I want to know what their plan is over there. Please."

The world was still a blur to Cass of morning light and color, yet she was already annoyed as she recalled how Arthur had labeled her "obsessed" with the children, as if this were an unhealthy trait. She healthily did not want to leave them. But Ella swore she'd keep them close and implored Cass to go.

Cass, in the blue bedroom, appreciated Ella's unsmiling, clear-eyed beauty; her frowning, mustached dark-hairedness, the fine way between right and necessity that Ella trod. Giving in to Ella's wishes was a simple decision. And Cass rolled over, wanting love in the simple tense, the present, where there is no indication of where things are going, or if they're completed. Where all is constant. All is in reach. Daisy blinked open her eyes and watched the ceiling coolly.

The walk to Lance's truck was long and uphill. Cass had a list from Ella folded in her hand and a set of instructions which would apparently start to make sense as she carried them out.

272

Lance explained that he'd filled and triple-parked Ella's, David's and his own vehicle at the passing place, before the wedding started. That way, no matter how full the lane became, they could get out, if they needed to. He'd also packed their trucks with essentials, just in case—water and food, and fire equipment.

"Why are you so happy?" he asked her.

"So much quiet foresight in you," she said.

"Do you want to drive?"

They set off. It was promising to be the first excessively hot day in a while. Lance pulled down the visor to shield his eyes, then he took from his bag a fist-sized lozenge of greaseproof paper and opened it to reveal leftovers from the wedding feast.

"Thank you." She pinched bites into her mouth as she drove. "I almost don't believe he's really sold it, do you? Or do you?"

"I don't know. I think he has. Ella, this morning, showed me a map. He has somewhere to go."

"Ella is very clear, isn't she, in how she speaks."

"Crystal."

Cass liked the shape of Lance's arms. The line of his nose. His smell. But mostly it was the peacefulness that she liked. He instigated no loud chatter in her. Everything was even. She tried to foment a fury about the sale of Eigleath, and found she couldn't in his presence.

She shifted gear and smiled, with the sun in her eyes. At least her husband wasn't coming back. At least they had a place to go. At least she could go there with Lance and her children.

She was alive, however, to the possibility that she was simply sedated by Lance's size and scent, and that face. If he weren't around, she'd surely be more scared of the situation, and scared for the children. If her sedating husband had never left her bed in the first place, maybe they'd still be in The City, choking to death, murdered by Gaia. Sedation was not sensible.

"It'll be the next left," Lance said.

"OK."

She indicated.

"You are really beautiful, Cass."

He said it gravely, like this was a burden to him, and she almost laughed, except that she felt enveloped by the words, by the way he said them: a druggy, time-slowing, gorgeous laze came over her. It seemed that she was turning the car around the corner for whole minutes.

"I've got weird eyes, though," she said, to leaven his solemn declaration. Why did it have such an effect on her, that he thought she was beautiful? *It shouldn't mean so much.* Being so easily flattered had left her open to so much manipulation.

"Your eyes are *great*," he said. "I've never been with anyone who was really beautiful before."

"Who have you been with?"

"Ah." He took his time. "I've been lucky. I've been with good people."

"Like the woman who runs the pub?"

"She's *definitely* not a bad person."

"You're not a bad person."

He considered this. "I will not compromise," he said. "Which could be a good thing about me. Or a bad."

"You will not compromise, or you will not compromise yourself?"

"Yes, that, the latter."

"The latter always comes later." She imagined what Nathaniel would have said to this: "How charming," in a patronizing way that suggested her charm was mannered.

"Better things come later."

They were driving by old warehouses, through to the ring road, and then into small market-town streets. Cass was amazed by the normal structures of life she saw here; to think this had been so nearby all this time. A billboard, and an industrial bin. Signs directing you to parking places. A school entranceway, and a crossing. But also she saw deeply ingrained impoverishment. Nothing was splendid. Nothing was fresh. The town cast Eigleath in stark relief. She wondered what Ally would have made of all this, whether even she would have been able to block it out. Cass realized she was looking for Ally on the streets walking in a wide-brimmed hat, as well as for Jem.

They passed a crew of kids eating from cereal boxes who seemed too little to be out by themselves. They passed a wall of graffiti that had been overwritten with large letters: "GAIA IS COMING." "I'm suffercating." "We are the end of the line." Cass jumped because she thought she'd caught sight of Jem, but they doubled back and it wasn't her. The lines for the shops along the pavements were not vibrant like they'd been back in The City. The mood was dour.

We are the end of the line.

She slowed down and stopped for a red light. Lance hadn't spoken for a while. Their windows were open. They were each leaning away from the other and out the open windows. Gathering themselves.

A group of people hanging out on the pavement, some of them drinking shine from large glass bottles. Two of them were arguing, the rest ignoring. One, slumped back against the wall, made eye contact with Cass. He cut through the argument with a bark and drew the group's attention to Lance's truck, which they collectively studied. They were all adolescent-thin, their shoes looked too heavy on their legs, yet they bounced from foot to foot. They agreed on something. A young woman among them—emaciated—started toward the truck. She was stooped, jangly of leg, her body both dancing and begging. The others followed her. The junction up ahead was clear; Cass considered jumping the light to avoid them.

"Hey. Hey. Hey," the woman said. Her voice was honeyed. Perhaps it was like a song remembering the days before she got hooked. "Hey. You're from Eigleath, aren't you?" She held her body out away from her legs at an angle, like a challenge. Her eyes were flares. All their eyes were flares. Scabs all over their arms. A young man on crutches— he could have been Vasaly's age. But aged. He was aged.

"With a nice ride like that, you're from Eigleath," said the man, using his crutches at a sprinting pace to reach them.

"Here, can you give Arthur a message from me?" The woman had curled her fingers over the edge of Lance's window. Lance was turning around in his seat and reaching for something in the back.

"Here, it's important, love. Please. Please, sister, please."

"I can tell him," Cass said.

"You're a love. You're a love. Isn't she a love?" she heralded to no one, or to a great omniscient judge in the air around her. "Tell him this, yeah? Tell him it's Lauren, and tell him I'm good for it, yeah? I'm good for it now."

"Please, sister, please," said a man up the back.

"Tell him: don't give up on us, we're good for him. He'll have us back. Please tell him that, yeah. Tell him," Lauren said. "Laur. En. Don't forget. Oh, are you sure?"

Lance was passing the woman bottles of water and more paper packages of wedding food from the back seat.

275

"Are you sure?" the woman repeated. "Oh, thank you. You're that one, aren't you? You're that one! With the food for our kiddies. I've seen you with her. With—what's her name? I never . . . Can you remember her name?" She turned to her group, who were showing that they were each trying hard to remember. "Who's that one you're always with? Who's always helping?"

"Ella," said Lance.

"That's it! You and Ella. You're angels here. No, seriously, I mean it. Angels. You know that? You know how much we appreciate you? Here, were you at the wedding? We were going to come."

"We were going to!" said the man on crutches.

"Only, I wasn't sure. I wasn't sure that Arthur would like it. I don't want to upset him. Because I love him"—with her plaintive wide eyes—"I care about him. I know it sounds weird. But like he's my own."

"We all do," said the man.

"Tell him that, yeah. Tell him you saw us."

"Lauren. Eat something," Lance said. "We've got to keep moving." Then, to Cass: "That light's broken. It's stuck on red, you çan go."

"Bless you," said Lauren.

"God bless, yeah," the others said.

Cass drove off very slowly. She saw Lauren opening the water in the rear view.

"Arthur's a bad person," Lance said.

Cass didn't reply. Lance smelled like that coat he'd given her, and his skin retained the taste of rain, even on that first truly hot day of the year, when she slowly edged across the junction and pulled over, licked his face in the car, to find his mouth.

What healthy woman taught you to be like this?

No one person. I worked it out. From various women, though, all women.

God bless those women.

They were headed for the main pub, The Tavern, at the center of a warren of streets, where there was a meeting that Ella had said needed to be "gauged." They turned onto the high street and parked up. Lance had his bearings completely. They crossed a square and entered down some steps into the low-ceilinged spaces of The Tavern.

51

The meeting had been going on for over an hour by the time they arrived, and The Tavern was full. People were alert, jostling. There were handwritten signs propped about the place saying the beer was off but shine could be had. There was an old hat turned over on the bench, marked on the inner rim with what happened to be Cass's father's initials. There was an old lady, in a baby's bonnet, sucking a pacifier. The glasses of shine were passed over heads by a line of staff who were standing on something behind the bar so that they could see over the crowd and catch orders and coins. Cass scanned the faces of the barmaids in case any of them reacted to Lance, but she picked up on nothing at all.

There was a man shouting from a small stage, and the people who listened gave noise back to him in agreement and, occasionally, dismay. The place was so overcrowded that Lance could put his hand between Cass's legs from behind, and leave it there, and no one could tell. The man was shouting about some sort of thing; but Lance was blowing in Cass's ear, extremely discreetly. He held her from beneath. And then he moved his fingers like he was pressing down on keys. What was anyone saying? ". . . and no matter what they say . . . we will defend against Gaia, we will defend against immigrants," declared the high-voiced man on the stage. Cass let her weight fall entirely onto Lance's body behind her and he was steady. Lance had brought his other hand around Cass's front now. Too much. Cass spun around quickly and kissed him fully and he reddened.

"I'm going to go do Ella's things," she said.

"Meet me by the car?" he said. "In how long?"

"Two hours? Where's Shoe Street?"

Ella's list was specific. Cass should be on Shoe Street at number 24 at 11:30 in order to deliver a small package of antibiotics; she was to be back at the main square at 11:45 to deliver a letter to an elderly lady who would be sitting out on a beach chair; then to a road off Shoe Street, where at 12:10 she was expected to pick up another package. It was heavy. Knives sharpened, the man explained. She passed him back an enormous chunk of cash, which had been pre-counted and was rolled in her pocket—but the man refused to take it, said it was too much, until Cass showed him the instructions written in Ella's hand, and the unmistakable amount, and he cried huge real tears that collected in the crevices of his face. Cass hesitated to touch him in case he was ashamed, but then she realized that she was using her knuckle to wipe his tears, and he grabbed her hand with both of his and held it to cover his face as he wept wetly. When he said, "I'm OK now," she bent her head to look in his eyes and check, and he offered her a cup of tea, which she declined by waving her list in the air. He directed her to Wellington Place, and told her: take care. At 6 Wellington Place she returned a book, and passed over some strong painkillers to a lady who had answered the door with a teaspoon in her mouth, which made a sucking sound as she released the bowl of it off her tongue. To another address on Wellington Place, this time to pass on the knives. At each stop the residences seemed more decrepit, and the person behind the door more disappointed that Ella hadn't come herself. But they all entreated Cass to stay and take their hospitality. Cass kept waving the list cheerfully and not stopping. Everyone left her with messages for Ella: "Tell her I will never forget her goodness, no matter what happens."

Next, Cass had to walk down to the harbor and deliver a bundle of letters, tied up in ribbon, to the harbormaster, who was wearing an apron and came to the door with a plastic razor in his hand.

Cass had asked Ella if she could change the order of the list and try the doors at different times; that way she could do all her visits to each street in one set, and be more efficient. But Ella had said profoundly, "No. There is method in my madness here." The effect of this was that Cass crossed and recrossed the main square several times on her errands. It was as if Ella wanted Cass to be seen, or perhaps to increase Cass's chances of seeing, of spotting Jem. She felt paraded, very visible. There was no anonymity here: everyone could identify her as an outsider. How they stared at her. She was quite surprised that they did not look away when she caught them looking. And she remembered, fondly again, a little of her days in The City, when on her commute to work she could pass hundreds of faces in a single morning, anonymously. Everyone in The City had agreed not to stare at one another. She would sip through a plastic hole at the top of a takeout coffee cup, and sneak glances at strangers, and go on unnoticed.

She began to affectionately recall her old journey to work on the train, and her daily walk across the bridge. How she'd loved jumping in her little car and driving straight through the center of town on a Sunday to visit a friend and have lunch. How she knew all the back routes. Her music in her car in her city. Or the pattern on the seats in the train. And it was particularly funny, just then, that she passed a parked car which was the exact same make and model as her own—the one she'd had since before she met Nathaniel even, and kept and kept. Her first and only car. She'd driven it all over the place. It had been so reliable. She'd actually been quite sad when she'd had to leave it at Eden's. Or would have been, if there had been time for such regrets. And wasn't the universe funny, showing her this little car again, just when she'd been remembering her old physical freedoms? It was a message, telling her, perhaps, to pick her happiness back up from the path where she'd left it. The universe had such a slick sense of humor. How appropriate it was, to see this car, in this moment, exactly her make and model and color.

And license plate.

It had the same license plate. The numbers and the letters appeared there. They appeared there in the right order, appeared there, and forced themselves into Cass's brain and slotted into the correct holes.

Daisy's blanket was over the headrest of the passenger seat. And that was Cass's *Mona Lisa*, hanging from its keychain on the mirror. There was what was hers.

Cass's legs carried her, running, back to the pub. She was tripping down the steps. Lance had moved from where she'd left him. She couldn't see him. A new man was speaking from the stage: "Already today, who are all these people?" he said. "No offense or anything, but there are people in this room here today who I've never seen even once in my life. So hello, to them, to you, and no, not welcome, because where are you going to sleep tonight? Not my place. In your car? In the field? You can't come here. Where do we take your garbage? There's no place for it here." There was Lance; he'd moved to the other side of the room. He seemed to be standing among friends, women he seemed to know, sharing his little space with them at the edge of the pub. Cass couldn't get to him. He looked totally different to her once more. He was close, yet unreachable. She had not seen him from her current angle before. It felt like chaos was catching up with her again and it was introducing a veil of estrangement all around her. The man on the stage: "They're going to bring their shit here. And who's on their tails? Gaia. That's who." Cass started to wave to get Lance's attention. It was undignified and desperate. One of the women beside him noticed her, and queried with her eyes, her fingers: *You want him?* And then that woman placed her hand on Lance's upper arm, too familiar, and spoke into his ear, and pointed out Cass.

"There is only one way to scare them off, and scare them off we must. And that way, the only way we have, I'm sorry to say it, but there's only one way: that way is fires."

There were cheers.

"Got to go. To. Go!" Cass mouthed at Lance.

"Jem?" he mouthed back.

She shook her head: "No."

He did not come toward her. Instead he pulled the car keys from his pocket, and was passing them to someone in the crowd, and as he did so he pointed out Cass. Her heart fell—that the keys were coming to her, but not him. The keys were passed five times from hand to hand, over heads, and then they were in Cass's reach. All the while Lance stayed where he was. And both he and Cass watched the passage of the keys.

When she held up the bronze ring of keys, to show him that she had them, he smiled, exactly as if he was hiding something.

A woman was taking to the stage. "I'm sorry but I've got to—I've got to disagree with you, John. What we've got coming up here . . . These people are fleeing Gaia, they're looking for safe places, with their children. More fire helps none of us. We have to help each other."

Cass didn't understand why Lance was staying. What was going to be achieved at this meeting? Wouldn't the arguments only circle around? Wasn't this nothing more than an exercise in letting people speak publicly to no avail, but to let off steam? Why didn't he come with her? But she could not care. She ran through a list of suspicions in her mind, and the one that undid their morning and had Lance hanging around for his ex-girlfriend barmaid, or some other woman in The Tavern, occupied her the least. Maybe she'd misread him, like she'd misread everyone. There were more urgent ideas to attend to, larger and more devastating: someone had brought her car all the way up here. Who? She was leaving The Tavern and running to Lance's truck.

Was it possible that Eden had come, alone, using Cass's car? Had she come alone, dashing through the broken border, to claim her grandchildren? Or if not completely claim, then nestle herself among them, under the guise of harmlessness?

No, it had to be Nathaniel. He was back. He was going to join himself back to Cass and the children. He was stopping in town to collect himself after the long journey from Eden's. Did that add up? Was he alone? Was he going to punish her for being with Lance?

Where was Petal in this? Cass realized she was about to discover, in person, the extent to which her husband had commingled with a new woman. And what if Petal needed help? What if Petal didn't know what she had gotten herself into?

Cass reassessed, rearranged the parts: Eden had to be near, Cass could feel the dread of it.

And Tim? No, that was ridiculous. Cass had to watch her thoughts and rank them according to likelihood.

Enough. The panic was in her mouth. Cass could taste-hear on the air the pitch of the conversation in which Eden would have informed Nathaniel that Cass was mad, unsafe. That he had to get his children back.

If Eden had come to stake her claim on the children, armed with the children's father, hadn't she come at the perfect time? Hadn't Cass been wrapping herself up in another man she barely knew, and taking her eye off her mothering? Eden would pry the children from her. Eden, Nathaniel, and Petal had come, and they would encourage each other to form a family around Nathaniel's children. And how Eden would relish Cass's humiliation. There was no way that Eden would miss out on witnessing it. Eden delighted in female humiliation. Her only stories about other women were ones in which they were left, or emptied out, or dressed-up and embarrassed. Eden would do the same to Petal. But she'd do it to Cass first.

And then Cass would be left with Lance, who was fine, but just now he felt like a bit part while her husband wrote the play. And her husband would make Lance look unimportant. Her husband had that secret desperation that makes a man great: he clung onto, and pulled down, anyone he could, to scramble up. Lance did not have this. He was too good. He was too peaceful. Wasn't he? Why, after being so burnt, had she trusted anybody?

Cass had to get back to her children immediately. What had she been thinking, diverting her attention to another man?

That morning, Maggs had fed porridge to her toy bear, Shark, and then washed the porridge off him, standing on a chair that she'd dragged to the sink. And then she'd taken Shark outside to dry; she'd propped him up against a flowerpot and "read" a book to him, by making up the story in her own lolloping sentences. Meanwhile, Daisy had been walking back and forth across the court-yard, with her hands held out at the level of her eyebrows, making noises like a goose. Vi had gone off with the other Children of the House before Cass woke. *Shit.* She needed them back.

What if her husband could give his new woman all the things he had shown, but not fully given, Cass? What if her own children learned from their father to honor a different woman's body?

Cass drove with a fury back the way she'd come, straight through the red light, the sun apocalyptic again.

*

At Eigleath, most of the cars had cleared from the lane. Ella came out, holding Daisy, opening Cass's door while the engine was still running.

Ella nodded to herself, confirming something to herself, deducing something from the way in which Cass took Daisy from her arms.

"What happened?" Ella asked.

"I saw my car. I saw my car. I left it at Eden's with the keys in it. It wouldn't start. I left it. She started it. She's here."

"Right." Ella seemed unsurprised. "What does that mean?"

Cass caught the tail end of a particular type of fleeting idea. *Did you make me walk around town like that on purpose, Ella? Did you use me today, to confirm your suspicion, that Eden was in town? Why weren't you upfront about it?* But she didn't want to say this out loud. If she began mistrusting Ella, she'd have no one. Instead she said, "They're here. I think they're all here. I don't know what to do."

"Let's go inside."

Ella led Cass wordlessly inside, made Cass a tea, adding drops of something dark to it, and blew over its surface, to cool it.

Maggs entered and said, "Mommy! Come play with me."

"You set up the game, baby, and I'll be there in a sec."

"Can it be an adventure game?"

"Yes. You set it up."

"Jem is terrified of Eden," Ella said.

"Me too." Cass was laying her forehead on Daisy for comfort; she'd never leaned on a daughter for her own comfort before, only to supply it. Daisy patted Cass's ear in a way that was slightly patronizing. This made Cass almost laugh and almost forget herself for a moment, so she was truly taken aback when Ella said, "Jem thinks Eden turned the water off herself."

"What the fuck . . ." Cass looked up.

Ella shrugged. "Could be. I don't know."

She could believe it. "If that were true . . ." If that were true . . . what did that mean? If Eden had turned the water off herself, to force Jem and then Cass to Tim's, to give him something, to please him . . .

"Mommy," said Maggs, "are you OK?"

If that were true, it meant, surely, that Eden actively despised the younger women. She despised them for their sexual power, which she wanted to have and use herself. She'd claimed it as her own, and sent them as carriers of it to Tim.

If Eden turned the water off herself . . . It meant she had used Cass's and Jem's love against them, to override their agency. She had exploited their fear that their loved ones might die of dehydration. She had managed to take the earth's natural resources, which should have been so abundantly available, and made the young women dance and debase themselves for access to them. This all revealed itself to Cass: an Old World pattern rising up to the surface.

The pattern of the swirl of hair on top of Daisy's head was so distinct, like a large fingerprint.

"Mommy's OK. You're a sweetheart," Cass said to Maggs.

Shifting sands beneath her feet: But how could Eden despise them that much? In order to despise or love a person, you had to be able to see them. Eden did not understand Jem or Cass as individuals in that way. They were only the holders of the gifts she wanted.

Eden could not admire or bask in the gifts of youth that were present in her sons' partners: she needed to obliterate the holder of the gifts, and take the gifts. She could not even admit her natural jealousy. She wanted their things—their motherhood, their access to her sons, their skin, their warmth—without the inconvenience of having to accept that they, the temporary holders of these things, existed. She had only tried to obliterate them. She needed to obliterate them. She was not done.

"Ella," Cass said. "I think Eden was here at the wedding. I think she was watching us."

The small figure at the clearing. The passing resemblance in the crowd. The way Jem saw a ghost and disappeared.

How Eden must have watched Cass undress and watched Lance kiss her between the legs.

"Do we take it that Jem's run away, then?" Ella said. "From Eden?"

"She doesn't want to be here at all."

Maggs was throwing two balls in the air, pretending she could juggle.

"Mom, look!" she said. "Are you looking?"

"I am looking, baby," Cass said. "That's really good."

"Mom, look! Are you looking at me?"

"I'm looking."

"Mom! Look at me!"

"I am literally looking." Cass's eyes filled with tears. She leaned in closer to Ella, to whisper, "They're going to take my children away from me."

"Who are?"

"Eden and Nathaniel."

"No. No. You're wrong. You're seeing this wrong."

"Mom! Come on! We've set up the game!" It was Vi, in his most demanding voice.

"I'm coming," said Cass, trying not to cry.

Ella said, "We have to find Jem. We need to show Jem that we protect her. We won't let her get left behind, it would be awful. Look."

Ella nodded to indicate the kitchen window behind Cass, where nuclear-seeming blooms of smoke were beginning to rise from various points on the horizon. Fires to keep people away.

Daisy, standing on Cass's lap, banged her little palm on Cass's breasts and bounced her bottom up and down.

"And even in all of this," said Ella, "Bluebell insists on a honeymoon."

"They've gone on honeymoon? Where on earth . . . ?"

"Oh, I didn't ask"—and despite it all, they shared in a little kind of desperate laughter.

52

Early evening. The very last of the revelers had been forced off the land by David and Vinnie brandishing deer rifles and calling for the wolfhounds, who had disappeared.

Cass, from her bedroom window, saw that Lance had returned and was walking circles in the meadow with Ella, talking and talking. Maggs was following them. When Lance noticed Maggs, he picked her up. They appeared together, several minutes later, outside Cass's room. Maggs declared that Lance was going to read her a story.

He was comically bad at reading out loud. Vi seemed to find this endearing and hovered over him, hoping to be of use. Maggs thought Lance's monotone was disappointing and funny all at once.

"Why do you say it like that?" she asked him. "Mom makes her voice go more la-li-la, more uppy-downy."

"Yeah, well. That's your mom," he said.

When Cass convinced the children to join Daisy in the bed, she followed Lance into the hallway, holding the door closed behind her.

"OK?" he asked.

"I saw my car."

"I know. Ella told me."

"What happened when I left?"

"Nothing. Butcher drove me back."

Vi called, "Mom!" from the bed.

"Hey," Lance said, gentle as the laps at the edges of a harbored sea, "I'll be right here. I'll sleep downstairs."

"I'm worried Eden's going to come in the middle of the night and surprise me."

"I know. But the surprise is the only bad part of that. She can't actually do anything."

Cass raised her eyebrows, then she said, "You don't have to get involved in this, by the way. Leave me to it."

"OK." He considered what she'd said more carefully. Vi called for her again. "Get away from them, though, yeah? But not on my account—for yourself." His eyes smiled.

"Nah. Not on your account."

He kissed her hungrily.

*

Cass woke in a sweat, in a very quiet part of the night, because she could hear children coughing down the hall.

Her daughters and son were hot and sleeping beside her. Daisy slept with her hips opened out, legs shaped like a diamond, like Cass did.

The evening sky outside was glowing, smeared orange and rose now.

She put Lance's T-shirt on, and her own loose pants, and went to close the windows in the children's bunk rooms. There was a thin smokiness in the air.

From the top of the stairs, she could hear Arthur's voice going in and out. She went down to him; she wanted to know his mind.

"I'm gonna burn it all down by myself to the ground, before that fire gets here," Cass heard him say. "I want to be the one that ends it."

"I just don't know what to say to you anymore," came Ella's voice. She sounded completely worn down.

They were both still in remnants of their wedding gear. Ella had unusual hollows under her eyes, while Arthur's eyes were rimmed red; he was sniffing, possibly high and drunk.

"I've got no choice," he was saying. "I'm not handing this place over, to the fire, or to no one. I take it back. I take back the sell."

"You can't do that."

"Watch me."

The kitchen air had grown misty with smoke. Cass could see it swirling sinister around the high-up paneless window. They had go-bags packed by the door.

"No. Arthur. No," said Ella, finding a final strength. "We're going to board it up. Pack it away. So there's something that remains. We've got to move now. So let's do these things we need to do, and go."

"What about Jem?" Cass asked from the doorway.

Arthur swung around to see her. Her question had a debilitating effect on him. He bent double and brought his hands to his knees, letting out a frustrated shout.

Jem was missing. They had to leave. But if they left without her, they'd be leaving her to wildfire and to Gaia. Arthur would not move from Eigleath until he was certain that she was missing for good, and this he would never accept. It was going to be impossible to wait for him. Cass was about to propose that she and Ella leave before morning, and at least get the children further away from the fires, when there was a loud knock, and they all three jumped. Someone outside was trying to get in the front door.

"Is everyone locked in?" Ella asked.

"Yeah," said Arthur, getting up menacingly. In the hall, they saw the front door handle being moved from the outside. Then there was another loud knock.

Arthur reached the door first. Cass could see the boyish hop in his stride when he thought that maybe it was Jem, trying to get back in. He undid the bolts at the top and the bottom of the door, then turned the key and opened it a little.

"Hello," he said through the gap. He opened the door wider, so that the man behind it was revealed.

And the man standing on the porch saw his wife, wearing a big T-shirt.

53

Once: she'd yearned for him to come home every single day. And now she wanted him to go away. He smiled in a way she didn't know or care to find out about. His fingers looked tapered and disgusting. He looked green.

"Hello, Cass," he said. His voice no longer like a match.

Then he nodded at his brother, and said his name.

They were all distracted for a moment by the thought of what Arthur might do next. He surprised them all by throwing his arms around his brother and swaying with him from side to side.

Nathaniel closed his eyes and the two men stood in their embrace. Eventually Nathaniel slapped Arthur's back—the signal to release—but Arthur held on. Nathaniel caught eyes with Cass over his brother's shoulder, and looked happy.

She was totally and unexpectedly pinned in place there by an overwhelming sadness for him—her feelings for him came rushing back, bewildering—all the stupid things he did. Wasn't he only a fool? His presence sparked up a system of hundreds of small but powerful points in her body. Given the crazed circumstances, wasn't it a miracle that he'd made it back to her. If he had died at war, she would have wept, for the good part of him, the true part, for the rest of her life.

"Sober, I see," Nathaniel said to Arthur.

Arthur clasped his glass of shine, having tipped a fair bit of it down Nathaniel's back. "Desperate times," he said. "Come, let's get you a drink."

"Not for me." He stood gazing at his wife. "I've come about a girl."

"Yeah, you two want somewhere to talk? Here: this way."

Cass would never know whether it was with unthinking drunkenness, or by design, that Arthur led them into The Good Room, waved them in ahead of him, so they were in the center of the room, and then turned the light on, with a flourish, to reveal Lance deeply asleep on the sofa, jumping awake too quickly.

Cass witnessed Lance and her husband clock each other, and she thought she was going to be sick. She immediately retreated back into the hall. She could hear Nathaniel—not apologizing for waking a sleeping man, not asking Arthur if they could find a different room, but saying, "Thanks, mate," as she imagined Lance pulling his pants from the floor.

"Mate" made her cringe.

Lance came out, walked past her. She was about to leap to his ear, but he trailed his fingers calmly across her belly as he passed. He seemed satisfied, having sized Nathaniel up. Lance's confidence wasn't a trick, and there were no ways around it.

Arthur followed Lance out, raised his eyebrows at Cass, and whispered, "Good luck, *mate*."

She entered The Good Room and closed the door.

Nathaniel wasn't standing. For some reason she'd expected him to be standing, but he was sitting, very comfortably, on the spot where Lance's head had been. Nathaniel's arm was spread along the back of the sofa. He was waiting for her to sit with him. From this alone she could see that they were not on the same page, or even in the same story. He had the poise of someone who expected to slip back in exactly where they'd left off. She sat, cautiously, at the furthest end of the sofa.

"You're very far away there," he said.

"Uh-huh."

He reached and took her hand, which fell limp in his.

"Do you remember me, my Cassandra?" He was searching her face.

"I really missed you," she said.

"Me too."

"I really needed you."

"Oh, Cass."

He scooted up to her and wrapped his arms around her. She could melt into this. She could forget everything. Maybe the pregnant girl had been her misunderstanding. Maybe Cass was home now.

She would learn later that, back in the kitchen, Arthur was silently loading the deer rifle, and Lance was pacing back and forth the length of the room, and Ella was sitting on one of the tables, meditating, or chanting, or invoking great powers.

"Tell me everything," she said, pulling away, open.

"Oh, darling, let me look at you first. I can't believe it. Where are the children?"

"They're upstairs. They're fine, happy. They're beautiful. Very grown-up. They're asleep."

"I'll go and look in on them, in a bit. But first . . ." He started running the back of a finger up and down her arm, up and down. Then he moved that same hand to her neck, and thumbed the indentation at her throat. She had to lean her head back, to make his touch bearable. She could hear from his breathing that he intended to get off before they discussed anything. And in normal circumstances that would have been fine. He communicated best physically, anyway. But—

"Wait. Let's talk," she said.

"I have really, truly missed you." His jaw was slack, his legs apart.

She felt bad for him. He probably wouldn't be able to concentrate until he got his end away. Where had she got that expression from? "Get his end away?" It was horrible. From her mother?

"Speak first," she said. "What happened?"

"Oh, my love. I am just so happy to see you."

"I know. So tell me."

"That I love you?"

"How did you get back?"

"I made it."

"But how?"

"On a . . . on a plane?" he said with a first hint of frustration.

"And what happened while you were away?"

"Oh, Cass, can't we just be? Just be. For a while."

"I need to know. Before I can do anything."

"I'm going to need that drink." He looked about.

"Have this." She picked up Lance's glass of shine from the floor. Nathaniel gulped some and then winced. He held up the glass to look at it like it was a joke. "Now. Tell me," she said.

"Right. Won't you just sit next to me while we talk? So I can touch you."

"I'm fine over here."

291

That was when he seemed to catch up with her version of events. It was also when he shape-shifted, into something younger and more betrayed, his glad tidings melted, and he looked up at her darkly.

"Can I see the children now?"

"No."

"I don't need your permission, really."

"Don't wake them."

"OK, so let's do this. Let's have it out like all good married couples do. This is what we sign up for, isn't it? These fights." He was up and moving around. "I used to hate fighting with you."

"We didn't fight."

"We fought all the time." He said this slowly, in an injured way. She stood.

"Can't we just love each other, baby, please?" he said, soft again.

"Sure. Why wouldn't we? Or has something happened to make that not possible? Something you don't want to talk about?"

"I feel like I'm giving you a lot of chances here," he said.

"Chances to do what?"

"Make amends? I make it so easy for you, Cass. I know about you, about you and what you did, what you had to do."

"What did I do?"

"And I understand. I really truly do. I forgive you."

"For which bit?"

"You know, I know it all, baby, the undertaker. You got upset. You ran away. I won't use my mother's word for it."

"What word? What are you talking about, 'undertaker'?"

"The caretaker. I mean the caretaker. The artist guy. What's-his-name."

"Tim?"

"Bingo."

"I never met him."

"Whatever. Whatever. It doesn't matter now." He was looking at her so weakly, not in vulnerability, but in childlike anticipation of her fix.

"What word?"

"Pardon?"

"What was your mother's word?"

His voice deepened, took on a serious phrasing. "She said you got upset over the man and you *kidnapped* the children."

She'd known Eden would use that word. "I didn't kidnap anyone," she said. "It was Eden who locked us up."

"Shhhhhh . . ." Slushing into her anger. "It's OK," he said, vacantly moving her hair from her face.

A certainty arrested her: she was furious and also intoxicated by the void he had dragged her into. There was only one thing she needed from him. "Tell me about her," she said. "About Petal." She could not believe that he was allowing her to feel like this. She could not believe that he was taking her to this place where she was mesmerized by jealousy.

He shifted away from her, set his mouth, and nodded discreetly. He drew up a drawbridge.

"Look. Cassandra. I don't believe—I don't believe—I think it's insane, these days, to believe in the Victorian institution of marriage. We're better than that." He appealed to her again with a new face. She could tell he was recollecting—was begging her to recapture—the cool girl he had once known her to be, the one with light in her hair, and his semen down her thighs. He so clearly wanted it to be that girl in front of him. This new Cass was inconvenient.

"We are . . . You know we are . . . We need freedom," he said. "We need to be free to love. We can only truly love each other if we are free, not forced to love. Because look where it got us, Cass. Look where all that control, and policing of each other, look where it has led us. And I don't mean just us. I mean the world. The cruelty of marriage, it has made us cruel, and the earth has had enough of our cruelty."

He was wearing his wedding ring. He was tired. The sky through the window had been growing increasingly orange as the night developed.

The truth, she realized, was that nothing could ever stand in this man's way. He was a doctor and he spoke like money. He would always be able to find his sort of people, around whom he was needed, and paid, and respected. He'd always find somewhere safe for himself. The rich, the politicians, the lawyers, they would always recognize him as one of their own and help him out. It was possible that, from a purely practical perspective, he was the safest port in the storm for Cass and the children—or maybe he was the safest option for only the children.

293

He continued, "Marriage is a spell. And it works a charm, I'll tell you. It really . . ." Searching for words, he held his fingers together and rubbed them vigorously as if he were seasoning an average meal with some foreign spice he'd never caught the name of. "I've done it three times! I will always be amazed, amazed, that we found each other. We were meant to be together. You know that. I know you feel that. We would have found each other no matter what. I would recognize you through lifetimes. And nothing can come between that. Nothing."

"But something has."

He fell back, exasperated. "It's very normal to fall in love with more than one person. We didn't mean to get pregnant. I thought she'd stay over there, and I'd leave and come back here, to you. I wanted to do that so much, you have no idea. But I couldn't leave my baby there. Not in that place. I couldn't do it. Maybe a better man would have managed it. But I'm not sure, on balance, that he'd be the better man. Cass, I couldn't look myself in the eye if I'd done that."

Cass was crying now. He didn't go toward her. He watched. As if he'd cut her, and was watching her bleed out, while telling her why, with words, in a loving way. As if this pain was something she was obligated to feel. But why did she have to feel like this? What law made it so? The sky was burning through the night outside.

He had an idea, and it left his lips with a set of fingertips indicating inspiration: "Talk to all the hippies in this place. They know how it works. Arthur must have fathered dozens of babies by different women by now. This is the way of the world, Cass. The real world. Not the pretend society invented by The Man. The Ad Man invented it all. And it's not real. You know that."

Somehow he seemed to have moved himself so he was now kneeling in front of her, holding her hands once more. All she felt was wretched, stupid, slightly comforted on an infantile level by the pain.

"You sold their home!" was all she could say.

"This place? This place is not their home. We'll find somewhere that will be the children's real home."

A little crying yelp escaped her. "The children" included his new baby with Petal.

"You can't stop loving me," he said.

"I can."

"But you can't stop loving me."

She nodded that she could.

"You cannot remove me from your head. I know you can't. No one knows you better than I do. And you are the strongest, most beautiful person I ever met. If you were weak you would walk away from our confusion of real painful love, but you are not weak. You can take this."

They were quiet for a bit. Cass had been waiting for him to tell her that he didn't love his pregnant other woman. But he was not saying that. Quite the opposite.

"You cannot stop loving me," he said again, so gently, not like a plea but like something they both had to sweetly admit, like little ill-fated, love-struck teenagers. "That's not who you are."

She heard herself speaking, unpleasantly, through her tears: "I was not put on this earth to always carry you around in my head no matter how much you hurt me."

"Oh" and "Cassandra"—he drew her down to kneel with him on the floor, and she went, because her legs required it. "I hurt you. I hurt you. But I can make this better."

"How? How on earth?" Kneeling face to face in front of the stone fireplace.

"We'll leave here, in the morning. Mom knows a place. A friend of hers, of course. We're trying to arrange a boat. Do you have another car here? I don't think we'll all fit in your old banger, unless you and Mom take a kid each on the lap."

She understood whom he meant by "we," but she couldn't quite believe it. The car seated five: him, Petal, Eden, Cass, and one child, leaving two children on laps.

"Arthur's bought a place," she said.

"I won't go with him. No way." He smirked exactly like his brother. "I will not let my children live with him."

"But you're the same."

"Come on, Cass. You know that's not true."

She said, "Tell me yourself exactly who you mean by 'we.' Is she coming, this woman? Say it. I want to hear you say it."

"I told you, I couldn't leave her behind. It was a nightmare getting her a visa to fly. That's why I didn't come back sooner. But I had to help her, I simply had to. You'll understand when you meet her. She's in town now with Mom."

Did he expect her to get in a car alongside a heavily pregnant woman who was carrying her husband's child, as soon as tomorrow morning? How would they explain that to the children? Was she going to go with him again because his alignment with power and money would protect her children? If so, would she be his wife? Would she have to share him? Like how? By rotation, or would it be decided by his dick?

He was still talking, but more brightly now. "She actually gets on really well with Mom. So that takes the heat off a bit. They're chattering constantly. In foreign, I might add! Although Petal's English is getting better and, you know, she could teach the kids some languages. Turns out: she's a great cook. I had no idea until I got to Mom's." He paused and looked solemn. "You're always my wife, Cassandra. You're top billing, forever. And there's nothing you can do about that."

Cass stood. She felt very, very hazed. If she did not go with him, would he try to take the kids? This is what she needed to know.

"Tell me what you're thinking," he said.

"I am thinking that I have to let you leave my head now. I wasn't put on this earth to carry you everywhere like this. You make me insane. But I am not an insane person. I have to believe that."

He was on his feet now too, voice louder. "How do I make you insane? Describe precisely how? You can't stop thinking about a person, you can't stop loving a person, just because you will it. That's not how humans work."

"Watch me. I will not hold you in my head for long. I will not be able to. You're too much."

"Well, if you don't hold me in your head, who will?" he shouted.

"I don't know. Your mother, maybe?" She did not shout.

He ignored that.

"If you—if *you*—the one person who understands me, the one person I love, if I don't exist in your head, where do I exist?" He was incandescent. "Where? Show me, where?" He looked most like Arthur when he raged. It was easier for her to see spaces around his words when he got angry. She moved into one.

"I want to see the children," he said.

"I don't want you to wake them."

"Why are you so unkind? Who made you like this?"

"You did."

"OK," he said. He passed his hands, palms down, through the air in front of his chest. He breathed like she knew he did when a patient on a table took an unexpected turn, and Dr. Maguren had to gain the confidence of the room. "Alright, alright," he said. He took another loud breath and he was calm. It was as if he'd just remembered that he was not talking to a rational person but an unhinged female patient, and he regained his surety. "Look, it's time to get out of here. I'll come back in the morning. I'll see the children in the morning. And then we'll leave together." He was going to carry them all out of this situation on the back of his reason. "It's actually nice to see the old place one last time," he said casually, because everything was lining up for him now, arranging in his head as he wished it to be. But after a pause of fruitlessly looking around the room, he added, "The children hold me—in their minds."

"Of course."

"Will you help me with them, at least?"

"What do you mean?"

"Well, I think it's becoming clear to me now, I mean, I don't know what you've told them about me."

"I've never told them anything. I help them love you."

"Help them? Help them! Why would my children need your help in that?"

"I didn't mean that, I meant—"

Again, shouting: "How can I father them if you don't protect their image of me? How can I love them if they don't love me?"

"Easily. It's not meant to be quid pro quo with them. You love your children no matter what they think of you."

"Oh, it's not quid pro quo with them, but it is with you, apparently. You'll only love me if I accept certain conditions of imprisonment. Your love is *very* conditional."

"I'm not your mother. It's not meant to be unconditional with me. I was not put on this earth to forgive your rebellions for independence."

"'Not put on this earth'? 'Not put on this earth'? What is this shit? Why do you keep saying that? Are you wondering what on earth you were put on this earth for? Because I am, I am right now, Cassandra: what were you put on this earth for, if not to do this?" He took one of her hands and moved it onto his chest, pushing it down over his heart, the source of all this feeling.

He placed his other hand firmly, decisively, below her left clavicle. She knew that he pictured her heart anatomically beneath it. He'd told her: her heart was not beautiful, it was literally a meaty organ, located behind her tripartite sternum, off-center. To perform CPR properly, he'd once reminded her, you had to push down so hard that you hear the sternum crack. To bring people back to life, he'd cautioned when she'd spoken admiringly of his job, you sometimes had to commit acts of violence. He held his hand over her heart and she remembered that it had chambers in it like the ones he had put his fingers through in the lamb's heart in the biology lab, when he was fourteen and scared of being a virgin.

And now he was crying—"What were you put on earth for, if not to do this, if not to feel this, Cassandra?"—and he spread his fingers on both his hands, to cover both of their hearts. "This was what we were put on earth to do, to find each other. To love each other. No matter what."

They were both crying.

"I can't believe you brought her here," Cass said.

"Oh, darling." He held her hand against his heart more softly.

They had gone all the way through.

She tried to picture the web of veiny tissues that connected her heart to her hand from the inside, and she felt a depression of life spreading through them.

And they were done for the night. All spent.

She kissed him, out of habit, between the eyes, and then she said, "I've got to go to bed."

"OK," he said. He took her hand from his chest and kissed it before releasing her. He went to sit heavily on the sofa. "I'll come back in the morning," he said throatily. He looked like he needed to be saved, all haunted and sad.

She exited and clicked the door shut quietly behind her.

54

Everything—the stairs, the side table, the plaster, the doors, the neck-laces, his wristwatch on her wrist—everything came in very close. She saw all her jewelry, and her husband's watch, for what they were: only metal loops encasing her neck and wrists. The house was dead; wood, and stone, and chalk, held in a structure above her head, and there were partitions, and separations, and rules of timekeeping and decency that kept you away from your real feelings, and your deeper connections.

She wanted him to disappear. And she also wanted him to fuck her, and never, ever, ever wish, try, nor care to fuck another. And she wanted him to never leave.

But maybe none of these mental positions were her feelings. Maybe they were his. She'd never actually been able to tell the difference.

When you are caught in a fire, synthetic materials will melt into your skin, but natural materials will burn right off.

The dial of his watch on her wrist was pretty. It was opulent, like the inside of a particularly thick, well-found oyster shell. It was eyeless, and mouthless.

There were three places she could reach within the time it would take the fastest hand on the watch to circle once around the dial: she could reach her children upstairs; the people in the kitchen; or she could go outside.

The second hand departed twelve and she crossed the hall, unlocked, opened, and closed another door behind her, and she was outside, where her heartbeat resounded so loudly in her head that she mistook it for an external sound coming from the center of the earth, just left of a deep delicate bone. She put her hands over her face and in the anguish left over from the conversation with her husband she let out a noise like a laboring thing.

Enough.

The wind was hot. The sky was ochre. Something flying past caught on her ankle as it spun by with the wind-taken leaves, and it burnt her in a quick stinging slice. She took the smoky air deeply into her lungs and walked on. The fires were strong, or close. They were no longer protected in the valley.

Cass sought her own counsel as she went.

The world is on fire. And what will you do?

You should go with the marriage unit: it offers you the most visible protection. The children should be with their father. And he will find a way to make a good situation for himself, and for you, if you are with him. You may have to quieten your soul, but at least you will get to keep your children close and they will be materially well provided for.

There were dark black leaves against a pink-orange sky. All the tones and contrasts of the world had changed.

No. Go to Arthur's place. Take yourself and the children from their father.

But he will fight this. And Eden will help him fight. You cannot live under the constant threat of Eden's tactics. Eden turned the water off herself.

Go with Nathaniel and lose your dignity; or leave Nathaniel and lose the children. Are these the only two options?

"There are never only two options, baby." Ally's voice in her head.

The wind was so hot. The trees would not stand it. The dust in the air. How would they breathe?

What the hell does it matter who you go with, or whether you are being true to yourself, when you cannot breathe?

You can only do what is safest for the children. That is the only option.

The children will have a better chance of survival if you go with your husband. If they have two adults with them, who are related to them, fighting for them at every turn, they will be better off.

And you cannot allow Lance to influence your decision. Lance is heaven, but heaven never lasts. It's always heaven at the beginning.

It cannot hold.

"But I want to go with Lance," she said, aloud.

No one can guarantee that Lance will be able to put himself on the line for another man's children. Nor that he would like to. If he were up against it, would Lance have their father's killer instinct, could he fight for them?

But their father left. His instinct absconded.

She stopped walking. The burning winds felt under her skin. She closed her eyes and tried to picture her lungs as spongy, natural things, because the sensation in them was increasingly becoming that of a more calcified substance; she couldn't get the air in.

Open your eyes.

The sky was as wide as the mind, and all orange. She could not inflate her lungs. She needed higher ground.

Up ahead stood the first of Arthur's three pyres. The ladder was still propped up against its side.

As she approached the pyre all her feelings for her husband rose again. She was overcome with a fear that, if she entertained even the smallest amount of compassion for him and his pregnant girlfriend, if she made peace with them for the children's sake, then her husband would take advantage of this, he would take everything. He would allow Cass to serve the pregnant girl. He would reach over Cass's wishes for his own ease. The physical sensations produced by this pattern of thought were too much to bear. Her proximity to her own debasement: the new worst thing.

The ladder was at a sturdy angle—leaning into the pile of wooden slats, and oak roots, and broken gates. She climbed the rungs. At the top there was a pallet, secure enough that she could crawl onto it. She could hold her face up to the landscape, with the fire at her back, could kneel and breathe slightly more easily.

There, she settled. Asked herself, *What were you worried about again, my love? Oh. Him.*

Husband. And how he might change you into his lesser wife. How he might embarrass, exceed, and defeat you.

How you might strive to keep him close only because you do not trust him. How you might strive to keep him close, not because you want him, but in order to prevent him falling too much in love with someone else. You have to release him.

You know how he will help himself to all of your good parts in perfect entitlement. How he might open you, and take from you, in the same manner that he opened his mother's cupboards and helped himself to food. And that would be alright. You could give of yourself to him. Yes, you may give of yourself freely.

So long as you hold—and all are held—by the proviso that you are allowed to withdraw yourself, if he hurts you.

And there was the rub. *Your self-protection will only ever make him furious and spiteful.*

Stop it.

She spoke the words reluctantly at first, released them, released him. "I release him," she said. She had been holding on to him because she did not trust him.

"I release you," she said. "I release."

It came in like a click. A click of the door, a click of the stove, a click in the wrist, a click of golden charms near the heart, the watch, click of the tongue. Resolve: all alight. Resolve:

It will be you alone who will lead the children. You will hold them until they are grown enough to leave you safely. The other players can align themselves around this, or fall away, as they wish. You will drive the children to Arthur's new place, and if it isn't suitable, if you do not feel your agency there, you will simply take the children and start again, elsewhere. Their father can see them whenever he likes, but you do not have to fall in with him. This future cannot be impossible. You could even go to it in your own car.

And Lance in this? Lance was a distraction. Not only a distraction, but he was self-sufficient. It was probably best that he went his own way now. Lance had reminded her of something, and brought her back to herself. And perhaps she had done the same for him, in some way. It was physical. The person who pulls you out of the mire is rarely the person you continue forward with. They're just the getaway car.

She would throw a cape over herself and the babes and lead them somewhere safer, lightly, slowly, meaningfully, with a message undulating to the confines of their existence: *I know the way, I will keep you safe.*

She closed her eyes and drew in air between her bared teeth. It whistled a slight way in and had a taste to it, like she was confronting something strange—not the smoke, but something else, something that would never cease.

She kept her eyes closed. Her children's mothers. With her. The dead wives. They'd never been real to her. She'd pretended not to know. But they were with her. They were at her back. She bowed her head and let out a sob of total recognition. It was a prayer she shared with them.

She opened her eyes. The sky was empty apart from the dark orange everywhere. There were no arcs. All ahead was flat, and hers, but beckonless. There was an eerie beauty in this beckonlessness. A peculiar kingdom. She felt like the Queen of Nothing. And she was not, as she had long believed, of the same substance as her husband. Unlike him, she did not ask, anymore, to be filled, and therefore she could not be in debt and taken.

She felt she could stay like this, in this way, on the pyre, forever. Breathing fire. Seeing concentric, geometric shapes swimming in everything. Witnessing her kingdom.

55

It was Jem's body that broke her focus.

A pair of birds were flying overhead: escaping. They were companions; they held a beautiful distance between them. She wondered at them; at what integrity, what discernment, what privacy, and what magic were required to allow for this type of partnering.

Then her eyes flitted to the landscape below the birds, because she saw a creature there, whose timing and pose made Cass's laugh trill out. The figure, coming up from the woods, a figure with her hair all wild and wet, and her skirts pulled up, and with a look of furious determination in her shoulder-led posture: It was Jem.

This was even better.

Cass called Jem's name. But Jem couldn't hear over the burning and the dawn chorus, which had begun spooling out even though there were hours to go until dawn, the birds all confused by the bright lights of the fires. All their song in disarray. Cass laughed more because Jem looked so brutal, like she could take on a dozen warriors, and yet hadn't they all been so worried about her? Here Jem was, striding out like the hero, followed by two dogs, more like wolves.

Cass might have climbed down hurriedly and run over to Jem, but she did not want to disturb Jem's feelings or her own. She had a sense that—in both their cases—some fresh sensibilities had been hard-won and were nascent. Jem went over the ridge and disappeared.

This was even better and Cass was reassured: the coming evacuation from Eigleath felt all at once more stable. If Jem was back safe then Arthur would concentrate again. And, what was more, if Arthur felt strong, Nathaniel would not. Nathaniel's loss of self was instantaneous when his brother was empowered. And if Nathaniel was on the back foot, and in vigilance, he would not feel so bold nor so able to stake his claim on Cass. He might even begin to feel embarrassed by his appearance here, with his pregnant friend. This was the story Cass ran through. And it fitted. It would give her more time to puzzle her way to the next safe space, where she could work out how to anticipate what she wanted, rather than accept what she was told she must have.

From the pyre, Cass climbed down. She walked a loop once around the perimeter of the house, as if to tie up a promise and say goodbye.

At the front, where the mist, which was smoke, was creeping low through the distant boughs, she spotted her own old car parked a little way up the lane, driven there by Nathaniel. He hadn't left yet.

She noticed that two pink candles were lit in the window of The Good Room. Arthur was surely taunting Nathaniel with those.

Cass went up to her bed, completely spent. They'd leave in a few hours. She shook her loosely laced boots off and left them at the foot of her bed. She crawled in between her children and, making a diamond shape with her legs around her Daisy-Baby, she dropped off for a bit. The children were most themselves when she was alright.

She was quickly dreaming: dropping a plumb line down. To a real world. A beckonless kingdom. Where she sat, mesmerically, with all things. And the waters moved. And she was complicit with life. It floated through her, finding no resistance. Like transparent green cloaks, full of light. A light that grew stronger and started blinding the world in flashes, sending her down a further level into deeper sleep.

56

Vi whispered, "Mom" in the night.

"Mom," Vi whispered. "Mom . . . Mom. I cannot sleep . . . Mom. I can't, Mom. It's in the air."

"OK," she said, waking slowly. Her eyes remained closed. Maggs was hugging Cass's head in her sleep, which is to say that Maggs had Cass's head in a viselike grip. Cass kissed the little girl and rolled over to Vi, throwing her own arm heavily across him.

"No, Mom," he said gently. "The smoke."

She opened her eyes.

This was not the thin veil of smoke from the wildfires, which had begun to inhabit Eigleath earlier. This was thicker smoke.

It was pouring in around the edges of the door.

It was coming up through the floorboards. Turning the blue of the room colder.

She had her boots back on almost instantly, but she took care, took the time, even in her haste, to lace them up properly. "Don't-worry-don't-worry," she intoned to her son, even finding herself holding his face in both of her hands. "Don't worry." All the necessary actions that were to follow were aligning already in her like dominoes; but she still caught herself taking a look into her son's face and thinking, *My God, you are so beautiful. You will have such beautiful children.* She went from him and opened the bedroom door a crack, to find that the hall outside was filled with the blackest, most tumbling of smokes, and there was a new sound within the building. It was a terrifying sound that was exploring the place like an animal. Something had been released and was trapped in between the four walls. She could not see a thing. Her senses were reconfiguring. She started shouting for Ella, but the smoke came right into the central channels of her lungs, making her hack.

She closed herself back in the bedroom to cough it out. Then, "It's fine," she said to Vi. It seemed that the smoke was worse within the house than without it. She opened the windows. "Stay here," she told him. "Two minutes." The girls remained asleep.

The hallway was in blackness and cloaking. She went a few steps, she could make out that the seat of the fire, the intense heat and brightness, was coming from the bottom of the stairwell. The closest exit via the front door was blocked by vibrant flames. But there were windows, she told herself, and there were other people, behind doors, with instincts, goodness. And there was a voice in her head screaming a number, over and over. *Nine.*

It was safest to leave her children where they were for two minutes while she grabbed a chance for them all. She dashed for the stairs that led up to the floor above, taking them two at a time. She was in Ella's room and screaming, "Get up, get up, get up, get up."

She ran into the other bedroom on that level, Jem and Arthur's room. It was empty.

Ella was already gone when Cass re-entered her room and turned the taps on in the sink in the corner, picking up piles of clothes and wetting them. The bedsheets. She raced back down the stairs with the wet pile in her arms; she angled her face into it, for shielding; but daring to look up as she reached the lower landing, she was able to make out Ella, who was frantic at the door to one of the children's bunk rooms.

"Handle's too hot." Ella had to shout in Cass's ear to be heard over the fire. Cass released the wet things onto the floor, retrieved one item from the pile and was trying to use it to cover the handle and turn the knob. But it slipped. But it didn't work. There was desperate crackling around them. And the heat. And the coughing. Cass took a big pace backward and kicked at the door with her boot. She kicked it again, in exactly the right spot, below the handle. It swung open. First one door, then the other—Cass kicked them in. Then Ella was in there for the children, she was setting about tenting the wet things over the children's heads.

A shift in the fire's mood, like a drawback of breath before it exhaled: here was a small change in the density of smoke, so Cass was able to see down the hallway to David's closed door. She rushed at it. It wasn't fully shut; she had only to tap it with her boot and it opened.

Behind it, David's bedroom was remarkably untouched by the flames. Only small black-gray tendrils were just beginning to rise through the gaps in the bare floorboards. David's daughter's drawings, which were taped along their top edges to the wall opposite his bed, were rising and falling in the blowing heat from the fire coming from below. It was all coming from below.

On the bed: there was David, asleep on his back, like a stone man atop a tomb, with his palms crossed. And beside him slept Lance, on his front, with one arm dangling off the side of the bed. This was a gift—"Up! Get up!" That's all she screamed into the room, and she was gone. It took seconds. But each second was playing out to her in slow time, like tree time, and the few minutes that she left her own children closed in her bedroom played out like an eternity.

Cass was back in her own room. All three of her children were awake now. They were not crying. They were sitting up on the bed, awaiting her return, in complete trust that she'd come back. Her face welcomed their faces. She grabbed the sling from the corner. Her hands slid over her children's heads in a comforting way as she clipped Daisy into the sling on her front, took Vi on her back, and held Maggs up on her hip. They left the blue room.

Lance was in the hallway then, pressing a wet towel over Daisy. "We can't take those stairs down," he was shouting. He reached automatically, offering his arms for Vi, and the boy climbed willingly onto the scaffolding of the man.

"The stairs look about to blow," David shouted; the other children had been partially closed back in their rooms, for safety. David had one hand shading his eyes and the other on Lance's shoulder. Shades of purple fire, and flashes that blinded, and filings of the gold, rolling, rolling up from the base of the stairwell.

Now began an appalling, chemical sound. A hissing from the stairwell. The sound seemed to be reaching some sort of crescendo, and all the adults in the hallway simultaneously flinched from it, turning their bodies from the stairs and covering the children they were carrying.

But the sound was Vinnie. He was coming up with a small fire extinguisher. "There's a gap!" Vinnie shouted. "Now! Now!" He took a second small extinguisher from under his arm and handed it to David, who struggled with the pin and got it out.

The partially closed doors were elbowed open once more. And some of the children were lifted, or told to hold hands, they were told to hold their breath, and were shown to hold the wet things over their noses and mouths. Cass began to lead them down, following Vinnie, whose extinguisher was faltering. David started his from behind. They led the children down the curve of the staircase.

Toward the bottom, the fire was too bright and too close. But the front door was already open; the orange shape of night that was visible through it pulled them forward.

They were out. A deep breath of outside air did not bring relief, it smelled of burning plastic. There were embers flying like snow on fire. Cass pointed to the bank at the edge of where the lane began: "There. Go!" Vi was sliding down from Lance's back; he took his sister's hand and launched away, across the gravel.

She followed them with Daisy crying in the sling. When the heat on her back was bearable enough to face, she turned to check that the other children were leaping to keep up with her. She stopped to count them. There was Lance's silhouette against the terrifying hall, which was aflame, and she could see how he grabbed the remaining children roughly when they reached the bottom of the stairs, how he seized their arms and pulled them from the extravagant light into the world, where Vinnie caught them and sent them fleeing to Cass. Cass heard Vinnie shout to Lance, "Nine! There should be nine kids!" They were all counting. There was number eight, there was number nine, running past Cass now. Who did that leave?

She watched Lance reach into the fire light again, and he caught Ella, and found David, almost simultaneously. And that was fourteen of them.

Ella had taken in too much smoke. She could not stand. David was propping her up.

Lance caught his breath to shout, "Where's Arthur?"

Eigleath let out a great puff of pungent air and it began to groan. All the adults ran away from it—a new, more urgent plume of smoke beginning to rush from the back of the building.

"Where's Arthur?" Lance repeated.

"His room was empty," said Cass. "He must have got out."

They headed for the bank, where the children were. Cass put her arm around Ella. She could feel Ella wheezing.

They reached the children and were counting them again, for reassurance. They were all panting and in confusion. Cass put her ear close to each child's mouth, to listen for clear breathing.

"They weren't in their room," she said as Vinnie and Ella sank to the ground together and started coughing.

"Who?" David asked.

"Arthur and Jem," she said.

"They're not here." David said this quite aggressively, because he was sure of it. "This is everyone from inside."

"Arthur's in there," said Ella between bouts of productive coughing.

"No, he's not. His truck's gone," said David. "He went out tonight. I saw him go out."

"His truck is there," Cass shouted, pointing at the vehicle. "And Jem came back. She came back tonight."

"No," David said. "Jem is missing," he explained very clearly. "And I saw Arthur go out." He said it kindly. "I saw him leave. Don't worry. He's not in there."

"I saw Jem come home," Cass said. "And that wasn't Arthur. You must have seen Nathaniel leaving. Look!" she implored. "Arthur's truck is there." She was shocked that David would speak with such certainty while refusing to see what was in front of him.

"Nathaniel?"

"I'm sure Arthur got out," said Lance. "He must be around the back."

"Nathaniel didn't leave!" said Ella, drawing shallow breaths. "He stayed—in The Good Room. David, you saw Arthur leaving in his truck. He left to pick up Eden. But then he came back."

"So, hold on," Lance said, both hands in the air. "Is Arthur here or not?"

Cass was trying to understand and simultaneously explain something, but they'd escaped through comprehending one another bodily, it had been efficient and the best they could do; and now they were outside and they couldn't tell what speech meant. Lance was looking at Cass like she was speaking in tongues.

But Cass noticed that he was slowly beginning to hear Ella. So Cass fell silent, and listened, too, to what Ella was saying: "Arthur went out in his truck to get Eden, and Petal for Nathaniel. I went to bed. I

310

was so tired. I'm so sorry. I was so tired. I went to bed. But Arthur's truck is here now. So he must have come back."

Vinnie said, "They weren't in the kitchen. I woke up in the kitchen."

Cass could feel her face all contorted. "Jem is in there. I saw Jem come back."

"But *where is she*?" cried Lance.

"Nathaniel was in The Good Room," said Ella. "They were all going to talk."

The Good Room, they could see through its smashed windows, was the center of the blaze.

"And they all . . . all in there?" said Cass. "There were candles. I saw two candles. Were they all in The Good Room?"

"I don't know, I don't know . . ." Ella had her forehead in her hands. "I'm so sorry."

57

In the end, Vi never found Nature a comfort in the way his mother did. His mother always told him that the natural world returned her to herself. But Vi, when he saw a glorious night sky, could not help but picture it on fire. When he encountered some unbelievable natural spectacle, he could not help but lay over it the image of his mother, running toward a burning building to save his father. She ran back into the fire that night with no hesitation. She was going, absolutely, into the center of the blaze. Her trajectory was like an arrow released; there was nothing you could do about it.

Then Vi saw the man, whom he liked to call the Beast Man, who like some kind of dial turned his mother up. The Beast Man ran so fast after Cass toward the burning building that very soon he was running ahead of her. It looked like he would beat her to the center of the blaze. Vi assumed then that the Beast Man would save his father, and this was preferable to his mother going back into a burning building. But, instead, the Beast Man swerved around and did the impossible. He caught an arrow mid-flight, before it hit its target: he picked Vi's mother up off the ground, and he held her. She scrambled against him, but once he had her he was unmoving.

Vi's sisters were worried and uncomprehendingly upset at the time but, watching this scene, Vi felt an overwhelming sense of calm, and he dropped his anchor right then and there, not into the flabbergasting beauty of the natural world, not learning, nor making, nor theory; he dropped his sense of self, and life, and safety, into other people then: into true community. *And you will be a happy man,* they said to him. And he was.

And when his mother was a little old woman, smiley and frail, with lines that had developed over her entire face like a map leading the

way to her ridiculous eyes—and when his sisters were away, somewhere out in the world, in their dignity, which they never did quite
learn to question—he went to collect his little old mother, to drive
her to the doctor. And she came slowly out to meet him, in her lovely
comfortable clothes, and she thanked him, so sincerely, and she looked
so unassuming. But he remembered what she was like, at the burning
house, on that night when she was still young, and they were children.

Lance held Cass against him and he said to her, "We cannot go back
in." And he said, "The children need you." And he said to her, "Listen
to me—no—*listen to me*. It is too late. I know. I know it is too late."

And she was desperately wailing, "I can't leave him in there. I can't
leave him."

Lance held her in that state. In her mind, against the fire, she was
seeing and reseeing the two candles in the window of The Good
Room. She'd thought Arthur had put them there, being ironic. Being
a dick. Parodying his mother.

Those candles: Eden's nightly ritual. Maybe Eden had lit those
candles. Ella had said that Arthur had gone into town *to collect Eden
and Petal and bring them to Eigleath*. Maybe, when Cass looped once
around the house, before she went to bed, maybe Eden was already
in there.

And maybe Eden, Eden who switched the water off herself, maybe
Eden had done something even worse here.

In a good fire, every single thing is moving. Nothing is still. This is how
Nature goes. Watch the sea, look into it: nothing is still down there.
Slow down, to tree time, and watch the growth of a leaf, or the growth
of a child. In terms of the pattern of its relentless movement, fire is only
living, sped up.

Lance managed to pull Cass further away from the blaze. He held
her against him and tried to speak to her. But her eyes were darting around to solve this catastrophe and—"Wait," she said, landing
her gaze in the particular spot where, earlier . . . "Wait. My car." She
couldn't see it. It wasn't where it had been. It wasn't where Nathaniel
had left it.

"*We've got to go!*" Lance insisted.

"It's not here. Oh my God. My car was here. Nathaniel drove
it here."

"Cass?"

"Who took my car?"

"OK."

"OK?"

"This is great. This means they got away. In your car." Lance's voice was filling with relief at this new possibility.

"They got away in my car. And they *left us in there?*"

"I don't know, Cass. I don't know. But look at that—look in there. It's an inferno. If they managed to get out, they wouldn't have thought for a moment they could save us."

"Fucking Vinnie did. Vinnie woke up in the kitchen and thought he could save us."

"Yeah, but that's fucking Vinnie, isn't it? Look, maybe"—he was preferring this version of events—"maybe they all got out of there, they got in your car, and they left."

Cass was panning for the bits of solid fact. So, according to Ella, when Cass had left The Good Room, Nathaniel had gone and convinced Arthur to collect Eden and Petal from town, and bring them to Eigleath. Which Arthur had done in his truck. He'd gone and he'd returned. Then Cass had seen the two candles in the window of The Good Room. And what did this mean? Did it mean that when Eden had arrived at her old Eigleath she had lit her two candles in her old Good Room, and had her two boys with her at last? She wouldn't leave them again. And was this where Jem had found them? Vengeful Jem. Jem who had passed the pyres looking like the hero.

Eden who had switched the water off herself.

Cass's car was definitely gone, so someone got away.

Nothing is still in a good fire.

She calculated: Eden, Nathaniel, Arthur, Jem, and Petal. That's five. They'd fit perfectly in Cass's car. But was it real? Or were they still in there? Or did only Jem get away? Or only Eden? Only Petal, with quickening maternal resolve?

Lance had not released his hold on Cass. "It's too late," he said. "We have to go. You have to give up. You have to give in."

A part of the building crashed down on itself and they reacted by mirroring it, crouching to the earth. Lance still did not let go of Cass. Even once he had got her into his truck, he kept hold of her clothes with one fist. She was the only one wearing shoes.

314

Vinnie was shouting in Lance's ear from the back seat: "A lot of this isn't even coming from the house. There's fire coming on every side."

The sound of the fire was like being directly under the impact of a waterfall. It was ceaseless and regenerating.

Ella and David were in the truck ahead with five of the kids. Lance, Cass, and Vinnie had the other four. They wrapped clothing around their heads. They drove slowly up the lane. Lance was sure the tires would burst. They drove in and out of pockets of extreme heat. Each time they entered one, Lance held his breath. The wipers became too full of ash to work effectively, so, at the passing place, Vinnie and David got out, Vinnie pulling on Cass's boots, and with their mouths covered they used blankets to clear the windows a bit. But they were in a gale of hell. They wanted to pour water into one of the engines, but they couldn't get the hood up in the hot wind.

In the two trucks they reached the top of the lane and took to the flat main road, where they joined other vehicles traveling in the same direction, away from the fires, toward the town. This proved to be a hopeless destination when, rounding the corner, they saw that there was nothing but towering flames coming from the town. They had assumed that things were at their very worst in their dip at Eigleath, but when they gained higher ground they found that Eigleath had been comparatively sheltered by its valley. It was all out of hand. There were lights from a couple of helicopters above.

"What are we going to do?" Cass was shouting. But you couldn't really hear anything over the roar.

There was so little visibility on the road. Lance flashed his lights at David's vehicle until David stopped. Lance carefully overtook him, and drove extremely slowly. David understood that Lance wanted them to be almost bumper to bumper, so they didn't lose each other. Lance continued and then took a counterintuitive turn onto a road that led back in the direction they'd come, but toward the coast.

This set them on a journey down abandoned roads, around fallen trees; they went toward the harbor, took the street that ran alongside it, then traced the coast back, and then forth, on a winding road; they went over by two bays, came to the top of a hill, and kept on going.

As soon as they climbed the last rise, the cacophony fell away. The land to their side was still kindling—you could see the roots of the

315

trees harboring molten, underground ovens—but Cass could open her window a little, and her trusting, big-eyed Daisy caught a vein of sea air in her mouth.

"Where are we going?" They could hear each other a little more now. It was Maggs's sweet voice asking, and it sounded so nice.

"Plan D," said Lance. "I mean: Plan E. Ella's mad plan."

"What happened to Plan A, B, and C?" Maggs asked.

"And D," said Lance.

Cass was not thinking along with them. Cass was picturing scenes: Nathaniel, after she left him, asserting himself, deciding to stay in the house. He would not go back to the town that night. Maybe he was worried that Cass would make a run for it with the children, without him. So he asked Arthur to drive to town and collect Eden, collect Petal. And Arthur did. Arthur was too drunk to drive, but this never usually stopped him. He knew the roads. Ella had said that Arthur drove off, and then he came back. Presumably with his mother and his brother's pregnant girlfriend. They sat in The Good Room, to talk, and make plans. Eden had a proposal. Perhaps she wanted them all to go on to the next place together. Both her sons, and all their lovers, and herself in the most important position: the elder. (A degraded elder, grabbing cheap-won honor out of disaster. Taking advantage of the situation.) Eden had lit her two candles happily. Maybe Arthur, there in presence but in avoidance of his family, sat with them and drank shine until he was unconscious. Maybe Nathaniel, exhausted, did the same. And the pregnant girl would be tired in that pregnant way. They all passed out on the sofas in The Good Room, having heard Eden's plans. And Eden would have sat with them, satisfied. Did she sleep? And then Jem came like the hero from over the hill. And what did Jem do?

The Good Room was usually locked. The key for it had been moved during the wedding to hang from a hook on the back of the door— Cass had seen it there. Did Jem set the flames and get out? Had she discovered her anger? Did she try to lock them in? Did she lock them in? But how would she get away with Cass's car? Did Nathaniel leave the keys in the ignition? Or did Eden stop Jem from getting away? Did Eden get away herself?

Eden—Eden who switched the water off herself. Maybe Eden had killed her sons, and their lovers, with her two candles. It was not a huge leap to make. Eden could easily have killed them with the ritual she had long used to mourn them. And she would say, if she got away, "as God is my witness," that it was a horrible accident. Plausible deniability. Always. Eden, who switched the water off herself.

Could the fire gutting Eigleath have been an accident? A simple accident. Did they all talk? Make plans about leaving as one, putting rifts aside for the emergency? Was Jem brought on side, Arthur delighted to see her? He must have been over the moon to see her. They all drank shine and toasted farewell to Eigleath and nodded off, and woke too late, they thought, to save anyone but themselves, and got away? Or they never woke. Someone had gotten away in Cass's car.

What was true and what was safe?

Lance turned down a track that came out onto a headland. They parked the trucks with all the others. You could hear the sea. They shouldered Lance's supplies, and their children, and scrambled the boulders down to the beach. To the sea.

Where there were boats. Dozens and dozens of boats. Anchored not far out, but far enough to be safe from fire.

And there were children. Not just nine children from Eigleath. Hundreds: little evacuees. The beach was covered in their footprints. They were in various stages of being sorted into boats.

A little group of children were shrieking as they waded toward one of the smaller vessels to be rowed out.

Cass did not stop to ask. She simply carried her two girls, one on her front, one on her back, with one hand free for her son, and with a clear, rich voice she called the other Children of the House to follow her. She walked directly into the water. And she stood there with it cold and beautiful around her calves, and waited silently for her turn, which came about quickly.

Before long they were listening to the oars carrying them out to sea.

Cass was the only one in their boat to be facing back to shore, so she was the only one who had the flames of the land reflected in her eyes. She trailed her hand in the flecked water, and did not think about diving.

The orange of the sky was clearing.

The morning stars, in the new pink tones, were delinquently bright.

317

It was easier than Cass had anticipated for everyone to climb out of the boat and board the larger vessel. The boatman helped them onto his ship. Cass went last. He held his hand out for her; it was stronger than it looked, his hand: muscle-smooth. Cass glimpsed David, Vinnie, and David's daughter ascending a ladder onto a large fishing boat nearby, where they joined a group of strangers. Cass watched to check that the strangers were friendly, and read in seconds that they were. Meanwhile, on Cass's boat, eight children, Lance, and Ella. There was a little cabin, and the children went in there, where they were wrapped in blankets by the boatman, and given sugary biscuits from Lance's big bag.

Everyone, on all the boats, was exceedingly quiet.

The boats rocked. The boats' wood creaked.

There were dozens of vessels, full of children and their adults, holding their breath, hearing the fires peaking and cracking, over the water.

Cass, in the cabin, kissed eight children and then went out onto the deck alone. After a while, Lance came out to offer her the last segments of a small greenhouse orange.

"How was this sorted?" Cass asked. She bit into the fruit.

"Ella," he replied with a forced clarity. "You took the letters down to the harbor. When you left town, I went around, talked to them all individually about it. But Ella's masterplan, this. I didn't think we'd have to use it, honestly. This was all for if . . . in case there was nowhere else safe to wait it out on land. I don't believe there was," he said. His breath all of oranges.

"She didn't tell me," Cass replied, her breath of oranges too. She thought that the angle of the gaze between his eyes and her lips was perhaps the same as the angle from the boats to their seabedded anchors, along anchor chains which she could picture, but not see.

"No. Tomorrow we could start out, navigate further, like, out and up." He made an approximating gesture with a free hand, which indicated that he didn't really know the way. They laughed together. "The sailors know how to do it. And Ella has the location of Arthur and Jem's new place."

"Arthur and Jem's new place."

"Yes."

The creak of dozens of boats held at sea in the morning light; it was a lonely sound, a reminder that grief would be lonely.

And Cass said, "OK." Then she said to him, "I really like your face."

Several thousand versions of him sprang from that face, and from each of those another thousand.

She sat down on the low, painted wooden shelf, and they stayed without speaking for a while. Then he moved, she assumed, to sit beside her, but he nodded toward the horizon, as if entrusting it to her, and went back inside the cabin. She was glad. She focused her attention on the place where the sun was rising like a line of milk, under where the stars were coming through more and more, as the smoke cleared from the sky.

The sunrise was diffuse, so wide and long, gentle and gradual. But it certainly stirred the children. They responded to it by raising their voices. Some of them started calling out to each other between the boats. Cass heard the unmistakable sounds of her own three; Ella was making them giggle inside the cabin. There was a rise in activity. There were typical childhood sounds, like disagreements, elegies of unfairness, particularly over food, a little cry of "But he hurt me . . ." and a song with which many joined in.

The sun was rising. The children's voices could be heard scattering out like starlight, skipping and skimming over the lapping sea. You could hear the children's voices, and they were unafraid.

A NOTE ON THE TEXT

Ally's line "What are you pretending not to know today, Sweetheart?" is taken from Toni Cade Bambara's essay "The Education of a Storyteller," which I know Ally read.

Jem's reply, when asked what she would save if her house was on fire (she says: "The fire") echoes Jean Cocteau's in a radio interview conducted in 1951 with André Fraigneau. For David's lecture at The Circle Place and Ella's wedding sermon I am indebted to the influence of *The Great Cosmic Mother: Rediscovering the Religion of the Earth*, by Monica Sjöö and Barbara Mor, 1987.

The line "It was no longer possible to secure a liveable future for all" is lifted from the summary of the Intergovernmental Panel on Climate Change, March 2023, which states: "There is a rapidly closing window of opportunity to secure a liveable and sustainable future for all (very high confidence)."

BIBLIOGRAPHY

Bambara, Toni Cade, "The Education of a Storyteller," *Deep Sightings and Rescue Missions: Fiction, Essays, and Conversations*, Pantheon, New York, 1996.

Cocteau, Jean, and André Fraigneau, *Jean Cocteau: Entretiens avec André Fraigneau*, Bibliothèque 10/18, Paris, 1965.

Intergovernmental Panel on Climate Change, "Summary for Policymakers," in *Climate Change 2023: Synthesis Report*, edited by Hoesung Lee and José Romero, pp. 1–34, Geneva, 2023.

Sjöö, Monica, and Barbara Mor, *The Great Cosmic Mother: Rediscovering the Religion of the Earth*, HarperCollins, New York, 1987.

ACKNOWLEDGMENTS

My deepest thanks, first and foremost, to my agent Eleanor Birne, who is a wonder, and to everyone at PEW Literary, without whom, none of this.

Thank you to everyone at The Overlook Press for guiding me through. My thanks to my US editors Chelsea Cutchens and Abby Muller, and to Deb Wood for the perfect cover. At Bloomsbury in the UK I would like to thank Alexis Kirschbaum, for her edits and her excellence. Thank you to Allegra Le Fanu, Silvia Crompton, Fabrice Wilmann, Anna Massardi, and the whole team there.

My love and thanks to Toby Lichtig, Zita Nevile, Lily Sykes, Alan Murrin, Charlotte Pusey, Jo-anne Carlyle, Sam Solnick, Polly Brown, Izzy McEvoy, Stefanos Kokotos, and Lee Jordan. To Heather Dineen and Mike Dineen (1948–2000).

My thanks to a further list of people too numerous to name here who taught me things, held me, printed out this book for me at a moment's notice, found me for coffee, met me for drinks, cooked me dinner, held parties in their warm homes, helped me with money, helped me with courage, agreed to go with me to the uncool concert, cried at the school gate, watched my kids, sang for me, made me a photoshoot on their balcony; a million scenes in a tapestry of light, all held together with your faces. When life isn't brief and it isn't *very* it is really fucking beautiful.

And to Matt Gold, who will always get his own line. Thank you. Rarest, sickest beast.

And finally, Willow and Sidney; Sid and Willow. Listen: if you ever read this (and you really don't have to) don't look for yourselves in here. I borrowed precisely two things from you. Sid: it was you who thought the expression "you're a lifesaver" was actually "you're a lightsaber." And Willow, the description of Vi learning to read is yours

(but unlike him, you weren't doing it to impress anybody). Other than that, I made it all up. Don't look for yourselves here. I've written you down elsewhere, all the little childhood things you did and do, so we don't forget them. I've written you all over the walls and the ceiling of my heart, which is also the sky. I love you. It is nothing but an honor.
Mummy x

A NOTE ON THE AUTHOR

ROZ DINEEN spent thirteen years as an editor and writer at the *Times Literary Supplement*. Born in Brighton in 1983, she studied English literature at Trinity College Dublin and received a master's degree in international studies and diplomacy from SOAS University of London. She lives with her two children in South London.

A NOTE ON THE TYPE

The text of this book is set in Linotype Sabon, a typeface named after the type founder, Jacques Sabon. It was designed by Jan Tschichold and jointly developed by Linotype, Monotype, and Stempel in response to a need for a typeface to be available in identical form for mechanical hot metal composition and hand composition using foundry type.

Tschichold based his design for Sabon roman on a font engraved by Garamond, and Sabon italic on a font by Granjon. It was first used in 1966 and has proved an enduring modern classic.